PRIZE STORIES 1981
The O. Henry Awards

PRIZE STORIES 1981
The O. Henry Awards

EDITED AND WITH
AN INTRODUCTION
BY WILLIAM ABRAHAMS

DOUBLEDAY & COMPANY, INC.
GARDEN CITY, NEW YORK
1981

The Library of Congress Cataloged This Serial as Follows:

Prize stories. The O. Henry awards. 1919–
Garden City, N. Y., Doubleday [etc.]

v. 21 cm.

Title varies: 1919–46, O. Henry memorial award prize stories.
Stories for 1919–27 were "chosen by the Society of Arts and Sciences."
Editors: 1919–32, B. C. Williams.—1933–40, Harry Hansen.—1941–
Herschel Brickell (with Muriel Fuller, 19 –46)

1. Short stories. I. Williams, Blanche Colton, 1879–1944, ed. II. Hansen, Harry, 1884– ed. III. Brickell, Herschel, 1889– ed. IV. Society of Arts and Sciences, New York.
PZ1.O11 813.5082
Library of Congress [150q830] Official

ISBN: 0-385-15977-3
Library of Congress Catalog Card Number: 21-9372

Printed in the United States of America
First Edition

CONTENTS

PUBLISHER'S NOTE

This volume is the sixty-first in the O. Henry Memorial Award series.

In 1918, the Society of Arts and Sciences met to vote upon a monument to the master of the short story, O. Henry. They decided that this memorial should be in the form of two prizes for the best short stories published by American authors in American magazines during the year 1919. From this beginning, the memorial developed into an annual anthology of outstanding short stories by American authors, published, with the exception of the years 1952 and 1953, by Doubleday & Company, Inc.

Blanche Colton Williams, one of the founders of the awards, was editor from 1919 to 1932; Harry Hansen from 1933 to 1940; Herschel Brickell from 1941 to 1951. The annual collection did not appear in 1952 and 1953, when the continuity of the series was interrupted by the death of Herschel Brickell. Paul Engle was editor from 1954 to 1959 with Hanson Martin coeditor in the years 1954 to 1960; Mary Stegner in 1960; Richard Poirier from 1961 to 1966, with assistance from and coeditorship with William Abrahams from 1964 to 1966. William Abrahams became editor of the series in 1967.

In 1970 Doubleday published under Mr. Abrahams' editorship *Fifty Years of the American Short Story*, and in January 1981, *Prize Stories of the Seventies*. Both are collections of stories selected from this series.

The stories chosen for this volume were published in the period from the summer of 1979 to the summer of 1980. A list of the magazines consulted appears at the back of the book. The choice of stories and the selection of prize winners are exclusively the responsibility of the editor. Biographical material is based on information provided by the contributors and obtained from standard works of reference.

INTRODUCTION

In *Unforgettable People,* the most recent and, regrettably, the last of the splendidly illustrated calendars he devised for the Metropolitan Museum of Art, the late A. Hyatt Mayor begins one of his commentaries on the paintings he included with a not unfamiliar but ever valuable generalization: "The more spontaneous a work of art appears, the more apt it is to have been reworked many times." The immediate occasion for the remark is a double portrait by John Singer Sargent, "Mr. and Mrs. Isaac Newton Phelps Stokes," and Mayor goes on to tell us that "When Sargent painted Mrs. Stokes in London during the summer of 1897, the sparkle of her smile challenged him to scrape out and repaint her face nine times. The dazzle of casualness had taken him so long to achieve that when he finally got ready for the Great Dane that was to nuzzle her right hand, its owner had taken it out of London, so he filled the background shadows with Mr. Stokes . . ."

That painters rework, scrape out, repaint; that writers revise, cross out, rewrite—this news will hardly come as a surprise, the craft beneath the art, one might say, but it is good to be reminded of it, especially in an age like ours that puts so high a value on the seemingly casual and spontaneous: the work of art as a happening. I think it reasonable to suggest that the story that simply happens—and no matter that a generous editor welcomes it into print—is a story that would have benefited if it had challenged its author much as Mrs. Stokes's sparkling smile had challenged her painter. (A bad, complacent painter, let it be said, would not have even felt the challenge.) Again and again, reading for the collection this year as in years past, I have been struck by those stories that fall into the category of "almost but not quite": the story, say, that aims for spontaneity but is overly and recognizably contrived; or the story that, for all its air of casualness, can't conceal the self-consciousness of its self-approving style.

No need to fall back on the wisdom of the inventor of the electric light who assured us, in a burst of mock candor or mock modesty, that genius is 1 percent inspiration and 99 percent perspiration, or the author of *Work Amongst Working Men* who is remembered today for her familiar quotation that "Genius is an infinite capacity for taking pains." We know all too well that many are the authors who plentifully perspire, many who take pains from here to infinity to master their craft, and who still write badly. But there is an irreducible good sense, sustained by the practice of too many artists who confirm it in their experience, that allows for work or craft, as well as for art or inspiration, in the writing of a story or the painting of a picture.

Inspiration—the word and the idea alike—is viewed with a good deal of justifiable suspicion nowadays: Who has not listened to a canting TV "preacher" in the throes of his "inspiration" and not fallen into despair? And yet, for all one's cynicism and distrust of the very word itself, there are certain otherwise inexplicable stories —very rarely encountered—where one feels the author has been inspired, has received the story and returned it to us in a single breath, without pausing for the interventions and manipulations of craft. Mere mastery is not sufficient to account for the quality of art that has been given us, and we say that the author has been inspired.

Such a story, I believe, is "The Shawl" by Cynthia Ozick to which I have awarded First Prize in this year's collection. It is an extraordinary work, and I should say at once, in fairness to the author, that for all I know she may have written the story as many as nine times before achieving the effect of inevitability, imaginative truth, and moral courage that make "The Shawl" so moving to read and, very possibly, so unforgettable.

For the sake of convenience one might place this very beautiful and painful work in a category where it would be virtually alone: a tale or parable of the Holocaust. Conventional wisdom, of course, would have us believe that the subject is "too great," "too important," "too difficult" for fiction. The magnitude of the historical event is beyond art—I am summarizing the argument against the imaginative writer taking up the subject at all—and it is better left to scholars and journalists. The facts in all their terribleness speak for themselves: What can the artist add?

Cynthia Ozick is an artist, and she does not add. Rather, she goes in her own way, trusting to the imagination, released from the tyranny of fact—whose validity she would never question—to evoke the most delicate of emotions. Who, reading "The Shawl" will not feel an anguish of the heart? Yet the word Holocaust itself never appears in the story; nor the word Jew; nor concentration or death camp, nor ovens, nor incineration: all those facts, whose immensity, piled one on another, silence us or shame us or arouse a kind of moral idiocy—the wish to believe that it did not really happen.

My own belief is very simple. As the facts recede into history and become the province of scholars, art—as it expresses itself in "The Shawl"—will endure: not, if you like, a "story," but a "memory" to haunt whoever reads it.

All the stories in this present volume are, by definition, O. Henry Award winners, and in accordance with the tradition of the series, I have awarded a First Prize to Cynthia Ozick for "The Shawl." But the traditions of the series further require that the editor shall award a Second and Third Prize. This year, at least, it seems to me that the tradition is better served by being ignored.

Frankly, I have found the task of awarding First, Second and Third Prizes the most vexing of editorial obligations. A First Prize generally can be justified without too much argument, if only because in a given year one story does dramatically stand out, and one does not feel oneself trapped into invidious comparisons. But thereafter difficulties begin. Sometimes in the past I have felt the chief though unacknowledged purpose of the Second and Third Prizes was to stir up controversy among readers who would have chosen differently. (This, I note, happens far less frequently with the First Prize.) "Oh yes," I have heard in one form or another, "the Second Prize story—or the Third Prize—is good, but I would have chosen X, Y, or Z." This year I leave that vexing pleasure to readers of the collection. To them I say, Here are twenty-one prize-winning stories. Confer upon them your respect and admiration, and even your affection—they are worthy of them all.

—William Abrahams

PRIZE STORIES 1981
The O. Henry Awards

THE SHAWL

CYNTHIA OZICK

Cynthia Ozick is the author of *Trust*, a novel (New American Library); *The Pagan Rabbi and Other Stories* (Knopf), nominated for a 1972 National Book Award; *Bloodshed and Three Novellas;* and *Levitation: Five Fictions*. She has also published essays, poetry, criticism, reviews, and translations in numerous periodicals and anthologies, and has been the recipient of several prizes, including the Award for Literature of the American Academy of Arts and Letters. Her home is in New Rochelle, New York.

Stella, cold, cold, the coldness of hell. How they walked on the roads together, Rosa with Magda curled up between sore breasts, Magda wound up in the shawl. Sometimes Stella carried Magda. But she was jealous of Magda. A thin girl of fourteen, too small, with thin breasts of her own, Stella wanted to be wrapped in a shawl, hidden away, asleep, rocked by the march, a baby, a round infant in arms. Magda took Rosa's nipple, and Rosa never stopped walking, a walking cradle. There was not enough milk; sometimes Magda sucked air; then she screamed. Stella was ravenous. Her knees were tumors on sticks, her elbows chicken bones.

Rosa did not feel hunger; she felt light, not like someone walking but like someone in a faint, in trance, arrested in a fit, someone who is already a floating angel, alert and seeing everything, but in the air, not there, not touching the road. As if teetering on the tips of her fingernails. She looked into Magda's face through a gap in the shawl: a squirrel in a nest, safe, no one could reach her inside the little house of the shawl's windings. The face, very round, a pocket mirror of a face: but it was not Rosa's bleak complexion, dark like cholera, it was another kind of face altogether, eyes blue as air, smooth feathers of hair nearly as yellow as the Star sewn into Rosa's coat. You could think she was one of *their* babies.

Rosa, floating, dreamed of giving Magda away in one of the villages. She could leave the line for a minute and push Magda into the hands of any woman on the side of the road. But if she moved out of line they might shoot. And even if she fled the line for half a second and pushed the shawl-bundle at a stranger, would the woman take it? She might be surprised, or afraid; she might drop the shawl, and Magda would fall out and strike her head and die. The little round head. Such a good child, she gave up screaming, and sucked now only for the taste of the drying nipple itself. The neat grip of the tiny gums. One mite of a tooth tip sticking up in the bottom gum, how shining, an elfin tombstone of white marble gleaming there. Without complaining, Magda relinquished Rosa's teats, first the left, then the right; both were cracked, not a sniff of milk. The duct crevice extinct, a dead volcano, blind eye, chill hole, so Magda took the corner of the shawl and milked it instead. She sucked and sucked, flooding the threads with wetness. The shawl's good flavor, milk of linen.

It was a magic shawl, it could nourish an infant for three days and three nights. Magda did not die, she stayed alive, although very quiet. A peculiar smell, of cinnamon and almonds, lifted out of her mouth. She held her eyes open every moment, forgetting how to blink or nap, and Rosa and sometimes Stella studied their blueness. On the road they raised one burden of a leg after another and studied Magda's face. "Aryan," Stella said, in a voice grown as thin as a string; and Rosa thought how Stella gazed at Magda like a young cannibal. And the time that Stella said "Aryan," it sounded to Rosa as if Stella had really said "Let us devour her."

But Magda lived to walk. She lived that long, but she did not walk very well, partly because she was only fifteen months old, and partly because the spindles of her legs could not hold up her fat belly. It was fat with air, full and round. Rosa gave almost all her food to Magda, Stella gave nothing; Stella was ravenous, a growing child herself, but not growing much. Stella did not menstruate. Rosa did not menstruate. Rosa was ravenous, but also not; she learned from Magda how to drink the taste of a finger in one's mouth. They were in a place without pity, all pity was annihilated in Rosa, she looked at Stella's bones without pity. She was sure that Stella was waiting for Magda to die so she could put her teeth into the little thighs.

Rosa knew Magda was going to die very soon; she should have been dead already, but she had been buried away deep inside the magic shawl, mistaken there for the shivering mound of Rosa's breasts; Rosa clung to the shawl as if it covered only herself. No one took it away from her. Magda was mute. She never cried. Rosa hid her in the barracks, under the shawl, but she knew that one day someone would inform; or one day someone, not even Stella, would steal Magda to eat her. When Magda began to walk Rosa knew that Magda was going to die very soon, something would happen. She was afraid to fall asleep; she slept with the weight of her thigh on Magda's body; she was afraid she would smother Magda under her thigh. The weight of Rosa was becoming less and less; Rosa and Stella were slowly turning into air.

Magda was quiet, but her eyes were horribly alive, like blue tigers. She watched. Sometimes she laughed—it seemed a laugh, but how could it be? Magda had never seen anyone laugh. Still, Magda laughed at her shawl when the wind blew its corners, the bad wind with pieces of black in it, that made Stella's and Rosa's eyes tear. Magda's eyes were always clear and tearless. She watched like a tiger. She guarded her shawl. No one could touch it; only Rosa could touch it. Stella was not allowed. The shawl was Magda's own baby, her pet, her little sister. She tangled herself up in it and sucked on one of the corners when she wanted to be very still.

Then Stella took the shawl away and made Magda die.

Afterward Stella said: "I was cold."

And afterward she was always cold, always. The cold went into her heart: Rosa saw that Stella's heart was cold. Magda flopped onward with her little pencil legs scribbling this way and that, in search of the shawl; the pencils faltered at the barracks opening, where the light began. Rosa saw and pursued. But already Magda was in the square outside the barracks, in the jolly light. It was the roll-call arena. Every morning Rosa had to conceal Magda under the shawl against a wall of the barracks and go out and stand in the arena with Stella and hundreds of others, sometimes for hours, and Magda, deserted, was quiet under the shawl, sucking on her corner. Every day Magda was silent, and so she did not die.

Rosa saw that today Magda was going to die, and at the same time a fearful joy ran in Rosa's two palms, her fingers were on fire, she was astonished, febrile: Magda, in the sunlight, swaying on her pencil legs, was howling. Ever since the drying up of Rosa's nipples, ever since Magda's last scream on the road, Magda had been devoid of any syllable; Magda was a mute. Rosa believed that something had gone wrong with her vocal cords, with her windpipe, with the cave of her larynx; Magda was defective, without a voice; perhaps she was deaf; there might be something amiss with her intelligence; Magda was dumb. Even the laugh that came when the ash-stippled wind made a clown out of Magda's shawl was only the air-blown showing of her teeth. Even when the lice, head lice and body lice, crazed her so that she became as wild as one of the big rats that plundered the barracks at daybreak looking for carrion, she rubbed and scratched and kicked and bit and rolled without a whimper. But now Magda's mouth was spilling a long viscous rope of clamor.

"Maaaa—"

It was the first noise Magda had ever sent out from her throat since the drying up of Rosa's nipples.

"Maaaa . . . aaa!"

Again! Magda was wavering in the perilous sunlight of the arena, scribbling on such pitiful little bent shins. Rosa saw. She saw that Magda was grieving for the loss of her shawl, she saw that Magda was going to die. A tide of commands hammered in Rosa's nipples: Fetch, get, bring! But she did not know which to go after first, Magda or the shawl. If she jumped out into the arena to snatch Magda up, the howling would not stop, because Magda would still not have the shawl; but if she ran back into the barracks to find the shawl, and if she found it, and if she came after Magda holding it and shaking it, then she would get Magda back, Magda would put the shawl in her mouth and turn dumb again.

Rosa entered the dark. It was easy to discover the shawl. Stella was heaped under it, asleep in her thin bones. Rosa tore the shawl free and flew—she could fly, she was only air—into the arena. The sunheat murmured of another life, of butterflies in summer. The light was placid, mellow. On the other side of the steel fence, far away, there were green meadows speckled with dandelions and deep-colored violets; beyond them, even farther, innocent tiger lilies, tall, lifting their orange bonnets. In the barracks they spoke of "flowers," of "rain": excrement, thick turd-braids, and the slow stinking maroon waterfall that slunk down from the upper bunks, the stink mixed with a bitter fatty floating smoke that greased Rosa's skin. She stood for an instant at the margin of the arena. Sometimes the electricity inside the fence would seem to hum; even Stella said it was only an imagining, but Rosa heard real sounds in the wire: grainy sad voices. The farther she was from the fence, the more clearly the voices crowded at her. The lamenting voices strummed so convincingly, so passionately, it was impossible to suspect them of being phantoms. The voices told her to hold up the shawl, high; the voices told her to shake it, to whip with it, to unfurl it like a flag. Rosa lifted, shook, whipped, unfurled. Far off, very far, Magda leaned across her air-fed belly, reaching out with the rods of her arms. She was high up, elevated, riding someone's shoulder. But the shoulder that carried Magda was not coming toward Rosa and the shawl, it was drifting away, the speck of Magda was moving more and more into the smoky distance. Above the shoulder a helmet glinted. The light tapped the helmet and sparkled it into a goblet. Below the helmet a black body like a domino and a pair of black boots hurled themselves in the direction of the electrified fence. The electric voices began to chatter wildly. "Maamaa, maaamaaa," they all hummed together. How far Magda was from Rosa now, across the whole square, past a dozen barracks, all the way on the other side! She was no bigger than a moth.

All at once Magda was swimming through the air. The whole of Magda traveled through loftiness. She looked like a butterfly touching a silver vine. And the moment Magda's feathered round head and her pencil legs and balloonish belly and zigzag arms splashed against the fence, the steel voices went mad in their growling, urging Rosa to run and run to the spot where Magda had fallen from her flight against the electrified fence; but of course Rosa did not obey them. She only stood, because if she ran they would shoot, and if she tried to pick up the sticks of Magda's body they would shoot, and if she let the wolf's screech ascending now through the ladder of her skeleton break out, they would shoot; so she took Magda's shawl and filled her own mouth with it, stuffed it in and stuffed it in, until she was swallowing up the wolf's screech and tasting the cinnamon and almond depth of Magda's saliva; and Rosa drank Magda's shawl until it dried.

INTERIOR SPACE

JOHN IRVING

John Irving was born in Exeter, New Hampshire, in 1942. His short stories have appeared in *Antaeus, Esquire, Fiction, Penthouse, Playboy,* and other magazines; his essays and reviews in *The New Republic* and the New York *Times Book Review*. He is the author of the novels *Setting Free the Bears* (1969), *The Water-Method Man* (1972), *The 158-Pound Marriage* (1974), and *The World According to Garp* (1978); his fifth novel, *The Hotel New Hampshire,* will be published in 1981.

George Ronkers was a young urologist in a university town—a lucrative situation nowadays; the uninformed liberality of both the young and old college community produced a marvel of venereal variety. A urologist had plenty to do. Ronkers was affectionately nicknamed by a plethora of his clientele at Student Health. "Raunchy Ronk," they said. With deeper affection, his wife called him "Raunch."

Her name was Kit; she had a good sense of humor about George's work and a gift for imaginative shelter. She was a graduate student in the School of Architecture; she had a Teaching Assistantship, and she taught one course to undergraduate architecture students called "Interior Space."

It was her field, really. She was completely responsible for all the interior space in the Ronkers home. She had knocked down walls, sunk bathtubs, arched doorways, rounded rooms, ovalled windows; in short, she treated interior space as an illusion. "The trick," she would say, "is not letting you see where one room ends and another begins; the concept of a *room* is defeating to the concept of *space;* in space, you can't make out the boundaries. . . ." And so on; it was her field.

George Ronkers walked through his house as if it were a park in a foreign but intriguing city. Theories of space didn't bother him one way or another.

"Saw a girl today with seventy-five warts," he'd say. "Really an obvious surgery. Don't know why she came to *me.* Really should have seen a *gynecologist* first."

The only part of the property that Ronkers considered *his* field was the large, lovely black walnut tree beside the house. Kit had spotted the house first; it belonged to an old Austrian named Kesler whose wife had just died. Kit told Ronkers it was repairable inside because the ceilings were at least high enough. But Ronkers had been sold on account of the tree. It was a split-trunked black walnut, growing out of the ground like two trees, making a high, slim V. The proper black walnut has a tall, graceful, upshooting style—the branches and the leaves start about two stories off the ground, and the leaves are small, slender, and clustered very closely together; they are a delicate green, turning yellow in October. The walnuts grow in a tough rubbery pale-green skin; in the fall they reach the size of peaches; the skins begin to darken—even blackening in spots—and they start to drop. Squirrels like them.

Kit liked the tree well enough, but she was ecstatic telling old Herr Kesler what she was going to do with his house after he moved out. Kesler just stared at her, saying, occasionally, "Which wall? *That* wall? You're going *this* wall to down-take, yes? Oh, the *other* wall too? Oh. Well . . . what will the ceiling up-hold? Oh . . ."

And Ronkers told Kesler how *much* he liked the black walnut tree. That was when Kesler warned him about their neighbor.

"*Der Bardlong,*" Kesler said. "He wants the tree down-chopped but I never to him listened." George Ronkers tried to press old Kesler to explain the motives of his would-be neighbor Bardlong, but the Austrian suddenly thumped the wall next to him with the flat of his hand and cried to Kit, "Not *this* wall too, I hope not! Ah, this wall I always *enjoyed* have!"

Well, they had to be delicate. No more plans out loud until Kesler moved out. He moved to an apartment in another suburb; for some reason, he dressed for the occasion—like a Tyrolean peasant, his felt Alpine hat with a feather in it and his old white knees winking under his lederhosen, he stood in a soft spring rain by his ancient wooden trunks and let George and Kit hustle the furniture around for him.

"Won't you get out of the rain, Mr. Kesler?" Kit asked him, but he would not budge from the sidewalk in front of his former house until all his furniture was in the truck. He was watching the black walnut tree.

Herr Kesler put his hand frankly on Kit's behind, saying to her, "Do not let *der pest Bardlong* the tree down-chop, okay?"

"Okay," said Kit.

George Ronkers liked to lie in bed in the spring mornings and watch the sun filter through the new green leaves of his black walnut tree. The patterns the tree cast on the bed were almost mosaic. Kit had enlarged the window to accommodate more of the tree; her term for it was "inviting the tree in."

"Oh, Raunch," she whispered, "isn't it lovely?"

"It's a lovely tree."

"Well, I mean the *room* too. And the window, the elevated sleeping platform . . ."

"*Platform?* I thought it was a bed."

There was a squirrel who came along a branch very near the window—in fact, he often brushed the screen with his tail; the squirrel liked to tug at the new nuts, as if he could anticipate autumn.

"Raunch?"

"Yup . . ."

"Remember the girl with seventy-five warts?"

"*Remember* her!"

"Well, Raunch . . . *where* were the warts?"

. . . and *der pest Bardlong* gave them no trouble. All that spring and long summer, when workmen were removing walls and sculpting windows, the aloof Mr. and Mrs. Bardlong smiled at the confusion from their immaculate grounds, waved distantly from their terraces, made sudden appearances from behind a trellis—but always they were neighborly, encouraging of the youthful bustle, prying into nothing.

Bardlong was retired. He was *the* Bardlong, if you're at all familiar with the shock absorber and brake systems magnate. In the Midwest, you may have seen the big trucks.

BARDLONG STOPS YOU SHORT!

BARDLONG TAKES THAT SHOCK!

Even in retirement, Bardlong appeared to be absorbing whatever shock his new neighbors and their renovations might have caused him. His own house was an old red-brick mansion, trimmed tastefully with dark green shutters and overcrawling with ivy. It imitated a Georgian version of architecture; the front of the house was square and centered with tall, thin downstairs windows. The depth of the house was considerable; it went back a long way, branching into terraces, trellises, rock gardens, manicured hedges, fussed-over flower beds, and a lawn as fine as a putting green.

The house took up a full corner of the shady, suburban street. Its only neighbor was the Ronkers' house, and the Bardlongs' property was walled off from George and Kit by a low slate-stone wall. From their second-floor windows, George and Kit looked down into Bardlong's perfect yard; their tangle of bushes and unkempt, matted grass was a full five feet above the apparent dike which kept their whole mess from crushing Bardlong as he raked and pruned. The houses themselves were queerly close together, the Ronkers' having once been servant quarters to the Bardlongs', long before the property was divided.

Between them, rooted on the raised ground on Ronkers' side of the slate-stone wall, was the black walnut tree. Ronkers could not imagine whatever had prodded old Herr Kesler to think that Bardlong wanted the demise of the tree. Perhaps it had been a language problem. The tree must have been a shared joy to Bardlong. It shaded *his* windows, too; its stately height towered over his roof. One veer of the V angled over George and Kit; the other part of the V leaned over Bardlong.

Did the man not care for unpruned beauty?

Possibly; but all summer long, Bardlong never complained. He was there in his faded straw hat, gardening, simply puttering, often accompanied by his wife. The two of them seemed more like guests in an elegant old resort hotel than actual residents. Their dress, for yard work, was absurdly formal—as if Bardlong's many years as a brake systems businessman had left him with no clothes other than business suits. He wore slightly out-of-style suit trousers, with suspenders, and slightly out-of-style dress shirts—the wide-brimmed straw hat shading his pale, freckled forehead. He was complete with an excessively sporty selection of two-toned shoes.

His wife—in a lawn-party dress and a cream-white Panama with a red silk ribbon round the bun at the back of her nail-gray hair—tapped her cane at bricks in the terrace which might dare to be loose. Bardlong followed her with a tiny, toylike pull-cart of cement, and a trowel.

They lunched every midafternoon under a large sun umbrella on their back terrace, the white iron lawn furniture gleaming from an era of hunt breakfasts and champagne brunches following a daughter's wedding.

A visit of grown-up children and less grown-up grandchildren seemed to mark the only interruption to Bardlong's summer. Three days of a dog barking and of balls being tossed about the pool-table symmetry of that yard seemed to upset the Bardlongs for a week following. They anxiously trailed the children around the grounds, trying to mend broken stalks of flowers, spearing on some garden instrument the affront of a gum wrapper, replacing divots dug up by the wild-running dog who could, and had, cut like a halfback through the soft grass.

For a week after this family invasion, the Bardlongs were collapsed on the terrace under their sun umbrella, too tired to tap a single brick or repair a tiny torn arm of ivy ripped from a trellis by a passing child.

"Hey, Raunch," Kit whispered. "Bardlong takes that shock!"

"Bardlong stops you short!" Ronkers would read off the trucks around town. But never did one of those crude vehicles so much as approach the fresh-painted curb by Bardlong's house. Bardlong was, indeed, retired. And the Ronkers found it impossible to imagine the man as ever having lived another way. Even when his daily fare had been brake systems and shock absorbers, the Ronkers couldn't conceive of Bardlong having taken part.

George once had a daydream of perverse exaggeration. He told Kit he had watched a huge BARDLONG STOPS YOU SHORT! truck dump its entire supply in Bardlong's yard—the truck with its big back-panel doors flung wide open, churning up the lawn and disgorging itself of clanking parts: brake drums and brake shoes and great oily slicks of brake fluid, rubbery, springing shock absorbers mashing down the flower beds.

"Raunch?" Kit whispered.

"Yup . . ."

"Were the warts actually *in* her vagina?"

"In it, on it, all around it . . ."

"*Seventy-five!* Oh Raunch, I can't imagine it."

They lay in bed dappled by the late summer sun, which in the early morning could scarcely penetrate the thick weave of leaves fanned over their window by the black walnut tree.

"You know what I love about lying here?" Ronkers asked his wife. She snuggled up to him.

"Oh no, tell . . ."

"Well, it's the *tree,*" he said. "I think my first sexual experience was in a tree house and that's what it's like up here. . . ."

"You and the damn tree," Kit said. "It might be my *architecture* that makes you like that tree so much. Or even *me,*" she said. "And *that's* a likely story—I can't imagine you doing it in a tree house, frankly—that sounds like something one of your dirty old patients told you. . . ."

"Well, actually, it was a dirty *young* one."

"You're awful, Raunch. My God, seventy-five *warts* . . ."

"Quite a lot of surgery for such a spot, too."

"I thought you said Tomlinson did it."

"Well, yes, but I *assisted.*"

"You don't *normally* do that, do you?"

"Well, no, but this wasn't *normal.*"

"You're really awful, Raunch. . . ."

"Purely medical interest, professional desire to learn. You use a lot of mineral oil and twenty-five percent podophyllin. The cautery is delicate . . ."

"Turds," Kit said.

But summer soon ends, and with the students back in town Ronkers was too busy to lie long abed in the mornings. There is a staggering host of urinary tract infections to be discovered in all corners of the globe, a little-known fringe benefit of the tourist trade; perhaps it is the nation's largest unknown summer import. A line of students waited to see him each morning, their summer travel ended, their work begun in earnest, their peeing problems growing more severe.

"Doc, I think I picked this up in Izmir."

"The question is, how much has it gotten around *since?*"

"The trouble," Ronkers told Kit, "is that they all know perfectly well, at the first sign, what it is they've got—and, usually, even from *whom*. But almost all of them spend some time waiting for it to go away—or passing it on, for Christ's sake!—and they don't come to me until they can't *stand* it any more."

But Ronkers was very sympathetic to his venereal patients and did not make them feel steeped in sin or wallowing in their just rewards; he said they should not feel guilty for catching anything from absolutely anybody. However, he was tough about insisting that they inform the original hostess—whenever they knew her. "She may not *know*," Ronkers would say.

"We are no longer communicating," they'd say.

And Ronkers would charge, "Well, she's just going to be passing it on to someone else, who in turn . . ."

"Good for them!" they'd holler.

"No, *look*," Ronkers would plead. "It's more serious than that, for *her*."

"Then *you* tell her," they'd say. "I'll give you her number."

"Oh, *Raunch!*" Kit would scream. "Why don't you make *them* do it?"

"How?" Ronkers would ask.

"Tell them you won't *fix* them. Tell them you'll let them pee themselves *blind!*"

"They'd just go to someone else," Ronkers would say. "Or they'd simply tell me that they've already told the person—when they haven't, and never intend to."

"Well, it's absurd, *you* calling up every other woman in the damn town."

"I just hate the long-distance ones," Ronkers would say.

"Well, you can at least make *them* pay for the calls, Raunch!"

"Some of the these students don't have any money."

"Tell them you'll ask their *parents* to pay, then!"

"It's tax-deductible, Kit. And they're not all students, either."

"It's awful, Raunch. It really *is*."

"How much higher are you going to make this damn sleeping platform?"

"I like to make you work for it, Raunch."

"I know, but a *ladder*, my God . . ."

"Well, it's up in your favorite tree, right? And you like that, I'm told. And anyone who gets me has got to be athletic."

"I may get maimed trying."

"Raunch! Who are you calling *now*?"

"Hello?" he said to the phone. "Hello, is this Miss Wentworth? Oh, *Mrs.* Wentworth, well . . . I guess I would like to speak to your *daughter*, Mrs. Wentworth. Oh. You don't *have* a daughter? Oh. Well, I guess I would like to speak to *you*, Mrs. Wentworth. . . ."

"Oh, Raunch, how *awful!*"

"Well, this is Dr. Ronkers. I'm a urologist at University Hospital. Yes, *George* Ronkers. Dr. George Ronkers. Well . . . hi. Yes, *George*. Oh, *Sarah*, is it? Well, Sarah . . ."

And with the end of summer there came an end to the rearrangements of the Ronkers' interior space. Kit was through with carpentry and busy with her teaching and her school work. When the workmen left, and the tools were carried off, and the dismantled walls no longer lay heaped in the Ronkers' yard, it must have become apparent to Bardlong that reconstruction—at least for this year—was over.

The walnut tree was still there. Perhaps Bardlong had thought that in the course of the summer building, the tree would go—making way for a new wing. He couldn't have known that the Ronkers were rebuilding their house on the principle of "inviting the tree in."

With autumn coming on, Bardlong's issue with the black walnut tree grew clear. Old Herr Kesler had not been wrong. George and Kit had a premonition of it the first cool, windy night of the fall. They lay on the sleeping platform with the tree swirling around them and the yellowing leaves falling past them, and they heard what sounded like a candlepin bowling ball falling on their roof and thudding its way down the slope to score in the rain gutter.

"Raunch?"

"That was a goddamn *walnut!*" Ronkers said.

"It sounded like a brick out of the chimney," Kit said.

And through the night they sat bolt upright to a few more:

when the wind would loose one or a squirrel would successfully attack one, *whump!* it would strike, and roll *thunker-thunker-thunker-thunker dang!* into the clattering rain gutter.

"That one took a squirrel with it," Ronkers said.

"Well," said Kit, "at least there's no mistaking it for a prowler. It's too obvious a noise."

"Like a prowler dropping his instruments of burglary," Ronkers said.

Whump! thunker-thunker-thunker-thunker dang!

"Like a prowler shot off the roof," Kit groaned.

"We'll get used to it, I'm sure," Ronkers said.

"Well, Raunch, I gather Bardlong has been slow to adapt . . ."

In the morning Ronkers noticed that the Bardlong house had a slate roof with a far steeper pitch than his own. He tried to imagine what the walnuts would sound like on Bardlong's roof.

"But there's surely an attic in that house," Kit said. "The sound is probably muffled." Ronkers could not imagine the sound of a walnut striking a slate roof—and its subsequent descent to the rain gutter—as in any way "muffled."

By mid-October the walnuts were dropping with fearful regularity. Ronkers thought ahead to the first wild storm in November as a potential blitzkrieg. Kit went out to rake a pile of the fallen nuts together; she heard one cutting loose above her, ripping through the dense leaves. She thought against looking up—imagining the ugly bruise between her eyes and the blow of the back of her head driven into the ground. She bent over double and covered her head with her hands. The walnut narrowly missed her offered spine; it gave her a kidney punch. *Thok!*

"It *hurt*, Raunch," she said.

A beaming Bardlong stood under the dangerous tree, watching Ronkers comfort his wife. Kit had not noticed him there before. He wore a thick Alpine hat with a ratty feather in it; it looked like a reject of Herr Kesler's.

"Kesler gave it to me," Bardlong said. "I had asked for a *helmet.*" He stood arrogantly in his yard, his rake held like a fungo bat, waiting for the tree to pitch a walnut down to him. He had chosen the perfect moment to introduce the subject—Kit just wounded, still in tears.

"You ever hear one of those things hit a slate roof?" Bardlong asked. "I'll call you up the next time a whole clump's ready to drop. About three A.M."

"It *is* a problem," Ronkers agreed.

"But it's a *lovely* tree," Kit said defensively.

"Well, it's *your* problem, of course," Bardlong said, offhanded, cheerful. "If I have the same problem with my rain gutters this fall as I had last, I *may* have to ask you to remove the part of your tree that's over *our* propertv, but you can do what you want with the rest of it."

"*What* rain gutter problem?" Ronkers asked.

"It must happen to *your* rain gutters, too, I'm sure . . ."

"*What* happens?" asked Kit.

"They get full of goddamn walnuts," Bardlong said. "And it rains, and rains, and the gutters don't work because they're clogged with walnuts, and the water pours down the side of your house; your windows leak and your basement fills with water. That's all."

"Oh."

"Kesler bought me a mop. But he was a poor old foreigner, you know," Bardlong said confidingly, "and you never felt like getting *legal* with him. You know."

"Oh," said Kit. She did not like Bardlong. The casual cheerfulness of his tone seemed as removed from his meaning as the shock absorber trade was from those delicately laced trellises in his yard.

"Oh, I don't mind raking up a few nuts," Bardlong said, smiling, "or waking up a few times in the night, when I think storks are crash-landing on my roof." He paused, glowing under old Kesler's hat. "Or wearing the protective gear," he added. He doffed the hat to Kit, who at the moment she saw his lightly freckled dome exposed was praying for that unmistakable sound of the leaves ripping apart above. But Bardlong returned the hat to his head. A walnut began its descent. Kit and George crouched, hands over their heads; Bardlong never flinched. With considerable force the walnut struck the slate-stone wall between them, splitting with a dramatic *kak!* It was as hard and as big as a baseball.

"It's sort of an *exciting* tree in the fall, really," Bardlong said. "Of course, my wife won't go near it this time of year—a sort of prisoner in her own yard, you might say." He laughed; some gold fillings from the booming brake systems industry winked in his mouth. "But that's all right. No price should be set for beauty, and it *is* a lovely tree. *Water damage,* though," he said, and his tone changed suddenly, "is *real* damage."

Bardlong managed, Ronkers thought, to make "real" sound like a legal term.

"And if you've got to spend the money to take down half the tree, you better face up to taking it all. When *your* basement's full of water, that won't be any joke." Bardlong pronounced "joke" as if it were an obscene word; moreover, the implication in Bardlong's voice led one to suspect the wisdom in thinking *anything* was funny.

Kit said, "Well, Raunch, you could just get up on the roof and sweep the walnuts out of the rain gutters."

"Of course *I'm* too old for that," Bardlong sighed, as if getting up on his roof was something he *longed* to do.

"Raunch, you could even sweep out Mr. Bardlong's rain gutters, couldn't you? Like once a week or so, just at this time of the year?"

Ronkers looked at the towering Bardlong roof, the smooth slate surface, the steep pitch. Headlines flooded his mind: DOCTOR TAKES FOUR-STORY FALL! UROLOGIST BEANED BY NUT! CAREER CUT SHORT BY DEADLY TREE!

No, Ronkers understood the moment; it was time to look ahead to the larger victory; he could only win half. Bardlong was oblique, but Bardlong was clearly a man with a made-up mind.

"Could you recommend a tree surgeon?" Ronkers asked.

"Oh, *Raunch!*" said Kit.

"We'll cut the tree in half," Ronkers said, striding boldly toward the split trunk, kicking the bomb-debris of fallen walnuts aside.

"I think about *here,*" Bardlong said eagerly, having no doubt picked the spot years ago. "Of course, what *costs,*" he added, with the old shock absorber seriousness back in his voice, "is properly roping the overhanging limbs so that they won't fall on my roof (*I hope they fall* through *your roof, Kit thought*). Whereas, if you cut the whole tree down," Bardlong said, "you could save some time, and your money, by just letting the whole thing fall along the line of the wall; there's room for it, you see, before the street . . ." The tree spread over them, obviously a *measured* tree, long in Bardlong's calculations. A terminal patient, Ronkers thought, perhaps from the beginning.

"I would like to keep the part of the tree that doesn't damage your property, Mr. Bardlong," Ronkers said; his dignity was good; his distance was cool. Bardlong respected the sense of business in his voice.

"I could arrange this for you," Bardlong said. "I mean, I know a good tree outfit." Somehow, the "outfit" smacked of the fleet of men driving around in the Bardlong trucks. "It would cost you a little less," he added, with his irritatingly confiding tone, "if you let me set this up. . . ."

Kit was about to speak but Ronkers said, "I would really appreciate that, Mr. Bardlong. And we'll just have to take our chances with *our* rain gutters."

"Those are new windows," Kit said. "They won't leak. And who cares about water in the old basement? God, *I* don't care, I can tell you. . . ."

Ronkers tried to return Bardlong's patient and infuriatingly *understanding* smile. It was a Yes-I-Tolerate-My-Wife-Too smile. Kit was hoping for a vast unloading from above in the walnut tree, a downfall which would leave them all as hurt as she felt they were guilty.

"Raunch," she said later. "What if poor old Mr. Kesler sees it? And he *will* see it, Raunch. He comes by, from time to time, you know. What are you going to tell him about selling out his tree?"

"I didn't sell it out!" Ronkers said. "I think I saved what I could of the tree by letting him have his half. I couldn't have stopped him, legally. You must have seen that."

"What about poor Mr. Kesler, though?" Kit said. "We *promised.*"

"Well, the tree will still be here."

"Half the tree. . . ."

"Better than none."

"But what will he think of us?" Kit asked. "He'll think we agree with Bardlong that the tree is a nuisance. He'll think it will only be a matter of time before we cut down the rest."

"Well, the tree *is* a nuisance, Kit."

"I just want to know what you're going to say to Mr. Kesler, Raunch."

"I won't have to say anything," Ronkers told her. "Kesler's in the hospital."

She seemed stunned to hear that, old Kesler always having struck her with a kind of peasant heartiness. Those men must live forever, surely? "Raunch?" she asked, less sure of herself now. "He'll get *out* of the hospital, won't he? And what will you tell him when he gets out and comes around to see his tree?"

"He won't get out," Ronkers told her.

"Oh *no*, Raunch. . . ."

The phone rang. He usually let Kit answer the phone; she could fend off the calls that weren't serious. But Kit was deep in a vision of old Kesler, in his worn lederhosen with his skinny, hairless legs.

"Hello," Ronkers told the phone.

"Dr. Ronkers?"

"Yes," he said.

"This is Margaret Brant." Ronkers groped to place the name. A young girl's voice?

"Uh. . . ."

"You left a message at the dorm to have me call this number," Margaret Brant said. And Ronkers remembered, then; he looked over the list of the women he had to call this week. Their names were opposite the names of their infected partners-in-fun.

"Miss Brant?" he said. Kit was mouthing words like a mute: *Why* won't old Mr. Kesler ever get out of the hospital? "Miss Brant, do you know a young man named Harlan Booth?"

Miss Brant seemed mute herself now, and Kit whispered harshly, "*What?* What's wrong with him?"

"Cancer," he whispered back.

"Yes. *What?*" said Margaret Brant. "Yes, I know Harlan Booth. What is the matter, please?"

"I am treating Harlan Booth for gonorrhea, Miss Brant," Ronkers said. There was no reaction over the phone. "Clap?" Ronkers said. "Gonorrhea? Harlan Booth has the clap."

"I know what you mean," the girl said. Her voice had gone hard; she was suspicious. Kit was turned away from him so that he couldn't see her face.

"If you have a gynecologist here in town, Miss Brant, I think you should make an appointment. I could recommend Dr. Caroline Gilmore; her office is at University Hospital. Or, of course, you could come to see me. . . ."

"Look, who *is* this?" Margaret Brant said. "How do I know you're a doctor? Someone just left a phone number for me to call. I never had anything to do with Harlan Booth. What kind of dirty joke is this?"

Possible, thought Ronkers. Harlan Booth had been a vain, uncooperative kid who had very scornfully feigned casualness when asked who else might be infected. "Could be a lot of people," he'd said proudly. And Ronkers had been forced to press him to get even one name: Margaret Brant. Possibly a virgin whom Harlan Brant disliked?

"You can call me at my home phone after I hang up," Ronkers said. "It's listed in the book: Dr. George Ronkers . . . and see if it's not the same number you have now. Or else I can simply apologize for the mistake; I can call up Harlan Booth and tell him off. And," Ronkers gambled, "you can examine yourself for any discharge, especially in the morning, and see if there's any inflammation. And if you think there's a possibility, you can certainly see *another* doctor and I'll never know. But if you've had relations with Harlan Booth, Miss Brant, I . . ."

She hung up.

"Cancer?" Kit said, her back still to him. "Cancer of what?"

"Lungs," Ronkers said. "The bronchoscopy was positive; they didn't even have to open him up."

The phone rang again. When Ronkers said hello, the party hung up. Ronkers had a deplorable habit of visualizing people he had only spoken with on the phone. He saw Margaret Brant in the girls' dormitory. First she would turn to the dictionary. Then, moving lights and mirrors, she would *look* at herself. What *should* it look like? she would be wondering. And perhaps a trip to the rack of medical encyclopedias in the library. Or, last, a talk with a friend. An embarrassing phone call to Harlan Booth? No, Ronkers couldn't see that part.

He could see Kit examining her walnut-bruise in the multi-imaged mirror which was suspended beside the inverted cone—also suspended—which was the flue for the open-pit fireplace in their bedroom. One day, Ronkers thought, I will fall off the sleeping platform into the open-pit fireplace and run screaming and burning through the bedroom seeing myself times five in that multi-imaged mirror. Jesus.

"One walnut sure makes a lot of bruises," Ronkers said sleepily.

"Please don't touch it," Kit said. She had wanted to bring up another subject tonight, but her enthusiasm had been stolen.

Outside, the doomed tree—the would-be amputee—brushed against their window the way a cat brushes against your leg. In that high room, the way the wind nudged under the eaves made sleep feel precarious—as if the roof might be suddenly lifted off the house and they'd be left there, exposed. The final phase of achieving perfect interior space.

Sometime after midnight, Ronkers was called to the hospital for an emergency. An old woman, whose entire urinary system Ronkers had replaced with bags and hoses, was suffering perhaps her last malfunction. Five minutes after he left the house, Kit answered the phone. It was the hospital saying that the woman had died and there was no need to hurry.

George was gone two hours; Kit lay awake. She had so much she wanted to say when George got back that she was overwhelmed with where to begin; she let him fall asleep. She had wanted to discuss once more whether and when they would have children. But the night seemed so stalked by mayhem that the optimism of having babies struck her as absurd. She thought instead of the cool aesthetics, the thin economy, which characterized her leanings in the field of architecture.

She lay awake a long time after George fell asleep, listening to the restless rubbing of the tree, hearing the patternless, breakaway falls of the walnuts hurtling down on them—dropping into their lives as randomly as old Herr Kesler's cancer, as Margaret Brant's possible case of clap.

In Ronkers' office, waiting for him even before his receptionist had arrived, was a bird-boned girl with a yogurt-and-wheat-germ complexion who couldn't have been more than eighteen; her clothes were expensive-looking and conservative—a steel-toned suit her mother might have worn. A cream-colored, softly scented scarf was at her throat. Ronkers thought she was beautiful; she looked as if she'd just stepped off a yacht. But, of course, he knew who she was.

"Margaret Brant?" he asked, shaking her hand. Her eyes were a complement to her suit, an eerie dawn-gray. She had a perfect nose, wide nostrils in which, Ronkers thought, hair would not dare to grow.

"Dr. Ronkers?"

"Yes. Margaret Brant?"

"Of course," she sighed. She eyed the stirrups on Ronkers' examining table with a bitter dread.

"I'm awfully sorry, Miss Brant, to have called you, but Harlan Booth was not the most cooperative patient I've ever had, and I thought—for your own good—since *he* wouldn't call you, *I* should." The girl nodded, biting her lower lip. She absently removed her suit jacket and her English buckle shoes; she moved toward the examining table and those gleaming stirrups as if the whole contraption were a horse she was not sure how to mount.

"You want to *look* at me?" she asked, her back to Ronkers.

"Please relax," Ronkers begged her. "This isn't especially unpleasant, really. Have you had any discharge? Have you noticed any burning, any inflammation?"

"I haven't noticed *anything*," the girl told him, and Ronkers saw she was about to burst into tears. "It's very unfair!" she cried suddenly. "I've always been so careful with . . . sex," she said, "and I really didn't allow very much of *anything*, with Harlan Booth. I *hate* Harlan Booth!" she screamed. "I didn't know he had anything *wrong* with him, of course, or I never would have let him *touch* me!"

"But you *did* let him?" Ronkers asked. He was confused.

". . . *touch* me?" she said. "Yes, he touched me . . . *there*, you know. And he kissed me, a *lot*. But I wouldn't let him do anything *else!*" she cried. "And he was just *awful* about it, too, and he probably knew then that he was giving me *this!*"

"You mean, he just *kissed* you?" Ronkers asked, incredulous.

"Well, yes. And *touched* me, you know," she said, blushing. "He put his hand in my pants!" she cried. "And I *let* him!" She collapsed against the bent-knee part of one stirrup on the examining table and Ronkers went over to her and led her very gently to a chair beside his desk. She sobbed, with her little sharp-boned fists balled against her eyes.

"Miss Brant," Ronkers said. "Miss Brant, do you mean that Harlan Booth only touched you with his *hand?* You didn't have *real* sexual intercourse . . . Miss Brant?"

She looked up at him, shocked. "God, *no!*" she said. She bit the back of her hand and kept her fierce eyes on Ronkers.

"Just his *hand* touched you . . . *there?*" said Ronkers, and he brushed the lap of her suit skirt when he said "there."

"Yes," she said.

Ronkers took her small face in his hands and smiled at her. He was not very good at comforting or reassuring people. People seemed to misread his gestures. Margaret Brant seemed to think he was going to kiss her passionately on the mouth, because her eyes grew very wide and her back stiffened and her quick hands came up under his wrists, trying to shove him away.

"Margaret!" Ronkers said. "You *can't* have the clap if that's all that happened. You don't often catch a venereal disease from someone's *hand.*"

She now held his wrists as though they were important to her. "But he *kissed* me, too," she said worriedly. "With his *mouth,*" she added, to make things clear.

Ronkers shook his head. He went to his desk and gathered up a bunch of medical pamphlets on venereal disease. The pamphlets resembled brochures from travel agencies; there were lots of pictures of people smiling sympathetically.

"Harlan Booth must have wanted me to embarrass you," Ronkers said. "I think he was angry that you wouldn't let him . . . *you* know."

"Then you don't even have to *look* at me?" she asked.

"No," Ronkers said. "I'm sure I don't."

"I've never *been* looked at, you know," Margaret Brant told him. Ronkers didn't know what to say. "I mean, *should* I be looked at?—sometime, you know. Just to see if everything's all right?"

"Well, you might have a standard examination by a gynecologist. I can recommend Dr. Caroline Gilmore at University Hospital; a lot of students find her very nice."

"But *you* don't want to look at me?" she asked.

"Uh, no," Ronkers said. "There's no need. And for a standard examination, you should see a gynecologist. I'm a urologist."

"Oh."

She looked vacantly at the examining table and those waiting stirrups; she slipped into her suit jacket very gracefully; she had a bit more hardship with her shoes.

"Boy, that Harlan Booth is going to *get* it," she said suddenly, and with a surprising authority in her small, sharp voice.

"Harlan Booth has already *got* it," Ronkers said, trying to lighten the situation. But tiny Margaret Brant looked newly dangerous to him. "Please don't do anything you'll regret," Ronkers began weakly. But the girl's clean, wide nostrils were flaring, her gun-gray eyes were dancing.

"Thank you, Dr. Ronkers," Margaret Brant said with icy poise. "I very much appreciate your taking the trouble, and putting up with the embarrassment, of calling me." She shook his hand. "You are a very brave and *moral* man," she said, as if she were conferring military honors on Ronkers.

Watch out, Harlan Booth, he thought. Margaret Brant left Ronkers' office like a woman who had strapped on those stirrups for a ride on the examining table—and won.

Ronkers phoned up Harlan Booth. He certainly wasn't thinking of warning him; he wanted some right names. Harlan Booth took so long to answer the phone that Ronkers had worked himself up pretty well by the time Booth said a sleepy "Hello."

"You lying bastard, Booth," Ronkers said. "I want the names of people you've actually slept with—people who actually might have been exposed to your case, or from whom you might even have *gotten* it."

"Oh go to hell, Doc," Booth said, bored. "How'd you like little Maggie Brant?"

"That was dirty," Ronkers said. "A rather young and innocent girl, Booth. You were very mean."

"A little prig, a stuck-up rich bitch," Harlan Booth said. "Did you have any luck with her, Doc?"

"Please," Ronkers said. "Just give me some names. Be kind, you've got to be kind, Booth."

"Queen Elizabeth," Booth said. "Tuesday Weld, Pearl Buck . . ."

"Bad taste, Booth," Ronkers said. "Don't be a swine."

"Bella Abzug," Booth said. "Gloria Steinem, Raquel Welch, Mamie Eisenhower . . ."

Ronkers hung up. *Go get him if you can, Maggie Brant; I wish you luck!*

There was a crush of people in the waiting room outside his office; Ronkers peered out the letter slot at them. His receptionist caught the secret signal and flashed his phone light.

"Yes?"

"You're supposed to call your wife. You want me to hold up the throng a minute?"

"Thank you, yes."

Kit must have picked up the phone and immediately shoved the mouthpiece toward the open window, because Ronkers heard the unmistakably harsh *yowl* of a chain saw (maybe, *two* chain saws).

"Well," Kit said, "this is some tree outfit, all right. Didn't Bardlong say he'd fix it up with a good *tree* outfit?"

"Yes," Ronkers said. "What's wrong?"

"Well, there are three men here with chain saws and helmets with their names printed on them. Their names are Mike, Joe, and Dougie. Dougie is the highest up in the tree right now; I hope he breaks his thick neck. . . ."

"Kit, for God's sake, what's the matter?"

"Oh, Raunch, they're not a *tree* outfit at all. They're Bardlong's men—you know, they came in a goddamn BARDLONG STOPS YOU SHORT truck.

"They'll probably kill the whole tree," Kit said. "You can't just hack off limbs and branches without putting that *stuff* on, can you?"

"Stuff?"

"Goop? Gunk?" Kit said. "You know, that gooey black stuff. It *heals* the tree. God, Raunch, you're supposed to be a *doctor*, I thought you'd know something about it."

"I'm not a *tree* doctor," Ronkers said.

"These men don't even look like they know what they're doing," Kit said. "They've got ropes all over the tree and they're swinging back and forth on the ropes, and every once in a while they buzz something off with those damn saws."

"I'll call Bardlong," Ronkers said.

But his phone light was flashing. He saw three patients in rapid order, gained four minutes on his appointment schedule, peeked through the letter slot, pleaded with his receptionist, took three minutes off to call Bardlong.

"I thought you were hiring *professionals*," Ronkers said.

"These men are *very* professional," Bardlong told him.

"Professional *shock absorber* men," Ronkers said.

"No, no," Bardlong said. "Dougie used to be a tree man."

"Specialized in the walnut tree, too, I'll bet."

"Everything's fine," Bardlong said.

"I see why it costs me less," Ronkers said. "I end up paying *you.*"

"I'm retired," Bardlong said.

Ronkers' phone light was flashing again; he was about to hang up.

"Please don't worry," Bardlong said. "Everything is in good hands." And then there was an ear-splitting disturbance that made Ronkers sweep his desk ashtray into the wastebasket. From Bardlong's end of the phone came a rending sound—glassy, Baroque chandeliers falling to a ballroom floor? Mrs. Bardlong, or some equally shrill and elderly woman, hooted and howled.

"Good *Christ!*" Bardlong said over the phone. And to Ronkers he hastily added, "Excuse me." He hung up, but Ronkers had distinctly heard it: a splintering of wood, a shattering of glass, and the yammer of a chain saw "invited in" the house. He tried to imagine the tree man, Dougie, falling with a roped limb through the Bardlongs' bay window, his chain saw still sawing as he snarled his way through the velvet drapes and the chaise longue. Mrs. Bardlong, an ancient cat on her lap, would have been reading the paper, when . . .

But his receptionist was flashing him with mad regularity, and Ronkers gave in. He saw a four-year-old girl with a urinary infection (little girls are more susceptible to that than little boys); he saw a forty-eight-year-old man with a large and exquisitely tender prostate; he saw a twenty-five-year-old woman who was suffering her first bladder problem. He prescribed some Azo Gantrisin for her; he found a sample packet of the big red choke-a-horse pills and gave it to her. She stared at them, frightened at the size.

"Is there, you know, an *applicator?*" she asked.

"No, no," Ronkers said. "You take them *orally*. You *swallow* them."

The phone flashed. Ronkers knew it was Kit.

"What happened?" he asked her. "I *heard* it!"

"Dougie cut right through the limb *and* the rope that was guiding the limb away from the house," Kit said.

"How exciting!"

"Poked the limb through Bardlong's bathroom window like a great pool cue . . ."

"Oh," said Ronkers, disappointed. He had hoped for the bay . . .

"I think Mrs. Bardlong was in the bathroom," Kit said.

Shocked at his glee, Ronkers asked, "Was anyone hurt?"

"Dougie sawed into Mike's arm," Kit said, "and I think Joe broke his ankle jumping out of the tree."

"God!"

"No one's hurt badly," Kit said. "But the tree looks *awful*; they didn't even finish it."

"Bardlong will have to take care of it," Ronkers said.

"Raunch," Kit said. "The newspaper photographer was here; he goes out on every ambulance call. He took a picture of the tree and Bardlong's window. Listen, this is *serious*, Raunch: Does Kesler get a newspaper on his breakfast tray? You've got to speak to the floor nurse; don't let him see the picture, Raunch. Okay?"

"Okay," he said.

Outside in the waiting room the woman was showing the Azo Gantrisin pills to Ronkers' receptionist. "He wants me to *swallow* them. . . ." Ronkers let the letter slot close slowly. He buzzed his receptionist.

"Entertain them, please," he said. "I am taking ten."

He slipped out of his office through the hospital entrance and crossed through Emergency as the ambulance staff was bringing in a man on a stretcher; he was propped up on his elbows, his ankle unbooted and wrapped in an ice pack. His helmet said "Joe." The man who walked beside the stretcher carried his helmet in his one good hand. He was "Mike." His other hand was held up close to his breast; his forearm was blood-soaked; an ambulance attendant walked alongside with his thumb jammed deep into the crook of Mike's arm. Ronkers intercepted them and took a look at the cut. It was not serious, but it was a messy, ragged thing with a lot of black oil and sawdust in it. About thirty stitches, Ronkers guessed, but the man was not bleeding too badly. A tedious debridement, lots of Xylocaine . . . but Fowler was covering Emergency this morning, and it wasn't any of Ronkers' business.

He went on to the third floor. Kesler was in 339, a single room; at least a private death awaited him. Ronkers found the floor nurse, but Kesler's door was open and Ronkers stood with the nurse in the hall where the old man could see them; Kesler recognized Ronkers, but didn't seem to know *where* he recognized Ronkers from.

"*Kommen Sie hinein, bitte!*" Kesler called. His voice was like speech scraped on a file, sanded down to something scratchier than old records. "*Grüss Gott!*" he called.

"I wish I knew some German," the nurse told Ronkers.

Ronkers knew a little. He went into Kesler's room, made a cursory check on the movable parts now keeping him alive. The rasp in Kesler's voice was due to the Levine tube which ran down his throat to his stomach.

"Hello, Mr. Kesler," Ronkers said. "Do you remember me?" Kesler stared with wonder at Ronkers; they had taken out his false teeth and his face was curiously turtlelike in its leatheriness—its sagging, cold qualities. Predictably, he had lost about sixty pounds.

"*Ach!*" Kesler said suddenly. "Das house gebought? You . . . *ja!* How goes it? Your wife the walls down-took?"

"Yes," Ronkers said, "but you would like it. It's very beautiful. There's more window light now."

"*Und der Bardlong?*" Kesler whispered. "He has not the tree down-chopped?"

"No."

"*Sehr gut!*" Herr Kesler said. That is pronounced *zohr goot.* "*Gut boy!*" Kesler told Ronkers. *Goot buoy.* Kesler blinked his dull, dry eyes for a second and when they opened it was as if they opened on another scene—another time, somewhere. "*Frühstück?*" he asked politely.

"That means breakfast," Ronkers told the nurse. They had Kesler on a hundred milligrams of Demerol every four hours; that makes you less than alert.

Ronkers was getting out of the elevator on the first floor when the intercom paged "Dr. Heart." There was no Dr. Heart at University Hospital. "Dr. Heart" meant that someone's heart had stopped.

"Dr. Heart?" the intercom asked sweetly. "Please come to 304. . . ."

Any doctor in the hospital was supposed to hurry to that room. There was an unwritten rule that you looked around and made a slow move to the nearest elevator, hoping another doctor would beat you to the patient. Ronkers hesitated, letting the elevator door close. He pushed the button again, but the elevator was already moving up.

"Dr. Heart, room 304," the intercom said calmly. It was better than urgently crying, "A doctor! Any doctor to room 304! Oh my God, *hurry!*" That might disturb the other patients and the visitors.

Dr. Hampton was coming down the floor toward the elevator.

"You still having office calls?" Hampton asked Ronkers.

"Yup," Ronkers said.

"Go back to your office, then," Hampton said. "I'll get this one."

The elevator had stopped on the third floor; it was pretty certain that "Dr. Heart" had already arrived in 304. Ronkers went back to his office. It would be nice to take Kit out to dinner, he thought.

At the Route Six Ming Dynasty, Kit ordered the sweet and sour bass; Ronkers chose the beef in lobster sauce. He was distracted. He had seen a sign in the window of the Route Six Ming Dynasty, just as they'd come in the door. It was a sign about two feet long and one foot high—black lettering on white shirt cardboard, perhaps. It looked perfectly natural there in the window, for it was about the expected size—and, Ronkers falsely assumed, about the expected content of a sign like TWO WAITRESSES WANTED.

Ronkers was distracted only now, as he sipped a drink with Kit, because only now was the *real* content of that sign coming through to him. He thought he was imagining it, so he excused himself from the table and slipped outside the Route Six Ming Dynasty to have another look at that sign.

Appallingly, he had *not* imagined it. There, vividly in a lower corner of the window, plainly in view of every customer approaching the door, was a neatly lettered sign which read: HARLAN BOOTH HAS THE CLAP.

"Well, it's *true*, isn't it?" Kit asked.

"Well, yes, but that's not the point," Ronkers said. "It's sort of unethical. I mean, it *has* to be Margaret Brant, and I'm responsible for releasing the information. That sort of thing should be confidential, after all. . . ."

"Turds," said Kit. "Good for Margaret Brant! You must admit,

Raunch, if Harlan Booth had played fair with you, the whole thing wouldn't have happened. I think he deserves it."

"Well, of course he *deserves* it," Ronkers said, "but I wonder where *else* she put up signs."

"Really, Raunch, just let it be. . . ."

But Ronkers had to see for himself. They drove to the Student Union. Inside the main lobby, Ronkers searched the giant bulletin board for clues.

> '70 BMW, LIKE NEW . . .
>
> RIDERS WANTED TO SHARE EXPENSES AND DRIVING TO NYC, LV. THURS., RETURN MON. EVE, CALL "LARRY," 351-4306 . . .
>
> HARLAN BOOTH HAS THE CLAP. . . .

"My God."

They went to the auditorium; a play was in progress. They didn't even have to get out of their car to see it: a NO PARKING sign had been neatly covered and given the new message. Kit was hysterical.

The Whale Room was where a lot of students drank and played pool and danced to local talent. It was a loud, smoke-filled place; Ronkers had several emergency calls a month involving patients who had begun their emergency in the Whale Room.

Somehow, Margaret Brant had warmed the bartender's heart. Above the bar mirror, above the glowing bottles, above the sign saying CHECKS CASHED FOR EXACT AMOUNT ONLY, were the same neat and condemning letters now familiar to Ronkers and Kit. The Whale Room was informed that Harlan Booth was contagious.

Fearing the worst, Ronkers insisted they take a drive past Margaret Brant's dorm—a giant building, a women's dormitory of prison size and structure. Ivy did not grow there.

In the upcast streetlights, above the bicycle racks—seemingly tacked to every sill of every third-floor window—a vast sewn-together bedsheet stretched across the entire front of Catherine Cascomb Dormitory for Women. Margaret Brant had friends. Her friends were upset, too. In a massive sacrifice of linen and labor, every girl in every third-floor, front-window room had done her part. Each letter was about six feet high and single-bed width.

"Fantastic!" Kit shouted. "Well done! Good show! Let him have it!"

"Way to go, Maggie Brant," whispered Ronkers reverently. But he knew he hadn't seen the end of it.

It was two A.M. when the phone rang and he suspected it was not the hospital.

"Yes?" he said.

"Did I wake you up, Doc?" said Harlan Booth. "I sure *hope* I woke you up."

"Hello, Booth," Ronkers said. Kit sat up beside him, looking strong and fit.

"Call off your goons, Doc. I don't have to put up with this. This is harassment. You're supposed to be *ethical*, you crummy doctors . . ."

"You mean you've seen the signs?" Ronkers asked.

"*Signs?*" Booth asked. "*What* signs? What are you talking about?"

"What are *you* talking about?" Ronkers said, genuinely puzzled.

"You know goddamn well what I'm talking about!" Harlan Booth yelled. "Every half-hour a broad calls me up. It's two o'clock in the morning, Doc, and every half-hour a broad calls me up. A *different* broad, every half-hour, you know perfectly well . . ."

"What do they say to you?" Ronkers asked.

"Cut it out!" Booth yelled. "You know damn well what they say to me, Doc. They say stuff like, 'How's your clap coming along, Mr. Booth?' and 'Where are you spreading your clap around, Harlan old baby?' You *know* what they say to me, Doc!"

"Cheer up, Booth," Ronkers said. "Get out for a breath of air. Take a drive—down by Catherine Cascomb Dormitory for Women, for example. There's a lovely banner unfurled in your honor; you really ought to see it."

"A *banner?*" Booth said.

"Go get a drink at the Whale Room, Booth," Ronkers told him. "It will settle you down."

"*Look*, Doc!" Booth screamed. "You call them off!"

"I didn't call them *on*, Booth."

"It's that little bitch Maggie Brant, isn't it, Doc?"

"I doubt she's operating alone, Booth."

"Look," Booth said. "I can take you to court for this. Invasion of privacy. I can go to the papers, I'll go to the *university*—expose Student Health. You've got no right to be this unethical."

"Why not just call Margaret Brant?" Ronkers suggested.

"*Call* her?"

"And apologize," Ronkers said. "Tell her you're sorry."

"*Sorry?!*" Booth shouted.

"And then come give me some names," Ronkers said.

"I'm going to every newspaper in the state, Doc."

"I'd love to see you do that, Booth. They would crucify you. . . ."

"Doc . . ."

"Give yourself a real lift, Booth. Take a drive by Catherine Cascomb Dormitory for Women. . . ."

"Go to hell, Doc."

"Better hurry, Booth. Tomorrow they may start the bumper sticker campaign."

"Bumper stickers?"

" 'Harlan Booth has the clap,' " Ronkers said. "That's what the bumper stickers are going to say. . . ."

Booth hung up. The way he hung up rang in Ronkers' ear for a long time. The walnuts dropping on the roof were almost soothing after the sound Booth had made.

"I think we've got him," Ronkers told Kit.

" 'We,' is it?" she said. "You sound like you've joined up."

"I *have*," Ronkers said. "I'm going to call Margaret Brant first thing in the morning and tell her about my bumper sticker idea."

But Margaret Brant needed no coaching. In the morning when Ronkers went out to his car, there was a freshly stuck-on bumper sticker, front and back. Dark blue lettering on a bright yellow background; it ran half the length of the bumper.

HARLAN BOOTH HAS THE CLAP

On his way to the hospital, Ronkers saw more of the adorned cars. Some drivers were parked in gas stations, working furiously to remove the stickers. But that was a hard, messy job. Most people appeared to be too busy to do anything about the stickers right away.

"I counted thirty-four, just driving across town," Ronkers told Kit on the phone. "And it's still early in the morning."

"Bardlong got to work early, too," Kit told him.

"What do you mean?"

"He hired a real *tree* outfit this time. The tree surgeons came right after you left."

"Ah, real tree surgeons . . ."

"They have helmets, too, and their names are Mickey, Max, and Harv," Kit said. "And they brought a whole tub of that black healing stuff."

"*Dr. Heart,*" said Ronkers' receptionist, cutting in. "*Dr. Heart, please, to 339.*"

"Raunch?"

But the receptionist was interrupting because it was so early; there just might not be another doctor around the hospital. Ronkers came in early, often hours ahead of his first appointment —to make his hospital rounds, yes, but mainly to sit in his office alone for a while.

"I've got to go," he told Kit. "I'll call back."

"Who's Dr. Hart?" Kit asked. "Somebody new?"

"Yup," Ronkers said, but he was thinking: No, it's probably somebody *old.*

He was out of his office, and half through the connecting tunnel which links the main hospital to several doctors' offices, when he heard the intercom call for Dr. Heart again and recognized the room number: 339. That was old Herr Kesler's room, Ronkers remembered. Nurses, seeing him coming, opened doors for him; they opened doors in all directions, down all corridors, and they always looked after him a little disappointed that he did not pass through *their* doors, that he veered left instead of right. When he got to Kesler's room, the cardiac resuscitation cart was parked beside the bed and Dr. Heart was already there. It was Danfors—a better Dr. Heart than Ronkers could have been, Ronkers knew; Danfors was a heart specialist.

Kesler was dead. That is, technically, when your heart stops, you're dead. But Danfors was already holding the electrode plates alongside Kesler's chest; the old man was about to get a tremendous jolt. Ah, the new machines, Ronkers marveled. Ronkers had once brought a man from the dead with five hundred volts from the cardioverter, lifting the body right off the bed, the limbs jangling—like pithing a frog in Introductory Biology.

"How's Kit, George?" Danfors asked.

"Just fine," Ronkers said. Danfors was checking the i.v. of sodium bicarbonate running into Kesler. "You must come see what she's done to the house. And bring Lilly."

"Right-O," said Danfors, giving Kesler five hundred volts.

Kesler's jaw was rigid on his chest and his teeth were clenched together fast, yet he managed to force a ghastly quarter-moon of a smile and expel a sentence of considerable volume and energy. It was German, of course, which surprised Danfors; he probably didn't know Kesler was an Austrian.

"*Noch ein Bier!*" Kesler ordered.

"What'd he say?" Danfors asked Ronkers.

"'One more beer,'" Ronkers translated.

But the current, of course, was cut. Kesler was dead again. Five hundred volts had woken him up, but Kesler did not have enough voltage of his own to keep himself awake.

"Shit," Danfors said. "I got three in a row with this thing when the hospital first got it, and I thought it was the best damn machine alive. But then I lost four out of the next five. So I was four-and-four with the thing; nothing is foolproof, of course. And now this one's the tie breaker." Danfors managed to make his record with the heart machine sound like a losing season.

Now Ronkers didn't want to call Kit back; he knew Kesler's death would upset her. But she called him before he could work it out.

"Well, good," Ronkers said.

"Raunch?" Kit asked. "Kesler didn't see the paper, did he? They put the picture right on the front page, you know. You don't think he saw it, do you?"

"For a fact, he did not see it," Ronkers said.

"Oh, good," she said. She seemed to want to stay on the phone, Ronkers thought, although she wasn't talking. He told her he was awfully busy and he had to go.

Ronkers was in a mean mood when he sat down to lunch with Danfors in the hospital cafeteria. They were still on the soup course when the intercom pleasantly asked for Dr. Heart. Since he was a heart specialist, Danfors answered most of the Dr. Heart calls in the hospital whenever he was there, even if someone beat him to the elevator. He stood up and drank his milk down with a few swift guzzles.

"*Noch ein Bier!*" Ronkers said.

At home, Kit—the receiver of messages, the composer of rooms—had news for him. First, Margaret Brant had left word she was dropping the Harlan Booth assault because Booth had called and begged her forgiveness. Second, Booth had called and left Kit with a list of names. "Real ones," he'd said. Third, something was up with Bardlong and the infernal tree. The tree surgeons had alarmed him about something, and Bardlong and his wife had been poking about under the tree, along their side of the slate-stone wall, as if inspecting some new damage—as if plotting some new attack.

Wearily, Ronkers wandered to the yard to confront this new problem. Bardlong was down on the ground on all fours, peering deep into the caves of his slate-stone wall. Looking for squirrels?

"After the men did such a neat job," Bardlong announced, "it came to their attention that they should really have taken the whole thing down. And they're professionals, of course. I'm afraid they're right. The whole thing's got to come down."

"Why?" Ronkers asked. He was trying to summon resistance but he found his resistance was stale.

"The roots," Bardlong said. "The roots are going to topple the wall. The *roots*," he said again, as if he were saying, *the armies! the tanks! the big guns!* "The roots are crawling their way through my wall." He made it sound like a conspiracy, the roots engaged in strangling some stones, bribing others. They crept their way into revolutionary positions among the slate. On signal, they were ready to upheave the whole.

"That will surely take some time," Ronkers said, thinking, with a harshness that surprised him: That wall will outlive *you* Bardlong!

"It's already happening," Bardlong said. "I hate to ask you to do this, of course, but the wall, if it crumbles, well . . ."

"We can build it up again," Ronkers said. Ah, the *doctor* in him!

As illogical as cancer, Bardlong shook his head. Not far away,

Ronkers saw, would be the line about hoping not to get "legal." Ronkers felt too tired to resist *anything.*

"It's simple," said Bardlong. "I want to keep the wall, you want to keep the tree."

"Walls can be rebuilt," Ronkers said, utterly without conviction.

"I see," Bardlong said. Meaning what? It was like the five hundred volts administered to Kesler. There was a real effect—it was visible—but it was not effective at all. On his gloomy way back inside his house, Ronkers pondered the effect of five hundred volts on Bardlong. With the current on for about five minutes.

He also fantasized this bizarre scene: Bardlong suddenly in Ronkers' office, looking at the floor and saying, "I have had certain . . . relations, ah, with a lady who, ah, apparently was not in the best of . . . health."

"If it would, Mr. Bardlong, spare you any embarrassment," Ronkers imagined himself saying, "I could of course let the, ah, lady know that she should seek medical attention."

"You'd do that for me?" Bardlong would cry then, overcome. "Why, I mean, I would, ah . . . pay you for that, anything you ask."

And Ronkers would have him then, of course. With a hunting cat's leer, he would spring the price. "How about half a walnut tree?"

But things like that, Ronkers knew, didn't happen. Things like that were in the nature of the stories about abandoned pets, limping their way from Vermont to California, finding the family months later, arriving with bleeding pads and wagging tails. The reason such stories were so popular was that they went pleasantly against what everyone knew *really* happened. The pet was squashed by a Buick in Massachusetts—or, worse, was perfectly happy to remain abandoned in Vermont.

And if Bardlong came to Ronkers' office, it would be for some perfectly respectable aspect of age finally lodging in his prostate.

"Kesler's dead, Kit," Ronkers told her. "His heart stopped, saved him a lot of trouble, really; he would have gotten quite uncomfortable."

He held her in the fabulous sleeping place she had invented. Outside their window the scrawny, pruned tree clicked against the rain gutter like light bones. The leaves were all gone; what few walnuts remained were small and shriveled—even the squirrels ignored them, and if one had fallen on the roof it would have gone unnoticed. Winter-bare and offering nothing but its weird shadows on their bed and its alarming sounds throughout their night, the tree seemed hardly worth their struggle. Kesler, after all, was dead. And Bardlong was so *very* retired that he had more time and energy to give to trivia than anyone who was likely to oppose him. The wall between Ronkers and Bardlong seemed frail, indeed.

It was then that Ronkers realized he had not made love to his wife in a very long time, and he made the sort of love to Kit that some therapist might have called "re-assuring." And some lover, Ronkers thought later, might have called dull.

He watched her sleep. A lovely woman; her students, he suspected, cared for more than her architecture. And she, one day, might care more for them—or for *one* of them. Why was he thinking *that?* he wondered, then pondered his own recent sensations for the X-ray technician.

But those kinds of problems, for Kit and him, seemed years away—well, *months* away, at least.

He thought of Margaret Brant's sweet taste of revenge; her mature forgiveness surprised and encouraged him. And Harlan Booth's giving in? Whether he was converted—or just trapped, and evil to the core—was quite unknowable at the moment. Whether *anyone* was . . . Ronkers wondered.

Danfors' season with the heart machine now stood at four-and-six. What sort of odds were those in favor of human reproduction?—Ronkers' and Kit's, especially. . . . And even if all the high school principals and parents in the world were as liberal and humorous and completely approachable concerning venereal disease, as they might be sympathetic toward a football injury, there would *still* be rampant clap in the world—and syphilis, and more.

Kit slept.

The brittle tree clacked against the house like the bill of a parrot he remembered hearing in a zoo. Where was that? *What* zoo?

In an impulse, which felt to Ronkers like resignation, he moved to the window and looked over the moonlit roofs of the suburbs—many of which he could see for the first time, now that the leaves were all gone and a winter view was possible. And to all the people under those roofs, and more, he whispered, wickedly, "Have fun!" To Ronkers, this was a kind of benediction with a hidden hook.

"Why *not* have children?" he said aloud. Kit stirred, but she had not actually heard him.

Putney, Vermont
1974

THE RUNNER

JAMES TABOR

James Michael Tabor was born in Newport News, Virginia, raised in West Hartford, Connecticut, and educated at the University of Vermont and The Johns Hopkins University, where he studied with John Barth. He lives presently in Silver Spring, Maryland, with his wife and one son. In classic writerly fashion, he has worked as a dockhand, laborer, baggage clerk, chauffeur, bartender, ski instructor, manager, ad writer, cop, and farmer. But he has never *been* anything but a writer.

He has been published in literary magazines, the Washington *Post*, *The Washingtonian Magazine*, and other periodicals. Currently he is working on a collection of short stories, a novel, and a nonfiction book about police work.

Out of a silver heat mirage he ran. Two lanes of blacktop stretched straight and flat in front of him, straight and flat behind. August-tall corn walled in the road and its red-sand shoulders. A half mile away was a blue-dark wall of woods.

On the road it was neither cool nor dark. The sky burned, and under him the paving was a black mirror reflecting sun-fire. Sweat sprayed from his skin with each footstrike, so that he ran in a hot mist of his own creation. With each slap on the softened asphalt, his soles absorbed heat that rose through his arches and ankles and the stems of his shins. It was a carnival of pain, but he loved each stride because the running distilled him to essence and the heat hastened this distillation.

He wore a pair of blue Etonic Streetfighters, faded red gym shorts, a neck chain hung with two battered dog tags, and nothing else. The plates of his stomach muscles rippled with each stretched-out stride that floated him over the roadway. In the heat he heard the light *hsssss* of his own breathing, and the rhythmic *click-cleck click-cleck* of his footstrikes. Beyond these, in the sound-discouraging heat, there were only snakes rustling in the rows of corn for something to kill.

He enjoyed running here, in the flat red corn country of Maryland's Eastern Shore. The roads were straight, traffic infrequent, problems few. And that was not unimportant to him. He wore his hair a little long for such original country, but he knew that the district's lone trooper was a whiskey drunk with all road love burned out of him. So here he could run without trouble, and he could rent a cheap clean room with a window over water, and he could make a few dollars working fishing boats that slid daily onto the Bay. That was all he wanted. He did not think it was too much.

From the distance a sound reached him, but he saw nothing. At first it was such a faint sound that he mistook it for the buzz of a diving bee, and prepared to swat it from his path. Then he saw a spot wavering on the horizon, and it grew larger.

A motorcycle. Jesus can't you keep them in the God-damned cities?

Rushing toward him, growing by the second, the cycle revealed itself: a fat chopped Honda, front fork pushed out, the frame an intestinal tangle of glistening chrome. He hated cycles, and not only for their buzzing snarls that fractured the peace of his running and filled the air with stink. Once, running in New Hampshire on the roads that coil around Winnipesaukee, he had been corralled by a gang from the Grafton races. For them at first it had been fun, circling their hogs around him on the dusty deserted road, spraying him with beer and urine, laughing, then readying to leave. But he was one of those men whose skin does not thicken into armor against the forces of lunacy. An eternal innocent, he existed in a state of near-constant amazement at the flaws in his universe. So he had cracked the throat of one with the flat edge of his hand, and then they had exacted a toll of torn flesh and splintered bones that had kept him from the roads for seven months.

The rider of this lone cycle reclined as though on a lounge, his back sloped against the sissy bar, his legs splayed and feet propped on high pegs. He wore tennis shoes and cutoff blue jeans and a yellow tank top. A full Bell helmet's black visor hid his face. When he roared by, blasting the runner with grit, scorched air, and exhaust stench, he made a languid salute: one middle finger, stiffly uplifted.

I seem unable to elude them. They cover the country like locusts, he thought, not only about the motorcyclists. But he could not really say to himself, as he ran between the green walls of corn, that he was surprised. Long ago he had realized that the world was divided, and he had begun trying to live his life free from the interference of a certain kind of people, who *drive station wagons, hunt deer, live near cities, watch television, mow lawns* (he ticked them off in rhythm to his footstrikes) *read newspapers play softball go shopping buy insurance smile marry vote pay taxes pray.*

He was neither an indigent nor a criminal. In fact he was educated, and a decorated veteran of combat, and a man who had once fit comfortably into a satisfactory niche. In Vermont, he had taught in a college. But, finally unable to bear the dooming of rich young minds, he had abandoned that to teach skiing. Later, in Montana, he had trained sled dogs. In California he had rescued mountain climbers and worked in a sleeping-bag factory. In Florida he had guided men to good bonefish flats. In Maryland, now, he worked the high-prowed boats, and ran. He had always run for solace, even before the tide of things he despised began washing him from his progressively less satisfactory niches. Now he had stayed nearly a year in the cove-locked shore towns, liking the red country and the great Bay and the people whose faces, as flat and red and unkind as the land, asked him nothing. But he felt, as the dinosaurs must have felt, something troubling the air. And far into the darkness of certain nights, sitting with a candle and a bottle of Glenfiddich on the unvarnished table in his room, he wondered how long it would be.

He ticked off six miles with reaching strides, his rhythm rolling on itself, like coasting downhill on oiled bearings. He passed a narrow dirt lane, a channel for tractors, but he did not think of turning off. He did not want such lanes. They were thin and blocked at their ends. He ran on, settling back into himself after the motorcycle, filling his body with breathing. A mile, another, the rhythm hypnotic. And then he was startled by an engine close behind him.

Somehow he had not heard the car coming up. Either the hot breeze had been wrong, or he had been hypnotized by heat shimmer, or entranced by the smooth commotion of his muscles. But now he heard it, and glanced over his shoulder to see a wallowing Cadillac, its yellow paint new and bright. One green-tinted window powered down as the car came on. He saw a hand flash whitely against the dark interior. A full brown bottle of Budweiser, capped, shot toward him. It exploded against the pavement, spraying him with glass splinters and beer. Faces, tinted corpse-green by the glass, jeered at him. As the car sped on he saw them, their features deformed by laughter.

"Screw you," he shouted, and hurled a rock at them. His rock fell far short and the Cadillac hurtled away, merging finally with the shimmering distance. Then he saw twin points of red light and a quick swirl, like the silver dart of barracuda in the flats he had once fished.

Coming back. They want to throw something else at me. Why don't they ever throw money?

He looked behind himself at the empty miles. Ahead, the Cadillac shot toward him down the straight black barrel of the road.

No more dancing. Jesus was a fool.

He picked up a baseball-sized stone, held it in his right hand, and kept running.

Come on.

Come they did. Angling out of the center of the road so that its right wheels balanced on the pavement's edge, the Cadillac veered in toward him. When it was twenty feet away, he lofted his rock gently into the air. Then he dove into the corn. The Cadillac, roaring on, shattered its windshield against the languidly descending stone.

He reclaimed his road to the screams of skidding rubber. Without breaking stride, he glanced back at the giant car slewing sideways, its four fat tires spraying smoke. The car rocked to a stop. Three doors banged open. Two fat men and a woman labored out. Rolls of flesh jiggled on their bodies. Sweat darkened their clothing immediately. Their full lips spewed curses. The woman waved a bottle. One of the men lumbered to the car's trunk, threw it open, and lifted out a shotgun. He shouldered the weapon and fired. The runner saw a blue puff of smoke, then heard buckshot whistle by to his left. Anticipating the man's correction, he moved left and ducked again into the corn, running at an angle away from the road. Stalks hit his shoulders like slalom poles. The leaves, curling down like wide green ribbons, flicked his face as the shotgun fired again and he heard the *thack thack* of buckshot striking stalks. Then he heard doors slamming and the engine roaring and tires squealing and they were coming after him. He was not surprised.

Empty country. Clear and open and empty. Good country for killing. They do intend to kill me. The one cop asleep in his own puke. Come, then.

He ran out of the corn onto one of the narrow dirt lanes that crossed the main road. For an instant he did not move. At that same instant the Cadillac passed by on the road. He knew they had seen him. The car stopped, reversed, and turned down the tractor lane. He began running toward the dark woods that were another quarter mile away, looking over his shoulder once to see the broad car bulling its way down the narrow strip of dirt, spraying green stalks out from its fenders like water curving off the bow of a ship.

He entered the woods 25 yards ahead of them and ran on, hurdling fallen logs, twisting through brambles, padding silently on the pine-needle-cushioned floor. The woods smelled sweetly damp and ancient.

He heard their doors open and close, and he heard them enter the woods. He was kneeling behind a boulder, and the two men were walking straight in, about 25 feet apart, moving with noisy disdain. He drifted 50 feet to his left, lay flat on his stomach, and waited while they passed. They walked hunched over, like hunters, and the one who carried the shotgun looked as though he might actually have done some hunting. The other looked like a city man, hands nervously swatting at branches and gnats. Both of them wore loud sport shirts and fresh beach sunburns. They went on through the woods, making so much noise that he did not have to disguise his own as he slipped back from tree to tree and stopped at the woods' edge, not far from the car. He entered the corn rows, circled silently, and came up behind the woman, who stood facing the woods with one flesh-heavy hip propped against the car and a bottle of Almaden wine tilted to her mouth. She was swallowing noisily as he threw his dog tags and chain around her neck, garroting her, collapsing the larynx before she could scream. The bottle dropped from her hand but she tore at his eyes with her fingers. He had expected that and drove her face-first into the dirt, then planted both knees in the small of her back and hauled up on her slippery chin with all his strength until her neck snapped. Her toes, kicking reflexively, threw little spurts of dust behind her body. Voided urine stained a circle around her hips. He rested a moment, then lifted her into the back seat of the Cadillac and leaned her against the closed door so that she appeared to be asleep. With a flat rock he cracked the bottle of Almaden wine. When it broke well, with the slim neck and one long shard forming a dagger, he took it as an omen and went back into the woods.

He thought that the men would come out in thirty minutes, but they lasted only twenty. They were a hundred feet away when he heard them, cursing through the undergrowth, and when they clambered out blinking in the sunlight the one with the shotgun said, ". . . the hell is she doing? That God-damned wine put her to sleep?"

Both of their backs were to him as he made his rush, focusing all his momentum into the flabby back of the one nearest, hitting him so hard that saliva burst in a white spray from the man's mouth. The glass dagger drove in as though into cheese, loosing a column of blood. The runner supported the fat man, so that he absorbed the buckshot when the second man fired once before he was knocked over by their combined impact. The runner watched the living fat man writhe beneath the dead wet weight of the companion he had just killed. When finally he struggled from beneath the corpse, he made no further move, because the runner was pointing the twelve-gauge shotgun into his face.

"You're crazy," the fat man whispered.

The runner's vision blurred from dripping sweat. Objects wavered before him now like plucked strings. Then, as he waited, everything clarified. The fat man was down on one knee, both hands flat in the dust, his head upraised. Dirt lined his flesh's creases. Sweat and new blood plastered his clothing to the rounded contours beneath. His eyes were soiled with hate and fury.

"Look what you've done. You're . . . you've killed two people. Jesus, you . . ."

"You're not people," the runner said. For a long time he had known that God was no more just than man was pure. He had sensed that the way to salvation was pain, and had run that road. Now his vision sharpened into an undeniable clarity. The air seemed to hum. Murder, he saw, was no longer the greatest sin.

He racked a shell into the shotgun's chamber and fired. Then he took off his shorts and wiped the gun free of fingerprints. He wiped his prints off of the shard of glass and the Cadillac. Then he put his shorts back on and ran out to the road, still shimmering under the afternoon sun.

ST. STEPHEN'S GREEN

KAY BOYLE

Kay Boyle was born in St. Paul, Minnesota. She has published seven collections of short stories, a collection of short novels, three volumes of poetry, fourteen novels, three children's books, and a book of memoirs. Doubleday published her *Fifty Stories* in 1980.

Among many other honors, she was awarded O. Henry Prizes for the best short story of the year in 1934, and again in 1941. In 1978 she was elected to the National Academy of Arts and Letters.

Since 1963 she has been a member of the English and Creative Writing Departments at San Francisco State University. After seventeen years of living in San Francisco, she is now beginning a new interval of travel from country to country.

She had come to Ireland with one suitcase and little more than the long blue denim coat she was wearing. It had been bought in Virginia two years before, where there are no revolutionaries to speak of, yet the coat had a fiery red silk lining that had a tendency to ravel out at the hem. She had also brought with her two pairs of walking shoes: the red leather ones she had on her feet when she walked into St. Stephen's Green, and the beige suede pair that was champing its snaffle and curb in the lowly chamber of the bed-and-breakfast place, with only Samuel Beckett to keep it company. There he sat on the paper cover of *That Time*, Beckett himself looking straight into the heart and soul of all mankind, the long fingers of his right hand resting on his knee, and his left hand, alive as a question mark, pressed fanwise to his chin. On the back of this slender volume, the publisher had seen fit to say: "In the darkness of an empty stage an old white face is seen.

Out of the darkness come to him voices—his own—which speak of the past: nostalgic, regretful, elegiac, fragmentary." And on the back as well was the price: a staggering 50p.

She was not in Ireland for the sake of the scenery or in search of forebears. That much she knew. Brendan Behan had once said, or maybe sang off-key as was his wont, that the Irish and the Jews don't have a nationality but simply a psychosis. It might be that the explanation for why she was here, without rhyme or reason or name of friend, was a need to be a part of that grave disorganization of personality (as Webster's dictionary defines the troubled area or homeland of psychotic pain) which her ancestors from Donegal had given her title to. With her youth interred alive behind her, she sat on a bench in St. Stephen's Green, wondrously and curiously at home. If a tourist of any stripe had happened to speak to her of the terrible beauty of the Irish countryside, or the amazing hospitality of the Irish people she would have grown faint and withered away before his eyes.

She had found this oasis the first day in Dublin. The foliage, dense as a wall on the other side of the pond, was luxuriant enough to have wooed camel caravans to stretch their necks and nibble with yellow teeth and hanging underlips at the tender leaves as they passed by. Quacking ducks and venomous gulls were skidding left and right on the water, for there were no lanes marked on the shimmering surface, no traffic signs forbidding U-turns or the spread of irate wings or snapping bills, no white-gloved authority telling the feathered and web-footed when to stop and when to go. The sun was warm on her denim coat, and the woman unbuttoned it slowly, wondering if the satin of zebras' necks, or the mottled throats of shy giraffes, might not reach across her shoulder at any moment and seek to drink. Once a grandchild—gone, gone now, as all grandchildren go into their own lives or deaths—had asked if it was a map painted on a giraffe's hide, and a voice she could no longer identify had answered: "Yes, it is the map of the whole world."

On the green sward behind the bench there were no long-legged, endangered species, but office workers, or bank or shop clerks, as well as the unemployed, stretched out in comfort for the lunch hour, some feigning sleep, some clasped in one another's arms. From a long way away, bells were ringing in high noon when a young man burst without warning on the scene. He wore a gray tweed jacket and tan slacks, and he sat down almost in impatience, without casting a glance toward the other end of the bench, and ran his fingers through his chestnut brown hair. His wrists were broad, and as hard to the eye as anvils, and his hand was startlingly out of scale with the minute notebook he had just taken from his pocket. He began at once to write in it with a pen small enough for a leprechaun to have handled. Line after line he wrote on the minuscule pages, writing earnestly, his lips forming the words in silence as he set them down. Whether he was Irish or English, the woman was still too new to the country to know. But because he glanced every now and then at the traffic of birds on the water, she thought it must be the history of their conflict he was desperately compiling, his red knuckles humped around the tiny pen.

Then, unexpected as a shot from a sniper's gun, the young man leapt up from the bench and the dwarfed notebook and pen fell to the paving at his feet. He rushed like a man demented to the water's edge and smashed his hands together in a thunderous clap that startled every bird into flight. Mother ducks abandoned in panic their trail of young, and with the sound of tearing silk winged to shelter in the jungle green of the other side, while gulls flapped upward, white and strong as canvas sails, screaming their imprecations at everyone below.

"Get out, bandits! Clear out!" the man shouted, and again he struck his broad, raw palms together. And now the clerks and office workers sat upright on the grass, as startled as the birds.

"Ow, let them be, limey!" a man's voice called out, the accent so different from that of the man in the tweed jacket that he might have been speaking a foreign tongue.

"It's the blasted gulls!" the man cried out, turning on the people now. "The ducks and all the rest of them, the small ones, they're cut off every time they try to eat!"

"That's life, man. That's the way it is in the old country," another man's voice called from the emerald grass, and laughter ran lazily from couple to couple as the dark-haired girls lay down and took their men into their soft, bare arms again for the little time that was left to them, and the men's arms drew the girls' waists close, as they had before.

But the Englishman, alone in his anger, stood there, flushed and boyish-looking, not knowing if it was the gulls or the humans he should turn on the spit of his ire. Then he stooped to pick up the notebook and pen, both so infinitesimal that they disappeared from sight in the palm of his hand.

"One of those long-haired Americans who had the bloody cheek," he said aloud to himself as he sat down. Then he glanced uneasily toward the other end of the bench and revised the wording. "The incredible cheek," he said, appalled that he, of all men, should have been called that name. "A hippie trying to pass for an Irishman, I dare say," he told the reassembling birds.

"I wouldn't take it as an insult," the woman said, looking down at the red shoes that had trod the soil of California just a day and a half before. He was maybe a schoolteacher here on holiday, she thought, and the blasting of his hands was the one gesture of discipline left to him now that the four walls of a classroom were no longer there. What she wanted to say to him was that drakes are a disgrace to the society of birds, and their wives must be out of their minds to put up with it. Drakes, as is common knowledge, she could have told him, were off with a flick of the tail with someone else the moment the business of procreation was over. Never a toe of his webbed foot, or a feather of his burnished wing, did wife or child see of him again, except if he happened to be skimming by with another woman on his mind. But instead the stranger to Ireland in her blue denim coat gave the Englishman another piece of information. "I've been told the name came from the custom of giving lime juice to the British Navy men on those long sea outings patrolling the coastlines of the colonies. It prevents scurvy," she said.

"I'm afraid I wouldn't know anything about that," the Englishman said, the words she had spoken a contamination in themselves. His brows were glowering at the gulls, trim as well-groomed yachts, as they cruised nearer to the shore. The ducks were settling again into their customary patterns: ducklings yellow as dandelions and lighter than dandelion fluff whipped from side to side after flies or waltzing spiders, losing and finding and losing again their mother's rippling wake; while one or two of the half-grown, isolated in their virginity, put their heads under their dark wings and slept, rocking as if at anchor on the gentle tide.

"I'm a writer," the Englishman went on saying. It seemed he had come from London to Dublin to compile, to edit, to examine in depth, the letters that the famous Irish dead had written in their old age to the equally famous English dead. "I set my thoughts down here so they won't escape me," he said, tapping the innocent notebook with his forefinger. "Habit they have of getting away." The young people who had lain prone on the green were beginning to get to their feet and drift away now, moving out of the sun and back to their shopkeeping, their bank wickets, their ledgers. "The Irish were always great letter-writers—Lady Gregory, Yeats, James Stephens, O'Casey," the Englishman said in a low voice, not certain, it must have been, if such names would have meaning to the average ear.

"Samuel Beckett's letters are very brief. Four or five lines is about his limit," the woman said, and she was struck suddenly with wonder that living poets and playwrights might at this noon hour be sitting on secluded benches in St. Stephen's Green, writing urgently, eagerly, in loneliness, to one another.

"Ah, that I'm not informed about," the Englishman said, his eye fixed on the watchful gulls who were maneuvering closer. But he was prepared to say that in the two months he had been here his views had been somewhat modified; not changed, but slightly modified. He crossed his long legs, and one foot in the glossy English leather of his shoe began to tap nervously on the Irish air. "I think the Irish are a heartless lot of murderers," was how he put it.

"Well, you may be right," the woman said, reflecting on it. "I'm sure you know of the time when Yeats wouldn't open the door of Maud Gonne's house to her, her own house which she had lent to him, looking right out over there on St. Stephen's Green. Of course, it was late at night," she said, "and he knew the police were after her, and that might have meant an unpleasant experience. Yeats," she said without rancor. "Despite his poetry, a senator's medal where his heart was supposed to be."

"I was referring to the Irish as a whole, not to the great writers," the Englishman managed to say.

"Well, that was some years before Yeats had his monkey gland transplant," the woman said, musing on it. "But think of the monkey who was deprived of his procreative organs. That was a very heartless act. Oh, I agree with you," she said.

The young man looked at her, startled, his eyes, like a runaway horse's, gone a little wild.

"I'm outraged at what they do to their children," he said in a low, fierce voice. In a moment he might wrench the shoe from his tapping foot and fling it either at her or at the gulls. "It's scarcely the fault of very young Irish children that their parents are genetically prone to alcoholism," he said, and the woman asked herself what she was doing, sitting here in the heart of Dublin, listening to an Englishman holding forth on the state of his pride. Would he have listened if O'Casey had tapped him gently on the shoulder then and told him that the three gates of Dublin are castles of poverty, penance, and pain? "Until puberty, or a little beyond," the Englishman was saying, "Irish children believe in the categorical promises that are made to them from the pulpit and in the confessional. And then when they find out they've been royally tricked, they follow without deviation the second path their parents have beaten for them straight to the bar of every public house that will let them in."

Now it was time for a miracle to take place. Even if it meant standing on the tracks and flagging down the laboring freight train of his thoughts, the woman knew it must be done. The cars, with axles and hinges creaking, the wheels barely able to turn because of the decades of rust that clogged their joints, must be brought to a halt. If it required that she fling herself in her blue denim coat and red shoes before it on the tracks, she would do that too. But the miracle was performed by fate itself as the children the Englishman had been holding forth about came running across the stretches of grass which the shop clerks and office workers had vacated just in time.

The younger children came more slowly, hand in hand with teachers or mothers or aunts, or perhaps even older sisters, and not one of the women seemed to be under the influence, as the saying goes. It was true, the woman noticed at once, there were no fathers or uncles, no grandparents among them, the males of the city of Dublin perhaps already rioting in the pubs, and the grandmothers, bless their iron-gray locks, at home tippling to their hearts' content. But the children, from whatever questionable source they had sprung, had a look of belief still in their dark, clear eyes. Their glossy black hair was cut straight across their foreheads, except for those among them with curly hair as bright as fire, and their eyes were blue as any Saxon's. The girls wore pleated green jumpers and flowered blouses, the boys wore tan shorts, and as they ran past the bench and across the pavings to the water's edge, their voices were as happy as bagpipes or flutes, and not a screech or a whine from the thirty or more of them. Some carried crumpled brown paper bags in their hands, and the armada of floating gulls knew at once and no longer hesitated. The black leather paddles of their feet went into motion, and, shouldering ducks and one another aside, the gulls advanced on the shore.

The Englishman surely saw them coming, the water rippling silkily behind their white tails, but still he did not stir. The woman looked away from the sight of the children kneeling down in homage to all birds, whatever their names might be, and she saw that the Englishman's whole being was held fast to the bench, as if in a vise of pain. For one quick instant she thought of saying to him that the thing that matters is not what the dead Irish wrote or didn't write to one another, but that cob swans alternate with their wives in sitting on the eggs atop the solid tower of twigs and reeds and estuary mud they build together once the time of honeymooning is past. She wanted to say that in every country on earth, when the young are able to edge themselves on their skinny elbows into the water, the father swan encircles them with his beauty and courage as the cygnets follow the mother the perilous way through the enemy territory of treacherous currents and lurking lily pads. She wanted to give him some kind of final reassurance about women and men, fish and fowl, saying there is a choice of roles to play in life, and perhaps even in death, and that pigeons, and the mourning doves who sob their hearts out in the spring, like swans, have but one love in their lives. But before she could speak, the Englishman stood up abruptly from the bench.

"The children," he began saying, and stopped.

"Why don't the sea gulls bring their children with them the way the ducks do?" asked one of the smallest of the black-haired girls who knelt at the edge, tossing crumbs from her bag to the screeching, quacking birds. And it was one of the squatting, red-headed boys who answered.

"It's like this," he said, meting out his store of dry bread carefully, frugally, in the direction of the warring birds. His thighs were covered with copper-colored fuzz, and the tight tan shorts which clasped his bottom seemed about to split in two. "It's because the children might get shot," he said.

The Englishman seemed not to have heard them speak, and now he singled out one of the teachers, or mothers, or aunts, to address. She stood in a faded lavender cotton dress near the water, holding a young child in her arms, and into its hand she had placed a crust of bread.

"The children," he said, the word itself a rebuke, "should not, absolutely *should* not, allow the gulls to deprive—"

"Ah, they must be free to do as they like about that," the woman in her faded dress interrupted him softly. There were small gold earrings shining through the strands of gray in her black hair, and the ups and downs of her brogue were enough to make the heart stand still. "They've come a long way, and they're certainly doing no one any harm," she said.

"But the injustice of it!" the Englishman cried out, and the color rose along his jaw.

"Ah, yes, injustice is the air they breathe every day of their lives," the woman said, speaking gently, patiently, to him.

"Here in Dublin?" the Englishman asked, with something like derision in his voice.

"Not Dublin, no," the woman said. "They're down here for the holidays. They come from the north, from Belfast," she said, all the while seeking to close the small fingers of the child she held around the crust of bread; but he seemed in mortal fear of the screaming of the birds.

The Englishman stood uncertainly there a moment longer, his notebook and pen held fast in his hand, and then he turned and left the scene, his arms swinging wildly, like a great gull flapping toward the sea.

THE WOMEN WHO WALK

NANCY HUDDLESTON PACKER

Nancy Huddleston Packer grew up in Birmingham, Alabama, and now lives in California where she teaches at Stanford University. She is the author of *Small Moments*, a collection of stories.

In the days right after Malcolm left her, Marian began to notice the women who walked the deserted streets near the university campus. They were a flash of color in the brilliant June sunlight at a distant intersection, a single shape thrusting through the shadows of the giant sycamores along the sidewalk. She did not at first differentiate one from another. She was too absorbed in her own suffering. Images of Malcolm that last day spun through her mind. The thin ankle over the thin knee as he sat on his luggage in the front hall. The silver lighter touched to the black cigarette. Well, Marian, he said. She pulled the car over to the curb and gave herself up to the blurring tears, the sudden thunder in her chest.

Soon, quieter, she looked around the empty streets. Had anyone seen her? She saw in the distance a lonely figure, walking, walking.

Two weeks had passed and she had not yet told the children. She had said, "He's out of town, he's at a conference, he's giving a lecture, he'll be back." One evening as they sat in the dying sun in the patio, Joseph, who was eleven, said,

"When? When will he be back?"

A bluebird squawked in the high branches of the silver maple. "Your father . . ." she began. She felt suffocated by the heat in her throat. Molly began to cry and buried her face in Marian's lap. Joseph grew red and he ran into the house. Later that night,

Marian called Malcolm at the backstreet hotel where he had taken a room. "I can't tell them," she managed to say, and quickly hung up.

Next day, Malcolm carried the children away for lunch. After that, each evening he spoke to them on the telephone. On the following Saturday, he took Joseph to a Giants game. On Sunday, he and Molly visited a horse farm in the hills. Marian longed to know what he had said, whether he had spoken of her. But they did not tell her.

Finally she asked. Molly grew somber, hooded, afraid. Joseph became moody and glared at the floor. Molly said,

"Daddy says we're not to carry tales back and forth."

"You're my children," she said.

"His too," said Joseph, "just as much as yours."

She felt an explosion and a wind and a fire, but she sat silent and staring.

The first few weeks, women she had counted as friends called her on the phone, invited her to lunch, came by to visit. From behind the living room curtain, she saw them walk up the drive, often in tennis whites, practicing an overhead slam or a low backhand as they waited for her to answer their knock. When she opened the door, their faces were grave. They sat on the sofa and put their sneakers on the coffee table and frowned and shook their heads in sympathy.

She could not speak of him. She tried to talk of other things, but all paths through her mind led back to the injustice she had suffered, of which she could not speak. The silence soon weighed too heavily on them, and their faces grew round and flat as moons, and pale. They knew they could not help her. They must leave now, they said, but they would return. They wished her well. They were her friends. She heard their tires sighing as they escaped down the street.

They were not her friends. They were the wives of his friends, the mothers of his children's friends, the neighbors who were no more than friends of his house. She had no friends. She would never be able to speak of herself, to share herself with friends. He had exiled her to an island of silence. She stood up and began to move around the room, shifting ashtrays, picking lint from the floor. She felt a restless, angry energy gathering in her.

During the summer, Marian frequently saw the woman in the large black coat walking rapidly on the outskirts of the university or the residential streets bordering the business area of the town. She thought the woman was an older faculty wife who apparently spent her leisure doing good works, carrying petitions door-to-door or collecting for the Cancer Society or the Red Cross.

The woman wore sandals and heavy dark socks, a floppy straw hat, and the black coat. The coat was shaped like a wigwam, with sloping shoulders and a wide skirt that struck her just above the ankles. Marian thought the woman wore it like a burnoose, a protection against the dog-day heat of late August and September. The woman was obviously a character, a throwback to the days when faculty and faculty wives were rather expected to be eccentric. Marian liked her, liked her independence and freedom from vanity. Often Marian waved as she drove by, but the woman never seemed to see her. She kept her eyes down, as if she were afraid she might stumble as she rushed along in her waddling, slue-footed gait.

One hot day in late September as Marian waited for a stoplight, the woman in the black coat started across the street in front of the car. Marian had never seen her so close before. She was much younger than she looked from a distance, about thirty-five or so, Marian's age. And still quite pretty, with a high-bridged, delicate nose and delicate fine lips and a soft-looking pale skin. When she came even with the front of the car, she abruptly twisted her head and glanced at Marian through the windshield. As their gazes met, Marian knew that she had seen the woman before how long ago, under what circumstances she could not recall, perhaps at a university party, a meeting, at the sandbox or the swings of the city park. She would never forget those startled pale gray eyes.

Marian waved but the woman ducked her head again and hurried on to the sidewalk. Watching her—the hunched tension of her neck and shoulders, the awkward, powerful, rushing gait—Marian felt that when they had met, they had been drawn together in one of those rare moments of intense though inexplicable intimacy. And now Marian longed to recapture the strange, treasured feeling.

She drove around the block and pulled into a driveway in the woman's path. She got out and stood leaning on the fender, waiting, smiling. The woman walked straight at her, heedless, but at the last moment, without lifting her gaze from the ground, veered clumsily aside. Marian reached out and touched her shoulder. "Wait," she said. "Don't I know you?"

The woman stopped and after a long moment lifted her head. Her gaze whipped from Marian to the sky to the trees. She pulled her coat collar up around her face. Marian said, "What is it? Can I help you?"

The woman threw back her head, like a colt shying, and opened her mouth. Marian heard the sound—distant, muted—of a strangled voice and she thought the voice said, "I'm so very cold." For an instant the woman stared at Marian, and then she lowered her head and rushed down the street.

Malcolm came late one evening to settle details. He sat in the red leather chair he had always sat in. He looked handsome, tanned, his graying hair tousled and longer than he had ever worn it. When he asked how everything was, he was charming and attentive, his smile warm and pleasing, as if she were his dinner partner. She sat on the edge of the wing chair, her knees close, her hands kneading each other, and told him the lie he wanted to hear. Yes, everything was fine. He nodded at her approvingly, no longer angry and irritated with her.

"Well, now," he began, and leaned forward. She did not want to hear it all just then, and she stood up.

"I'll get some coffee," she said. "Turkish coffee," she pleaded. He sighed and nodded.

She went into the kitchen and turned on the faucet. She waited for her heartbeat to slow. When she heard his footsteps, she busied herself with cups and saucers. He stood in the doorway and gazed around him, smiling at the wall decorated with dinner plates from different countries.

"I always liked that one," he said, pointing at a Mexican plate he had brought to her from Mexico City where he had gone for a conference. But, he hastened to assure her, she needn't worry, all he wanted were a few mementos, keepsakes that had been in his family for a long time. The tintype of his great-grandmother and of course its antique frame and the silver ladle his great-aunt had saved from the Yankees. He smiled. Everything else was hers, absolutely, he didn't want anything else. Nothing.

Nothing? she wanted to ask. Nothing? No memento, no keepsake of our fifteen years together?

"Nothing besides coffee?" she asked. "Some fruit?" She picked up an immense pineapple from the straw basket on the counter. It was just ripe, soft and yellow. He had always loved pineapples. "It's just ripe," she said. "I'll cut it for you." When he shook his head, she held it close to his face. "Smell it," she pleaded.

"I do not want to smell it, for God's sake," he said. For an instant his composure dropped away and she saw what she had remembered all these months: the rigid shoulders, the pinched mouth, the hard, irritated eyes. She could easily drag the sharp points of the pineapple across his face. She watched little specks of blood ooze from his skin, swell into a long thick ruby streamer that marked his cheek like a savage decoration. She put the pineapple down and handed him a cup of coffee. Back in the living room, he sat again in the red chair and put his feet up on the matching ottoman.

Molly and Joseph were already in bed, but when they heard his voice they ran into the living room. Joseph stood in the doorway, smiling quizzically. Molly climbed over Malcolm's legs and onto his lap. He set the coffee down and Molly burrowed under his arm, into his armpit. He stroked her hair. Marian felt an uneasiness, a tension, and then she was suddenly shaken by a yearning —to be held, to be stroked—and she felt dizzy, as if she might faint.

"Run along now," said Malcolm to the children, "and I'll see you Sunday." As the children left the room, he explained. "They're coming to my new place for lunch on Sunday. If that's all right with you?" She nodded. "Did you know I had a place? It's not exactly elegant, but I like it much better than the hotel. I like having a place of my own."

"This is yours. " She slid off her chair and dropped to her knees beside him. She pressed her face against his thigh. He did not move beneath her caresses. When she looked up, she saw the prim set of his lips. She stood up.

"Now about the arrangements," he said. "Here's what I thought, but I want you to be thoroughly satisfied."

He pulled a folded-up piece of paper from his wallet. It was covered with words and figures in his neat small handwriting. She saw the words "Insurance" and "Automobile."

"You really should get a lawyer," he said. She seized upon the kindness in his voice.

"Who should I get?"

He drew one of the black cigarettes from the box. He tamped it against the back of his hand and lighted it with his silver lighter. After a moment, he said, "You've got to start making that kind of decision for yourself, you know."

"Don't you see that it's too late?" she whispered.

He stood up, tapped ashes into the ashtray, drank off the last of the coffee, gathered together his cigarettes and lighter and wallet. "You're a perfectly competent woman," he said, "as no one knows better than I. After all," he went on, smiling at her, his voice remote, jocular, false, "you managed to get me through graduate school. I don't forget that. I'll always be grateful for that."

She went to the window and stared out at the darkness. "Then how can you desert me like this?" Her voice was hoarse, choked.

"There's no point going over this again," he said in an exasperated voice. "I know it's right for both of us."

She heard his sigh, the sound of the ottoman scraping over the floor as he pushed it aside, his footsteps brushing across the rug. The sky was cloudless, moonless, starless. The leaves of the eucalyptus shivered. Dark spaces opened within her. She spoke softly to the windowpane.

"Can't you stay just tonight?"

"Now, Marian," he said, moving into the hallway.

"Just to hold me," she whispered, "in the dark, a last time."

"Good night," he called from the front door. Soon the lights of his car vanished into the dark. She stood at the window a moment longer. She felt the agitation rising, the fury, the rush of movement through her body. She felt the hardness gather in the center of her chest and she could make no sound.

The rains came early, and by the middle of November the ground was soggy. For days the sky was close in and gray. Through the autumn Marian had become aware of the woman in white, seen as a flash of light out of the corner of her eye as she drove along. The woman was probably a nurse, cutting through the campus on her way to the university hospital. She was about five nine or five ten and very very thin, like a wraith. She was swaybacked and as she walked she lifted her knees high, her feet far out in front of her, like a drum majorette on parade. The knobby joints between her long thin bones made her look even more awkward and absurd. Yet she walked without self-consciousness, head high, as if she had better thoughts to ponder than the amusement of people driving by in their big cars. This lack of vanity was one of the characteristics shared by the women who walked. That, and the vigorous, almost heedless, way they moved.

Marian had only seen the wraith—as she came to think of her—in the vicinity of the university until a drizzly Sunday afternoon in early December when she saw her on a downtown street. The children had eaten lunch with Malcolm and she had contrived to pick them up. Malcolm lived in a cottage behind a large Spanish house close by the freeway. Often she had driven past and stared down the overgrown path that ran alongside the house. Baskets of ferns and Wandering Jew hung from the roof of the little dilapidated porch, and there were bright flowered curtains behind the windows. Though appealing in the way that dark, shabby little cottages sometimes are, the charm of this one seemed utterly foreign to everything she believed she knew of Malcolm's taste. He had always insisted that their house be neat, clean, sparse. Something had changed in him, and she thought that if only she could see inside the place, she might at last understand what had gone wrong between them. And so she had told him that she was going on an errand and since she didn't want the children to return to an empty house, she would pick them up.

But even before she had turned off the ignition, she saw Molly running down the path toward her, and Joseph sauntering behind. Malcolm, in a bright green sweatshirt and jeans, stood on the porch and waved to her as if she were only the mother of children visiting at his house. She was filled with shame at her scheme, and with disappointment at its failure, and then with relief.

Joseph got in the front seat. He looked sullen, moody, as he often did after the Sundays with his father. Molly climbed in back and grasped Marian's ears and said, "Giddap." Marian patted Molly's hands. And she said, "I'll bet anything you had—let's see—bologna on store-bought bread and Coke. And of course Oreos." The thought of Malcolm's providing such a dreary lunch gave her pleasure, and revving the motor she laughed aloud.

"No," said Joseph. He crossed his arms and dropped his head. "We had chicken with some kind of orange stuff all over it," said Molly. "I didn't like it but that lady said I had to eat it since she made it special."

Joseph turned to the back seat. "You're stupid," he said. "Nobody can trust you, you're a baby."

Marian thrust her foot against the accelerator and the car jumped from the curb, bucked, almost died, caught, sped away. That lady. A woman. No one had told her there was a woman. But who would? Who did she have to tell her anything? Yet she should have known. She was the stupid one. The secrecy. The children's silence. The shabby place with its shabby charm. The ferns. The bright curtains. And behind the curtains, a woman peering out at her, perhaps laughing at her. The rejected wife. The discard. Garbage.

"I didn't mean to tell," said Molly. She patted Marian's shoulder. "I'm sorry."

Marian drove in silence, beneath the immense white oaks, past the fine old mansions, past the run-down rooming houses and flats. No life stirred. Even the downtown streets were empty. The car moved through empty gray streets. The day was cold, damp, dark. She saw a flash of shimmering white. Without thinking, she said,

"One of the walkers."

The woman strutted toward them on her long heron legs. She had on a pale pink jacket over her white dress. As the car drew near Marian saw that the jacket was short-sleeved, that it barely covered the woman's breasts, that it was loose-fitting, flimsy, crocheted. That it was a bed jacket. As Marian stared, the woman turned toward her. Her eyes were narrowed, glittering, defiant. She grinned fiercely.

"What walker?" asked Joseph. He dropped his feet from the dashboard and sat up to see. Marian pressed the accelerator and the car jerked forward and threw Joseph against the seat.

"Never mind. We've passed her." Marian flushed with embarrassment. She felt she had somehow humiliated the woman in front of Joseph and Molly.

"I saw her," said Molly. "She had on pink and white. Joseph just doesn't look."

Joseph spun toward her. "You shut up, you shut up," he said. His voice trembled. Marian touched his shoulder.

"Please don't quarrel," she said.

He pulled away from her hand. "I hate you and Daddy," he shouted. "You don't care about us, you don't care what you do to us."

"Mommy didn't do it, did you?" said Molly. "It was Daddy and that lady."

"He wouldn't have just left," said Joseph. "It was her fault, too."

Hot moisture bubbled into her eyes, and shrill sounds rose into her ears. She pulled the car over to the curb. Now she would tell them. Her fault? Her fault too? Now she would unleash her suffering, she would engulf them in her anguish. She would tell them, she would tell them. She turned to Joseph. His eyelids were slightly lowered and his nose and mouth were stretched down and pinched. She twisted to see Molly.

"Don't," said Molly. "Please don't look like that. Don't cry, please don't cry. You're so ugly when you cry. Please don't."

Marian pressed her fingers into her skull. She held her neck muscles taut. She pushed out her chest and belly to make room for the expanding pressure. They were her children. They were all she now had. She must protect them from misery and pain. From herself. In the rearview mirror, she could make out in the gray distance the comic cakewalk of the woman in white, alone, in the cold.

Over the next weeks, she longed to tell Malcolm that she knew about the lady. She longed to taunt him. How typical, how trite, how sordid. He had deserted his family for the sleaziest of reasons, another woman, a younger woman, probably a graduate student. Malcolm with his dignity and pride. How comical it was. She saw herself pick up the telephone and dial his number. She heard her contemptuous yet amused voice ringing through the wires. Sleazy and comical, she heard herself say.

But she did not call him. She was afraid. His voice would be hard and irritable, and he would say hateful things to her that she could not bear to hear. She imagined his saying, I never loved you, not even at the beginning. She heard him say, I married you only so I could finish my degree. He would infect her memories with doubt and ruin the past for her. He would leave her with nothing. While he had his lady.

Through the winter months, she spent hours at a time daydreaming about Malcolm and his woman. Often, she sat at her bedroom window and watched the rain break against the pane. She believed that if she concentrated hard enough, she would be able to conjure up an image of his woman. But always as the face began to form on the film of the glass, the wind swept the image away.

One day as the outline of the eyes appeared, she leaned close to fasten the face to the windowpane. She saw her own reflection, and she saw that her eyes were more haggard than she remembered, her lips thin, her nose taut. She had grown suddenly old and ugly. She drew back from the windowpane, and as she did, her reflection began to move away from her, as if the image were running to a distant point in the street. She saw her reflection grow smaller and smaller, and then vanish.

She jumped from the chair and rushed into the living room. She must come out of her misery. She had lost touch with the world, gone stale and sour inside herself. Her life had lost its shape. She had no purpose. She had been only marking time, waiting for relief that would never come. She had to build her life again, become a person again.

She sat down in the red chair, Malcolm's chair. No, she thought, it's my chair. She pulled the *New York Times Magazine* from the mahogany rack by the chair. The magazine was six months old. She dumped all the magazines on the floor, the *New Republic, Harper's,* the *New York Review.* They were all stiff and yellow with age. Malcolm's magazines. He had taken the subscriptions with him, and she had not even missed them. She had read nothing in months.

The blood rose to her head and pounded behind her eyes. She had once been an attractive, interesting woman who kept up, who could talk of anything. Yes, talk so that men listened to her and admired her and desired her. Malcolm had taken all that from her. That, too. Slowly, slowly. Over the years he had frequently said hurtful things to her—that she chattered, that she told everything in boring detail. Hurtful things that made her feel inadequate or silly and that broke her confidence. She had given up, content to let him do the talking, content with the warmth of his brilliance. To please him, she had become a cipher. And when he thought he had completed her destruction, he had deserted her.

But he was wrong: she was not destroyed. Free of him, she was ready to become the attractive woman she had once been. Everything was still there, ready to emerge from the half-life she had lived all these years. She felt that her powers were flooding back to her, washing away her fear of him, her timidity.

Exultant, triumphant, she rushed to the telephone and dialed his number at the university. But when a soft young female voice answered, she could not speak. She heard Malcolm ask, "Who is it, Teddy?" and then "Hello" into the phone. She could not remember what she had intended to say to him. A pressure began, swelled larger and larger until she feared it would explode in her chest, crash through her eardrums, shatter the delicate membrane of her nostrils and eyes. She opened her mouth to let the sounds out, but no sounds came.

Marian had often noticed the woman in the red plastic coat who walked with one hand palm up at her shoulder and the other on her hip. Her white hair was burnished to a metallic sheen and it stood high above her face like a chef's cap. She wore multicolored platform shoes with six-inch heels that threw her forward, and she took quick little mincing steps as if hurrying to catch up with her top before it fell. She was, Marian decided, probably a prostitute.

But prostitute or not, she was a human being and a woman, and a woman obviously mistreated by men. And so seeing her on a drizzly March afternoon walking with the red coat held straight-armed above the elaborate hair-do, Marian decided to give the woman a lift. She drew the car alongside the curb and leaned across the passenger seat to lower the window.

And then she noticed the sores on the woman's bare legs. Some of the sores were black holes with diameters the size of a pencil and some were raw looking with moist crusts and some were fresh, suppurating, leaving faint trails down her calves.

The woman turned. Her face was mottled and skull-like and Marian thought the flesh had already begun to rot back from the bones. Marian felt a hard spasm in her lower belly, as if a steel hand had fastened around her groin. The woman grinned then, a terrible grin of complicity, as if she had anticipated, had desired, now shared the sudden hatred Marian felt surging through her. As Marian reared back from the window and twisted the steering wheel toward the street, she heard a muffled, constricted whimpering, and she knew it was her own.

One Sunday afternoon in June, Malcolm came into the house with the children. It had been nearly a year since he had left; the divorce was final. He stood in the hallway and leaned casually against the wall. He was deeply tanned and his gray sideburns were long and bushy and somehow boyish. He seemed cheerful and lighthearted, qualities she thought he had long ago given up to his seriousness, his image of himself as a scholar. He wore his new happiness like an advertisement and he apparently expected her to rejoice with him.

He said, "I've got a plan I know you're going to like."

Her resentment was like a coagulant. As he spoke her blood and her energy ceased to flow, and she felt sullen, dull, thick.

He told her that he would take the children for July to one of the San Juan Islands off Seattle. No electricity, he exulted. No cars. No telephone. Just man against nature, with the necessities flown in, he said, laughing archly. He had never been there, of course, but—he paused no more than a heartbeat—he knew someone who had. He began to describe the island, as if he were enticing her to come along, the cliffs, the immense trees, the wild berries, the birds.

"This will be one of the best experiences of their lives," he said, "and you'll be free for a whole month."

"Free to do what?" she asked. Her tongue was thick and heavy, and her voice hardly rose to her mouth.

"See you next Sunday," he called to the children, and waving, waving, he backed out the front door.

"I'm going to have a shell collection," Molly said.

"There's a lot of driftwood," said Joseph, "so you can carve things and all."

"Teddy says the shells are beautiful and I'm going to make you a beautiful shell necklace."

"Be quiet," said Joseph.

"I've never been to an island," said Molly. "I wish you could come too."

"Yeah," said Joseph.

After her hot bath, she lay in bed in the dark, staring at the odd shapes the moon cast against the draperies. The moon on the water and the sandy beaches and the shadows of trees. The wind blew in her open window and the draperies billowed. She saw people in the moving folds. Heads. Bodies. Lovers moving against each other in the dark shadows. Malcolm and his lady. She drew her hands along her hips, squeezed her breasts between her fingers. No one would ever hold her, whisper to her in the night. For a moment she feared that she would scream out in her anguish, and she threw back the covers and sat up on the side of the bed.

If only she had someone to talk to, to whom she could tell her suffering. She thought of her parents, both dead, and of the brother she had not seen in years. The faces of girls she had been close to came to her, and one in particular who had blond hair in a Dutch boy cut and who had moved away when they were both eleven. She thought of a boy whose name she could not recall who had given her chocolates in a heart-shaped box and had kissed her clumsily on the ear. And of the boy who had loved her in high school and whom she had loved until she had met Malcolm. All these, and others she might have talked to, were gone.

She got up to close the window against the wind and she saw a light beneath Joseph's door. Molly had already deserted her, had said "Teddy" in an affectionate, accepting way. But Joseph, her first-born, suffered, too.

She went to his room. He lay prone on his bed, propped on his elbows, a book open in front of him. She said, "I want to talk to you."

He folded the book over his finger and turned over. He lay back against the headboard. The light from the bullet lamp fell across the side of his face. He looked frail and sad.

She sat down in the desk chair and dragged it closer to the bed. "You're going away," she said, "with them." She held his gaze.

"Mom, please don't," he said. His shadowed face turned away from her. "We're not supposed to talk about the other one. He never talks about you."

"Never? Has he never said anything?"

"All he ever said was he had a right to try to be happy," Joseph said in a soft, fretful, placating voice. He drew his knees up and folded his arms across them and buried his head in his arms. "Please don't talk to me, please," he said.

As he lifted his face to her, his head seemed to rise above the knees, disembodied. As she stared at him, his face grew larger and larger and whiter and whiter. It swelled toward her, a pale disc, like the moon. She got to her feet.

"Sleep well," she said.

She went to the kitchen to make sure she had turned off the oven and the burners. She checked the locks on outside doors. She listened for the sound of a forgotten sprinkler. The house was still and dark and hot. She felt dull and sluggish, and yet excited, too restless to stay inside.

She went into her bathroom and took her old flannel robe off the hook on the back of the door. She got in the car and drove over to the university lake. In the springtime, the students boated and swam and sunned at the lake, and often she and Malcolm had brought the children there to search for tadpoles and frogs. Now, in June, the lake was slowly drying into a swamp.

She sat on the dark bank and breathed in the cool night air. The moon shimmered in the puddles on the lake bottom. It was the end of Spring term and she heard the murmur of student lovers and the rustle of dry leaves. She imagined bodies touching, and the soft delicious look of desire on their mouths and in their eyes. She had known that ecstasy. She remembered the first night she and Malcolm had been together. They had been on Cape Cod. She saw them lying in a little pocket of leafy brush, protected from the wind by an overhanging cliff. She had felt nothing existed but the two of them, and nothing mattered but the act of love they performed.

And in the moonlight, sitting on the damp bank of the swampy lake, she began to cry. Her crying was a moan that returned to her as the sound of soft thunder. And then she saw movement in the shadows of the trees. The students, the lovers, were moving away from her along the shores of the lake. She had driven them away. In her groin was the pain that was like lust, like fear, like hatred. She didn't care what the lovers or anyone thought of her. Her chest swelled with sobs. They seemed to be exploding through her ribs, bursting from her armpits, ripping through her ears and eye-sockets.

She stood up. The streets were empty. She clutched her bathrobe tighter against the suddenly chilly night, and she began to walk quickly, recklessly, in the direction of the moon. As she walked, she felt the power of her thrusting stride, the rising flood of her energy, the release of her torment.

BETWEEN THE LINES

LEE SMITH

Lee Smith was born in Grundy, Virginia, a small coal town in southern Appalachia which serves as the setting for most of her recent work. Her fourth novel, *Black Mountain Breakdown*, was published by Putnam's in January 1981. She has published stories in *Carolina Quarterly*, *Redbook*, *McCall's*, *Southern Exposure*, and other periodicals. She and her husband, James Seay, live with their two sons in Chapel Hill, North Carolina. Smith teaches fiction writing at the University of North Carolina.

"Peace be with you from Mrs. Joline B. Newhouse" is how I sign my columns. Now I gave some thought to that. In the first place, I like a line that has a ring to it. In the second place, what I have always tried to do with my column is to uplift my readers if at all possible, which sometimes it is not. After careful thought, I threw out "Yours in Christ." I am a religious person and all my readers know it. If I put "Yours in Christ," it seems to me that they will think I am theirs because I am in Christ, or even that they and I are in Christ *together*, which is not always the case. I am in Christ but I know for a fact that a lot of them are not. There's no use acting like they are, but there's no use rubbing their face in it, either. "Peace be with you," as I see it, is sufficiently religious without laying all the cards right out on the table in plain view. I like to keep an ace or two up my sleeve. I like to write between the lines.

This is what I call my column, in fact: "Between the Lines, by Mrs. Joline B. Newhouse." Nobody knows why. Many people have come right out and asked me, including my best friend Sally Peck and my husband Glenn. "Come on, now, Joline," they say.

First appeared in *Carolina Quarterly*, Winter 1980, Vol. 32, No. 1. Reprinted by permission.

"What's this 'Between the Lines' all about? What's this 'Between the Lines' supposed to mean?" But I just smile a sweet mysterious smile and change the subject. I know what I know.

And my column means everything to folks around here. Salt Lick community is where we live, unincorporated. I guess there is not much that you would notice, passing through—the Post Office (real little), the American oil station, my husband Glenn's Cash 'N' Carry Beverage Store. He sells more than beverages in there, though, believe me. He sells everything you can think of, from thermometers and rubbing alcohol to nails to frozen pizza. Anything else you want, you have to go out of the holler and get on the interstate and go to Greenville to get it. That's where my column appears, in the *Greenville Herald*, fortnightly. Now there's a word with a ring to it: fortnightly.

There are seventeen families here in Salt Lick—twenty, if you count those three down by the Five Mile Bridge. I put what they do in the paper. Anybody gets married, I write it. That goes for born, divorced, dies, celebrates a golden wedding anniversary, has a baby shower, visits relatives in Ohio, you name it. But these mere facts are not what's most important, to my mind.

I write, for instance: "Mrs. Alma Goodnight is enjoying a pleasant recuperation period in the lovely, modern Walker Mountain Community Hospital while she is sorely missed by her loved ones at home. Get well soon, Alma!" I do not write that Alma Goodnight is in the hospital because her husband hit her up the side with a rake and left a straight line of bloody little holes going from her waist to her armpit after she yelled at him, which Lord knows she did all the time, once too often. I don't write about how Eben Goodnight is all torn up now about what he did, missing work and worrying, or how Alma liked it so much in the hospital that nobody knows if they'll ever get her to go home or not. Because that is a *mystery*, and I am no detective by a long shot. I am what I am, I know what I know, and I know you've got to give folks something to hang on to, something to keep them going. That is what I have in mind when I say *uplift*, and that is what God had in mind when he gave us Jesus Christ.

My column would not be but a paragraph if the news was all I told. But it isn't. What I tell is what's important, like the bulbs coming up, the way the redbud comes out first on the hills in the spring and how pretty it looks, the way the cattails shoot up by the creek, how the mist winds down low on the ridge in the mornings, how my wash all hung out on the line of a Tuesday looks like a regular square dance with those pants legs just flapping and flapping in the wind! I tell how all the things you ever dreamed of, all changed and ghostly, will come crowding into your head on a winter night when you sit up late in front of your fire. I even made up these little characters to talk for me, Mr. and Mrs. Cardinal and Princess Pussycat, and often I have them voice my thoughts. Each week I give a little chapter in their lives. Or I might tell what was the message brought in church, or relate an inspirational word from a magazine, book, or TV. I look on the bright side of life.

I've had God's gift of writing from the time I was a child. That's what the B. stands for in Mrs. Joline B. Newhouse—Barker, my maiden name. My father was a patient strong God-fearing man despite his problems and it is in his honor that I maintain the B. There was a lot of us children around all the time—it was right up the road here where I grew up—and it would take me a day to tell you what all we got into! But after I learned how to write, that was that. My fingers just naturally curved to a pencil and I sat down to writing like a ball of fire. They skipped me up one, two grades in school. When I was not but eight, I wrote a poem named "God's Garden" which was published in the church bulletin of the little Methodist Church we went to then on Hunter's Ridge. Oh, Daddy was so proud! He gave me a quarter that Sunday, and then I turned around and gave it straight to God. Put it in the collection plate. Daddy almost cried he was so proud. I wrote another poem in school the next year, telling how life is like a merry-go-round, and it won a statewide prize.

That's me—I grew up smart as a whip, lively, and naturally good. Jesus came as easy as breathing did to me. Don't think I'm putting on airs, though: I'm not. I know what I know. I've done my share of sinning, too, of which more later.

Anyway, I was smart. It's no telling but what I might have gone on to school like my own children have and who knows what all else if Mama hadn't run off with a man. I don't remember Mama very well, to tell the truth. She was a weak woman, always laying in the bed having a headache. One day we all came home from school and she was gone, didn't even bother to make up the bed. Well, that was the end of Mama! None of us ever saw her again, but Daddy told us right before he died that one time he had gotten a postcard from her from Atlanta, Georgia, years and years after that. He showed it to us, all wrinkled and soft from him holding it.

Being the oldest I took over and raised those little ones, three of them, and then I taught school and then I married Glenn and we had our own children, four of them, and I have raised them too and still have Marshall, of course, poor thing. He is the cross I have to bear and he'll be just like he is now for the rest of his natural life.

I was writing my column for the week of March 17, 1976, when the following events occurred. It was a real coincidence because I had just finished doing the cutest little story named "A Red-Letter Day for Mr. and Mrs. Cardinal" when the phone rang. It rings all the time, of course. Everybody around here knows my number by heart. It was Mrs. Irene Chalmers. She was all torn up. She said that Mr. Biggers was over at Greenville at the hospital very bad off this time, and that he was asking for me and would I please try to get over there today as the doctors were not giving him but a 20 per cent chance to make it through the night. Mr. Biggers has always been a fan of mine, and he especially liked Mr. and Mrs. Cardinal. "Well!" I said. "Of course I will! I'll get Glenn on the phone right this minute. And you calm down, Mrs. Chalmers. You go fix yourself a Coke." Mrs. Chalmers said she would; and hung up. I knew what was bothering her, of course. It was that given the natural run of things, she would be the next to go. The next one to be over there dying. Without even putting down the receiver, I dialed the beverage store. Bert answered.

"Good morning," I said. I like to maintain a certain distance with the hired help although Glenn does not. He will talk to anybody, and any time you go in there, you can find half the old men in the county just sitting around that stove in the winter or outside on those wooden drink boxes in the summer, smoking and drinking drinks which I am sure they are getting free out of the cooler although Glenn swears it on the Bible they are not. Anyway, I said good morning.

"Can I speak to Glenn?" I said.

"Well now, Mrs. Newhouse," Bert said in his naturally insolent voice—he is just out of high school and too big for his britches—"He's not here right now. He had to go out for a while."

"Where did he go?" I asked.

"Well, I don't rightly know," Bert said. "He said he'd be back after lunch."

"Thank you very much, there will not be a message," I said sweetly, and hung up. I *knew* where Glenn was. Glenn was over on Caney Creek where his adopted half-sister Margie Kettles lived, having carnal knowledge of her in a trailer. They had been at it for 30 years and anybody would have thought they'd have worn it out by that time. Oh, I knew all about it!

The way it happened in the beginning was that Glenn's father had died of his lungs when Glenn was not but about ten years old, and his mother grieved so hard that she went off her head and began taking up with anybody who would go with her. One of the fellows she took up with was a foreign man out of a carnival, the James H. Drew Exposition, a man named Emilio something. He had this curly-headed dark-skinned little daughter. So Emilio stayed around longer than anybody would have expected, but finally it was clear to all that he never would find any work around here to suit him. The work around here is hard work, all of it, and they say he played a musical instrument. Anyway, in due course this Emilio just up and vanished, leaving that foreign child. Now that was Margie, of course, but her name wasn't Margie then. It was a long foreign name which ended up as Margie, and that's how Margie ended up here, in these mountains, where she has been up to no good ever since. Glenn's mother did not last too long after Emilio left, and those children grew up wild. Most of them went to foster homes, and to this day Glenn does not know where two of his brothers are! The military was what finally saved Glenn. He stayed with the military for nine years, and when he came back to this area he found me over here teaching school and with something of a nest egg in hand, enabling him to start the beverage store. Glenn says he owes everything to me.

This is true. But I can tell you something else: Glenn is a good man, and he has been a good provider all these years. He has not ever spoke to me above a regular tone of voice nor raised his hand in anger. He has not been tight with the money. He used to hold the girls in his lap of an evening. Since I got him started, he has been a regular member of the church, and he has not fallen down on it yet. Glenn furthermore has that kind of disposition where he never knows a stranger. So I can count my blessings, too.

Of course I knew about Margie! Glenn's sister Lou-Ann told me about it before she died, that is how I found out about it originally. She thought I *should* know, she said. She said it went on for years and she just wanted me to know before she died. Well! I had had the first two girls by then, and I thought I was so happy. I took to my bed and just cried and cried. I cried for four days and then by gum I got up and started my column, and I have been writing on it ever since. So I was not unprepared when Margie showed up again some years after that, all gap-toothed and wild looking, but then before you knew it she was gone, off again to Knoxville, then back working as a waitress at that truck stop at the county line, then off again, like that. She led an irregular life. And as for Glenn, I will have to hand it to him, he never darkened her door again until after the birth of Marshall.

Now let me add that I would not have gone on and had Marshall if it was left up to me. I would have practiced more birth control. Because I was old by that time, thirty-seven, and that was too old for more children I felt, even though I had started late of course. I had told Glenn many times, I said three normal girls is enough for anybody. But no, Glenn was like a lot of men, and I don't blame him for it—he just had to try one more time for a boy. So we went on with it, and I must say I had a feeling all along.

I was not a bit surprised at what we got, although after wrestling with it all for many hours in the dark night of the soul as they say, I do not believe that Marshall is a judgment on me for my sin. I don't believe that. He is one of God's special children, is how I look at it. Of course he looks funny, but he has already lived ten years longer than they said he would. And has a job! He goes to Greenville every day on the Trailways bus rain or shine and cleans up the Plaza Mall. He gets to ride on the bus, and he gets to see people. Along about six o'clock he'll come back, walking up the holler and not looking to one side or the other, and then I give him his supper and then he'll watch something on TV like the Brady Bunch or Family Affair, and then he'll go to bed. He would not hurt a flea. But oh, Glenn took it hard when Marshall came! I remember that night so well and the way he just turned his back on the doctor. This is what sent him back to Margie, I am convinced of it, what made him take up right where he had left off all those years before.

So since Glenn was up to his old tricks I called up Lavonne, my daughter, to see if she could take me to the hospital to see Mr. Biggers. Why yes she could, it turned out. As a matter of fact she was going to Greenville herself. As a matter of fact she had something she wanted to talk to me about anyway. Now Lavonne is our youngest girl and the only one that stayed around here. Lavonne is somewhat pop-eyed, and has a weak constitution. She is one of those people that never can make up their mind. That day on the phone, I heard a whine in her voice I didn't like the sound of. Something is up, I thought.

First I powdered my face, so I would be ready to go when Lavonne got there. Then I sat back down to write some more on my column, this paragraph I had been framing in my mind for weeks about how sweet potatoes are not what they used to be. They taste gritty and dry now, compared to how they were. I don't know the cause of it, whether it is man on the moon or pollution in the ecology or what, but it is true. They taste awful.

Then my door came bursting open in a way that Lavonne would never do it and I knew it was Sally Peck from next door. Sally is loud and excitable but she has a good heart. She would do anything for you. "Hold on to your hat, Joline!" she hollered. Sally is so loud because she's deaf. Sally was just huffing and puffing—she is a heavy woman—and she had rollers still up in her hair and her old housecoat on with the buttons off.

"Why, Sally!" I exclaimed. "You are all wrought up!"

Sally sat down in my rocker and spread out her legs and started fanning herself with my *Family Circle* magazine. "If you think I'm wrought up," she said finally, "it is nothing compared to what you are going to be. We have had us a suicide, right here in Salt Lick. Margie Kettles put her head inside her gas oven in the night."

"Margie?" I said. My heart was just pumping.

"Yes, and a little neighbor girl was the one who found her, they say. She came over to borrow some baking soda for her mama's biscuits at seven o'clock A.M." Sally looked real hard at me. "Now wasn't she related to you all?"

"Why," I said just as easily, "why yes, she was Glenn's adopted half sister of course when they were nothing but a child. But we haven't had anything to do with her for years as you can well imagine."

"Well, they say Glenn is making the burial arrangements," Sally spoke up. She was getting her own back that day, I'll admit it. Usually I'm the one with all the news.

"I have to finish my column now and then Lavonne is taking me in to Greenville to see old Mr. Biggers who is breathing his last," I said.

"Well," Sally said, hauling herself up out of my chair, "I'll be going along then. I just didn't know if you knew or not." Now Sally Peck is not a spiteful woman in all truth. I have known her since we were little girls sitting out in the yard looking at a magazine together. It is hard to imagine being as old as I am now, or knowing Sally Peck—who was Sally Bland, then—so long.

Of course I couldn't get my mind back on sweet potatoes after she left. I just sat still and fiddled with the pigeonholes in my desk and the whole kitchen seemed like it was moving and rocking back and forth around me. Margie dead! Sooner or later I would have to write it up tastefully in my column. Well, I must say I had never thought of Margie dying. Before God, I never hoped for that in all my life. I didn't know what it would do to *me*, in fact, to me and Glenn and Marshall and the way we live because you know how the habits and the ways of people can build up over the years. It was too much for me to take in at one time. I couldn't see how anybody committing suicide could choose to stick their head in the oven anyway—you can imagine the position you would be found in.

Well, in came Lavonne at that point, sort of hanging back and stuttering like she always does, and that child of hers Bethy Rose hanging on to her skirt for dear life. I saw no reason at that time to tell Lavonne about the death of Margie Kettles. She would hear it sooner or later, anyway. Instead, I gave her some plant food which I had ordered two for the price of one from Montgomery Ward some days before.

"Are you all ready, Mama?" Lavonne asked in that quavery way she has, and I said indeed I was, as soon as I got my hat, which I did, and we went out and got in Lavonne's Buick Electra and set off on our trip. Bethy Rose sat in the back, coloring in her coloring book. She is a real good child. "How's Ron?" I said. Ron is Lavonne's husband, an electrician, as up and coming a boy as you would want to see. Glenn and I are as proud as punch of Ron, and actually I never have gotten over the shock of Lavonne marrying him in the first place. All through high school she never showed any signs of marrying anybody, and you could have knocked me over with a feather the day she told us she was secretly engaged. I'll tell you, our Lavonne was not the marrying sort! Or so I thought.

But that day in the car she told me, "Mama, I wanted to talk to you and tell you I am thinking of getting a d-i-v-o-r-c-e."

I shot a quick look into the back seat but Bethy Rose wasn't hearing a thing. She was coloring Wonder Woman in her book.

"Now Lavonne," I said. "What in the world is it? Why, I'll bet you can work it out." Part of me was listening to Lavonne, as you can imagine, but part of me was still stuck in that oven with crazy Margie. I was not myself.

I told her that. "Lavonne," I said, "I am not myself today. But I'll tell you one thing. You give this some careful thought. You don't want to go off half-cocked. What is the problem, anyway?"

"It's a man where I work," Lavonne said. She works in the Welfare Department, part-time, typing. "He is just giving me a fit. I guess you can pray for me, Mama, because I don't know what I'll decide to do."

"Can we get an Icee?" asked Bethy Rose.

"Has anything happened between you?" I asked. You have to get all the facts.

"Why *no!*" Lavonne was shocked. "Why, I wouldn't do anything like that! Mama, for goodness' sakes! We just have coffee together so far."

That's Lavonne all over. She never has been very bright. "Honey," I said, "I would think twice before I threw up a perfectly good marriage and a new brick home for the sake of a cup of coffee. If you don't have enough to keep you busy, go take a course at the community college. Make yourself a new pantsuit. This is just a mood, believe me."

"Well," Lavonne said. Her voice was shaking and her eyes were swimming in tears which just stayed there and never rolled down her cheeks. "Well," she said again.

As for me, I was lost in thought. It was when I was a young married woman like Lavonne that I committed my own great sin. I had the girls, and things were fine with Glenn and all, and there was simply not any reason to ascribe to it. It was just something I did out of loving pure and simple, did because I wanted to do it. I knew and have always known the consequences, yet God is full of grace, I pray and believe, and his mercy is everlasting.

To make a long story short, we had a visiting evangelist from Louisville, Kentucky, for a two-week revival that year. John Marcel Wilkes. If I say it myself, John Marcel Wilkes was a real humdinger! He had the yellowest hair you ever saw, curly, and the finest singing voice available. Oh, he was something, and that very first night he brought two souls into Christ. The next day I went over to the church with a pan of brownies just to tell him how much I personally had received from his message. I thought, of course, that there would be other people around—the Reverend Mr. Clark, or the youth director, or somebody cleaning. But to my surprise that church was totally empty except for John Marcel Wilkes himself reading the Bible in the fellowship hall and making notes on a pad of paper. The sun came in a window on his head. It was early June, I remember, and I had on a blue dress with little white cap sleeves and open-toed sandals. John Marcel Wilkes looked up at me and his face gave off light like the sun.

"Why, Mrs. Newhouse," he said. "What an unexpected pleasure!" His voice echoed out in the empty fellowship hall. He had the most beautiful voice, too—strong and deep, like it had bells in it. Everything he said had a ring to it.

He stood up and came around the table to where I was. I put the brownies down on the table and stood there. We both just stood there, real close without touching each other, for the longest time, looking into each other's eyes. Then he took my hands and brought them up to his mouth and kissed them, which nobody ever did to me before or since, and then he kissed me on the mouth. I thought I would die. After some time of that, we went together out into the hot June day where the bees were all buzzing around the flowers there by the back gate and I couldn't think straight. "Come," said John Marcel Wilkes. We went out in the woods behind the church to the prettiest place, and when it was all over I could look up across his curly yellow head and over the trees and see the white church steeple stuck up against that blue, blue sky like it was pasted there. This was not all. Two more times we went out there during that revival. John Marcel Wilkes left after that and I have never heard a word of him since. I do not know where he is, or what has become of him in all these years. I do know that I never bake a pan of brownies but what I think of him, or hear the church bells ring. So I have to pity Lavonne and her cup of coffee if you see what I mean, just like I have to spend the rest of my life to live my sinning down. But I'll tell you this: if I had it all to do over, I would do it all over again, and I would not trade it in for anything.

Lavonne drove off to look at fabric and get Bethy Rose an Icee, and I went in the hospital. I hate the way they smell. As soon as I entered Mr. Biggers' room, I could see he was breathing his last. He was so tiny in the bed you almost missed him, a poor little shriveled-up thing. His family sat all around.

"Aren't you sweet to come?" they said. "Looky here, honey, it's Mrs. Newhouse."

He didn't move a muscle, all hooked up to tubes. You could hear him breathing all over the room.

"It's Mrs. Newhouse," they said, louder. "Mrs. Newhouse is here. Last night he was asking for everybody," they said to me. "Now he won't open his eyes. You are real sweet to come," they said. "You certainly did brighten his days." Now I knew this was true because the family had remarked on it before.

"I'm so glad," I said. Then some more people came in the door and everybody was talking at once, and while they were doing that, I went over to the bed and got right up by his ear.

"Mr. Biggers!" I said. "Mr. Biggers, it's Joline Newhouse here."

He opened one little old bleary eye.

"Mr. Biggers!" I said right into his ear. "Mr. Biggers, you know those cardinals in my column? Mr. and Mrs. Cardinal? Well, I made them up! I made them up, Mr. Biggers. They never were real at all." Mr. Biggers closed his eye and a nurse came in and I stood up.

"Thank you so much for coming, Mrs. Newhouse," his daughter said.

"He is one fine old gentleman," I told them all, and then I left.

Outside in the hall, I had to lean against the tile wall for support while I waited for the elevator to come. Imagine, me saying such a thing to a dying man! I was not myself that day.

Lavonne took me to the big Krogers in north Greenville and we did our shopping, and on the way back in the car she told me she had been giving everything a lot of thought and she guessed I was right after all.

"You're not going to tell anybody, are you?" she asked me anxiously, popping her eyes. "You're not going to tell Daddy, are you?" she said.

"Why, Lord no, honey!" I told her. "It is the farthest thing from my mind."

Sitting in the back seat among all the grocery bags, Bethy Rose sang a little song she had learned at school. "Make new friends but keep the old, some are silver but the other gold," she sang.

"I don't know what I was thinking of," Lavonne said.

Glenn was not home yet when I got there—making his arrangements, I supposed. I took off my hat, made myself a cup of Sanka, and sat down and finished off my column on a high inspirational note, saving Margie and Mr. Biggers for the next week. I cooked up some ham and red-eye gravy, which Glenn just loves, and then I made some biscuits. The time seemed to pass so slow. The phone rang two times while I was fixing supper, but I just let it go. I thought I had received enough news for *that* day. I still couldn't get over Margie putting her head in the oven, or what I had said to poor Mr. Biggers, which was not at all like me you can be sure. I buzzed around that kitchen doing first one thing, then another. I couldn't keep my mind on anything I did.

After a while Marshall came home, and ate, and went in the front room to watch TV. He cannot keep it in his head that watching TV in the dark will ruin your eyes, so I always have to go in there and turn on a light for him. This night, though, I didn't. I just let him sit there in the recliner in the dark, watching his show, and in the pale blue light from that TV set he looked just like anybody else.

I put on a sweater and went out on the front porch and sat in the swing to watch for Glenn. It was nice weather for that time of year, still a little cold but you could smell spring in the air already and I knew it wouldn't be long before the redbud would come out again on the hills. Out in the dark where I couldn't see them, around the front steps, my crocuses were already up. After a while of sitting out there I began to take on a chill, due more to my age no doubt than the weather, but just then some lights came around the bend, two headlights, and I knew it was Glenn coming home.

Glenn parked the truck and came up the steps. He was dog-tired, I could see that. He came over to the swing and put his hand on my shoulder. A little wind came up, and by then it was so dark you could see lights on all the ridges where the people live. "Well, Joline," he said.

"Dinner is waiting on you," I said. "You go on in and wash up and I'll be there directly. I was getting worried about you," I said.

Glenn went on and I sat there swaying on the breeze for a minute before I went after him. Now where will it all end? I ask you. All this pain and loving, mystery and loss. And it just goes on and on, from Glenn's mother taking up with dark-skinned gypsies to my own daddy and his postcard to that silly Lavonne and her cup of coffee to Margie with her head in the oven, to John Marcel Wilkes and myself, God help me, and all of it so long ago out in those holy woods.

SNOW

ALICE ADAMS

Alice Adams grew up in Chapel Hill, North Carolina, and graduated from Radcliffe; since then she has lived mostly in San Francisco. Her collection of stories, *Beautiful Girl*, was published by Knopf in 1979, and her fourth novel, *Rich Rewards*, was published in 1980, also by Knopf. This is her eleventh O. Henry story.

On a trail high up in the California Sierra, between heavy smooth white snowbanks, four people on cross-country skis form a straggling line. A man and three women: Graham, dark and good-looking, a San Francisco architect, who is originally from Georgia; Carol, his girlfriend, a gray-eyed blonde, a florist; Susannah, daughter of Graham, dark and fat and now living in Venice, California; and, quite a way behind Susannah, tall thin Rose, Susannah's friend and lover. Susannah and Rose both have film-related jobs—Graham has never been quite sure what they do.

Graham and Carol both wear smart cross-country outfits: knickers and Norwegian wool stockings. The younger women are in jeans and heavy sweaters. And actually, despite the bright cold look of so much snow, this April day is warm, and the sky is a lovely spring blue, reflected in distant small lakes, just visible, at intervals.

Graham is by far the best skier of the four, a natural; he does anything athletic easily. He strides and glides along, hardly aware of what he is doing, except for a sense of physical well-being. However, just now he is cursing himself for having dreamed up this weekend, renting an unknown house in Alpine Meadows, near Lake Tahoe, even for bringing these women together. He had hoped for a diversion from a situation that could be tricky, difficult: a visit from Susannah, who was bringing Rose, whom he had previously been told about but had not met. Well, skiing was a diversion, but what in God's name would they all do tonight? Or talk about? And why had he wanted to get them together anyway? He wasn't all that serious about Carol (was he?); why introduce her to his daughter? And why did he have to meet Rose?

Carol is a fair skier, although she doesn't like it much: it takes all her breath. At the moment, with the part of her mind that is not concentrated on skiing, she is thinking that although Graham is smarter than most of the men she knows, talented and successful, and really nice as well, she is tired of going out with men who don't *see* her, don't know who she is. That's partly her fault, she knows; she lies about her age and dyes her hair, and she *never* mentions the daughter in Vallejo, put out for adoption when Carol was fifteen (she would be almost twenty now, almost as old as Graham's girl, this unfriendly fat Susannah). But sometimes Carol would like to say to the men she knows, Look, I'm thirty-five, and in some ways my life has been terrible—being blond and pretty doesn't save you from anything.

But, being more fair-minded than given to self-pity, next Carol thinks, Well, as far as that goes Graham didn't tell me much about his girl, either, and for all I know mine is that way, too. So many of them are, these days.

How can he possibly be so dumb, Susannah is passionately thinking, of her father. And the fact that she has asked that question hundreds of times in her life does not diminish its intensity or the accompanying pain. He doesn't understand anything, she wildly, silently screams. Stupid, straight blondes: a *florist*. *Skiing*. How could he think that I . . . that Rose . . . ?

Then, thinking of Rose in a more immediate way, she remembers that Rose has hardly skied before—just a couple of times in Vermont, where she comes from. In the almost-noon sun Susannah stops to wait for Rose, half-heartedly aware of the lakes, just now in view, and the smell of pines, as sweat collects under her heavy breasts, slides down her ribs.

Far behind them all, and terrified of everything, Rose moves along with stiffened desperation. Her ankles, her calves, her thighs, her lower back are all tight with dread. Snow is stuck to the bottoms of her skis, she knows—she can hardly move them—

but she doesn't dare stop. She will fall, break something, get lost. And everyone will hate her, even Susannah.

Suddenly, like a gift to a man in his time of need, just ahead of Graham there appears a lovely open glade, to one side of the trail. Two huge heavy trees have fallen there, at right angles to each other; at the far side of the open space runs a brook, darkly glistening over small smooth rocks. High overhead a wind sings through the pines, in the brilliant sunlight.

It is perfect, a perfect picnic place, and it is just now time for lunch. Graham is hungry; he decides that hunger is what has been unsettling him. He gets out of his skis in an instant, and he has just found a smooth, level stump for the knapsack, a natural table, when Carol skis up—out of breath, not looking happy.

But at the sight of that place she instantly smiles. She says, "Oh, how perfect! Graham, it's beautiful." Her gray eyes praise him, and the warmth of her voice. "Even benches to sit on. Graham, what a perfect Southern host you are." She laughs in a pleased, cheered-up way, and bends to unclip her skis. But something is wrong, and they stick. Graham comes over to help. He gets her out easily; he takes her hand and lightly he kisses her mouth, and then they both go over and start removing food from the knapsack, spreading it out.

"Two bottles of wine. Lord, we'll all get plastered." Carol laughs again, as she sets up the tall green bottles in a deep patch of snow.

Graham laughs, too, just then very happy with her, although he is also feeling the familiar apprehension that any approach of his daughter brings on: *will* Susannah like what he has done, will she approve of him, ever? He looks at his watch and he says to Carol, "I wonder if they're O.K. Rose is pretty new on skis. I wonder . . ."

But there they are, Susannah and Rose. They have both taken off their skis and are walking along the side of the trail, carrying the skis on their shoulders, Susannah's neatly together, Rose's at a clumsy, difficult angle. There are snowflakes in Susannah's dark brown hair—hair like Graham's. Rose's hair is light, dirty blond; she is not even pretty, Graham has unkindly thought. At the moment they both look exhausted and miserable.

In a slow, tired way, not speaking, the two girls lean their skis and poles against a tree; they turn toward Graham and Carol, and then, seemingly on a single impulse, they stop and look around. And with a wide smile Susannah says, "Christ, Dad, it's just beautiful. It's great."

Rose looks toward the spread of food. "Oh, roast chicken. That's my favorite thing." These are the first nice words she has said to Graham. (Good manners are not a strong suit of Rose's, he has observed, in an interior, Southern voice.)

He has indeed provided a superior lunch, as well as the lovely place—his discovery. Besides the chicken, there are cherry tomatoes (called love apples where Graham comes from, in Georgia), cheese (Jack and cheddar), Triscuits, and oranges and chocolate. And the nice cool dry white wine. They all eat and drink a lot, and they talk eagerly about how good it all is, how beautiful the place where they are. The sky, the trees, the running brook.

Susannah even asks Carol about her work, in a polite, interested way that Graham has not heard from her for years. "Do you have to get up early and go to the flower mart every morning?" Susannah asks.

"No, but I used to, and really that was more fun—getting out so early, all those nice fresh smells. Now there's a boy I hire to do all that, and I'm pretty busy making arrangements."

"Oh, arrangements," says Rose, disparagingly.

Carol laughs. "Me, too, I hate them. I just try to make them as nice as I can, and the money I get is really good."

Both Rose and Susannah regard Carol in an agreeing, respectful way. For a moment Graham is surprised: these kids respecting money? Then he remembers that this is the seventies: women are supposed to earn money, it's good for them.

The main thing, though, is what a good time they all have together. Graham even finds Rose looking at him with a small, shy smile. He offers her more wine, which she accepts—another smile as he pours it out for her. And he thinks, Well, of course it's tough on her, too, meeting me. Poor girl, I'm sure she's doing the best she can.

"You all really like it down there in Hollywood?" he asks the two girls, and he notes that his voice is much more Southern than usual; maybe the wine.

"Universal City," Susannah corrects him, but she gives a serious answer. "I love it. There's this neat woman in the cutting room, and she knows I'm interested, so she lets me come in and look at the rushes, and hear them talk about what has to go. I'm really learning. It's great."

And Rose: "There're so many really exciting people around."

At that moment they both look so young, so enviably involved in their work, so happy, that Graham thinks, Well, really, why not?

Occasionally the wind will move a branch from a nearby tree and some snow will sift down, through sunlight. The sky seems a deeper blue than when they first came to this glade, a pure azure. The brook gurgles more loudly, and the sun is very hot.

And then they are all through with lunch; they have finished off the wine, and it is time to go.

They put on their skis, and they set off again, in the same order in which they began the day.

For no good reason, as he glides along, striding through snow in the early California afternoon, the heat, Graham is suddenly, sharply visited by a painful memory of the childhood of Susannah. He remembers a ferociously hot summer night in Atlanta, when he and his former wife, mother of Susannah, had quarrelled all through suppertime, and had finally got Susannah off to bed; she must have been about two. But she kept getting up again, screaming for her bottle, her Teddy bear, a sandwich. Her mother and Graham took turns going in to her, and then finally, about three in the morning, Graham picked her up and smacked her bottom, very hard; he can remember the sting on his hand—and good Christ, what a thing to do to a little baby. No wonder she is as she is; he probably frightened her right then, for good. Not to mention all the other times he got mad and just yelled at her—or his love affairs, the move to San Francisco, the divorce, more love affairs.

If only she were two right now, he desperately thinks, he could change everything; he could give her a stable, loving father. Now he has a nice house on Russian Hill; he is a successful man; he could give her—anything.

Then his mind painfully reverses itself and he thinks, But I was a loving father, most of the time. Susannah's got no real cause to be the way she is. Lots of girls—most girls—come out all right. At that overheated moment he feels that his heart will truly break. It is more than I can stand, he thinks; why do I have to?

Carol's problem is simply a physical one: a headache. But she never has headaches, and this one is especially severe; for the first time she knows exactly what her mother meant by "splitting headache." Is she going to get more and more like her mother as she herself ages? Could she be having an early menopause, beginning with migraines? She could die, the pain is so sharp. She could die, and would anyone care much, really? She's *lonely*.

Susannah is absorbed in the problem of Rose, who keeps falling down. Almost every time Susannah looks back, there is Rose, fallen in the snow. Susannah smiles at her encouragingly, and sometimes she calls back, "You're O.K.?" She knows that Rose would not like it if she actually skied back to her and helped her up; Rose has that ferocious Vermont Yankee pride, difficult in a fragile frightened woman.

It is breezier now than earlier in the morning, and somewhat cooler. Whenever Susannah stops, stands still, and waits for Rose, she is aware of her own wind-chilled sweat, and she worries, thinking of Rose, of wet and cold. Last winter Rose had a terrible, prolonged bout of flu, a racking cough.

Talking over their "relationship," at times Susannah and Rose have (somewhat jokingly) concluded that there certainly are elements of mothering within it; in many ways Susannah takes care of Rose. She is stronger—that is simply true. Now for the first time it occurs to Susannah (wryly, her style is wry) that she is somewhat fatherly with Rose, too: the sometimes stern guardian, the protector. And she thinks, Actually Graham wasn't all that bad with me, I've been rough on him. Look at the example he set me: I work hard, and I care about my work, the way he does. And he taught me to ski, come to think of it. I should thank him, sometime, somehow, for some of it.

Rose is falling, falling, again and again, and oh Christ, how much she hates it—hates her helplessness, hates the horrible snow, the cold wet. Drinking all that wine at lunchtime, in the pretty glade, the sunlight, she had thought that wine would make her brave; she knows her main problem to be fear—no confidence and hence no balance. But the wine, and the sun, and sheer fatigue have destroyed whatever equilibrium she had, so that all she can do is fall, fall miserably, and each time the snow is colder and it is harder for her to get up.

Therefore, they are all extremely glad when, finally, they are out of their skis and off the trail and at last back in their house, in Alpine Meadows. It is small—two tiny, juxtaposed bedrooms—but the living room is pleasant: it looks out to steeply wooded, snowy slopes. Even more pleasant at the moment is the fact that the hot-water supply is vast; there is enough for deep baths for everyone, and then they will all have much-needed before-dinner naps.

Carol gets the first bath, and then, in turn, the two younger women. Graham last. All three women have left a tidy room, a clean tub, he happily notices, and the steamy air smells vaguely sweet, of something perfumed, feminine. Luxuriating in his own full, hot tub, he thinks tenderly, in a general way, of women, how warm and sexual they are, more often than not, how frequently intelligent and kind. And then he wonders what he has not quite, ever, put into words before: what is it that women do, women together? What ever could they do that they couldn't do with men, and *why?*

However, these questions are much less urgent and less painful than most of his musings along those lines; he simply wonders.

In their bedroom, disappointingly, Carol is already fast asleep. He has not seen her actually sleeping before; she is always first awake when he stays over at her place. Now she looks so drained, so entirely exhausted, with one hand protectively across her eyes, that he is touched. Carefully, so as not to wake her, he slips in beside her, and in minutes he, too, is sound asleep.

Graham has planned and shopped for their dinner, which he intends to cook. He likes to cook, and does it well, but in his bachelor life he has done it less and less, perhaps because he and most of the women he meets tend to shy off from such domestic encounters. Somehow the implication of cooking *for* anyone has become alarming, more so than making love to them. But tonight Graham happily prepares to make pork chops with milk gravy and mashed potatoes, green peas, an apple-and-nut salad, and cherry pie (from a bakery, to be heated). A down-home meal, for his girlfriend, and his daughter, and her friend.

From the kitchen, which is at one end of the living room, he can hear the pleasant sounds of the three women's voices, in amiable conversation, as he blends butter and flour in the pan in which he has browned the chops, and begins to add hot milk. And then he notices a change in the tone of those voices: what was gentle and soft has gone shrill, strident—the sounds of a quarrel. He hates the thought of women fighting; it is almost frightening, and, of course, he is anxious for this particular group to get along, if only for the weekend.

He had meant, at just that moment, to go in and see if anyone wanted another glass of wine; dinner is almost ready. And so, reluctantly, he does; he gets into the living room just in time to hear Rose say, in a shakily loud voice, "No one who hasn't actually experienced rape can have the least idea what it's like."

Such a desperately serious sentence could have sounded ludicrous, but it does not. Graham is horrified; he thinks, Ah, poor girl, poor Rose. Jesus, *raped.* It is a crime that he absolutely cannot imagine.

In a calm, conciliatory way, Susannah says to Carol, "You see, Rose actually was raped, when she was very young, and it was terrible for her—"

Surprisingly, Carol reacts almost with anger. "Of course it's terrible, but you kids think you're the only ones things happen to. I got pregnant when I was fifteen, and I had it, a girl, and I put her out for adoption." Seeming to have just now noticed Graham, she addresses him in a low, defiant, scolding voice. "And I'm not thirty. I'm thirty-five."

Graham has no idea, really, of what to do, but he is aware of strong feelings that lead him to Carol. He goes over and puts his arms around her. Behind him he hears the gentle voice of Susannah, who is saying, "Oh Carol, that's terrible. God, that's *awful.*"

Carol's large eyes are teary, but in a friendly way she disengages herself from Graham; she even smiles as she says, "Well, I'm sorry, I didn't mean to say that. But you see? You really can't tell what's happened to anyone."

And Susannah: "Oh, you're right, of course you are . . ."

And Rose: "It's true, we do get arrogant . . ."

Graham says that he thinks they should eat. The food is hot; they must be hungry. He brings the dinner to them at the table, and he serves out hot food onto the heated plates.

Carol and Rose are talking about the towns they came from: Vallejo, California, and Manchester, Vermont.

"It's thirty miles from San Francisco," Carol says. "And that's all we talked about. The City. How to get there, and what was going on there. Vallejo was just a place we ignored, dirt under our feet."

"All the kids in Manchester wanted to make it to New York," Rose says. "All but me, and I was fixated on Cambridge. Not getting into Radcliffe was terrible for me—it's why I never went to college at all."

"I didn't either," Carol says, with a slight irony that Graham thinks may have been lost on Rose: Carol would not have expected to go to college, probably—it wasn't what high-school kids from Vallejo did. But how does he know this?

"I went to work instead," says Rose, a little priggishly (thinks Graham).

"Me too," Carol says, with a small laugh.

Susannah breaks in. "Dad, this is absolutely the greatest dinner. You're still the best cook I know. It's good I don't have your dinners more often."

"I'm glad you like it. I haven't cooked a lot lately."

And Rose, and Carol: "It's super. It's great."

Warmed by praise, and just then wanting to be nice to Rose (partly because he has to admit to himself that he doesn't much like her), Graham says to her, "Cambridge was where I wanted to go to school, too. The Harvard School of Design. Chicago seemed second-best. But I guess it's all worked out."

"I guess." Rose smiles.

She looks almost pretty at that moment, but not quite; looking at her, Graham thinks again, If it had to be another girl, why her? But he knows this to be unfair, and, as far as that goes, why anyone for anyone, when you come to think of it? Any pairing is basically mysterious.

Partly as a diversion from such unsettling thoughts, and also from real curiosity, he asks Carol, "But was it worth it, when you got to the city?"

She laughs, in her low, self-depreciating way. "Oh, *I* thought so. I really liked it. My first job was with a florist on Union Street. It was nice there then, before it got all junked up with body shops and stuff. I had a good time."

Some memory of that era has put a younger, musing look on Carol's face, and Graham wonders if she is thinking of a love affair; jealously he wonders, Who? Who did you know, back then?

"I was working for this really nice older man," says Carol, in a higher than usual voice (as Graham thinks, *Ah*). "He taught me all he could. I was pretty dumb, at first. About marketing, arranging, keeping stuff fresh, all that. He lived by himself. A lonely person, I guess. He was—uh—gay, and then he died, and it turned out he'd left the store to me." For the second time that night tears have come to her eyes. "I was so touched, and it was too late to thank him, or anything." Then, the tears gone, her voice returns to its usual depth as she sums it up, "Well, that's how I got my start in the business world."

These sudden shifts in mood, along with her absolute refusal to see herself as an object of pity, are strongly, newly attractive to Graham; he has the sense of being with an unknown, exciting woman.

And then, in a quick, clairvoyant way, he gets a picture of Carol as a twenty-year-old girl, new in town: tall and a little awkward, working in the florist shop and worrying about her hands, her fingers scratched up from stems and wires; worrying about her darkening blond hair and then deciding, what the hell, better dye it; worrying about money, and men, and her parents back in Vallejo—and *should* she have put the baby out for adoption? He feels an unfamiliar tenderness for this new Carol.

"You guys are making me feel very boring," says Susannah. "I always wanted to go to Berkeley, and I did, and I wanted to go to L.A. and work in films."

"I think you're just more direct," amends Rose, affectionate admiration in her voice, and in her eyes. "You just know what you're doing. I fall into things."

Susannah laughs. "Well, you do all right, you've got to admit." And, to Graham and Carol: "She's only moved up twice since January. At this rate she'll be casting something in August."

What Graham had earlier named discomfort he now recognizes as envy: Susannah is closer to Rose than she is to him; they are closer to each other than he is to anyone. He says, "Well, Rose, that's really swell. That's *swell*."

Carol glances at Graham for an instant before she says, "Well,

I'll bet your father didn't even tell you about his most recent prize." And she tells them about an award from the A.I.A., which Graham had indeed not mentioned to Susannah, but which had pleased him at the time of its announcement (immoderately, he told himself).

And now Susannah and Rose join Carol in congratulations, saying how terrific, really great.

Dinner is over, and in a rather disorganized way they all clear the table and load the dishwasher.

They go into the living room, where Graham lights the fire, and the three women sit down, or, rather, sprawl—Rose and Susannah at either end of the sofa, Carol in an easy chair. For dinner Carol put on velvet pants and a red silk shirt. In the bright hot firelight her gray eyes shine, and the fine line under her chin, that first age line, is just barely visible. She is very beautiful at that moment—probably more so now than she was fifteen years ago, Graham decides.

Susannah, in clean, faded, too tight Levi's, stretches her legs out stiffly before her. "Oh, I'm really going to feel that skiing in the morning!"

And Carol: "Me too. I haven't had that much exercise forever."

Rose says, "If I could just not fall."

"Oh, you won't; tomorrow you'll see. Tomorrow . . ." says everyone.

They are all exhausted. Silly to stay up late. And so as the fire dies down, Graham covers it and they all four go off to bed, in the two separate rooms.

Outside a strong wind has come up, creaking the walls and rattling windowpanes.

In the middle of the night, in what has become a storm—lashing snow and violent wind—Rose wakes up, terrified. From the depths of bad dreams, she has no idea where she is, what time it is, what day. With whom she is. She struggles for clues, her wide eyes scouring the dark, her tentative hands reaching out, encountering Susannah's familiar, fleshy back. Everything comes into focus for her; she knows where she is. She breathes out softly, "Oh, thank God it's you," moving closer to her friend.

IN THE GARDEN OF THE NORTH AMERICAN MARTYRS

TOBIAS WOLFF

Tobias Wolff is a native of Washington State. His short stories have appeared in *Antaeus*, the *Atlantic Monthly*, *Encounter*, *Mademoiselle*, *TriQuarterly*, and other magazines and reviews. He lives in Syracuse, New York, where he teaches literature and creative writing at Syracuse University. *In the Garden of the North American Martyrs* is the title story of a collection of stories to be published by Ecco Press in the fall of 1981.

When she was young, Mary saw a brilliant and original man lose his job because he had expressed ideas that were offensive to the trustees of the college where they both taught. She shared his views, but did not sign the protest petition. She was, after all, on trial herself—as a teacher, as a woman, as an interpreter of history.

Mary watched herself. Before giving a lecture she wrote it out in full, using the arguments and often the words of other, approved writers, so that she would not by chance say something scandalous. Her own thoughts she kept to herself, and the words for them grew faint as time went on; without quite disappearing they shrank to remote, nervous points, like birds flying away.

When the department turned into a hive of cliques, Mary went about her business and pretended not to know that people hated each other. To avoid seeming bland she let herself become eccentric in harmless ways. She took up bowling, which she learned to love, and founded the Brandon College chapter of a society dedicated to restoring the good name of Richard III. She memorized comedy routines from records and jokes from books; people groaned when she rattled them off, but she did not let that stop her, and after a time the groans became the point of the jokes. They were a kind of tribute to Mary's willingness to expose herself.

In fact, no one at the college was safer than Mary, for she was making herself into something institutional, like a custom, or a mascot—part of the college's idea of itself.

Now and then she wondered whether she had been too careful. The things she said and wrote seemed flat to her, pulpy, as though someone else had squeezed the juice out of them. And once, while talking with a senior professor, Mary saw herself reflected in a window: she was leaning toward him and had her head turned so that her ear was right in front of his moving mouth. The sight disgusted her. Years later, when she had to get a hearing aid, Mary suspected that her deafness was a result of always trying to catch everything everyone said.

In the second half of Mary's fifteenth year at Brandon the provost called a meeting of all faculty and students, to announce that the college was bankrupt and would not open its gates again. He was every bit as much surprised as they; the report from the trustees had reached his desk only that morning. It seemed that Brandon's financial manager had speculated in some kind of futures and lost everything. The provost wanted to deliver the news in person before it reached the papers. He wept openly and so did the students and teachers, with only a few exceptions—some cynical upperclassmen who claimed to despise the education they had received.

Mary could not rid her mind of the word "speculate." It meant to guess, in terms of money to gamble. How could a man gamble a college? Why would he want to do that, and how could it be that no one stopped him? To Mary, it seemed to belong to another time; she thought of a drunken plantation owner gaming away his slaves.

She applied for jobs and got an offer from a new experimental college in Oregon. It was her only offer so she took it.

The college was in one building. Bells rang all the time, lockers lined the hallways, and at every corner stood a buzzing water fountain. The student newspaper came out twice a month on wet mimeograph paper. The library, which was next to the band room, had no librarian and no books to speak of.

The countryside was beautiful, though, and Mary might have enjoyed it if the rain had not caused her so much trouble. There was something wrong with her lungs that the doctors couldn't agree on, and couldn't cure; whatever it was, the dampness made it worse. On rainy days condensation formed in Mary's hearing aid and shorted it out. She began to dread talking with people, never knowing when she would have to take out her control box and slap it against her leg.

It rained nearly every day. When it was not raining it was getting ready to rain, or clearing. The ground glinted under the grass, and the light had a yellow undertone that flared up during storms.

There was water in Mary's basement. Her walls sweated, and she had found toadstools growing behind the refrigerator. She felt as though she were rusting out, like one of those old cars people thereabouts kept in their front yards, on pieces of wood. Mary knew that everyone was dying, but it did seem to her that she was dying faster than most.

She continued to look for another job, without success. Then, in the fall of her third year in Oregon, she got a letter from a woman named Louise who'd once taught at Brandon. Louise had scored a great success with a book on Benedict Arnold, and was now on the faculty of a famous college in upstate New York. She said that one of her colleagues would be retiring at the end of the year, and asked whether Mary would be interested in the position.

The letter surprised Mary. Louise thought of herself as a great historian and of almost everyone else as useless; Mary had not known that she felt differently about her. Moreover, enthusiasm for other people's causes did not come easily to Louise, who had a way of sucking in her breath when familiar names were mentioned, as though she knew things that friendship kept her from disclosing.

Mary expected nothing, but sent a resume and copies of her two books. Shortly after that Louise called to say that the search committee, of which she was chairwoman, had decided to grant Mary an interview in early November. "Now don't get your hopes *too* high," said Louise.

"Oh, no," said Mary, but thought: Why shouldn't I hope? They would not go to the bother and expense of bringing me to the college if they weren't serious. And she was certain that the interview would go well. She would make them like her, or at least give them no cause to dislike her.

She read about the area with a strange sense of familiarity, as if the land and its history were already known to her. And when her plane left Portland and climbed easterly into the clouds, Mary felt as if she were going home. The feeling stayed with her, growing stronger when they landed. She tried to describe it to Louise as they left the airport at Syracuse and drove toward the college, an hour or so away. "It's like *déjà vu*," she said.

"*Déjà vu* is a hoax," said Louise. "It's just a chemical imbalance of some kind."

"Maybe so," said Mary, "but I still have this sensation."

"Don't get serious on me," said Louise. "That's not your long suit. Just be your funny, wisecracking old self. Tell me now—honestly—how do I look?"

It was night, too dark to see Louise's face well, but in the airport she had seemed gaunt and pale and intense. She reminded Mary of a description in the book she'd been reading, of how Iroquois warriors gave themselves visions by fasting. She had that kind of look about her. But she wouldn't want to hear that. "You look wonderful," said Mary.

"There's a reason," said Louise. "I've taken a lover. My concentration has improved, my energy level is up, and I've lost ten pounds. I'm also getting some color in my cheeks, though that could be the weather. I recommend the experience highly. But you probably disapprove."

Mary didn't know what to say. She said that she was sure Louise knew best, but that didn't seem to be enough. "Marriage is a great institution," she added, "but who wants to live in an institution?"

Louise groaned. "I know you," she said, "and I know that right now you're thinking 'But what about Ted? What about the children?' The fact is, Mary, they aren't taking it well at all. Ted has become a nag." She handed Mary her purse. "Be a good girl and light me a cigarette, will you? I know I told you I quit, but this whole thing has been very hard on me, very hard, and I'm afraid I've started again."

They were in the hills now, heading north on a narrow road. Tall trees arched above them. As they topped a rise Mary saw the forest all around, deep black under the plum-colored sky. There were a few lights and these made the darkness seem even greater.

"Ted has succeeded in completely alienating the children from me," Louise was saying. "There is no reasoning with any of them. In fact, they refuse to discuss the matter at all, which is very ironical because over the years I have tried to instill in them a willingness to see things from the other person's point of view. If they could just *meet* Jonathan I know they would feel differently. But they won't hear of it. Jonathan," she said, "is my lover."

"I see," said Mary, and nodded.

Coming around a curve they caught two deer in the headlights. Their eyes lit up and their hindquarters tensed; Mary could see them shaking as the car went by. "Deer," she said.

"I don't know," said Louise, "I just don't know. I do my best and it never seems to be enough. But that's enough about me—let's talk about you. What did you think of my latest book?" She squawked and beat her palms on the steering wheel. "God, I love that joke," she said. "Seriously, though, what about you? It must have been a real shockeroo when good old Brandon folded."

"It was hard. Things haven't been good but they'll be a lot better if I get this job."

"At least you have work," said Louise. "You should look at it from the bright side."

"I try."

"You seem so gloomy. I hope you're not worrying about the interview, or the class. Worrying won't do you a bit of good. Be happy."

"Class? What class?"

"The class you're supposed to give tomorrow, after the interview. Didn't I tell you? *Mea culpa*, hon, *mea maxima culpa*. I've been uncharacteristically forgetful lately."

"But what will I do?"

"Relax," said Louise. "Just pick a subject and wing it."

"Wing it?"

"You know, open your mouth and see what comes out. Extemporize."

"But I always work from a prepared lecture."

Louise sighed. "All right. I'll tell you what. Last year I wrote an article on the Marshall Plan that I got bored with and never published. You can read that."

Parroting what Louise had written seemed wrong to Mary, at

first; then it occurred to her that she had been doing the same kind of thing for many years, and that this was not the time to get scruples. "Thanks," she said. "I appreciate it."

"Here we are," said Louise, and pulled into a circular drive with several cabins grouped around it. In two of the cabins lights were on; smoke drifted straight up from the chimneys. "This is the visitors' center. The college is another two miles thataway." Louise pointed down the road. "I'd invite you to stay at my house, but I'm spending the night with Jonathan and Ted is not good company these days. You would hardly recognize him."

She took Mary's bags from the trunk and carried them up the steps of a darkened cabin. "Look," she said, "they've laid a fire for you. All you have to do is light it." She stood in the middle of the room with her arms crossed and watched as Mary held a match under the kindling. "There," she said. "You'll be snugaroo in no time. I'd love to stay and chew the fat but I can't. You just get a good night's sleep and I'll see you in the morning."

Mary stood in the doorway and waved as Louise pulled out of the drive, spraying gravel. She filled her lungs, to taste the air: it was tart and clear. She could see the stars in their figurations, and the vague streams of light that ran among the stars.

She still felt uneasy about reading Louise's work as her own. It would be her first complete act of plagiarism. It would change her. It would make her less—how much less, she did not know. But what else could she do? She certainly couldn't 'wing it.' Words might fail her, and then what? Mary had a dread of silence. When she thought of silence she thought of drowning, as if it were a kind of water she could not swim in.

"I want this job," she said, and settled deep into her coat. It was cashmere and Mary had not worn it since moving to Oregon, because people there thought you were pretentious if you had on anything but a Pendleton shirt or, of course, raingear. She rubbed her cheek against the upturned collar and thought of a silver moon shining through bare black branches, a white house with green shutters, red leaves falling in a hard blue sky.

Louise woke her a few hours later. She was sitting on the edge of the bed, pushing at Mary's shoulder and snuffling loudly. When Mary asked her what was wrong she said, "I want your opinion on something. It's very important. Do you think I'm womanly?"

Mary sat up. "Louise, can this wait?"

"No."

"Womanly?"

Louise nodded.

"You are very beautiful," said Mary, "and you know how to present yourself."

Louise stood and paced the room. "That sonofabitch," she said. She came back and stood over Mary. "Let's suppose someone said I have no sense of humor. Would you agree or disagree?"

"In some things you do. I mean, yes, you have a good sense of humor."

"What do you mean, 'in some things'? What kind of things?"

"Well, if you heard that someone had been killed in an unusual way, like by an exploding cigar, you would think that was funny."

Louise laughed.

"That's what I mean," said Mary.

Louise went on laughing. "Oh, Lordy," she said. "Now it's my turn to say something about you." She sat down beside Mary.

"Please," said Mary.

"Just one thing," said Louise.

Mary waited.

"You're trembling," said Louise. "I was just going to say—oh, forget it. Listen, do you mind if I sleep on the couch. I'm all in."

"Go ahead."

"Sure it's okay? You've got a big day tomorrow." She fell back on the sofa and kicked off her shoes. "I was just going to say, you should use some liner on those eyebrows of yours. They sort of disappear and the effect is disconcerting."

Neither of them slept. Louise chain-smoked cigarettes and Mary watched the coals burn down. When it was light enough that they could see each other Louise got up. "I'll send a student for you," she said. "Good luck."

The college looked the way colleges are supposed to look. Roger, the student assigned to show Mary around, explained that it was an exact copy of a college in England, right down to the gargoyles and stained-glass windows. It looked so much like a college that moviemakers sometimes used it as a set. *Andy Hardy*

Goes to College had been filmed there, and every fall they had an Andy Hardy Goes to College Day, with raccoon coats and goldfish-swallowing contests.

Above the door of the Founder's Building was a Latin motto which, roughly translated, meant "God helps those who help themselves." As Roger recited the names of illustrious graduates Mary was struck by the extent to which they had taken this precept to heart. They had helped themselves to railroads, mines, armies, states; to empires of finance with outposts all over the world.

Roger took Mary to the chapel and showed her a plaque bearing the names of alumni who had been killed in various wars, all the way back to the Civil War. There were not many names. Here too, apparently, the graduates had helped themselves. "Oh yes," said Roger as they were leaving, "I forgot to tell you. The communion rail comes from some church in Europe where Charlemagne used to go."

They went to the gymnasium, and the three hockey rinks, and the library, where Mary inspected the card catalogue, as though she would turn down the job if they didn't have the right books. "We have a little more time," said Roger as they went outside. "Would you like to see the power plant?"

Mary wanted to keep busy until the last minute, so she agreed.

Roger led her into the depths of the service building, explaining things about the machine, which was the most advanced in the country. "People think the college is really old-fashioned," he said, "but it isn't. They let girls come here now, and some of the teachers are women. In fact, there's a statute that says they have to interview at least one woman for each opening. There it is."

They were standing on an iron catwalk above the biggest machine Mary had ever beheld. Roger, who was majoring in Earth Sciences, said that it had been built from a design pioneered by a professor in his department. Where before he had been gabby, Roger now became reverent. It was clear that to him, this machine was the soul of the college, that indeed the purpose of the college was to provide outlets for the machine. Together they leaned against the railing and watched it hum.

Mary arrived at the committee room exactly on time for her interview, but it was empty. Her two books were on the table, along with a water pitcher and some glasses. She sat down and picked up one of the books. The binding cracked as she opened it. The pages were smooth, clean, unread. Mary turned to the first chapter, which began "It is generally believed that . . ." How dull, she thought.

Nearly half an hour later Louise came in with several men. "Sorry we're late," she said. "We don't have much time so we'd better get started." She introduced Mary to the men but with one exception the names and faces did not stay together. The exception was Dr. Howells, the department chairman, who had a porous blue nose and terrible teeth.

A shiny-faced man to Dr. Howells' right spoke first. "So," he said, "I understand you once taught at Brandon College."

"It was a shame that Brandon had to close," said a young man with a pipe in his mouth. "There is a place for schools like Brandon." As he talked the pipe wagged up and down.

"Now you're in Oregon," said Dr. Howells. "I've never been there. How do you like it?"

"Not very much," said Mary.

"Is that right?" Dr. Howells leaned toward her. "I thought everyone liked Oregon. I hear it's very green."

"That's true," said Mary.

"I suppose it rains a lot," he said.

"Nearly every day."

"I wouldn't like that," he said, shaking his head. "I like it dry. Of course it snows here, and you have your rain now and then, but it's a *dry* rain. Have you ever been to Utah? There's a state for you. Bryce Canyon. The Mormon Tabernacle Choir."

"Dr. Howells was brought up in Utah," said the young man with the pipe.

"It was a different place altogether in those days," said Dr. Howells. "Mrs. Howells and I have always talked about going back when I retire, but now I'm not so sure."

"We're a little short on time," said Louise.

"And here I've been going on and on," said Dr. Howells. "Before we wind things up, is there anything you want to tell us?"

"Yes. I think you should give me the job." Mary laughed when she said this, but no one laughed back, or even looked at her. They all looked away. Mary understood then that they were not really considering her for the position. She had been brought here to satisfy a rule. She had no hope.

The men gathered their papers and shook hands with Mary and told her how much they were looking forward to her class. "I can't get enough of the Marshall Plan," said Dr. Howells.

"Sorry about that," said Louise when they were alone. "I didn't think it would be so bad. That was a real bitcheroo."

"Tell me something," said Mary. "You already know who you're going to hire, don't you?"

Louise nodded.

"Then why did you bring me here?" Louise began to explain about the statute and Mary interrupted. "I know all that. But why me? Why did you pick *me*?"

Louise walked to the window. She spoke with her back to Mary. "Things haven't been going very well for old Louise," she said. "I've been unhappy and I thought you might cheer me up. You used to be so funny, and I was sure you would enjoy the trip —it didn't cost you anything, and it's pretty this time of year with the leaves and everything. Mary, you don't know the things my parents did to me. And Ted is no barrel of laughs either. Or Jonathan, the sonofabitch. I deserve some love and friendship but I don't get any." She turned and looked at her watch. "It's almost time for your class. We'd better go."

"I would rather not give it. After all, there's not much point, is there?"

"But you *have* to give it. That's part of the interview." Louise handed Mary a folder. "All you have to do is read this. It isn't much, considering all the money we've laid out to get you here."

Mary followed Louise down the hall to the lecture room. The professors were sitting in the front row with their legs crossed. They smiled and nodded at Mary. Behind them the room was full of students, some of whom had spilled over into the aisles. One of the professors adjusted the microphone to Mary's height, crouching down as he went to the podium and back as though he would prefer not to be seen.

Louise called the room to order. She introduced Mary and gave the subject of the lecture, not knowing that Mary had decided to wing it after all. Mary came to the podium unsure of what she would say; sure only that she would rather die than read Louise's article. The sun poured through the stained glass onto the people around her, painting their faces. Thick streams of smoke from the young professor's pipe drifted through a circle of red light at Mary's feet, turning crimson and twisting like flames.

"I wonder how many of you know," she began, "that we are in the Long House, the ancient domain of the Five Nations of the Iroquois."

Two professors looked at each other.

"The Iroquois were without pity," said Mary. "They hunted people down with clubs and arrows and spears and nets, and blowguns made from elder stalks. They tortured their captives, sparing no one, not even the little children. They took scalps and practiced cannibalism and slavery. Because they had no pity they became powerful, so powerful that no other tribe dared to oppose them. They made the other tribes pay tribute, and when they had nothing more to pay, the Iroquois attacked them."

Several of the professors began to whisper. Dr. Howells was saying something to Louise, and Louise was shaking her head.

"In one of their attacks," said Mary, "they captured two Jesuit priests, Jean de Brébeuf and Gabriel Lalemant. They covered Lalemant with pitch and set him on fire in front of Brébeuf. When Brébeuf rebuked them they cut off his lips and put a burning iron down his throat. They hung a collar of red-hot hatchets around his neck, and poured boiling water over his head. When he continued to preach to them they cut strips of flesh from his body and ate them before his eyes. While he was still alive they scalped him and cut open his breast and drank his blood. Later, their chief tore out Brébeuf's heart and ate it, but just before he did this Brébeuf spoke to them one last time. He said—"

"That's enough!" yelled Dr. Howells, jumping to his feet.

Louise stopped shaking her head. Her eyes were perfectly round.

Mary had come to the end of her facts. She did not know what Brébeuf had said. Silence rose up around her; just when she thought she would go under and be lost in it she heard someone whistling in the hallway outside, trilling the notes like a bird, like many birds.

"Mend your lives," she said. "You have deceived yourselves in the pride of your hearts, and the strength of your arms. Though you soar aloft like the eagle, though your nest is set among the stars, thence I will bring you down, says the Lord. Turn from power to love. Be kind. Do justice. Walk humbly."

Louise was waving her arms. "Mary!" she shouted.

But Mary had more to say, much more; she waved back at Louise, then turned off her hearing aid so that she would not be distracted again.

HOPE OF ZION

SANDRA HOLLIN FLOWERS

Sandra Hollin Flowers was born in Yuma, Arizona, in 1946. She received the B.A. and M.F.A. from the University of Arizona. Her work has appeared in *Quest: a feminist quarterly*, *Essence*, and *Redbook*. "Hope of Zion" is her first published short story.

Each year when Veronica returned for Hope of Zion's home-coming, she entered the church with a fervent prayer that something would have changed. Perhaps there would be new stained-glass contact paper on the windows, new offering and attendance banners, a different version of the Last Supper emblazoned on the wall behind the pulpit. And each year the prayer went unanswered.

This year, however, the change was in her, for today marked the last time she would make the eight-hundred-mile trip for home-coming. During the last six years she had resented her father's unarticulated assumption that she would be there. And as she approached the crooked, whitewashed building she felt good knowing that as her father beamed on her from the pulpit he'd have no idea that she'd made up her mind never to suffer through another of his meaningless, meandering sermons. Sermons (if they could be called that) of no use to any but Zion's dead and dying.

Let the dead bury their dead; but as for me and my house . . . Ah, she was mixing testaments again in the fashion of her father. Because she was embarrassed about being a bit late, she accepted, along with a program and an offering envelope, an extra hug in the fleshy arms and deep bosom of the head usher. "Hugging Sister Thorpe," she was called, her meaty arms always so extremely ready to enfold some body. Veronica had permitted these embraces more graciously as the years passed; and now, approaching her twenty-ninth birthday, she was more charitable than Hope of Zion had ever seen her. She pulled away from Sister Thorpe and tiptoed respectfully to her seat, third bench, left row, under the window.

Hope of Zion's lemon-oil-shined benches creaked under the unaccustomed weight of a full house. Unless sick or out of town, the faithful came every Sunday. The others, by far the majority, came on Christmas, Easter, Mother's Day and during hard times. And those, like Veronica, whose out-of-town addresses proclaimed them truly lost sheep, came for home-coming, the Sunday of Thanksgiving weekend.

In childhood Veronica had often spied on her father, the Reverend Douglas Fairfax, as he prepared and practiced his sermons. She remembered, with some anguish and embarrassment, how he would pore over his Bibles and clergyman's periodicals, searching for those certain passages that would make his Mother's Day and home-coming messages meaningful to somebody's mother. And how those mothers worshiped him for it! Outside after service they led their grown, God-strange children by the sleeve: "You remember my little Eugene (or Melvina or what-have-you), don't you, Rev?" Written all over the mother's face and sometimes spilling from her mouth: "Bless my baby—just say one word to keep him on the path." Written all over the baby's face: "Damn, I sure could use a smoke."

The deacons, rising at the end of passionate prayers delivered into dry, ashy hands, brought Veronica back to the service. Immediately a sharp *ding!* from the silver offering bell signaled the ushers to admit the latecomers. While these filed in, a saint in the front row began a garbled wail:

"*Beforethistimetomorrow Imaybeonmywaytoglory* . . ."

And the congregation, dissecting the dirge, drew each word out to its infinite possibilities, achieving harmony and logic without trying. Furtive glances were cast over perfumed and furred shoulders. Who was coming in; what were they wearing?

Latecomers seated, the choir halt-stepped up the center aisle, resplendent in red and gold.

"*The Lord is blessing me*
Right now—oh, yes, he is!"

When they reached the altar Veronica's father also blessed

them, simultaneously bringing the congregation to their feet with a majestic sweep of black-robed arms. He prayed for all those who had got out of their beds this morning to come to the House of the Lord and for all those who had otherwise been summoned to the House. He blessed the comings and goings of all people everywhere; and he invoked a particular blessing for the sick and the shut-in. With a last blessing he released the choir, who marched on, singing, into the choir stand.

"He woke me up this mor-aning . . ."

Rev. Fairfax knew the song to be one of Veronica's favorites. Had he asked the choir to sing it? she wondered uneasily. He might do that, she suspected, to make her feel remorseful and penitent about what he called the sin-filled life she led in Los Angeles. She craned her neck to get a look at him on the other side of the pulpit. His eyes were cast upward and he appeared lost in the ecstasy of the music.

Within a few minutes it was time for the first offering. The choir slipped smoothly into a soothing, lulling melody about the joys of giving. By the infrequency with which silver could be heard clinking against copper, Veronica judged the offering to be a generous one. Still blessing and praising, Rev. Fairfax approached the pulpit again.

"Our lesson this morning," he said, "comes from Luke fifteen. You know the story—hear me, Church. Say, 'There was a man who had two sons; and the younger of them said to his father, "Father give me the share of property that falls to me." And he divided his living between them. Not many days later, the younger son gathered all he had and took his journey into a far country, and there he squandered his property in loose living. And when he had spent everything, a great famine arose in that country, and he began to be in want.' "

Rev. Fairfax finished in a precise, low voice, slowing the words as though hypnotizing a reluctant subject. He paused and ceremoniously closed the Bible, fixing his stare on the door in the manner of one awaiting a long-desired visitor. The pianist tinkled some forlorn notes, which the choir picked up and turned into a mournful humming. The humming had a shape, the shape a song whose words need not be articulated, for everyone knew them.

"Coming home," they hummed, *"coming home. Lord, I'm coming home. . . ."*

Veronica refused to hum with the others, though she could not keep the words from tumbling through her mind as the song moved inexorably on. If they had stopped humming in mid-chorus, she would have been forced to finish out the song in her head; and this, she knew, was what was expected of her, what she had been conditioned for. "Train up a child," her father loved to quote to the despairing parents of his congregation, "in the way he should go, and when he is old he will not depart from it." Recalling the many times she had heard him issue that advice, Veronica tried to reason herself out of feeling that she had betrayed him, had even—she winced at the thought—betrayed God.

Rev. Fairfax was proceeding with his message, summarizing the parable and its happy ending. His voice, patient, compelling, was just as it had been the day Veronica told him she'd signed a contract as a back-up singer with a blues artist. But the note of desperation it had held then was missing now. This morning's listeners, hearing him that day, would not have believed him to be their pastor, God's voice with a ready, unvarying answer to every earthly problem. He had been objective at first, talking about the harshness of life in a big city. She answered all his arguments—she had a place to stay, a roommate waiting for her, a job, some savings to keep her going until her first check. Switching tactics, he had asked her what she knew about the life of "show people." She countered by asking where his faith was in his "train up a child" motto.

"I have built this church for you," he'd finally said in exasperation. "From a prayer circle of six souls to what it is today."

"And what is it?" she had asked. "A raggedy, patched-up hut I'd be ashamed to have strangers step into."

"Then you would be like Peter. But remember what the Lord said on the Mount: 'No man can serve two masters; for either he will hate the one and love the other, or he will be devoted to the one and despise the other. You cannot serve God and Mammon.' "

"Well, suppose I don't want to serve God?"

"What are you saying?" he had cried, throwing his hands over his ears. "Take it back right now, lest the anger of the Lord be kindled against you and he destroy you—"

"—from off the face of the earth," she interrupted, finishing the Scripture. "For God's sake, Daddy! You walk the paths of righteousness like a policeman on patrol. I don't want to do all that. I want to live before I die into your kind of eternal life."

"Veronica! You are blaspheming, you are dishonoring your father—"

"I know that!"

"Well, God protect and forgive you."

"But you drove me to it!" she shouted.

"Then God protect and forgive me," he said, slumping into his chair.

No, his congregation wouldn't have recognized him, she thought now, watching him pace himself through his sermon. She glanced at her watch, surprised that nearly ten minutes were past and he had not yet launched into the singsong harangue that all except her accepted as the Lord working through him for their souls' salvation. Today he was calm and delivered the message his text had promised.

"How many of us," he was saying, "would accept the return of the prodigal, or—and this is the real test—reward it? I hear what you thinking! 'What's that you say, Rev—reward the ungrateful spendthrift, reward a disobedient child for being a fool?' Say, 'That was all right in the Bible days when there was plenty to go around, but things pretty tight now.' "

"All right!" Hugging Sister Thorpe said with a short, rhythmic handclap.

"Well, sir," Rev. Fairfax continued, "go on and call your own child a fool; that's between you and the Lord. But while you acting contrarywise and refusing to reward your prodigal, remember that you have been told to 'answer not a fool according to his folly, lest you be like him yourself.' Proverbs twenty-six: four!"

"Amen!" and "Say on!" rang out among the younger worshipers while the elders offered a tentative, low-pitched "Well-l-l. . . ."

Veronica stared at her father questioningly. He avoided looking toward the row where she sat. She remembered his letters from the first few months after she'd left home, full of blistering pain couched in the guise of Biblical wisdom. He'd done everything short of opening his letters with "Dear Fool."

"The wise of heart will heed commandments," he had written once, "but a prating fool will come to ruin." That had been in response to someone's showing him an article in a rock magazine in which Veronica had given advice to youngsters who wanted to be back-up singers. Her few words, she felt, hardly deserved his accusation that she had switched from winning souls for the Lord to winning them for the devil. After trying unsuccessfully to pray over the question, she'd finally written back that she didn't see it his way. Immediately he responded that "the way of a fool is right in *her* own eyes, but a wise *woman* listens to advice." She began to dread his letters, letting them go unopened for days at a time.

And now he was saying it in public. Or was he? she wondered as he continued. "And you remember, don't you, children, that the prodigal, after wasting his inheritance, said to his father, 'I am no longer worthy to be called your son.' What ought we to do with a child who is not worthy, people? What would Jesus do—what would be his answer? Search your hearts, Church, and if the answer's not in there—search your Bibles!"

The "amens" got louder, the "wells" got longer, the old sisters in the saints' corner started tambourining their sturdy black shoes against the floorboards. Veronica grew uneasier. Her father was preaching as though to her, as though he had guessed her intention of never coming home again. She could almost believe that he did know, for he often had visions. When she'd been involved with the church, she too sometimes had had visions. Not clear, graphic ones like her father's, but distorted puzzles that he would help her rearrange and interpret like dreams. These days, though, she had nothing that could even pass for a vision. A sign of her weakened faith, she assumed, feeling a sense of loss and regret.

Shifting restlessly on the bench, she became annoyed. In Los Angeles such thoughts never occurred to her, but here there was no escape from them. Even the Fairfax home, which she had helped decorate years and years ago, seemed like an accusation: ceramic praying hands, crosses, pictures of Jesus with little shaded light bulbs over or under them. "Bless This House" and other prayers hanging from all the walls, in doorways, plastered under the glass of tables. Everywhere she turned she felt fingers pointing at her—backslider, backslider, they accused. Those that weren't pointing were beckoning her to come back to the fold.

Last month she had called to wish her father happy birthday, having forgotten, as usual, to send him a card. By this time, they had re-established enough rapport for him to tease her about her forgetfulness.

"But," he had said, "with me going on seventy, you won't have to be bothered with remembering too much longer."

He'd said it lightly enough, but the point was, he *had* said it. Rev. Fairfax had been widowed when Veronica was only ten, and since that time he had used his age as a sort of cold-war weapon whenever she showed signs of growing away from him. Born late into an until-then-childless marriage, Veronica had no one to share the burden with. She might have borne it well enough except that when she became a teen-ager, her father had begun sounding her out on the question of going into the ministry and carrying on Hope of Zion.

And the birthday call revealed that he'd not given up the idea, even with her having been away from home six years.

"I just don't want you to lose sight of what's here for you," he'd said. "I had my will done over yesterday—do that every year just before my birthday, you know. There's a lot here for you, baby—a lot more than you know."

"I'm sure you're right, Daddy, but at this point I just can't see coming back there."

"You might look at the church," he continued as though she hadn't spoken, "and think it's not much to whoop and holler about. But the land—now, the land is worth something. Why, you could tear the old building down and put up a new one—"

"Daddy—"

"—or leave the old one standing so you'd have some place to worship while you built a new sanctuary alongside it."

"Why won't you understand that my sanctuary is in Los Angeles?"

"Some young man?" he asked.

"That's not what I meant."

"Are you going to church?"

"Sometimes." It wasn't a full-fledged lie. Wasn't she always there at Hope of Zion's home-coming?

He said nothing for a moment. Obviously he was coming to some realization, for his voice was tired, discouraged, as they finished the conversation. She imagined the lines deepening in his face, felt his spirits declining with each sentence. Guiltily she hung up as soon as she decently could, resolved to quit holding out false hope to him by returning to the church once a year like an absentee landlord. . . .

Rev. Fairfax had concluded his sermon and was basking in the warmth that even Veronica could feel flowing through the congregation. What she had heard of his message had moved her, which she found surprising, for she long ago had stopped listening to his sermons, once she discovered that he never really *said* anything. His idea of preaching was to recite scriptures, call down blessings and reminisce over wraths that Job and Noah and the rest had suffered—as if he'd been right there by their side. All this was accompanied by shouts and posturings and frequent dabbing of his forehead with a neatly pressed handkerchief that doubled as a bookmark for his Bible.

Today, though, he had talked, had made himself accessible to the congregation, as though admitting he had no advantage over them, had had no secret meetings with God, or at least not any that they themselves couldn't bring about. She felt kindly toward him for making her last Hope of Zion service something worth remembering.

"Rev preached this morning, didn't he?" she heard one of the missionaries behind her whisper.

"Did," another answered. "But it was right strange, wasn't it? Nobody even got happy!"

Veronica rolled her eyes. Got happy! That was another thing that she had not missed about Hope of Zion—frenzied shouting and jerking that sometimes erupted into wild dancing and diving over benches. They would do that, some of the older women, when her father howled at them and when he was, as Veronica saw it, at the height of not making sense. It seemed to worry her father that she was apparently untouched by the spirit of the Lord during services, for he occasionally asked her if she ever felt anything at church. "Sometimes," she had admitted. But she didn't tell him that what she felt came from the music, not the preaching.

It was a strange feeling, and it made her so uncomfortable that she'd physically restrain herself to keep it from overpowering her. During these times she diverted herself by intellectualizing what was going on. An emotional overload, probably a tired body, a word or a chord that struck a charged nerve and set off an excess of adrenaline and ended in a physical reaction. And that, sisters, she mentally said to the missionaries, is all there is to getting happy.

Remembering the many times she had reasoned this out, Veronica smiled and felt the tension ease from her body. Surely God would find a subtler, more private way to touch her if He felt the need. She trusted His wisdom on this point; He knew what she needed. Hadn't He just led her father to a complete forgiveness and release of her? For thinking back on it, she felt sure now that that had been the meaning of his sermon. Pleased, she settled herself more comfortably, admiring the smoothness of her father's altar-call technique. One more offering, the benediction, and her last Hope of Zion service would be over.

Suddenly, as she was sometimes apt to do, as though overcome with the power of being able to make music—suddenly the pianist went wild. She pounded out a refrain on the bass keys, shouting as she played. Hugging Sister Thorpe gave one mighty yelp from the back of the church and Veronica heard what sounded like heavily clad feet running up the back of a bench. By this time, the choir and some of the congregation had started clapping and rocking to the music. Then, having gone from one end of the keyboard to the other, the pianist worked her way back to the choir's key and played a few bars of introduction. Eagerly the choir sang:

"Something
got a hold—got a hold
on me;
Oh, yes it did, right now!
Something . . ."

In seconds the whole church was afire, singing and clapping and shouting as Veronica had never known it. Her father was on his feet again, singing joyously, a radiant smile on his face as he directed the choir, the deacons, anybody who would look at him. Veronica knew the song; it was a favorite at Hope of Zion. But had she ever heard it sung with so much—what? So much urgency?

My God! she thought, looking around, feeling genuinely frightened, as though waking up to find herself in a place she'd never been. Have they gone crazy? The church sang as though the song would be taken from them any minute:

"I went to the meeting last night,
and my heart was not right—
ooooh—"

Veronica felt her knees knocking together. Her hands grew cold and clammy; the blood pounded in her head. They were drawing her into it; she was getting happy, she realized. And with that knowledge she remembered something her father had told her long ago: *If you ever get happy just once, baby, you will be the Lord's from then on!*

"No!" she cried into the shouting and singing. She pressed her thighs together; interlaced her fingers tightly; clenched her teeth, which had started to chatter. She gripped the edge of the bench, but the trembling and pulsating, the itching in her hands, the chills and the urge to weep, of all things, wouldn't go away.

The pianist hit the bass keys again, coming halfway up the scale, and broke into a new, faster rhythm as she went into the bridge. The hand clapping switched effortlessly to double time.

"*It was the Holy Ghost,*" the choir sang; ". . . *Holy Ghost,*" the congregation answered. Veronica saw her father lean across the pulpit rail, his hands outstretched to her. "Jesus will make a way!" she heard him shout. She shook her head. "Oh, yes!" he insisted.

"*The Holy Ghost,*" the choir chanted; ". . . *Holy Ghost,*" the church responded. Rev. Fairfax clapped his hands fiercely and shouted, "Thy will be done!" And the choir began prancing and shouting.

"*It made me walk right—*
Holy Ghost!
Talk right—
Holy Ghost!"

As though thrust from the bench, Veronica sprang up, her fists clenched, arms waving stiffly in the air, head thrown back and mouth stretched open in a silent scream of horrified joy.

THE ABORTION

ALICE WALKER

Alice Walker is a poet, novelist, short-story writer, essayist, biographer, and consulting and contributing editor of *Freedomways*, a quarterly journal of the Black Freedom Movement, and *Ms.* She is the author of eight books, and her work has appeared in the New York *Times Magazine* and *Book Review, Ms., Harper's, Mother Jones, The Black Scholar, Essence,* and other magazines.

She is the recipient of many honors, including a National Book Award Nomination. She was born in Eatonton, Georgia, in 1944.

They had discussed it, but not deeply, whether they wanted the baby she was now carrying. "I don't *know* if I want it," she said, eyes filling with tears. She cried at anything now and was often nauseous. That pregnant women cried easily and were nauseous seemed banal to her, and she resented banality.

"Well, think about it," he said, with his smooth reassuring voice (but with an edge of impatience she now felt) that used to soothe her.

It was all she *did* think about, all she, apparently, *could;* that he could dream otherwise enraged her. But she always lost when they argued. Her temper would flare up, he would become instantly reasonable, mature, responsible if not responsive, precisely, to her mood, and she would swallow down her tears and hate herself. It was because she believed him "good." The best human being she had ever met.

"It isn't as if we don't already have a child," she said in a calmer tone, carelessly wiping at the tear that slid from one eye.

"We have a perfect child," he said with relish. "Thank the good Lord!"

Had she ever dreamed she'd marry someone humble enough to go around thanking the good Lord? She had not.

Now they left the bedroom, where she had been lying down on their massive king-size bed with the forbidding ridge in the middle, and went down the hall—hung with bright prints—to the cheerful, clean kitchen. He put water on for tea in a bright yellow pot.

She wanted him to want the baby so much he would try to save its life. On the other hand, she did not permit such presumptuousness. As he praised the child they already had, a daughter of sunny disposition and winning smile, Imani sensed subterfuge and hardened her heart.

"What am I talking about?" she said, as if she'd been talking about it. "Another child would kill me. I can't imagine life with two children. Having a child is a good experience to have had, like graduate school. But if you've had one, you've had the experience and that's enough."

He placed the tea before her and rested a heavy hand on her hair. She felt the heat and pressure of his hand as she touched the cup and felt the odor and steam rise up from it. Her throat contracted.

"I can't drink that," she said through gritted teeth. "Take it away."

There were days of this.

Clarice, their daughter, was barely two years old. A miscarriage brought on by grief (Imani had lost her fervidly environmentalist mother to lung cancer shortly after Clarice's birth; the asbestos ceiling in the classroom where she taught first-graders had leaked for 40 years) separated Clarice's birth from the new pregnancy. Imani felt her body had been assaulted by these events and was, in fact, considerably weakened and was also, in any case, chronically anemic and run-down. Still, if she had wanted the baby more than she did not want it, she would not have planned to abort it.

They lived in a small town in the South. Her husband, Clarence, was—among other things—legal advisor and defender of the new black mayor of the town. The mayor was much in their lives because of the difficulties being the first black mayor of a small town assured, and because, next to the major leaders of black struggles in the South, Clarence respected and admired him most.

Imani reserved absolute judgment, but she did point out that Mayor Carswell would never look at her directly when she made a comment or posed a question, even sitting at her own dinner table, and would instead talk to Clarence as if she were not there. He assumed that as a woman she would not be interested in or even understand politics. (He would comment occasionally on her cooking or her clothes. He noticed when she cut her hair.) But Imani understood, for example, why she fed the mouth that did not speak to her; because for the present she must believe in Mayor Carswell, even as he could not believe in her. Even understanding this, however, she found dinners with Carswell hard to swallow.

But Clarence was dedicated to the mayor and believed his success would ultimately mean security and advancement for them all.

On the morning she left to have the abortion, the mayor and Clarence were to have a working lunch, and they drove to the airport deep in conversation about municipal funds, racist cops and the facilities for teaching at the chaotic, newly integrated schools. Clarence had time for the briefest kiss and hug at the airport ramp.

"Take care of yourself," he whispered lovingly, as she walked away. He was needed, while she was gone, to draft the city's new charter. She had agreed this was important; the mayor was already being called incompetent by local businessmen and the chamber of commerce, and one inferred from television that no black person alive knew what a city charter was.

"Take care of myself." *Yes,* she thought. *I see that is what I have to do.* But she thought this self-pityingly, which invalidated it. She had expected *him* to take care of her, and she blamed him for not doing so now.

Well, she was a fraud, anyway. She had known after a year of marriage that it bored her. "The Experience of Having a Child" was to distract her from this fact. Still, she expected him to "take care of her." She was lucky he didn't pack up and leave. But he seemed to know, as she did, that if anyone packed and left, it would be her. Precisely *because* she was a fraud and because in the end he would settle for fraud and she could not.

On the plane to New York her teeth ached and she vomited bile—bitter, yellowish stuff she hadn't even been aware her body produced. She resented and appreciated the crisp help of the stewardess who asked if she needed anything, then stood chatting with the cigarette-smoking white man next to her, whose fat hairy wrist, like a large worm, was all Imani could bear to see out of the corner of her eye.

Her first abortion, when she was still in college, she frequently remembered as wonderful, bearing as it had all the marks of a supreme coming of age and a seizing of the direction of her own life, as well as a comprehension of existence that never left her: that life—what one saw about one and called Life—was not a facade. There was nothing behind it which used "Life" as its manifestation. Life was itself. Period. At the time, and afterward, and even now, this seemed a marvelous thing to know.

The abortionist had been a delightful Italian doctor on the Upper East Side in New York, and before he put her under he told her about his own daughter, who was just her age and a junior at Vassar. He babbled on and on until she was out, but not before Imani had thought how her thousand dollars, for which she would be in debt for years, would go to keep his daughter there.

When she woke up it was all over. She lay on a brown naugahyde sofa in the doctor's outer office. And she heard, over her somewhere in the air, the sound of a woman's voice. It was a Saturday, no nurses in attendance, and she presumed it was the doctor's wife. She was pulled gently to her feet by this voice and encouraged to walk.

"And when you leave, be sure to walk as if nothing is wrong," the voice said.

Imani did not feel any pain. This surprised her. *Perhaps he didn't do anything,* she thought. *Perhaps he took my thousand dollars and put me to sleep with two dollars' worth of ether. Perhaps this is a racket.*

But he was so kind, and he was smiling benignly, almost fatherly, at her (and Imani realized how desperately she needed this "fatherly" look, this "fatherly" smile). "Thank you," she murmured sincerely: she was thanking him for her life.

Some of Italy was still in his voice. "It's nothing, nothing," he said. "A nice, pretty girl like you, in school like my own daughter, you didn't need this trouble."

"He's nice," she said to herself, walking to the subway on her way back to school. She lay down gingerly across a vacant seat and passed out.

She hemorrhaged steadily for six weeks and was not well again for a year.

But this was seven years later. An abortion law now made it possible to make an appointment at a clinic, and for $75 a safe, quick, painless abortion was yours.

Imani had once lived in New York, in the Village, not five blocks from where the abortion clinic was. It was also near the Margaret Sanger clinic, where she had received her very first diaphragm, with utter gratitude and amazement that someone apparently understood and actually cared about young women as alone and ignorant as she. In fact, as she walked up the block with its modern office buildings side by side with older, more elegant brownstones, she felt how close she was still to that earlier self. Still not in control of her sensuality, and only through violence and with money (for the flight and for the operation itself) in control of her body.

She found that abortion had entered the age of the assembly line. Grateful for the lack of distinction between herself and the other women—all colors, ages, states of misery or nervousness—she was less happy to notice, once the doctor started to insert the catheter, that the anesthesia she had been given was insufficient. But assembly lines don't stop because the product on them has a complaint. Her doctor whistled and assured her she was all right and carried the procedure through to the horrific end. Imani fainted some seconds before that.

They laid her out in a peaceful room full of cheerful colors. Primary colors: yellow, red, blue. When she revived she had the feeling of being in a nursery. She had a pressing need to urinate.

A nurse—kindly, white-haired and with firm hands—helped her to the john. Imani saw herself in the mirror over the sink and was alarmed. She was literally gray, as if all her blood had leaked out.

"Don't worry about how you look," said the nurse. "Rest a bit here and take it easy when you get back home. You'll be fine in a week or so."

She could not imagine being fine again. Somewhere her child—she never dodged into the language of "fetuses" and "amorphous growths"—was being flushed down a sewer. Gone all her or his chances to see the sunlight, savor a fig.

"Well," she said to this child, "it was you or me, Kiddo, and I chose me."

There were people who thought she had no right to choose herself, but Imani knew better than to think of those people now.

It was a bright, hot Saturday when she returned.

Clarence and Clarice picked her up at the airport. They had brought flowers from Imani's garden, and Clarice presented them with a stouthearted hug. Once in her mother's lap she rested content all the way home, sucking her thumb, stroking her nose with the forefinger of the same hand and kneading a corner of her blanket with the three fingers that were left.

"How did it go?" asked Clarence.

"It went," said Imani.

There was no way to explain abortion to a man. She thought castration might be an apt analogy, but most men, perhaps all, would insist this could not possibly be true.

"The anesthesia failed," she said. "I thought I would never faint in time to keep from screaming and leaping right off the table."

Clarence paled. He hated the thought of pain, any kind of violence. He could not endure it; it made him physically ill. This was one of the reasons he was a pacifist, another reason she admired him.

She knew he wanted her to stop talking. But she continued in a flat, deliberate voice.

"All the blood seemed to run out of me. The tendons in my legs felt cut. I was gray."

He reached for her hand. Held it. Squeezed.

"But," she said, "at least I know what I don't want. And I intend never to go through any of this again."

They were in the living room of their peaceful, quiet and colorful house. Imani was in her rocker, Clarice dozing on her lap. Clarence sank to the floor and held both of them in his arms. She felt he was asking for nurturance when she needed it herself. She felt the two of them, Clarence and Clarice, clinging to her, using her. And that the only way she could claim herself, feel herself distinct from them, was by doing something painful, self-defining but self-destructive.

She suffered his arms and his head against her knees as long as she could.

"Have a vasectomy," she said, "or stay in the guest room. Nothing is going to touch me anymore that isn't harmless."

He smoothed her thick hair with his hand. "We'll talk about it," he said, as if that was not what they were doing. "We'll see. Don't worry. We'll take care of things."

She had forgotten that the third Sunday in June, the following day, was the fifth memorial observance for Holly Monroe, who had been shot down on her way home from her high school graduation ceremony five years before. Imani *always* went to these memorials. She liked the reassurance that her people had long memories and that those people who fell in struggle or innocence were not forgotten. She was, of course, too weak to go. She was dizzy and still losing blood. The white lawgivers attempted to get around assassination—which Imani considered extreme abortion—by saying the victim provoked it (there had been some difficulty saying this about Holly Monroe, but they had tried), but they were antiabortionist to a man. Imani thought of all this as she resolutely showered and washed her hair.

Clarence had installed central air conditioning their second year in the house. Imani had at first objected. "I want to smell the trees, the flowers, the natural air!" she had cried. But the first summer of 110-degree heat had cured her of giving a damn about any of that. Now she wanted to be cool. As much as she loved trees, on a hot day she would have sawed through a forest to get to an air conditioner.

In fairness to him, he asked her if she thought she was well enough to go. But even to be asked annoyed her. She was not one to let her own troubles prevent her from showing proper respect and remembrance toward the dead, although she understood perfectly well that once dead, the dead do not exist. So respect, remembrance, was for herself, and today herself needed rest. There was something mad about her refusal to rest, and she felt it as she tottered about getting Clarice dressed. But she did not stop. She ran a bath, plopped the child in it, scrubbed her plump body while on her knees, arms straining over the tub awkwardly in a way that made her stomach hurt—but not yet her uterus—dried her hair, lifted her out and dried the rest of her on the kitchen table.

"You are going to remember as long as you live what kind of people they are," she said to the child, who, gurgling and cooing, looked into her mother's stern face with lighthearted fixation.

"You are going to hear the music," Imani said. "The music they've tried to kill. The music they try to steal." She felt feverish and was aware she was muttering. She didn't care.

"They think they can kill a continent—people, trees, buffalo—and then fly off to the moon and just forget about it. But you and me, we're going to remember the people, the trees and the fucking buffalo. Goddammit."

"Buffwoe," said the child, hitting at her mother's face with a spoon.

She placed the baby on a blanket in the living room and turned to see her husband's eyes, full of pity, on her. She wore pert green velvet slippers and a lovely sea green robe. Her body was bent within it. A reluctant tear formed beneath his gaze.

"Sometimes I look at you and I wonder, *What is this man doing in my house?*"

This had started as a joke between them. Her aim had been never to marry, but to take in lovers who could be sent home at dawn, freeing her to work and ramble.

"I'm here because you love me," was the traditional answer. But Clarence faltered, meeting her eyes, and Imani turned away.

It was a hundred degrees by ten o'clock. By eleven, when the memorial service began, it would be ten degrees hotter. Imani staggered from the heat. When she sat in the car she had to clench her teeth against the dizziness until the motor prodded the air conditioning to envelop them in coolness. A dull ache started in her uterus.

The church was not, of course, air conditioned. It was authentic Primitive Baptist in every sense.

Like the four previous memorials, this one was designed by Holly Monroe's classmates. All twenty-five of whom—fat and thin

—managed to look like the dead girl. Imani had never seen Holly Monroe, though there were always photographs of her dominating the pulpit of this church where she had been baptized and where she had sung in the choir—and to Imani, every black girl of a certain vulnerable age *was* Holly Monroe. And an even deeper truth was that Holly Monroe was herself. Herself shot down, aborted on the eve of becoming herself.

She was prepared to cry and to do so with abandon. But she did not. She clenched her teeth against the steadily increasing pain and her tears were instantly blotted by the heat.

Mayor Carswell had been waiting for Clarence in the vestibule of the church, mopping his plumply jowled face with a voluminous handkerchief and holding court among half a dozen young men and women who listened to him with awe. Imani exchanged greetings with the mayor, he ritualistically kissed her on the cheek, and kissed Clarice on the cheek, but his rather heat-glazed eye was already fastened on her husband. The two men huddled in a corner away from the awed young group. Away from Imani and Clarice, who passed hesitantly, waiting to be joined or to be called back, into the church.

There was a quarter hour's worth of music.

"Holly Monroe was five feet, three inches tall and weighed one hundred and eleven pounds," her best friend said, not reading from notes but talking to each person in the audience. "She was a stubborn, loyal Aries, the best kind of friend to have. She had black kinky hair that she experimented with a lot. She was exactly the color of this oak church pew in the summer; in the winter she was the color [pointing up] of this heart-pine ceiling. She loved green. She did not like lavender because she said she also didn't like pink. She had brown eyes and wore glasses, except when she was meeting someone for the first time. She had a sort of rounded nose. She had beautiful large teeth, but her lips were always chapped, so she didn't smile as much as she might have if she'd ever gotten used to carrying chapstick. She had elegant feet.

"Her favorite church song was 'Leaning on the Everlasting Arms.' Her favorite other kind of song was 'I Can't Help Myself—I Love You and Nobody Else.' She was often late for choir rehearsal though she loved to sing. She made the dress she wore to her graduation in Home Ec. She *hated* Home Ec . . ."

Imani was aware that the sound of low, murmurous voices had been the background for this statement all along. Everything was quiet around her; even Clarice sat up straight, absorbed by the simple friendliness of the young woman's voice. All of Holly Monroe's classmates and friends in the choir wore vivid green. Imani imagined Clarice entranced by the brilliant, swaying color as by a field of swaying corn.

Lifting the child, her uterus burning and perspiration already a stream down her back, Imani tiptoed to the door. Clarence and the mayor were still deep in conversation. She heard "Board meeting . . . aldermen . . . city council . . ." She beckoned to Clarence.

"Your voices are carrying!" she hissed.

She meant: *How dare you not come inside?*

They did not. Clarence raised his head, looked at her and shrugged his shoulders helplessly. Then, turning, with the abstracted air of priests, the two men moved slowly toward the outer door and into the churchyard, coming to stand some distance from the church beneath a large oak tree. There they remained throughout the service.

Two years later, Clarence was furious with her: What is the matter with you, he asked. You never want me to touch you. You told me to sleep in the guest room and I did. You told me to have a vasectomy I didn't want and *I did.* (Here, there was a sob of hatred for her somewhere in the anger, the humiliation: he thought of himself as a eunuch and blamed her.)

She was not merely frigid, she was remote.

She had been amazed after they left the church that the anger she had felt watching Clarence and the mayor turn away from the Holly Monroe memorial did not prevent her accepting a ride home with him. A month later it did not prevent her smiling on him fondly. Did not prevent a trip to Bermuda, a few blissful days of very good sex on a deserted beach screened by trees. Did not prevent her listening to his mother's stories of Clarence's youth as though she would treasure them forever.

And yet. From that moment in the heat at the church door, she had uncoupled herself from him, in a separation that made him, except occasionally, little more than a stranger.

And he had not felt it, had not known.

"What have I done?" he asked, all the tenderness in his voice breaking over her. She smiled a nervous smile at him, which he interpreted as derision—so far apart had they drifted.

They had discussed the episode at the church many times. Mayor Carswell—whom they never saw anymore—was now a model mayor, with wide biracial support in his campaign for the legislature. Neither could easily recall him, though television frequently brought him into the house.

"It was so important that I help the mayor!" said Clarence. "He was our *first!*"

Imani understood this perfectly well, but it sounded humorous to her. When she smiled, he was offended.

She had known the moment she left the marriage, the exact second. But apparently that moment had left no perceptible mark. They argued, she smiled, they scowled, blamed and cried—as she packed.

Each of them almost recalled out loud that about this time of this year their aborted child would have been a troublesome, "terrible" two-year-old, a great burden on its mother, whose health was by now excellent; each wanted to think aloud that the marriage would have deteriorated anyway, because of that.

THE LAST ABANDONMENT

JACK MATTHEWS

Jack Matthews is Distinguished Professor of English at Ohio University, in Athens. He has had five novels, two volumes of stories, and a book on collecting rare books published. He has received many honors, including a Guggenheim Fellowship in 1974–75.

"I'm going to fatten you up," she'd cried. "I'm going to put some meat on those bones!" At odd moments, her words came back to him, riding edgily on a voice that any man would have to admit was not attractive, not calculated to contribute to that essential restfulness which is what a man after all (he understood this now)—beyond all the turmoils and confusions of sex—wants from a woman.

Her voice wasn't something that swam to the murky surface of his mind when he was idle or at peace in the hammock on the back porch of the cabin. At such times, he might hear the voice of Tillie, his dead wife, saying something like, "Hal, don't forget your diet," or "Hal, don't strain yourself lifting that; you be careful!" (Of course, it had been a long time since he'd tried to lift anything heavier than a pair of shoes or a half-gallon carton of skimmed milk.)

No, it wasn't at such quiet times that he heard *her* voice, but in sudden tangles of crisis or tension: hearing a car horn blare from behind when he was caught napping at the wheel under a traffic light, or turning the corner on the gravel walk as he walked down the steep path to the lake, and hearing the pounding of footsteps behind him as the Larimer boys raced toward the canoe and passed him in a hot flush of air.

Then he would hear: "*I'm going to fatten you up!*" And momentarily Sylvia Kate Dunham's face would float like a balloon in the air, past his mind's eye, and one of Sylvia Kate's eyes would wink at him, as if it—though only imaginary—saw more, and knew more, than he saw or knew.

"Aren't you the *funniest* little old thing," Sylvia Kate had said the first time they'd met. But no, that was later. Maybe the third or fourth time. Sylvia Kate had been dressed in her spotted bikini (Hardly big enough to have spots *on* it, old Mrs. Cosgrove had murmured between scarcely-parted lips), and she'd been sitting in the big bucket chair on the big sun porch of the lounge when she'd said it.

His foot had slipped in the shower stall, and this is when it had all come back to him. (This memory, this time.) Most reality was made up of memories, now, even things that had just happened—Good God, they might as well have all happened forty years ago!

By the time his heart had stopped lurching (he might have fallen and broken his hip or elbow), Sylvia Kate's ghostly, remembered head had joined him, and her voice was cranking out that somehow-obscene utterance; and he was trying to remember when and where she had said it.

Then it was that he remembered: it had been on the sun porch of the lounge, and Sylvia Kate had been sitting in that bucket chair with her pretty knees sticking up higher than her heavy, plump, rounded hips, and her bleached hair white as a wedding cake, and her deep gray eyes as perfect as the inside of seashells, smooth and (like them) echoing of inhuman depths.

If it had been only the voice, it wouldn't have mattered. He could have coped with that, easily; a man doesn't collect all those years without learning *something*, he'd said. (But inside his mind, at this very moment, Sylvia Kate's head had been turned, talking to Mrs. Stillwell.)

No, that wasn't it. That voice would have sunk just about any woman's chances, but the first glance at Sylvia Kate was enough to tell you that she could have croaked like a frog or grunted like a pig and it wouldn't have made any difference. Because she was *just plain damned too much*; she was just so plain damned beautiful, it sort of hit you in the pit of the stomach, so that you were a little bit sick and thought of turning your head away so you could throw up.

And she wasn't just beautiful, she was overwhelming. She was tall, rawboned, with a stride that made you want to harness her to a sulkey. Broad-shouldered, heavy-breasted, and with a rounded bottom that a man could hug with both arms and close his eyes and whisper, "Thank you, God, for making this!" Yes, looking at Sylvia Kate, you would forgive her any kind of voice; she might have cawed like a crow or whooped like a baboon with pink side-burns . . . and you could forgive that voice saying anything . . . or (he told himself, plunking his teeth in the plastic water glass and staring at them) *almost* anything.

Why had she fastened on him? Did she guess he was lonely? Did she sense he had money? (Of course, you damned old fool, he told himself—and then forgot.) Could she perceive in his poor blasted old features the lineaments of a once-commanding and quite handsome profile? (Go back to the money, the voice inside his mind said—and he forgot again.)

And what was he doing here at the Pine Bluff Lodge (seventy dollars a day and smiling attentive help) when he knew that any time he stuck his old hawk-nose outside he'd be risking trouble. Better stay away from the world (he said, and listened), because it is out to get you sooner or later. But it was a little hard to think of Pine Bluff Lodge as the world . . . or at least it had been, until Sylvia Kate Dunham appeared. Which somehow turned it into *more* than the world . . . into Heaven or Hell, either one (he didn't know which) . . . but, he knew with a certainty that came from someplace deeper than his heartbeat, *one or the other*.

"What are you doing here, Mr. Sibley?" one of them asked. "Just taking a vacation? Taking it easy?"

He wasn't sure which one it was. One was named Treskell and the other was named Chambers. (Last names; he didn't know their first, and didn't care. Whichever one it was, this was the fat one.)

"I'm recovering from an illness," Howard Sibley answered. He started to say more, but then stopped. Instead, he looked out upon the lake, forgetting Treskell or Chambers, whichever one it was, and thinking: my granddaddy farmed land that is now somewhere at the bottom of that lake; if we could bring granddaddy back, he wouldn't know his land any more than if it was an alley on the moon.

"I hope you're feeling better," Treskell or Chambers said, touching the tips of his fingers together and sounding like he might be going to lead somebody in a prayer.

God, it had changed! Not just the land turned into water, but all the old ways, the people, the air blowing through the pines. He thought of the old song:

> *In the pines, in the pines*
> *Where the sun never shines,*
> *In the pines where the cold wind blows.*

But to save his life, he couldn't think of the melody. His dead wife, Tillie, would have remembered it. If he'd mentioned it, Tillie would have sung the music, as sure as spit hits the ground.

"You're all from this part of the country, aren't you?" Mr. Treskell said politely. (Yes, it was Treskell; Chambers was the little bald skinny one who wore fancy shirts open all the way down to his belt buckle.)

"I was born and raised near here," Howard Sibley told him, nodding at the lake. He almost said, "Sixty feet under water about two miles north of here," but that would have made Treskell start asking questions all over, like a barrel springing leaks. Sibley sneaked a glance at him, and saw the fat young man leaning far back in his chair, rubbing his hands idly. He was staring at the water, too, not realizing that he was practically looking at the old Sibley place right then.

"It all goes down the drain," Sibley said, and when Treskell said, "What? What?" he could have kicked himself for a damned fool, because now there'd be no stopping him. Treskell's eyes were too close together and he had a big mustache underneath a snub nose and had sort of bangs over his forehead. As if that wasn't enough, he had huge soft, fat, hairy arms and a sort of sissy voice. Briefly, he wondered if Chambers and Treskell were, you know, but then he dismissed the question from his mind as being deficient in interest.

And yet, he'd known Treskell's type way back before he'd gone North to make his fortune, turning his back on the land and people of his heritage. (He'd never felt guilty about it, but sometimes a little uneasy.) There was a type of sissy produced by the fierce old culture-maddened women and the Bible schools that Northerners had trouble understanding, especially when these sissies could upon rare occasions surprise you—cope with a lot more than you'd expect, and maybe even prove stalwart or vicious (depending, of course) when all the cards were on the table.

Then, too, there was that type of aggressive Southern woman, volted with charm and cunning, whose thoughts in a one-day period could provide a battalion of psychologists with enough enigmas for a year of study.

Tillie certainly had not been one of these. Tillie had been a pretty, bright, lovable, strong-spirited woman from Milwaukee, whom Hal (he'd become "Hal" six months after leaving the old plantation) Sibley had met when he was just starting to do pretty damned well by trading in commodities, which an acquaintance had once said is a little bit like trying to land Hereford steers with a fly rod. But that faintly offbeat simile notwithstanding, Howard ("Hal") Sibley had, by God, made good at it, and when his wife had died seven years ago, he'd been worth something like eight-hundred thousand dollars . . . even after a few spectacular losses in which the steers had smashed line, rod, and tackle.

When you get old, what happens is you make a lot of connections you didn't make as a younger person. Some people think that old people don't *make* connections, but this is wrong. They make too many; they are embarrassed by a richness of connections; connections, with the elderly, are too common to be respected, therefore they are treated with contempt, and sometimes (as is natural) forgotten or ignored. The connections you had made when you were younger no longer have quite the same authority they had then. The arbitrary character of most human meanings has finally sunken in, and you are not as gullible (i.e., *interested*) as you once were. At least, this is one way of looking at it.

Also, the connections that do remain are changed; the relations they form are altered. The lofty perspectives of time afforded by a long life see to this, so that recent events often rub shoulders presumptuously with those of long ago, and an old man may gaze upon a young girl who reminds him of a high school sweetheart, causing her image to merge (however briefly and inconsequentially) with that of a woman long dead, some of whose children, even, may be resting in the grave. What a resurrection is this; and what a connection!

Actually, however, Hal Sibley was not all this ancient. He had been ill, as he'd informed Treskell. He was certainly *getting* to be an old man, but he was not yet as old as a hickory tree or a carp can get. And the fact that he had never in all his life encountered a woman like Sylvia Kate Dunham was sufficient to relegate him to the helplessness and innocence of youth, if not to youth itself.

For he *had* never seen a woman like her. No one had. Discovering Sylvia Kate and hearing her speak for the first time (including what she said) was a significant moment for most men. As for most women, they preferred to ignore the whole business as best they could. Take Hal Sibley's poor dead wife, Tillie: if she had come upon Sylvia Kate in Hal's presence, she would have had a seizure. She would have smiled and carried on an intelligent conversation, but deep down underneath she would have been having a seizure. Tillie was a pretty woman—everybody said so—but Sylvia Kate was an act of God, like a tempest or a mud slide.

Not only that, she was politely tactless. Or perhaps she was merely tactfully impolite. Whatever it was, she probed, she manipulated, she *found out;* she was something of a bully. Hal could hear all the familiar accents, identify all the ploys and tactics (and, yes, real affection) he had known in the women who'd surrounded him as a little boy and youth . . . but none of them had put it all together the way Sylvia Kate did. And once Sibley found himself speculating that if he'd met a woman like this in those early days in Chicago, he would not have made a fortune in the commodities market; he probably would have become an idiot, or perhaps the sort of hebephrenic who giggles and dribbles and eats things like socks and matchboxes.

Out on the long deck of the lodge, Hal Sibley sat and waited. The day had been peaceful, and he was gratified that Sylvia Kate's words had not once obtruded upon his mind, startling even the nerves in his arms and legs. That morning, in his room, he had gazed upon himself in the mirror, and had recognized his thinness. (He had always faced up to facts, he frequently told himself.) Then he had said, "Thin, yes; emaciated, no."

But of course, Sylvia Kate had never said he was emaciated; she had said only that she was going to fatten him up. She had said only (also) that she was going to put some meat on his bones. She had said this at odd moments (but shrilly, unabashedly—as if Sylvia Kate could act in any other way); and yet, the context was unclear. Hal Sibley could not remember what had framed those memorable utterances, just as he could not fathom her glaring tactics. ("There are men just as rich as I," he said to himself, "who are younger and more vital by far!")

What he guessed he really wanted to do was just die in peace. No fuss; no theatrics. With as little static from others as possible. Especially Treskell and Chambers, and *especially* especially Sylvia Kate Dunham . . . who was somehow beginning to give the impression of *stalking* him.

"What does she want?" Sibley had cried deep in his spirit. This was also on that very morning, as he'd crawled out of bed and approached his grinning dentures in the water glass. And then, like a sigh of regret: "I have nothing to give her but money, and money is impersonal . . . worse, it is nothing; and it is everywhere." (Like many wealthy people, Hal Sibley thought wealth was available to all, practically for the asking; he had forgotten the poverty of his own youth.)

Before dinner, the guests usually gathered on the long porch and gazed out upon the vastness of the lake, discussing such topics as sunburns and fishing and the weather. Sibley liked such conversations, for they made no demands upon him, and yet they gave him a sense of community. But this afternoon, as he was sitting there (Treskell and Chambers had not appeared yet), he felt his head suddenly jarred forward, and Sylvia Kate's face leaned over in front, upside down, smiling brightly.

"Do you know, I've just always wanted to do that to a man!" she said to nobody in particular. Several older women were sitting nearby, however, and Sibley saw them lift the corners of their mouths in automatic smiles, as if they had been raked by the brief salvo of Sylvia Kate's words.

"Do what?" Sibley asked.

"Why, put a flower in a man's hair!"

"Do you mean . . ." Sibley started to ask, groping at his head. One of the smiling women nodded busily at him, and sure enough, he found a flower there.

"You looked just like a Polynesian Prince or somebody," Sylvia Kate cried, pouting and picking up the little white flower he'd dropped by his chair. "And now you've gone and thrown it aside."

Then she came at him again and grabbed him like a blacksmith about to shoe a horse, and stuck the damned flower in his hair. And it was at that instant he heard a sharp intake of breath and—startled more than he could ever have described—he turned ninety degrees to the side and saw Tillie sitting there . . . his dead wife, Tillie, dressed in baggy shorts and with her poor pointed nose red (the only unattractive feature in her face) and her dark-brown eyes sizzling like sausages as she watched the damned old fool fumbling at his hair, trying to extirpate the flower that Sylvia Kate had planted there just a second before.

He couldn't help noticing how pear-shaped Tillie had gotten since her death. Or he had forgotten how plump she'd gotten toward the end. Either one. Or perhaps both. Perhaps she had put on a lot of weight since she'd died, which wasn't at all fair, when you stopped to think about it.

That night it came to him: Sylvia Kate was crazy. All that utterly indescribable beauty marred (rendered human) by a whangy voice and a cracked brain. Nature is full of such compensations; Sibley knew this well. And he was not about to fool himself; he may have been old and in delicate health (he pored over his printed diet the way men once pored over homilies and sermons), but he had common sense and dignity.

He vowed that if the occasion arose, he would tell Sylvia Kate that. Come right out with it. Let her know the score, which was . . . well, that *he* knew the score. But that wouldn't really solve anything, and he knew it, because, damn it, Sylvia Kate Dunham *wanted* something. What was it?

Sibley shook his head and looked at the television set. This was evening. The TV set was moaning over there in the corner, flashing feebly in the darkness, so he walked over to it. The channel selector was set on an impossible channel. How had it gotten there?

He switched to channel 9, where there was a western playing . . . in fact, there was a gunfight, and when Sibley turned up the volume, the pop, pop of the guns filled him with a sort of muted horror at the thought of these grown men (now mostly dead, which increased the obscenity of it all) playing at death. The horror was sufficient to prod that old mechanism, and Sylvia

Kate's voice floated by saying, "I'm going to fatten you up if it's the last thing I *do!*"

He turned the set off and wandered out to the kitchenette. Through the window he could see the lake glowing dimly, framed by the pines beside the path. Where was Sylvia Kate now? Was she romping in the sack with some appropriate stud, her happy feet waving at the ceiling?

Sibley shook his head and made a face. "Crazy," he murmured to the growling refrigerator. "Crazy, crazy, crazy!" Only that wasn't really an answer to anything, and he knew it; for even if she was crazy, there was still a motive behind the crazy things she said and did (and said she was going to do) and it was *that* which perplexed him.

He went to the front door of his cabin and opened it. A fresh breeze washed over him, smelling of the lake. The dust of his granddaddy's farm, like that of his body, had long since been settled, quieted forever and ever. Sibley thought about this for a while, and then he wondered why, indeed, he had come back here to a changed place. How would he have answered Treskell if he had been forced to say something sensible?

Well, that was a mystery, too.

And then a little later, still standing in his lighted doorway, Sibley whispered to himself, "But God, how beautiful she is!"

Poor Tillie hadn't really been there. Nor had her ghost. Sibley knew this, and felt a brief spasm of comfort pass through him from the knowledge.

But if you live with a woman over forty years and love her (far more than a man could ever love that damned Sylvia Kate) and learn to fit comfortably into her ways (as she has learned to fit into yours) and learn to expect her voice, saying particular things upon particular occasions . . . why, there is little wonder that parts of her last on, sometimes even as visibly and tangibly as those more conventional presences we call living people. After all, a human being is not an electronic component; he is not wired so that when a particular circuit is cut, the sound and image fade swiftly, leaving a surface as cold and dead as a pearl. Most of our realities are internal, after all; and it is not really so strange that since Tillie's death, Hal Sibley had spoken more words to her than to any other human being.

This did not prevent his being mightily irritated with her, of course. It would be a long time before he could forgive her for that business on the porch, when Sylvia Kate had stuck the white flower (hell, he didn't even know what kind it was) in his hair. Tillie had acted as if it was all *his* doing! And all he had really been doing was sitting there looking at the lake. If it was true that he wasn't at that very moment thinking of Tillie (*remembering* her), it was equally true that he hadn't been thinking of Sylvia Kate, either.

What had he been thinking of? He groped and tried to remember. He was dawdling over his dessert in the Lodge Dining Room as he did so. His waitress was a little redhead named Brendalee, one word, and Sibley had commented on it one day, making him realize that Brendalee appeared never once to have given a single thought to her name.

Anyway, what he had been thinking of at that very moment was Treskell and Chambers. He didn't know what he had been thinking, but they were the subject of his thoughts. Very definitely. He was probably wondering where in the hell they were, since they spent so much time on the porch (the big fat one, Treskell, especially) and were such a damned nuisance, asking him questions and all.

Only this evening, they didn't ask questions. And as a matter of fact, they didn't show up until after Sylvia Kate had walked off, shouting in an old woman's ear as she held her two arms above her head in a sort of parentheses (God knows what she'd been talking about); and then Treskell and Chambers had crawled out on the porch, like creatures too afraid to risk the heat radiated by Sylvia Kate, and yet needful of the lake breeze on a hot evening.

When the subject had arisen, Sibley didn't know. He'd been sitting there half-listening to Treskell and Chambers talk, and then Treskell had said something directly to him, Sibley, and Sibley had said, "What?"

"I said," Treskell told him, popping each syllable distinctly in his mouth, "that you'd better be careful. That's all I said, isn't it?" He asked this of Chambers, who didn't answer but merely stared at Sibley appraisingly, and then let his gaze wander off as if he was suddenly tired of focusing his eyes.

"Be careful of what?" Sibley asked.

"He says be careful of what!" Treskell said, chuckling in the direction of his friend, who was now gazing at the sky above the trees.

"Why am I in danger?" Sibley asked, and was about to ask another question, when something strange happened: the image of Sylvia Kate was in his mind; she had just received a cue to speak, but then she stopped and waited.

"I think she pronounces her name Sylvia Kate Dunham," Treskell said; then he closed his eyes and bobbed his head up and down. Apparently, he was laughing.

"She has you in her sights," Chambers said with the corners of his mouth tucked up in a grin. "That's what he means."

"Nonsense," Sibley said in a scarcely audible voice.

"Not at all, not at all," Treskell said. "You'd better watch out! She shows all the signs."

"Signs of what?"

"Of having *plans* for you."

"She has you in her sights," Chambers repeated, looking up at the sky once again.

"What makes you think that?" Sibley asked, trembling a little.

"It's perfectly obvious," Treskell said, nodding and tapping the tips of his fingers together.

At precisely that instant, they heard Sylvia Kate's whooping laugh from somewhere deep inside the lodge. It was startling, as always . . . but also because Sibley had seen her go off in the direction of the lake. She'd circled. What was she doing inside the lodge?

"If she doesn't sound like a siren," Treskell said, "I don't know what does."

"She looks like one, too," Chambers said, savoring the twist in meaning.

"And *acts* like one," Treskell added. "I'm afraid for Mr. Sibley here. Afraid he might crash upon the rocks and never be heard of again."

"Nonsense," Sibley muttered, gripping the arms of his chair.

A sudden breeze from the lake had come up, agitating the flowers in the flower pots upon the railing. Sibley stared at them and realized that their petals were white. It had been one of these that Sylvia Kate had stuck in his hair.

"You'd better watch your step," Treskell went on. "She looks like dynamite, if you ask me. Too much for one man to handle."

"Oh, I don't know," Chambers said, gazing steadily at Sibley as he spoke. "I think Mr. Sibley has learned how to take care of himself by now!"

At that instant, there was a shout of laughter behind him. Sibley turned and saw two rockers nodding back and forth. They were empty, but they had the appearance of rockers that have just been abandoned by two people in a great hurry.

Could it have been the sudden wind rocking them?

Not at all.

Then who had been sitting there?

Treskell and Chambers suddenly drifted off, and Sibley was left alone, thinking of who might have been sitting in the rockers.

But of course, there was no question. None at all.

Tillie and Sylvia Kate had been sitting there together, and they had heard everything.

Later, Sibley remembered this conversation on the porch and took comfort in it. Treskell's and Chambers's awareness that Sylvia Kate was after him was reassuring—he had not been imagining it; it was really happening, all of it.

But the mystery of what she wanted from him still remained. Her attacks were so sudden and violent, and her departures so unexpected, that Sibley didn't know what to think. Sylvia Kate gave the impression of being visited by seizures of inscrutable responsibility that took her suddenly elsewhere; she gave the impression that as soon as she took care of various kinds of pressing business, she would turn her full attention upon Sibley and fulfill all those dire threats and prophecies of fattening him up that had been echoing in his head for over a week.

At times, Sibley thought she was talking about marriage. What else could she be talking about? How else would she fatten him up? How else could she put meat on his bones?

Sibley was walking down the path toward the lake as he contemplated these questions, and while stepping over a wrist-thick root in a particularly steep section of the path to the lake, he misjudged the height and tripped. The fall would have been spectacular, if anyone had been there to witness it: Sibley dived forward over the path, part of him taking a rather remote interest in this brief sensation of flight.

But such ecstasies are not to be trusted, and when Howard

Sibley came down, it was with brutal force, jamming his shoulder so hard the pain reached clear inside his ear, like a long-buried fishhook being suddenly yanked, and then a forlorn scalding ache spread like a seepage of hot mustard throughout his shoulder muscles; and his arm and hand were trembling; and he knew with clinical certainty that something had broken inside, for he was already remembering the heavy, dull cracking sound, like a pool cue being broken under water.

How long he lay there, and what dreams struggled like torpid fish through his mind, no one knows. Old Mr. Cosgrove was the next person to come down the path, and of course he saw Sibley lying there with his arm all crumpled and mashed beneath him. He cried out, and Vernon Peters, the lodge handyman, heard him, and sobered by Mr. Cosgrove's admonition not to touch the body he hurried up to the lodge and phoned for the emergency squad.

Sibley was taken to the hospital, where it was determined that he had broken his collarbone and dislocated his shoulder. The pain had been extreme, and it was no wonder he had passed out. The resident physician was a man named Gifford, and Sibley eventually decided that he was probably the grandson of a man he had known forty years before; but he did not ask Gifford about this, nor did he let on that he was anything but a random guest of Pine Bluff Lodge.

The day after next, Vernon Peters brought him back in the lodge station wagon, talking volubly upon various topics, including the fish not biting. Sibley, on the other hand, wanted to ask about Sylvia Kate Dunham; but he did not. And yet, he thought about her; he thought about her mightily, with a sort of yearning that was not unlike suffering a dislocated shoulder and broken collarbone; and once he even found himself wondering if Treskell and Chambers were still there at the lodge, or whether they had picked up and departed for parts unknown.

No one was waiting for him, and he took note of the fact, calling himself a damned fool for expecting anything else. His shoulder ached so badly he took one of the painkillers the doctor had given him, and then lay down on the bed, flat on his back.

He did not fall into sleep, but was rather sucked under . . . with a rapidity and force that would have proved a little bewildering, had he been more fully aware of it. The rush of darknesses, representing different layers of sleep, drifted upwards past the descending wafer of his mind . . . a wafer which normally disintegrated precisely as it sank, but in this instance (possibly because of the sting of the painkiller) resolutely retained its shape.

But then, just as suddenly, it popped into nothingness, and Howard Sibley was reduced to an equal Nothing. At least he would not remember anything afterwards, which is tantamount to a dream's not having existed at all (and which small enclaves of dark rhapsodists often cite as sufficient cause for our concluding that life itself is less than a dream, since eventually nothing is remembered).

Independently of this, Howard Sibley slept—whether the sleep of the wicked or the innocent, there is no way of knowing—and rose and fell on dim powerful waves of breathing, cross-currented by the systole and diastole of another rhythm deep down inside his after-all-sturdy body.

Sometime late in that dimness, he awoke and was startled to see dear Tillie sitting cross-legged in the velveteen-covered chair that came with the room. (How she would have despised that expensive but meretricious and vulgar chair when she was alive!) Seeing his dead wife, Sibley's heart went out to her. More than his heart, for he actually cried out, even as he told himself that this could not be as it seemed. Tillie seemed to understand and sympathize, for she smiled tiredly and nodded at him, lifting her hand and waving it as if to dispel the very illusion of herself.

But of course she did not disappear. She did not even ripple, so sturdy was she at this moment. And seeing this, Sibley could not help but notice once again that poor Tillie had put on considerable weight since her death, and her long pale gray shorts and blouse were mussed and wrinkled, as if they had been packed in a suitcase during her voyage from the dead, and she had not (poor woman!) had a chance to iron them out.

"Tillie!" Sibley groaned. "For God's sake, help me!"

But all Tillie said was, "Hal, you got yourself into this, so don't be surprised."

What she meant by that, only God could know; Sibley was so astonished that he could not even ask for a clarification. He lifted his arm and saw that it was in a sling, but suddenly nothing hurt. It was almost as if he had been faking it, for there was not even an echo of pain, not even the merest trickle left from that storm of agony that had inundated him the day before yesterday.

"I want to get out, Tillie," he said. He had had enough; he was too perplexed, too confused by the storms and turmoils within, too bewildered by the terrible galloping of existential cowboys across the neat lawns in his mind, firing their six-shooters and killing everything in sight . . . all of which managed somehow to come alive again, in time for the next reel being fitted on the spindle by inhuman hands.

But what Tillie said was the greatest surprise of all: what she said was, "Well, if you want to, go ahead."

And even then, even at that deepest moment in the mire, Sibley realized that she was not talking about the same thing at all; she was not talking about calling it quits.

The next day he felt a little better. In fact, there were times when he felt well enough to think of Sylvia Kate and her mysterious utterances. What would he say if Sylvia Kate proposed to him? (*Ridiculous Old Fool,* he cried in anguish, and then turned his head so he wouldn't hear.)

Long and grandiose scenarios of qualification unwound in his mind. Many had to do with his calm and dignified acknowledgment of the fundamentally mercenary character of her infatuation, along with his acceptance of this. "I am myself the power I have generated," he said in one of these scenarios, only to scratch it out in a spasm of disgust and self-loathing.

Later, however, he faced up to Sylvia Kate (inside his mind, of course, where all these adventures were happening), and said, "I do not intend to relinquish my diet."

"But I'm going to fatten you up!" she cried in that now familiar war call.

"Absolutely not!" Sibley thundered. "Don't you know that the doctors say that fatty foods and sugar will *kill* me?"

"But don't you know that those doctors don't know *anything*?" Sylvia Kate cried, shaking her head in an ecstasy of negation.

This dialogue ended inconsequentially, for it was not tied to reality . . . and Sibley very well knew it. And was content, for by dinner time he was feeling well enough to go to the lodge and face them all: Treskell, Chambers and above all, Sylvia Kate.

He lifted his arm and probed it carefully through his shirt

sleeve. The route it took was a delicate one, bordered on all sides by fiery pain, and his fist was weighted with lead. At four minutes till six, he was ready—his arm in the sling and the jacket thrown over it all, like Louis Hayward in an old movie from the time of his youth, ready to march forth (though wounded) to claim the heroine.

He walked—most carefully and yet with as nearly a lighthearted spirit as he had felt in years—toward the lodge, and entered in a fanfare of muted light glancing off the lake and vibrating subtly upon every niche and corner through the high windows.

After he ordered, he looked around and saw . . . no one he could remember from before. Treskell and Chambers, that obnoxious duo, were nowhere in sight. When he asked the waitress (not Brendalee, not redheaded, not familiar at all), she said that she thought they had both checked out. Eating quietly, he occasionally lifted his eyes to glance about the dining area. Mrs. Cosgrove was not there; Mr. Cosgrove was not there. Perhaps even Vernon Peters had gone, and was retired—living with a fat daughter and raising coonhounds somewhere under the water.

"Where?" he asked, but no one turned around.

Later, in the lobby, when he found out that Sylvia Kate had also left, he smiled at the clerk and nodded. That nod said that Sibley had known all along. He almost winked: he knew all the tricks. He could take care of himself, as Chambers had said. Indeed. He was almost frolicsome with the knowledge.

Even later, after sitting alone for over an hour on the porch, crowded with sudden strangers, Sibley returned to his cabin—stepping carefully—and went inside. He took another painkiller, and retired early. Softly, he drifted down through the layers of darkness; and later on that night when he awoke, he saw that Tillie was not sitting there in the velveteen-covered chair . . . and he was almost relieved, knowing that she was slender and pretty, as he remembered her, and free . . . knowing that some things, at least, last on even as they change.

After that, he felt the silence closing in; the stillness was absolute, like the darkness in a photograph. He knew that on the big porch of the lodge, all the rockers were still. He knew all of this and found it breathtaking, for in spite of its terrible beauty, he had to acknowledge that it was more awful and more true than anything he had ever known.

ADVENT

MARIAN NOVICK

Marian Novick was born in Brooklyn, New York, in 1951. Her fiction has appeared in *Epoch* and *The Massachusetts Review*. She lives in Brookline, Massachusetts, and is at work on a novel.

The problem is, I've never been very good at entrances. I usually have trouble finding the building, and then when I do, I ring the wrong doorbell so some fat Greek grandmother with stockings bagged around her ankles comes lurching down nineteen stairs and says through the crack in the door, "Who are *you?* Go vay." And then I have to explain. After ten minutes she points to the door I want; by now I can hear the music and probably would have found it anyway. Sometimes it's Scarlatti, and when the door opens on all these strange sober faces, and I can't find anyone I know or have even heard of (God knows why I'm invited to parties, I'm not even a particularly good conversationalist), I realize I should have at least brought a bottle of wine or a bag of whole wheat pretzels. But they ask me to come in anyway, and I usually manage to catch my toe on the umbrella stand, and I know it's going to be one of those evenings. And if it's not Scarlatti, if it's the Rolling Stones, say, I'm likely to step on some girl's fingers. I have terrible night vision. I've also been known to sit on the dope. But they keep on inviting me. At least they did.

Maybe it's because I'm good-looking, in a harmless, distracted, Gene Wilder sort of way that's become pretty popular lately. I have leonine curls. That's what a girl on Fisherman's Wharf told me just three weeks ago before I misplaced my pipe and decided for the hell of it to return East. I sort of wanted to see Alice. I wanted to see if she'd have me back, it being just before Christmas and everything. I figured I'd also see if the Dean would have me back. My mother's never forgiven me for dropping out of Harvard. I sort of figured it was time, as Mother says, to start putting my house in order, and I was determined that it wasn't going to be a house with any goddamn umbrella stand. I swear to you I didn't want any more clumsy entrances. But like it says in the song, you can't always get what you want. Which is one reason, I suppose, I've taken a room in the Y, where nobody gives a damn how you come in, or whether you come in at all. A second reason is that I can sit here in front of the window, melt a peephole with my palms, warm my hands on the radiator coil, and get a clear, comfortable view of Mass. Ave. And once every third day or so, if I'm lucky, I'll snatch a glimpse of Alice, or of someone who looks remarkably like her, as she walks to work in Central Square. Sometimes I wave, but she ignores me. As she should.

Ice-blonde Alice, silver-skinned Alice, Alice of the golden eyes and midwestern A's. I'd been used to my women short, dark, and broad-beamed, like sturdy night tables with secret drawers where they kept generations of recipes, Madison Avenue hopes, and a few genuine psychic bruises. They used to like to open themselves up to me, soul and body. Most of them were sort of cuddly. I even liked a few of them. But what usually happened was that after a month or so they'd start following me around, and they'd wait for me, like my own bad conscience, where they had no business being: in the balcony above the squash courts. Outside of phone booths. On the hood of my Volkswagen. By the Men's Room door in Widener Library. My mother would have loved them. But everybody loved Alice. Not the way I did, though; not as much. We got along well together, too. I'd met her in Epistemology and it turned out that our thought processes were amazingly similar. And then after a dozen or so walks along the Charles, she briefed her roommate Mary Louise about phone messages and hung her toothbrush next to mine. George and Rajiv didn't mind; there was room enough in the house on Dana Street, and compensation: Sunday mornings Alice would bake blueberry muffins and I'd make the coffee and Rajiv would get the *Times* and George would promise to do the dishes and we'd all sit around the trestle table for hours, pretending we were a family. In the evenings sometimes we'd play Botticelli, and Alice wouldn't even get angry when

George cheated. Nights she'd come to me all damp and rosy from the shower, and the world would close in as far as the bedposts. And every dawn was as good as our first, even when it was raining.

For about four months.

First it was the little things. Her homilies on the refrigerator door: "Hostess Twinkies are bad for you, Love." Her shoes lined up exactly even with the dresser legs. Her habit of plumping the toothpaste tube after I'd given it a good squeeze in the middle. Her pantyhose drip-drying from the shower knobs. Once I accidentally tore one of the stockings as I was about to step into the shower, and on a whim, God knows why else I did it, I stuck the thing over my head and I put on my Bogey trenchcoat and tiptoed downstairs. Alice was curled up on the sofa like a great cocker spaniel, crunching soya nuts and reading *Centennial*. She didn't hear a thing. I approached her from behind and gave her a big kiss on the top of her silken head. She giggled and squirmed a bit, and reached up to ruffle my hair as she usually did, and she discovered the stocking. Right then I knew I'd made a mistake. I began to explain, but she screamed anyway. George made a flying tackle from the kitchen doorway and I landed flat on my face, parallel with the coffee table. My nose began to bleed and we had a hell of a time getting the stocking off; Alice had to cut it with a cuticle scissors. I felt about as desirable as the tomato aspic at a retirement dinner. But she forgave me. She always did. She had a genius for it. She'd look up at me and smile, waiting for me to stroke her. Pat, pat. Sometimes I couldn't help it, I couldn't stand it, and I'd pick on her. For instance, I asked her didn't she wonder how Mary Louise was getting along in the dormitory. She gave me a foul look and ate her yogurt alone that night on the sun porch even though it was December. That really pissed me off. I talked to Rajiv and George about it.

Rajiv said, "When there is love between individuals, one must expect not all to go smoothly."

And George said, "Shit, Andy. She can cook. She can blow dope. She's damn good-looking. You're swimmin' in cream, baby; don't sweat it."

"O.K.," I said, "but what about Fraternity?"

"There is love, too, among brothers," Rajiv said.

"Thanks," I said, "but she's ruining me. I can't concentrate.

I'm flunking Kroeger's course and McMillan's been on my ass for two weeks."

George shrugged. "Listen, if you don't want her, *I'll* lay her, for Chrissake. True love, baby. That's the way it is."

It was the way it was, all right, but it wasn't love. At least I didn't think so at the time. Though for Christmas I bought her a little fish made of Steuben crystal; she'd been coveting it for as long as I'd known her. She knit me argyle socks. I tried them on right there under the tree, and for the moment things were good. I guess you might say we had a memorable evening. She was crying again by breakfast, though, and I didn't have the strength to find out why. A week later we had a talk. Yet, when the time came for me to actually *do* it, I couldn't face her, so I wrote her a note and stuck it under the fish. Dear Alice, it said, I've never loved anyone the way I love you. Please don't ever forget that. Remember our talk about angst? Well, I have to leave for a while. I'm truly sorry. Love, Andy Who Doesn't Deserve You.

That afternoon I took my toothbrush and a change of underwear and got in touch with Purnendoo, a Physics grad student friend of Rajiv's, and he said I could sleep on the couch in his office. Rajiv discovered me a day later and in his best Brahmin voice said, "All those 'loves.' She believed. We, too, believed. You should be filled with much shame, you asshole." I promised him the rent checks, but he didn't soften. So the next day I went West.

Why? you ask.

Manifest Destiny.

How?

It was easy. It was simply a matter of following the sun. Interstates all the way. I kept my eyes open for gold, for Bigfoot, and my soul alert for the spirit of Walt Disney, Bishop Pike's son, Jack Kerouac, the Sixties. I wanted to have something to tell my grandchildren. I wanted my crack at the myth. Sounds good, huh?

Wait. I lie. I wanted to get away. And I did, too. I met a horde of swell chicks and three honest-to-God genuine migrant farm workers. I sweated for ten months dipping sticks in the basement of an incense factory. And I thought about things. And one night I climbed the highest of the Berkeley Hills, and lay in dried grass the color of her hair, and mouthed the words to the stars: I made a mistake; I shouldn't have gone.

Granted, I was stoned. But the next morning when my head wouldn't clear I knew it was time. I threw all my excellent new camping gear onto the rear seat and roared through America's desiccated heart, back to her congested head. I even found a parking space free of snow, not a block from the house on Dana Street. It was a Friday, about four o'clock, pretty dark. Everything was covered with about two inches of snow. No one had plowed or shovelled yet, and when I tilted my head and squinted a little I was almost able to convince myself that I was back a hundred years on the main street of a country town, and any minute a carriage would ride by, and a girl in an ermine collar would wave to me from the window. I'd tip my hat. Then I'd knock my walking stick against my boot, and turn up my own gravelled path. After checking on the horses I'd get my man Clarence to drive me over to the club, where I'd drink brandy and play whist. I wasn't even sure what whist was, but I was sure playing it was preferable to freezing my ass off in the snow. So finally I acknowledged the Christmas lights and the trash cans and the row of battered subcompacts nose to tail at the curb, and I walked up to the house where someone resembling me, who in fact, unfortunately, *was* me, had lived less than a year before.

The names on the mailbox were too blurry to read, so after a minute I cupped my hands on the frozen glass and tried to peer through the window. I could tell first off that the curtains were different—filmy white stuff rather than the opulent Salvation Army red velvet we used to have, which I admit made our living room look a little like the lobby of a funeral home. Right away I started to feel uneasy. George had really liked those curtains. And then through the gauze and frost and dim yellow lights I discerned row upon row of coleus plants, and a big orange cat rubbing his side against the flowerpots. That clinched it. Rajiv was allergic to cats. I should have split immediately, or at least knocked and asked, but I was too preoccupied trying to convince myself that I simply had the wrong house or something. And when that didn't work, I began to wonder what my housemates had done with all those rent checks I had sweated for in that goddamn incense factory. I didn't even see her open the door.

"Hey, sweetheart," she said. I looked up. She was about my age, maybe a little older, good-looking in a dusky way. "I have a suggestion. Why don't you either ring the doorbell, or go loiter on someone else's stoop."

"I wasn't loitering."

"You were sightseeing, then?"

"Not exactly," I said. She smiled. She really was good-looking, and built, but I was preparing myself to hate her anyway. "Listen," I said, "I'm trying to find a couple of friends of mine, George Brooks and Rajiv Shastri. You don't happen to know them, do you?"

"Brooks. Let me see. Is he the tall, athletic type?"

"Yeah, the quintessential jock, that's George."

"And Shastri . . . from India?"

"Yes, yes." I stomped my feet a little, partly from excitement, partly to see if there was any feeling left in them. There wasn't much. "So you know them?"

"Never met them before in my life."

"Christ, then why—"

"Never met Him before, either."

I turned as disdainfully as I could, given the fact that my feet were numb, and headed for the steps.

"Wait a minute, Andrew, aren't you forgetting someone?"

Well *that* stopped me, all right. "How do you know my name? What are you, a witch or something?"

"My, my," she said, "there's no need to insult me; we've barely begun to get to know each other. Why don't you come in?"

"Why should I?"

"Because it's *cold* out, sweetheart. And because Alice is due home any minute. Come."

She drew me inside with a touch on the shoulder. I wish she had left me out there to freeze. I really do.

They'd painted the walls a sort of peaches-and-cream color, and in place of George's highway signs they'd hung a lot of woven squares that would've made great bath mats, and one of those twiny macramé things with the walnut shells and bits of sticks worked into it; you know the kind of thing I mean—it looks like a fishnet that's lost out to a hell of a big fish. They'd polished the coffee table. On it were half a dozen *Ms.* magazines spread into a neat little fan so you didn't exactly feel like picking one up and reading it, and next to the magazines, artfully off-center, was an abalone shell filled with imported hard candies. There was no ashtray or anything for the wrappers. And the couch—they'd covered it with one of these crocheted blankets that it must have taken someone's half-blind great aunt thirty years to make. It was white. I was afraid to sit down. That didn't matter, though, because the Dark One led me clear through the living room into the kitchen, over the red Oriental throw rug that I secretly knew was mine. I felt a sudden twist of affection for it, as I might've for a rediscovered birthmark on the chin of an old friend who'd had a sex change. Before I could reminisce, though, I'd been steered past the stove and refrigerator and into a yellow ladderback chair with daisies painted on it. I made a subtle statement of protest by clunking my elbows down, hard, on the unfamiliar glass-topped table. The table was too small to accommodate more than one Sunday *Times* reader and half a dozen muffins, but of course now there was room next to it for an avocado tree, a baby basket, a mustard colored rocker, and a shelf full of jars with things sprouting inside. There wasn't a trace of curry in the air, which instead was steamy with chicken soup and smelled faintly of onions and perfume. If you've ever eaten a turkey dinner in a Y, with a lot of old men, aftershave still wet on their cheeks, you'll have some idea of the air quality. It wasn't great. I considered asking to use the john and slipping out the back door, but I didn't think I'd be able to pull it off. So I sat there and listened to the soup bubble while she poked around in the kitchen cabinets. Finally we exchanged a few insincere pleasantries. I found out her name was Jacqueline and she'd been in Cambridge since September. When I asked her her star sign, she curled her lip at me and muttered something about protracted adolescence. Then I asked her if she liked Kurt Vonnegut and she sighed and said, "How about you stir the soup while I feed Tiresias, O.K.?" Tiresias was the cat. I checked later and sure enough, the poor thing had no nuts. I tell you, that Jacqueline was a real bitch. I was only trying to make conversation. But I stirred the soup anyway.

And then there was this noise on the stairs and I thought for a second that it was Alice and my blood rushed down into my Bean boots and I figured the best I could do would be to smile and say "Hi, Alice." Not too great for an opener. But it wasn't Alice. It was a huge fat girl. Some like them that way but I don't. Long shiny brown hair, large shiny forehead, wire-rim glasses, bovine eyes, diaper on her shoulder. An amplified, updated version of Vermeer's milk pourer; the kind of girl whose puffy hands are always gentle. She wasn't much to look at but she was a relief from Jacqueline, and to tell you the truth I sort of got a kick out of watching her take a baby bottle from the refrigerator and set it in a pot on the stove to warm. As soon as she'd done that, she ambled over to the basket which I suddenly realized had a baby in it. Then she leaned over it and started to talk, the way mothers do. She was O.K.

She must've sensed me watching, because she asked, "Do you want to see him?"

"O.K.," I said. I really didn't care, but I figured I'd do anything to pass the time. She lifted the kid and brought it over to me. I swear it looked just like my grandfather.

"How old is he?" I asked.

"Three months."

"Is he much trouble?"

"Not at all."

"Oh. Does your husband help you with him?"

"I don't have a husband," she said. Jacqueline made snorting noises over by the sink, which I thought was pretty damn rude.

"That's too bad," I said. And then she looked at me, and I looked at her, and we were both pretty embarrassed, so I asked, "What's his name?"

"Andrew," she said.

"That's funny," I said, "that's *my* name."

"I know," she said. "Do you want to hold him?"

I was about to say no, I didn't think so, when Jacqueline snorted again and said, "Don't let him; he's liable to drop it." What a honey.

"Now wait a minute," I said. I was starting to get angry. "You're not being the least bit fair. Whatever Alice told you, you can't know more than half the story."

"Two-thirds," Jacqueline said, "but why quibble?" She jabbed a spoon into the cat food. "Stick around, sweetheart; we'll fill you in. Here, for instance—" She swung the loaded spoon in an arc and stopped when it pointed to the fat girl, who patted the baby and pretended not to blush. "—is Maureen Benetto. A woman and an artist. One of the finest you'll ever hope to meet."

"Jacky, please—" Maureen interrupted. Ineffectual, but at least she was trying.

"—and this, Maureen, this—" Jacqueline waved the spoon at me. "—is Andrew Bergen. Andrew loves long walks in the woods and fireside chats. He's into T.M., Body Awareness, pottery, macrobiotics, ten-speed bicycles, and reggae."

"I am not," I said.

"Stir the soup," she said.

"Why do you hate me?" I asked, but I might as well have been talking to the television.

"—reggae, Meaningful Relationships, and travel. Andrew loves to travel."

"You're damn *right.*" I slammed the lid on the pot. "Stir your own goddamn soup," I said, "I'm leaving." *Le mot juste.* I was pretty pleased with myself, actually. With a sweeping flourish I whipped my jacket off the rungs of the ladderback, and bolted. I got halfway to the door before Maureen blocked it. For a fat girl, she really could move.

"You can't go," she said.

"Wanna make a bet?"

"Please. *Stay.*"

"Oh, let him go, for Chrissake," Jacqueline butted in.

"*No,*" Maureen insisted, "not yet."

And then they were at it:

"Give him another chance."

"He's had plenty."

"One more."

"Maureen, you're a sap."

"Well, you're a shrew."

I was almost interested enough to want to stick around, just to see who'd win. But it was getting late, and I had nowhere to crash. "Give Alice my love," I said. "Tell her I'll stop by again soon." I angled myself into a flying wedge, to squeeze through somehow.

But then there was this hand on my elbow, and Maureen shouting at me, "You're *not* going," and pressing the baby against my chest, and insisting, "Take him, take him." Well, I wasn't nuts about babies but the kid would've fallen to the linoleum if I hadn't held onto him. He felt sort of like a terrycloth football. And then he began to wail.

"Look," I said, "it's a nice kid and everything, but why don't you please take it and let me get the hell out of here."

"Take it from him before he drops it," Jacqueline said.

"No," Maureen said. And then to me, "Comfort him."

I jiggled it, just to appease her, but nothing happened. "See? He wants you." I looked at her pleadingly, I had to get *out* of there, but her face was about as yielding as a clam's. I got the feeling that she hated me even more than Jacqueline did. So I gave the kid another jiggle.

"That's better," she said. "You'll learn."

"Like hell I will. Take the baby."

"No. It's yours."

"That's very generous of you, but I can't accept it. Really. Take it."

"No," Maureen repeated. "You don't understand. It's yours. Yours and Alice's."

"What?" I said.

And she repeated, "It's yours." And Jacqueline chimed in like a goddamn Greek chorus, "It's yours."

At last, you say. He's finally figured it out. But I swear to God I had no idea. And you can picture me standing there, embracing those Harpies, and kissing the kid, and feeling for the first time my humanity and all that. But the truth is, it wasn't like that. I didn't feel anything at all, except for a vague desire for the kid to stop crying. And I didn't know what to do. So I laughed. And minutes later, that's how Alice found me, holding the kid and laughing. It was as serviceable an opener as any.

I had a hell of a time sleeping that night. For an hour or so I cursed the sofa which was a foot too short, and the decorative lumps on the great-aunt coverlet that poked through the bottom sheet and pressed on the nerves in my ribs. But after a while I had to stop blaming the sofa, start blaming the pictures—I couldn't get them out of my mind, they kept coming, like I was stuck in a double feature and the Management had locked the doors and even if I'd shouted "Fire!" it wouldn't have done any good, I'd have been forced to sit there and watch. Now it was re-runs of dinner's documentary in which Alice's hair was a little darker than I'd remembered, her face a little fuller, her eyes fixed on the carrots in her soup. And I don't know how it could have slipped my mind, but there, rising from the side of her jaw and disappearing behind her left ear lobe, was that little blue vein I used to trace with my tongue. Ah, Alice. Silver Alice. The rest wasn't so interesting: Maureen sliced the bread and passed the board around during the ten second spots between topics: Idi Amin, recombinant DNA, cholesterol levels, the benefits of jogging, alternative energy sources, the decline in verbal aptitude. When things got really dull we fell back on busing and the Red Sox. Once or twice no one said anything and I got nervous watching Maureen roll her bread into doughy pills, so I told a couple of funny stories about Manuel who'd worked next to me in the incense factory. No one laughed. Alice said about three words altogether, and went upstairs to take care of the kid. She didn't even ask if I wanted to hold it again or anything. I thought about this while I was helping Jacqueline with the dishes, and though I didn't mean to say it, it just slipped out: "I'd better go see how she is. Maybe she needs me." "Don't be silly," Jacqueline said, "she doesn't need you. Here—" And she handed me a dripping plate, which I dried.

Now as I was lying there after the fact with my knees drawn up I figured what the hell and I took a few liberties with the scenario, returning that wet plate to her a hundred times, each time refusing to dry it in terms wittier than the last, until finally, with Cyrano de Bergerac aplomb, I wing the plate out of the window, dash upstairs, garner my sullied maid and her poor wee babe, and drive off into the Friday night traffic. But then I couldn't imagine us beyond the second red light. So I sat up, ate some of the candy out of the dish, and read a couple of the *Ms.* magazines. I learned how women sometimes hate their own bodies but can fall in love with them eventually if they work at it. It was pretty depressing. Finally around two or three I must have drifted off, because I remember a series of dreams. In one I'm playing poker with George and Rajiv and some other guys around that ugly glass-topped table, and somehow my cards are reflected in the surface and everyone can see my hand just by looking down. But they all pretend they don't see anything. Another dream was about a green parakeet I had as a kid. In the dream the snow is about three feet deep and for some reason I have the parakeet outside with me, and it's shivering, and I know I should take it in, but I can't make it to the door of my house; one thing or another prevents me. I woke up sweating, twice.

Then on about four o'clock I dozed, and my son came down to haunt me. In this one he's a dirty, drippy-nosed five year old, but even I can tell he has potential. I invite him to sit on my lap, and though he says "Up yours, Daddy," he very graciously puts down the skateboard and beer can and comes over and leans against my knees. I lift him onto my lap; he weighs practically nothing. When I hug him I can feel his heart beating against my forearm. He squirms and mutters something about fags. So I take my arm away and he relaxes, and settles his bony rear end into my thigh. And we begin to talk. We discuss Idi Amin, the dissolution of the nuclear family, anomie, the Red Sox. He tries to convince me that ninety percent of our contemporary ills have been generated by multinational corporations. He has a particular aversion to the petrochemical industry. I say to him, "Where would we be without Saran Wrap?" but to tell you the truth I'm not too interested in his response, because by this time my thigh is really beginning to hurt. So I hoist him up with one arm, and slip my free hand into his back pockets and withdraw three marbles, a red candy heart, a wad of green stamps, and a hash pipe. I chuck the hash pipe under the sofa and tell him I love him, that we'll work it out somehow, but he doesn't appear to be interested. And suddenly I hear the click of high heels on the stairs, and both of us turn to watch Alice descend. When she reaches the end of the coffee table, the kid shouts "Mama!" and leaps from the sofa, and throws himself against her legs with a force that travels the length of her silver lamé torso and causes the cocktails she's carrying to converge in the center of her Budweiser tray. She says, "Now, now, Muffin, don't upset Mummy's dress," and then she winks at me, shakes her ass east-west, and disappears out the front door with my son clinging like a lamprey to her thigh.

Intending to go after them I awoke, reconsidered, ate some more candy, tried to go back to sleep, failed, looked out the window for a while, did a few push-ups, put on my jacket, put on my boots, tiptoed to the door, opened it, looked out the doorway for a while, closed the door, took off my jacket, sat on my hands to warm them, thought about the Pacific Ocean and multitudes of unmet receptionists, thought about bells and rice and white lace and in-laws and lawnmowers and Little League and report cards and orthodontist bills and credit agencies and wax-bagged lunches and rush hours and macaroni dinners and fifty years of the same bed and that blue vein. The ascent of that blue vein. The silver skin. The foggy mornings, and the glass fish, and the son who might or might not grow up to look like me and the mother upstairs, Alice above me, her skin outshining the ocean I might never see again. I stood up, left what I had known of myself on the sofa, and climbed the stairs. Her door was partly opened. I leaned in and whispered "Alice?" She stirred. I whispered again, "Hey, Alice? Can I come in?" This time she surely heard me; she sat up in bed, and we looked at each other. I took a few steps toward her and she didn't say anything. So I closed the door behind me and walked over to her. I held out my hand. She looked at it for a moment, then touched her finger to my palm. I sat down on the bed. "Take off your boots," she said. I did. She wouldn't let me hold her, but she didn't kick me out, either. At last I slept.

Changes were not immediately discernible. Unlike Gregor Samsa, I awoke mammalian, humanoid, in need of a shower, and hungry. I accepted the first two conditions, remedied the third, and took steps to alter the last, toward the nearest Pewter Pot where I bought a dozen blueberry muffins. In my absence the triumvirate convened to discuss my fate, and deemed me the prodigal papa, educable. They let me observe for a few hours, then Alice put me to the test.

"Diaper," I recited.

"Check," she said.

"Pants," I chanted.

"Check," she said.

"Baby Wipe," I suggested.

"Check," she said.

"Baby," I added.

"Very funny," she said. "Check."

"O.K.," I said. "How am I doing? I've got everything, right?"

"Check," she said.

"And should I begin?"

"Any time now."

I let time pass.

"Alice? Maybe you oughta do it."

"No."

"But what if I do it wrong?"

"His prick will fall off."

"Jesus Christ, don't say that!" I widened my eyes with horror that was only half-feigned. "Living with that goddamn Jacqueline, it's ruined your sensibilities," I said.

"Like hell it has. Go ahead."

"Aw, come on, Allie. Please."

"This isn't a heart transplant. What are you waiting for?"

"I think I need to watch a few more times."

"No. You need to *do* it," she said, and folded her arms across her bulwark of breasts.

So you see, she left me no choice. I looked my son in the eye and said This is it, kid, and gave him a reassuring pat on his distended little belly. Then I bared his bottom to the world. Wet only. To celebrate I held his feet between two fingers, lifted him like a trussed chicken, and powdered him twice. He sneezed. After the air cleared I took a good long look at him and rubbed him gently where I prayed no man but his father would ever rub him. I think he liked it. He smiled and beat his tiny fists against the ducks on his flannel blanket.

"Hey, Alice, I think he takes after me."

"We'll see."

"No, he does. I can tell already. He's a terrific kid. Take a look at those biceps. I'll teach him to play Frisbee; he'll be Frisbee champ of the block. Then when he's older I'll buy him an Irish setter. Come summers we'll rent a cabin on Winnipesaukee and we'll go out in a rowboat, he and I, and bring you back thousands of fish. How's that?"

"I hate fish."

I went on anyway. "And then he'll win a scholarship to Harvard, and go on to Harvard Med, and discover a cure for cancer. Won't you, Champ?" I tweaked his foot. Then I looked at Alice. "Hey? Why not? Why can't he?"

"You're putting his pants on wrong. The Honeybear goes on the back." She spoke into her necklace of donkey beads that was supposed to ward off bad luck, people of my ilk. I could hardly hear her. I lifted her chin. She was all quivery around the mouth, like she was going to cry.

"Don't cry," I said. "If he doesn't get into Harvard, he can always go to Johns Hopkins."

She swooped down on my son just as I was transferring his right leg into the right leg-hole.

"So what's the matter now," I said, "I was only trying to be funny. I did what you told me to do. Except for those goddamn pants, did I make a single mistake?"

"Does it rain in the Amazon?"

"What did I do? Tell me what I did wrong. Come on. Tell me."

That's what I said. Now imagine: The modern madonna, her back to me, her hair a tent over the kid pressed to her center, her tears falling soundlessly on the Indian print of her sleeves. Off to the left, a paint-chipped crib; suspended above it, instead of birds or butterflies, a mobile made of orange juice cans. In the crib, a plastic bottle with fuzz on the nipple, a gray terrycloth dog with no eyes, a mass of blue yarn macramėd into a huge salami. I took it all in. But because in a way it was my fault, and I couldn't do a thing about the decline of the church, the rise in the price index, food additives, and nuclear powerplants, I walked over to Alice and stroked her hair and said, "Hey, I'm sorry."

She turned to me and lay her cheek tentatively on my shoulder. The baby squirmed.

"Cheer up," I said, holding her. "At the very least he'll be a handsome son of a bitch with leonine curls."

"Yes," she agreed. "The poor thing."

I didn't argue.

An hour later we began Our Life Together. I pushed the carriage down Dana to Harvard, she down Harvard to Quincy, I down Mass. Ave. to Boylston. We split the distance to the river. On our promenade we each took half the handle: ours was to be a sharing relationship. I was optimistic. We made one shadow. The puddles parted at our approach. Two joggers peeked into the carriage on their way by; a cyclist smiled at us; an old woman called to us from her bench, "God bless you and Merry Christmas. Don't let the child watch television." "We won't," we promised, and hailed her in return, "Happy New Year. Be Well. Be Happy." And we walked. Alice's hand inched along the rubber grip and nested cat-like next to mine. I gave it a reassuring squeeze.

"I'll get a job," I said. "Monday. Nine o'clock. As soon as the stores open."

"The stores don't need anyone. I know," she said.

"But I'll find something. You'll see. I, too, shall be a Kelly Girl. You'll teach me to file. We'll type together. We can hire ourselves out as a team. It'll be temporary, you understand."

"It always is."

"No, I mean that I'll find something better, soon. After all, this is America. America—"

"Do me a favor, Andy," she said, pulling her half of the carriage to a halt. "Don't talk. Just don't say anything."

"But I—"

"No." She gave a resolute shrug of her shoulders and launched the carriage. I followed in her wake.

"Three words?" I persisted.

She shook her head. You should've seen the way her hair rippled over her collar. Pulled the plug on my old Puritan gut. I would've said anything.

"They're short words."

"No."

"I. That's the first word."

"I would have guessed."

"Love. That's the second."

"Shut up, Andy."

The bums on the benches were beginning to look.

"Two words, then." I clasped her nearer elbow. "Just two? Granted, one's a contraction. *Je*—"

"I'm not listening."

"*Je t'aime.*"

"I didn't hear you."

"Wait, I'll say it louder, then. *JE T'AIME.*"

It was almost a shout. The bums applauded.

"I'm leaving," she said.

"Softer?" I implored. And then I look her by her shoulders and pulled her toward me and whispered in her ear, "I love you." And then I kissed her cheek through the veil of her silvery hair. And then I kissed her eyes which were wet again. And then I realized what I had done, and I backed away and said, "Oh my God, I'm sorry." I was, too.

But then, then, Alice reached for me and hung on, and kissed *me*. And I held her against the scudding clouds, the river, the litter on the path, the benched men, the old woman she would become, the child in the carriage who would jog by some day and not bother to look in. And seconds later, the clouds having changed shape, the river having drained a unique quantity of water, we broke apart. In the movie version Alice tips her head onto my clavicle and we hold hands; the camera climbs our arms to our shoulders, takes a sharp right, and focuses on our glittering eyes, which in turn are focused on the horizon blurry with leafless trees. Then a quick shot of the interior of the carriage, a sweep of the bench bums, two seconds of the Christmas wreaths at the bridge's arch, a return to our sunlit cheekbones, and a final fade of the skyline, the John Hancock Building winking in time to Telemann's A-minor sonata. On an off day I might even pay two dollars to see it.

When I was a small child I believed in Santa Claus, but when I got to be about six or seven, my friend Roger Schatzwell, whose parents were Ethical Culturalists, told me that Santa was nothing more than a symbolic representation of American society's crass materialistic urge. I think those were the words he used. After a brief catechism I was able to accept the fact of Santa's non-being, but the reasons eluded me. Now, as then, the facts are clear: I know exactly what happened. We stopped in front of Schoenhoff's. I stayed outside and jiggled the carriage; Alice went inside and emerged six minutes later with a book of Norwegian Christmas carols. For you, she said, and kissed me. I thanked her. Then we reversed directions, switched roles; I ran into the Coop and bought Alice a gold sweater the color of her eyes. Kiss, kiss, reverse. We went into Bailey's and had peppermint sundaes. Then Alice said she had some more shopping to do and wouldn't I please take little Andrew into the Yard and walk around there for a while; she'd only be a half hour or so. Certainly, I said. I steered safely round Nini's Corner. I crossed with the light. I passed through the gates, and was drawn by the fiddle and the drum to the steps of Widener Library, where I stood for fifteen minutes with my cap down low and watched the Morris Dancers. I was hoping no one would recognize me and ask how're things. But as I was about to toss a quarter in the can and head toward the church, I heard someone call, "Andy, back from the dead?" I turned. It was Lola, Purnendoo's ex-girlfriend.

I said, "Oh, it's Lola," which seemed appropriate at the time.

"So how're things?" she asked.

"Fine," I said. "And how're things with you?"

"Serendipitous."

"Likewise. Hey, I'll see you around."

"Oh, look. A baby."

"Yeah."

"Isn't it cute?"

"Adorable. Peace be with you in the coming year."

With that, I prepared to sashay into the future, but Lola blocked the path. Suddenly she gave me the once-over and said, "It isn't yours, is it?"

"Of course not," I said.

"Well then, whose is it?" she asked.

"I think it belongs to that dancer, second from the left. You know how tough it is to find a babysitter these days." I fluttered my eyebrows at her and tapped a non-existent cigar.

"Oh, Andrew, you always *were* a jocular wag."

"No, a lapsed Unitarian."

Lola giggled.

"In fact," I added, "I think I'd better go pray. Right now. I'll see you around, Lola. Take care of things." And I started toward the church.

Now these are the facts: I got ten feet from that carriage, flung a glance over my shoulder for good luck, saw the carriage blaring its red plaid through the whirl and click of the dancers, saw no Lola, and kept walking. I walked halfway to the church. Then I cut across the crusty lawn and circled back to the library steps. I stopped for a moment at my aphelion, and yearned. Then I continued in stony orbit around my son, up the library steps, into the lobby, and stood behind the brass doors looking out. Even then I thought that at the last moment I might rush out and intercept Alice on her way to the carriage. But I didn't. I did hear her cry, though, when she arrived five minutes later and found me gone. It was more of a wail than a sob, and it lasted only a few seconds. I saw a leopard-coated lady offer Alice a Kleenex from her bag. Then a behemoth in an orange Gerry jacket buzzed over and blocked my view, so I focused on the solicitous arm he'd draped over the carriage handle. I might've gone down if he hadn't been half as large as my Volkswagen. But I didn't. And soon Alice was the hub, and the dancers were ignored. Unappreciated, they smoothed their ruffled kilts and migrated toward Mass. Ave. For a devastating instant I thought I smelled blueberry muffins. Again I did nothing. Four minutes later by the steeple clock, nine-tenths of the soul that had missed both Walt Disney and Jack Kerouac nested under the carriage hood and exited with Alice as she squared her shoulders and wheeled east, a straggling entourage at her tail. The remaining tenth bugged off unaccompanied and left no forwarding address.

But why? you ask. Why did you do it?

Manifest Destiny.

Explain?

I told you already; I can't explain. If you wish, say my eyes were open for gold; blame my actions on the Zeitgeist. You who left crackers and milk on the mantelpiece should be able to come up with something.

But just for the record, here's the rest of it. I wandered around till it got dark. I looked at the people, mostly; thumbed through a couple of magazines until the kid with the apron told me to get moving; stood on the corner and studied the time and temperature and practiced converting into centigrade. Then I caught a sort of a chill and decided to ride the Red Line to warm up. It was crowded down there in the subway: people puffed up in furs and down jackets, arms full of flowers and bottles and bakery boxes, legs straddling cartons, shopping bags overflowing, packs stuffed to the straps with ribboned boxes. A regular cornucopia of imminent generosity. Unnoticed, I flowed with the tide toward the tracks. At the edge of the platform I found myself staring into the hairline of a dumpy woman in a kelly green coat; on her velvet lapel was one of those battery operated reindeer-face pins: you pull on the string that hangs from the reindeer's chin and its nose lights up red. She smiled at me because she didn't know any better. Then some damp distance off from behind a stanchion came music, the stuttering chime of a hammer dulcimer. And people began to sing. At first I had trouble distinguishing the words, but then I heard:

> . . . snow lay round about,
> Deep and crisp and even.
> Brightly shone the moon that night,
> Though the frost was cruel . . .

The rest was drowned out in the rumble of the approaching train. I wish I could have been the person playing. Whoever it was.

When the train stopped I got on with everyone else. I rode nowhere for hours. Without any luck I looked for myself among the changing faces. Then on about nine-thirty I surfaced, retrieved my car, checked into the Y.

I heard it's going to snow so hard we'll be buried for a week.

THE MAN WHO LOVED LEVITTOWN

W. D. WETHERELL

W. D. Wetherell was raised in Garden City, New York. His stories and articles have appeared in a variety of publications, including *The Atlantic, Virginia Quarterly Review,* and the New York *Times.* He is presently working on a novel.

You realize what I had to do to get this place? It was thirty-odd years ago come July. I'm just out of the Army. Two kids, twins on their way, a wife who's younger than I am, just as naive, just as crazy hopeful. We're living in the old neighborhood with my folks four to a room. All along I've got this idea. Airplanes. P-40s, these great big 29s. We're slogging through Saipan, they're flying over it. DiMaria, I tell myself, this war is going to end, when it does that's where you want to be, up there in the blue not down here in the brown. Ever since I'm a kid I'm good with machines, what I do is figure I'll get a job making them. Grumman. Republic. Airborne. They're all out there on Long Island. I tell Kathy to watch the kids, I'll be back tonight, wish me luck. I borrow the old man's Ford, out I go. Brooklyn Bridge, Jamaica Avenue, Southern State, and I'm there.

Potato fields. Nothing but. French-fried heaven, not another car in sight. I stop at a diner for coffee. Farmers inside look me over like I'm the tax man come to collect. Bitter. Talking about how they were being run off their places by these new housing developments you saw advertised in the paper, which made me mad because here I am a young guy just trying to get started, what were we supposed to do . . . live on East 13th Street the rest of our lives? The being run off part was pure phooey anyhow, because they were making plenty on it, they never had it so good. But hearing them talk made me curious enough to drive around a little exploring.

Sure enough, here's this farmhouse all boarded up. Out in front is an ancient Chevy piled to the gunwales with old spring beds, pots and pans. Dust Bowl, Okies, *Grapes of Wrath* . . . just like that. I drive up to ask directions half expecting Marjorie Main. Instead there's this old man climbing up to the top of the pile. He's having a hell of a time getting up there. Once he does he stands with his hand shielding his eyes looking around the horizon like someone saying good-bye.

Maybe I'm just imagining it now but it seems to me it was so flat and smooth those days even from where I stood on the ground I could see just as far as he could . . . see the entire Island, right across the entire thing. Out to Montauk with waves breaking atop the rocks so green and bright they made me squint. Back this way over acres of pine trees, maybe one, maybe two lonely railroad tracks, nothing else except lots of ospreys which were still around those days. Then he turns, I turn, we look over to where the Jones Beach water tower is jutting up like the Leaning Tower of Pisa. Just this side of it the Great South Bay is wall-to-wall scallops and clams. You look left up the other way toward the North Shore there's these old ivy-covered mansions being torn down, pieces of confetti, broken champagne bottles all over the lawn. I have to squint a little now . . . I can just make out the shore of the Sound with all these sandy beaches that had "No Trespassing" signs on them, only a man in a yellow vest is walking along now ripping them down . . . not two seconds later the beach is crowded with little kids splashing in the waves. Then after that we both look the other way back toward New York . . . the old man tottering up there in the breeze . . . over these abandoned hangars at Roosevelt Field where everybody took off to Europe alone from back in the twenties, then out toward where the skyscrapers are in the distance. I see the Empire State Building . . . for some crazy reason I wave. Then in a little closer over one or two small villages, acres of potato fields, and no matter which way you look . . . Sound side, Bay side, South Shore, North Shore . . . there's the sound of hammers, the smell of sawdust, little houses going up in clusters, carpenters working barechested in the sun. The old man is looking all this over, then looks right down at me, you know what he says? "I hope it poisons you!" With that he fell off the bundle, his son had to prop him back up, they drove away in a cloud of dust.

Fine. I drive down the road a little farther, here are these new houses up close. Small ones. Lots of mud. Old potatoes sticking out of it like dried-up turds. Broken blocks off two-by-fours. Nails, bits of shingle. In front of each house or half house or quarter house is a little lawn. Fuzzy green grass. Baby grass. At every corner is an empty post waiting for a street name to be fitted in the slot on top. A man comes along in a jeep, shuffles through the signs, scratches his head, sticks in one says LINDBERGH, drives off. Down the street is a Quonset hut with a long line of men waiting out front, half of them still in uniform. Waiting for jobs I figure, like in the Depression . . . here we go again. But here's what happens. A truck comes along, stops in front of a house, half a dozen men pile out . . . in fifteen minutes they've put in a bathroom. Pop! Off they go to the next house, just in time, too, because here comes another truck with the kitchen. Pop! In goes the kitchen. They move on one house, here come the electricians. Pop! Pop! Pop! the house goes up.

There's no one around except this guy in overalls planting sticks in the little brown patches stamped out of the grass. "My name's DiMaria," I tell him. "What's yours?" "Bill Levitt," he says. "And what's the name of this place anyhow?" "Levittown." And then it finally dawns on me. What these men are lined up for isn't work, it's homes!

"How much does one of these babies cost?" I ask him casually. He picks at his nose, leans his shovel against the tree. "Seven thousand," he says, looking right at me. "One hundred dollars down." "Oh yeah?" I say, still casual. But I kind of half turn, take out my wallet, take a peek inside. "I only have eighty-three." He looks me over. "You a veteran?" "You bet. Four years' worth, I don't miss it at all either." He calls over to a man helping with the sinks. "Hey, Johnson!" he yells. "Take this guy's money and let him pick out whichever one he wants. Mr. DiMaria," he says, shaking my hand. "You've just bought yourself a house."

I will never until the day I die forget the expression on Kathy's face when I got back that night. Not only have I bought a house but that same afternoon Grumman hires me at three bucks an hour plus overtime. "Honey," I said, "get your things together, let's go, hubba, hubba, we're on our way home!"

I'm not saying it wasn't tough those first years. I worked to six most nights, sometimes seven. When I got home I fixed hamburgers for the kids since Kathy was out working herself. Minute she gets home, out I go pumping gas on the turnpike for mortgage money. Ten years we did that. But what made it seem easier was that everyone else on Lindbergh was more or less in the same boat. Young GI's from old parts of the city somewhere working at the big plants farther out. There were some pretty good men on that block. Scotty. Mike. Hank Zimmer. There wasn't anything we couldn't build or fix between us. I once figured out just among the guys on Lindbergh, let alone Hillcrest, we had enough talent to make ourselves an F-14. You know how complicated an F-14 is? Cabin cruisers, porches, garages . . . you name it, we built it. That's why this little boxes stuff was pure phooey. Sure they were little boxes when we first started. But what did we do? The minute we got our mitts on them we started remodeling them, adding stuff, changing them around.

There wasn't anything we wouldn't do for each other. Babysit, drive someone somewhere, maybe help out with a mortgage payment someone couldn't meet. You talk about Little League. Me and Mike are the ones *invented* it. We got the field for it, organized teams, umpired, managed, coached. Both my boys played; we once had a team to the national finals, we would have won if O'Brien's kid hadn't booted a grounder. But it was nice on summer nights to see dads knocking out flies to their kids, hearing the ball plop into gloves, see the wives sitting there on the lawns talking, maybe watering the lawn. The swimming pool up the block, the shops, the schools. It was nice all those things. People take them for granted nowadays, they had to start somewhere, right?

I'll never forget those years. The fifties. The early sixties. We were all going the same direction . . . thanks to Big Bill Levitt we all had a chance. You talk about dreams. Hell, we had ours. We had ours like nobody before or since ever had theirs. SEVEN THOUSAND BUCKS! ONE HUNDRED DOLLARS DOWN! We were cowboys out there. We were the pioneers.

I'll be damned if I know where the end came from. It was a little after the time I finished putting the sun roof over the porch. Kathy was in the living room yelling, trying to get my attention. "Tommy, come over here quick! Look out the window on Scotty's front lawn!" There planted right smack in the middle is a sign. FOR SALE! You know what my first reaction was? I was scared. Honest to God. I can't tell you why, but seeing that sign scared me. It scared me so much I ran into the bathroom, felt like being sick. Steady, DiMaria, I said. It's a joke like the time he put flounders under the hubcaps. Ginger needed a walk anyway, I snap a collar on her, out we go.

"So, Scotty, you kidding or what?" I say. Scotty just smiles. "We're pulling up, moving to Florida." "You mean you're taking a vacation down there? Whereabouts, Vero Beach?" He shakes his head. "Nope, Tommy. For good. I'm retiring. Twenty-five years of this is enough for anyone. The kids are on their own now. The house is too big for just the two of us. Carol and I are heading south. Thirty-nine thousand we're asking. Thirty-nine thousand! Whoever thought when we bought these shacks they would someday go for that?"

The twenty-five years part stunned me because it was like we'd all started yesterday as far as I was concerned. But the Florida part, that really killed me. Florida was someplace you got oranges from, where the Yanks spent March. But to actually move there?

"Come on, Scotty." I laugh. "You're kidding me, right?" "Nope. This guy is coming to look at the house this afternoon."

A guy named Mapes bought Scotty's place. A young kid worked for the county. I went over and introduced myself. "I've been here twenty-nine years," I said. "I knew Bill Levitt personally." "Who?" he asks. "Big Bill Levitt, the guy this town is named after." "Oh," he says, looking stupid. "I always thought that was an Indian name."

I should have known right there. But being the idiot I am, I take him out behind the house, show him the electricity meter. "Tell you a little secret," I whisper. "Got a screwdriver?"

I'd been helping myself to some surplus voltage ever since I got out there. Everyone on Lindbergh did. We were all practically engineers; when we moved in we couldn't believe it, all this electricity up there, all these phone lines going to waste. It was the Land of Milk and Honey as far as we were concerned; all we had to do was plug in and help ourselves. I'm telling Mapes this but he's standing there looking dubious. "Uh, you sure this is okay?" "You kidding? There's plenty more where that came from. They'll never miss it. Twist that, jig this, weld that there, you're in business." "Oh yeah," he says, but you can tell he doesn't get it because when I hand him the screwdriver he drops it. "Oops!" he giggles. Meantime his bride comes along. Beads. Sandals. No, repeat NO, bra. "Jennifer," he says, "this is Mr. DiMaria from next door." "Call me Tommy, how are you?" The first words out of her mouth, you know what they are? "How many live in your house?" "Uh, two. My wife, myself." She looks me over, puffs on something I don't swear was a Winston. "That's not many for a whole house. If you ever decide to sell my kid sister's getting married. They need a place bad. Let me know next week, will yah?"

That was Mapes. Silver, the sheepherder took over O'Briens', was even worse. "Hello, welcome to the neighborhood," I said walking across his lawn, my hand out. "That your dog?" he asks, pointing toward Ginger rolling in the pachysandra. "Yeah. Come here, Ginger. Shake the man's hand." "Dogs are supposed to be leashed, mister. If you don't get him off my property in five minutes I'm calling the pound and having the animal destroyed." With that he walks away.

Welcome to Lindbergh Street.

I'm not saying it was because of that but right about then a lot of the old-timers put their houses on the market. It was sad because before guys like Scotty could at least say they wanted to go to Florida, actually look forward to it. But now? Now the ones who ran out ran out because they were forced to. Taxes up, cost of living, heating oil, you name it. Here we'd had these homes for thirty years, broke our backs paying the mortgages off, you'd think it'd become easier for us now. Forget it. It was *harder*. It was harder keeping them than getting them.

What made it worse was the price everyone was getting. Forty thousand. Fifty thousand. The ones who stayed couldn't handle it anymore thinking they'd only paid seven. The real estate bastards dazzled them into selling even though they didn't want to. That was the sad part of it, seeing them try to convince themselves Florida would be nice. "We're getting a condominium," they'd say, the same somebody told you they were getting a valve bypass or a hysterectomy. "Well, I kind of like fishing," Mike said when he broke the news to me. "Don't they have good fishing down there?" "Sure they have good fishing, Mike," I told him. "Good fishing if you don't mind having your finger sucked by a water moccasin."

You think I'm exaggerating? You expect me to maybe say something good about the place? What if all your friends were taken away from you by coronaries, you wouldn't be too fond of heart disease, right? That's exactly the way I look at Florida. Guys like Buzz and Scotty think they're going to find Paradise down there, they're going to find mosquitoes, snakes, walking catfish, old people, that's it. This guy I know in the plant had his vacation down there. He thought it would be nice, no crime, no muggers. The first night there a Cuban breaks into his trailer, ties him up, rapes his wife, takes everything they had. Florida? You guys can have it. If Ponce de León were alive today he'd be living in Levittown.

But anyhow, nature hates a vacuum, the sheepherders moved in, started taking things over. You have to wonder about them to begin with. Here they are starting off where we finished, everything took us so long to get they have right away. They're sad more than anything . . . sadder than the old-timers moving south. You know what these kids who stayed on Long Island know? Shopping centers, that's it. If it's not in a mall they don't know nothing. And talk about dreams, they don't have any. A new stereo? A new Datsun? Call those dreams? Those aren't dreams, those are pacifiers. Popsicles. That's exactly what I feel like telling them. You find your own dream, pal, you're walking on mine. My generation survived the Depression, won the war, got Armstrong to the moon and back. And when I say *we* I'm talking about guys I know, not guys I read about. You think Grumman only makes F-14s? I *worked* on the landing module my last two years. Me, Tommy DiMaria. Nobody knows this but Scotty and me carved our initials on the facing under a transistor panel inside of the cabin. T.DM.S.S.H. right straight to the goddamn moon. But that's the kind of thing *we* did. What will the sheepherders be able to say they did when they get to be our age? . . . Evaded the draft. Bought a Cougar. Jogged.

It's like I told each of my kids when they were teenagers. "This town is where you grow up," I told them, "not where you *end* up." And they didn't either. They're scattered all over the place. I'm proud of them all. The only problem is like when Kathy got sick the last time it was a hell of a job getting everyone together. When I think about Kathy dying you know what I remember? Kennedy Airport. The TWA terminal. Going there to meet each of the kids, trying to figure out plane schedules, time zones, who I'm seeing off, who I'm meeting. The older I get the more I think what the real problem is in this country isn't *what* or *how* or *why* but *where*. *Where*'s the question, the country's so goddamn big. Where in hell do you put yourself in it? Where?

Each of the kids wanted me to move in with them after Kathy died. Candy's a psychologist, she told me I was crazy to live by myself in the suburbs. If it was one thing people in suburbs couldn't stand it was to see someone living alone. It threatened them, they'd do anything to get rid of that reminder the world wasn't created in minimum denominations of two . . . that's the way she talks. But I told her no because the very last thing Kathy said was, Tommy, whatever you do don't give up the house. She was holding my hand, it was late, I was there all by myself not even a nurse. "Tommy, don't give up the house!" "Shh, Kathy," I whispered. "Rest now. I won't. I won't ever give it up." She squeezed my hand. I looked around to see if the nurse had come in but it wasn't her, it was the lady in the next bed mumbling something in her sleep. "I'll never give it up, Kathy," I promised. I bent over. I kissed her. She smiled . . . she closed her eyes and it was like she had gone to sleep.

"Good-bye, Kathy," I said. "Sweet dreams, princess."

It was harder without her. I remember I'm in the back yard fixing up the garden for spring just like I would if she was still there, watching Ginger out of the corner of my eye, when Mapes's wife comes up the driveway. She stands there chewing gum. "I'm sorry about your wife, Mr. DiMaria," she says. "I guess you're going to sell your house now, huh?" When I told her no she acted mad. "We'll see about that!" she says.

Her little boy Ringo runs over to help me like he sometimes did. She pulls him away, stands there clutching him tight to her body like she's protecting him. "Never play with that dirty old man again!" she screams. "You old people think you can keep putting us down all the time! You think you can ask anything for a house we'll pay it on account of we're desperate! What's Janey supposed to do, live in Queens the rest of her life?" She's screaming, getting all worked up. Mapes comes over, looks embarrassed, tries to quiet her down . . . away they go.

A few days later I'm out there again, this time planting beans, when I hear voices coming from the porch. I'm just about to go inside to investigate when this guy in a suit comes around back with a young couple holding hands. "This is the yard!" he says, pointing. "It's a nice yard, good place for kids. Hello doggy, what's your name?" He walks around me like I'm not there, squeezes a tomato, leads them back around front. Ten minutes later they come out of the house. "You'll like it here, it's a good investment. Oh, hello," he says, "you must be the owner. I'm Mr. Charles from Stroud Realty, here's my card, these are the Canadays, they love your house." "Scram!" All three of them jump. "Go on, you heard me! Clear the hell out before I call the cops!" "But I'm showing the property!" the little guy squeaks. I had a hell of a time chasing them off of there.

The pressure really started after that. It was little ways at first. Kids that had been friendly before staying away because their mothers told them to. Finding my garbage can spilled across the lawn. Mail stolen, things like that. One morning there's a knock on the door, this pimple face is standing there holding a briefcase. "Mr. DiMaria?" "That's right, who are you?" "I'm from the county. We've come to assess your home." "It was assessed." He looks at his chart. "Yes, but twenty years ago. I'm sure it still can't be worth just four thousand now can it? Excuse me." He butts his way in, starts feeling the upholstery. He's there five minutes, he comes back to the door. "Nice place you got here, Mr. DiMaria. I can see you put a lot of work into it since we were last here. Let's say forty thousand dollars' worth, shall we? Your taxes will be adjusted accordingly."

"You're crazy!" I yell. I'm about to lose my temper but then I remember something. "Hey, you know D'Amato down at the county executive's office? Him and me grew up together." "Never heard of him," pimple face says, shaking his head. "Well, how about Gus Louis in the sheriff's office?" "Oh, we don't have much to do with them these days I'm afraid." He starts to leave. "Well, you're probably going next door now, right?" "Oh, no," he says. "This is the only house on the block we're checking." "Wait a second!" I yell. "That's bullshit. You're going to Mapes, then Silver or I'm calling my congressman. Discrimination's a crime, pal!" His eyes finally light up. "You mean Mr. Silver? Hell of a nice guy. His brother is my boss. Good-bye, Mr. DiMaria. Have a nice day."

I don't want to give the impression I didn't fight back. I did, because if there's one thing I know about Levittown it's this. People are scared of blacks moving in, only nowadays it isn't blacks, it's drug treatment centers. It terrifies everyone. It terrifies them because all they think about when they're not shopping is property values. So what does DiMaria do? I wait until the next time these sweet Seventh Day whatever ladies come around selling their little pamphlets. I always give them a dime, no one else on the street ever gives them a penny . . . they think the world of me. They're always very polite, a bit crazy. What I did when they rang the doorbell was invite them into the house for some coffee. That was probably enough right there to give most of the sheepherders a good scare. It's Saturday, they're all out there waxing their Camaros, here's two black ladies inside DiMaria's talking about God knows what, maybe thinking to buy it. But what I do is take them outside around back saying I wanted to show them my peach tree. These ladies are so sweet and polite, they're a bit deaf, besides they'll do anything I want.

I point to the side of the house. "This is where we'll put the rehabilitation room!" I say real loud. "Over here we'll have the methadone clinic!" The ladies are nodding, smiling, handing me new pamphlets, I'm slipping them fresh dimes. "AND OVER HERE'S THE ABORTION WING!" I see Mapes and Silver staring at us all upset; if they had a gun they would have shot me.

What really kept me going, though, was Hank Zimmer. He was the last cowboy left besides me. Every once in a while I'd get discouraged, he'd cheer me up, then he'd get discouraged, I'd cheer him up . . . we'd both get discouraged, we'd take it out working on my new den, maybe his. What we used to talk about was how there were no hedges on Lindbergh in the old days, no fences, no locked doors. Everyone's home was your home; we all walked back and forth like it was one big yard.

That was long since done with now. You think the sheepherders would have anything to do with other sheepherders? It was like the hedges we'd planted, the bushes and trees, had grown up so high they'd cut people off from each other. The only thing they wanted anymore was to pretend their neighbors weren't there.

I remember the last time he came over because it was just after I finished wallpapering the den. Ginger was whining to go out so I let her . . . that crap about leashes didn't bother me at all. Hank's telling me about school taxes going up again, how he didn't think he could pay his on Social Security, nothing else. "What we should do," he says, "is find other people in our position to organize a senior citizens' group to see if something can't be done." "Hank," I tell him. "No offense, but all of that what you just said is pure phooey. You join one of those senior citizens' groups, women's groups, queer groups, right away you put yourself in a minority, you're stuck there. All these people running around wanting to be in a minority just so they can feel all nice and persecuted. Forget it! We're humans, that puts us in the *majority!* We're humans, we should demand to be treated like it."

Hank runs his hands up and down the wallpaper, admires the job. "Yeah, you're probably right," he says. Humans. He never thought of it that way before. We go into the kitchen for some coffee. "Now what my idea is, we find out where Big Bill Levitt is these days, we get a petition together telling him how things have gone wrong here, all these young people moving in, taxes going up forcing us out. He'll find some way to make things right for us. I'd stake my life on it."

Hank nods, reaches for the cream. "By the way," he says. "You hear about Johnny Holmes over on Hillcrest? The guy who once broke his chin on the high board at the pool?" "What about him?" "He's moving to Fort Lauderdale, him and his wife. They bought this old house there. They're going to fix it up nice. Have a garden and all. He made it sound very appealing." "Oh, yeah?" I say. Then I remember myself. "Appealing, my ass. It'll collapse on him, he'll be back in a month. If you don't mind my saying so, Hank, change the subject before I throw up."

All of a sudden we hear this godawful roar from out front like a car accelerating at a drag strip, then brakes squealing, only I knew right away it wasn't brakes. "Ginger!" I jump up, knock the coffee over, run outside . . . There's this car fishtailing away up the street. In the middle of the pavement in a circle from the streetlight is poor Ginger. I run over, put her head in my lap, pet her, but it's too late, she's crying, kicking her legs up and down. Behind her head's nothing but blood. Hank's next to me nearly screaming himself . . . There's nothing to do but put her out of her pain with my bare hands because there's no other way. Then Hank's got his arm around me, I'm shivering, crying, cursing, all at the same time. He takes me back to the house, his wife comes over, they have me swallow something . . . the next thing I know it's morning, Hank's buried Ginger in the back near the birch tree she always liked to curl up against in the sun.

It was a while before I found out who did it. I kept on taking my walk around the block same as before, except I didn't have Ginger with me anymore. Maybe a month later I'm walking along past Silver's house, I see him out in his driveway with Mapes, a few other sheepherders. Silver is giggling. Mapes is standing to one side acting half ashamed, but smirking, too. "Hey, DiMaria!" Silver yells. "How's your dog?"

I didn't do anything right away. We had a tradition in the old days, you had a score to settle you took your time. I waited for the first stormy night, went over there with two buckets of the cheapest red paint money could buy.

It was pretty late. I shined a flashlight at the lamppost which if you ever want to try it is enough to put one of those mercury vapor jobs out of commission for a while. Then I propped my ladder against the side of his house facing Mapes, went to work. The first cross stroke on the left was pretty easy, the upper right hand one was tougher because I had to paint across a bay window O'Brien had put in years before. I was being careful not to drip any on the bushes. No matter what I thought of Silver I had a certain amount of respect for his shrubbery which had been planted by Big Bill Levitt back in the forties. It must have taken me two hours all told. I'm painting away humming to myself like it was something I did every night. When it was morning I woke up early, took my usual stroll right past Silver's house, there on the side looking wet and shiny in the sun is the biggest, ugliest, coarsest swastika you ever saw, painted right across the side of his house big as life, the only thing bothered me was the upper right stroke was a bit crooked after all.

There were pictures of it in the paper, editorials saying Levittown had gone to hell which was true but for the wrong reasons. The entire Island's gone sour if you ask me. The Sound's gone sour, the ocean's gone sour, the dirt's gone sour. We used to grow enough tomatoes to last the winter, these great big red ones, now you're lucky if you get enough to feed the worms. Great South Bay? Sick clams, dead scallops, that's it. I remember it wasn't that long ago we used to catch stripers bigger than a man's arm, me and Scotty, right off Fire Island a twenty-minute drive away. I remember going there before dawn, cooking ourselves breakfast over a fire we made from driftwood, not seeing another soul on the beach . . . just Scotty, me, the sun, the stripers. Nowadays? Nowadays you can't even fish without getting your reel gummed up in oil; you're lucky to take one crap-choked blowfish let alone stripers.

Looking back what I think happened was that guys like Scotty, Buzz, Mike, and me had the right dream in the wrong place. Long Island's gone sour. Sometimes I remember the first day I came out here, a know-nothing kid, watching that farmer, that last old farmer up there on the overloaded Chevy looking around saying good-bye at the same time cursing it once for all. Other times I walk around the house looking for something to do. What I usually end up doing is put the record player on. Mitch Miller doing "Exodus." I put it on real loud. When they sing, "This land is mine, God gave this land to me," I start singing too. Listening to it makes me feel stronger, so I keep turning it up, playing it again. After that I fix lunch for myself. Tuna fish, a cup of soup. After lunch I end up staring out the front window trying to figure out who lived where in the old days. Know something? It gets harder every year. O'Brien's and Scotty's are easy, but sometimes I get confused on the others.

It's like this morning I'm looking out across the street trying to remember if Buzz or Rich Ammons lived where this sheepherder name of Diaz lives now, when who do I see over on Zimmer's lawn but the same real estate bastard I chased off my place, Mr. Charles, with two young kids showing them around. This time I was really mad. I ran outside without even a coat, started screaming at them, telling them I'd call the cops, break every bone in his miserable little body if he didn't clear out and leave poor Hank alone. But what happened next was that Hank was outside, too. He was pleading with me to stop, but by then it was too late. Real estate man and kids are running into their car, locking the doors, racing away.

"Tommy!" Hank yelled, shaking his head. "They were going to pay me fifty-five thousand, Tommy!" "What are you talking about?" But now he looked away like he was ashamed. He took me inside the sun porch, sat me down on a lawn chair he unhooked from the wall.

"Tommy, we're moving south," he said. "Bullshit you are!" But he doesn't do anything, he just sits there. "We can't take it here anymore, Tommy," he whispered. "The cold gets to Marge. The taxes are too much for me. All these kids, what do we have in common with them? We're going to Florida. St. Pete. We bought a trailer."

It was probably the next to worst moment I ever had. "You can't do that, Hank," I said, just as quiet as him. "Not after what we've been through all these years. I was going to help you out with your den. Think of all the things we could do yet. There's another porch we could add on, we could add on a pool." But he was shaking his head again. "Let's face it," he said. "You've got nothing left to work on, Tommy. The house is finished. You hear me? Finished! There's nothing left." He took out his wallet, showed me some pictures. "My grandkids. Terri and Shawn. They live down there now. We want to be close to them. That's the main reason, Tommy. We want to be close to them the years we have left."

By now I was getting mad. "Grandkids my ass!" I yelled. "You think your grandkids give a damn about you? Maybe at Christmastime, that's it. To them you're an old smelly man they don't give a damn about, they never will. Take it from me, I know." But then I looked at him . . . seeing him blink, cover his face with his hands, I got feeling ashamed of myself. "Hank," I said, "don't leave me alone like this. Please, Hank. Just hold on a little while more."

"Fifty-five thousand, Tommy. I can't turn it down."

"Listen, Hank. We'll call Big Bill Levitt up. I'll say, Mr. Levitt, my name is Tommy DiMaria, I live on Lindbergh Street, you probably don't remember but you once let me have a house for eighty-three dollars down instead of a hundred. Remember that, Mr. Levitt? Remember those days? Well, a lot of us old-timers are having trouble hanging on to our places you built for us. We wondered if maybe you could help us out. We'll call him up, Hank. We'll call him up just like that."

"You and your Levitt! I'm sick of hearing about him! What has Levitt ever done? He built these places and never looked back. He made his pile, then didn't want to know nothing. Levitt? You're so crazy about Levitt, let me ask you something. Where is Levitt now? Tell me that! Where is he now? Where is Levitt now?"

Like a dope, like the idiot I am, I shake my head, whisper, "I don't know, Hank. Where?"

"Florida!"

"Hank," I said, "I hope you fry."

When I got back to my place there was a panel truck in front, two men standing on the sidewalk watching me cross the street. At the same time Mapes's wife is on her lawn pointing at me, yelling, "That's him, officer! That's your man!" One of the men came up to me the moment I reached the curb. "You Thomas A. DiMaria?" he said. "Beat it!" "You live at 155 Lindbergh?" "Beat it! You're trespassing on private property, pal!" "We're from the electric company. This is for you."

I'm feeling so tired by then I took the envelope, opened it up. Inside is a bill for $11,456.65. "You owe us for thirty-two years' worth," the man said. "If we want we can put you in jail. Stealing electricity is a crime." I looked back toward Mapes's house, sure enough there he is with that same half-ashamed smirk hiding behind his Cougar pretending he's polishing the roof.

"I'm not paying," I said. "Leave me alone." With that the other man, the one who hadn't said anything before, comes right up to me, waves a paper in my face. "You better pay, DiMaria!" he said with a sneer. "You don't, we take the house!"

I didn't waste any time after that. I went out to the tool shed, took a five-gallon can of gasoline, went back inside . . . took off the cap, taped a piece of cheesecloth over the spout, went into the den.

Sprinkle, sprinkle. Right over the desk. Sprinkle. Right over the wallpaper. Then after that I went into the bathroom. I remembered those men putting it in. I remembered redoing it with a bigger tub, new tiles, new cabinets. Sprinkle, sprinkle. Right over the cabinets. Right over the rugs. Next I went up the stairs I'd built with Scotty from lumber we helped ourselves to at a construction project on the turnpike . . . up to the dormer I'd added on for the kids. Their stuff was still there, all the kids' stuff, because they didn't want it, Kathy would never let me throw it away. There's a blue teddy bear called Navy, a brown one called Army. I took the can, poured some over their fur, propped them up in the corner, poured some over the bunk beds. I remembered the time Candy cried because she had the bottom one, she wanted the top. Thinking about that, thinking about the times I sat around the old DuMont watching *Mickey Mouse Club* with them waiting for Kathy to get home, almost made me stop right there.

I went back downstairs, the can getting lighter, leaving a little trail behind me . . . into the twins' room where I sprinkled some on the curtains Kathy sewed, sprinkled some on the Davy Crockett hat Chris used to wear every time she came out of the bathtub. Then after that I went into the kitchen. The kitchen cabinets. The linoleum. Sprinkle, sprinkle. Out to the porch where we used to eat in summer, right over the bar I made from leftover knotty pine. I stood there a while. I stood there remembering the party we had when we ripped the mortgage up, how Scotty got drunk and we had to carry him home only we carried him, dropped him in the pool instead. Sprinkle, sprinkle. Like watering plants. Like baptizing someone. Like starting a barbecue with lighter fluid, all the neighborhood there in my back yard. Into our bedroom, over the floor, the floor where the first night I brought Kathy home we had no bed yet so we lay there on the floor of what we still couldn't believe was our house, making love all night because we were so happy we didn't think we could stand it. Sprinkle. The fumes getting pretty bad now. Sprinkle. Outside to the carport, over the beams, over the tools, over everything. Sprinkle, sprinkle. Splash.

And that's where I am right now. The carport. The bill they handed me in one hand, a match in the other. I'm going to wait until Silver gets home first. I want to make sure everyone on the block gets to see what fifty-five thousand dollars, thirty-two years, looks like going up in smoke. A second more it'll be like kids, neighbors, house, never happened, as if it all passed in a twinkling of an eye like they say. One half of me I feel ready to start all over again. I feel like I'm ready to find a new dream, raise a new family, the works. Nothing that's happened has made me change my mind. I'm ready to start again, just say the word. I feel stronger, more hopeful than ever . . . how many guys my age can say that? That's all I want, one more chance. For the time being I'm moving back to the old neighborhood to my sister's. After that, I don't know. Maybe I'll head down south where it's warmer, but not, I repeat NOT, to Florida, maybe as far as Virginia, I'm not sure.

MUTILATED WOMAN

JOYCE CAROL OATES

Joyce Carol Oates' most recent novel is *Bellefleur* (Dutton). She was awarded the National Book Award in 1970 for her novel *Them*, and was recently inducted into the American Academy and Institute of Arts and Letters. Presently she is teaching at Princeton University.

Many years ago Constance Shea's favorite teacher—this was at the Hendon School in Connecticut—told her that she was a very special, a very peculiar, type.

Constance, thirteen years old at the time, was immensely flattered. A warm blush spread across her face.

Special? *Peculiar?*

The young woman fussed with a pen, and then nervously stroked the back of her neck, which had been neatly shaved. She told Constance that she was one of those people who, without desiring it, without encouraging it, exact homage from others throughout life.

Homage? Constance did not understand.

Admiration. Envy. . . . Homage.

I don't understand, Constance said. Her face grew warmer.

Such people, the teacher went on, talking rapidly now (for of course she must have realized her imprudence), such people often doubt their own self-worth, perversely. In fact they may secretly despise themselves. They may . . . even toy with the idea of suicide or self-mutilation, to mock the world's high estimation of them.

Constance, who had in fact consoled herself with silly dreams of "suicide"—vague vaporous cinematic notions—blushed even harder. She had begun to tremble and her eyes filled with angry tears.

"But in general such people tend to be strangely unconscious of their effect upon others," the woman said slowly. She swallowed, no longer looking at Constance. Her long fingers continued to stroke the back of her neck.

"I—I don't know what you're talking about," Constance said. "You—you're—It isn't true—"

The woman looked away. There was a long painful silence. Constance, about to burst into tears, finally hurried out of the classroom.

But time passed. Decades passed. And Constance came gradually to see—sometimes in anger, sometimes in bewilderment, sometimes with an inchoate pride—that the woman's words were fairly accurate. She never thought of suicide and certainly never of self-mutilation, but it was true that people fell in love with her. It was Constance Shea's misfortune that people, unbidden, fell in love with her.

The most recent was the young Lindenthal girl with the wild kinky black hair and the hectic, melancholy manner—though Mira was not *that* young, twenty-seven to Constance's fifty-two. She was a playwright whose first play had been successfully produced in a tiny theatre on Bleecker Street; she had acted in it herself, and though Constance had not seen the play—she never went to experimental plays, on or off Broadway—colleagues of hers whose judgment she respected informed her that it was really quite good, surprisingly good; and that Mira had acquitted herself well as an actress. But then that sort of play, highly energetic and "iconoclastic," a sort of satirical blend of Brecht, Ionesco, and Pinter, was difficult to assess. At any rate it had been warmly received by critics, and Mira had been written up last spring in the Sunday *Times* as one of the most promising of the younger woman dramatists. Constance remembered studying the young woman's photograph, touched by something raw and arrogant and hopeful in her strained smile, though of course she had not known Mira at the time. She had no idea of Mira, at the time.

Now it was October and Mira Lindenthal was visiting dramatist for one year at Elyria College, where Constance taught literature and a workshop in creative writing; and she went about the little college town of Fairfax, Maryland, speaking of Constance Shea in the most embarrassing terms. A beautiful woman, an extraordinary person, a writer of genius. The most remarkable person Mira had ever met, except possibly for Lillian Hellman, another of Mira's idols. (Lillian Hellman had helped Mira find a good director for her play, and had even given her some advice about revision.) Hidden away here in Fairfax, living almost in seclusion, a writer whose novels are obviously too exquisite and demanding for most of her students to appreciate—what a weird situation! But how fortunate for Elyria College! And for Mira most of all. "I consider it a great honor just to be on the same faculty as Constance Shea," Mira was reported to have said when the chairman of the Drama Department interviewed her. Her adulation must have been genuine, since she accepted the offer of a job, with noisy enthusiasm, before she was even told what her salary would be.

"Have you heard what Mira Lindenthal is saying about you?" Constance's colleagues inquired. "Evidently she worships you—did you know?"

"But I did nothing to encourage her," Constance said quickly.

A beautiful woman, a writer of genius. An extraordinary person.

All of which, Constance thought, might be true to some degree. (For though she was outwardly modest, and fairly shy in social situations, she never, in private, doubted her own high worth as a novelist.) But such histrionic claims, such exuberant bullying exclamations, were in very bad taste, and would have the effect—in Mira's mouth—of being merely embarrassing. "If only she were more restrained," Constance said with a wan smile. "If only she would leave me alone. . . ."

In recent years Constance had come to value quiet and privacy and near-anonymity. She supposed she was "famous" enough in the literary community though she had done nothing to pursue fame except write her novels, publishing only five during a thirty-year period; certainly she had the high esteem of her fellow writers, and was quite content with her position. A number of other colleges and universities had made her offers over the years, but she preferred to stay at Elyria, with its high tuition, its genteel pastoral tradition, and its fairly good students—all undergraduates, no graduate students, which was a relief; the president of the college respected her immensely, and the chairman of her department treated her with an urbane friendly caution she found distinctly gratifying. And then she was, in Fairfax, within an easy drive of Princeton and Hopewell and Pennington, where she had friends; and it was no problem to take the train to New York City for one of her infrequent visits with her publishers. Fairfax was hardly more than a village, a hamlet; it had no industry; no slums; no racial problems. The surrounding countryside was mainly farmland, hilly and remarkably attractive. Constance liked nothing so much as to drive out and go for long hikes, by herself, on warm autumn days. Coming to Elyria College had been a retreat of sorts but it had been absolutely correct. Constance thought with satisfaction that she was now settling into middle-age and that she would enjoy it, would take pleasure in it, as she had only infrequently enjoyed her young adulthood. In fact she often thought with a pang of excitement that she had slipped through relatively unscathed—she was now finished with all *that*.

At the age of thirty-six she had had her left breast removed, and in the months that followed that brutal—and, she thought, needless—operation she had undergone, rather too swiftly, a series of profound changes. At first she had felt, of course, sheer terror: a dizzying sense of panic: she had had to stop herself from clutching at the doctor's hands, as he told her his diagnosis, as he outlined the steps that must be taken at once. A biopsy, and if the growth is malignant, then the breast should be removed; even if the lymph glands are not affected the breast should be removed; so the doctor told her, and so she agreed. Afterward she wondered if she had acquiesced too readily. But then it was too late. But *then* . . . shouldn't she be grateful that the cancer had evidently been stopped, that the operation, radical as it was, had been a success . . . ? Yet, for a while, she felt anger; even fury. She could not determine if she loathed the doctor who had cut away her breast, or if she loathed herself, for being now so unwhole and unclean; a mutilated woman. She had not done it to herself but still she was mutilated and in time everyone would know. . . . Have you considered an operation to restore the breast, someone said, hesitantly, they have all sorts of miraculous techniques these days, the sister of a friend of mine was telling me that she flew to Texas for the operation and that it turned out beautifully. . . . Then, seeing Constance's rigid expression, the woman had gone silent.

At that time in her life Constance had been seeing a man, an old friend, really, in his fifties, who was newly divorced, and she was sickened at the prospect of his revulsion when he saw her hideous scarred chest. Though she had told him about the surgery—indeed, he'd known from the very first, even before her family, she had called him in tears from the doctor's office—and though he had been warmly sympathetic, she could not believe, she could not *really* believe, that he would not be disgusted. "I don't want to live," she had said tonelessly, calling from the doctor's office. "Where are you?" he said. "I'll come pick you up in a cab. Just stay there."

After the operation she refused to look at herself in mirrors, even when she was dressed. It was such a fraud, her image—such a blatant lie. Constance Shea from the outside was an attractive woman, somewhat tall, with dark blond hair neatly brushed back from her face to show her high, strong forehead, and to give prominence to her faint widow's peak which, she had been told as a child, is a sign of beauty. Her frank gray eyes had a customary quizzical expression. She was not pretty, had never been pretty, had long ago given up trying. Consequently the compliments of others surprised her; she did not *think* they were deliberately lying to her, or mocking her. Even after the operation she continued to look healthy, with her good coloring, her quick, graceful, almost lithe manner; and of course she told no one beyond her family and a few intimate friends about the operation. But her outward appearance was such a lie, she wanted at times to tear off her clothing, angrily, to undeceive her admirers. And what was she to do about her friend Perry, who continued to insist that he wanted to see her despite the mutilation. . . .

It was some time before Constance realized that she was not apprehensive of her friend's disgust; she was hoping for it. Because love—romantic, sexual, "companionable"—no longer interested her. It depended too much upon emotion, upon the subjective whims of the other; it was something she had outgrown. In a sense, Constance thought, it was a novel she herself had written, and had consequently outgrown.

During her first year at Elyria College a young English instructor named Thornton fell in love with her, quite openly. He was in his late twenties; he had published a few poems in literary journals, and was working on his first book. Constance was fond of him in her detached way, and offered to read his poetry, which he pressed upon her eagerly. His reverence for Constance Shea and his initial shyness in her presence were touching, when Constance did not find them ludicrous.

In the course of their peculiar eighteen months' friendship they were rarely alone together—he drove her up to Princeton one fine autumn day, to lunch at the Nassau Inn; he often escorted her to parties and college events. So far as Constance knew they touched only once, and then by accident—it was raining, Thornton was holding a large black umbrella over them both, Constance lost her footing on a slippery stone step and seized his arm to stop from falling. At once he squeezed her hand tight. But a moment later he released it, and neither alluded to the incident afterward.

Thornton was a burly, good-natured, soft-spoken young man with gingery curls and somewhat self-conscious mannerisms. Some of his students imitated him behind his back, others liked him immensely; he seemed frank, simple, open, unpretentious. His generosity surprised Constance, and began to annoy her as time passed: he gave her a 6-ounce bottle of French perfume, a potted rose tree for the terrace of her little rented house, a signed first edition of Katherine Anne Porter's *Flowering Judas*, and a small carved ivory figurine from Malaysia which represented the goddess of "light and wisdom" rather than fecundity, and which possessed, despite its flat, near-featureless face and elongated body, an eerie sort of beauty. She had tried to refuse the ivory figurine, arguing that it was too costly; but Thornton had seemed genuinely upset and in the end she relented. "But no more presents, please," she said.

About his poetry: she suspected that it was too timid, too mannered and fastidiously crafted for the Seventies, but it *was* promising, and she was reasonably sure that the young man did have talent. She even offered to write a letter to an acquaintance, an editor at a New York publishing house, to accompany Thornton's manuscript. From the very first he was boyishly grateful and could speak of nothing other than her "fantastic generosity." Constance told him that he must not exaggerate her influence, but he brushed her remarks aside. "You're just modest, Constance," he said, his voice rising. "Everyone knows you're absurdly modest."

But as Constance feared the manuscript was eventually returned, after a disgraceful delay of eight months, and her relationship with Thornton was immediately altered. At first he pretended not to care—the rejection letter was, after all, a kindly one, filled with apologetic reasons for declining the book. Then, as the weeks passed, he became quite odd: he stopped her in the corridor of the English Department, or in the library, or in the parking lot, asking with a queer strained smile if she had "heard anything more" from her friend in New York. Constance tried to explain that the editor was not a friend; a casual acquaintance at best; but Thornton seemed not to listen. At a party, before curious witnesses, he told Constance in a whining voice that the least she could do was try again. "You know dozens of editors," he said with a plaintive smile. "You have innumerable connections. After all, Constance, you're a famous writer. . . ."

She refused him curtly. And awaited his apology. (For he was, after all, a sensible, sane person; there was nothing to indicate that he was aggressive or opportunistic, or emotionally unbalanced.) But days passed and he did not apologize and Constance began to hear from colleagues that Thornton was speaking angrily of her, of her "betrayal"; he was planning to "expose" her. Eventually he sent her several long poems dedicated to her. They were unlike his earlier work: crudely done, spiced with obscenities and exclamations, quite vicious. Constance read them in disbelief, trembling. Such hatred! Such rage! A "Constance Shea" emerged who was selfish, cold, arrogant, vain, sterile, ugly, bodiless, loveless. In the nastiest poem, typed out in the shape of a highly stylized vagina, Thornton fantasized raping and killing the "famous authoress" with the sharp point of an umbrella.

Everyone at Elyria was sympathetic with Constance. They told her that Thornton was notoriously unstable; confronted with a student's complaint, his first semester at the college, he had actually burst into tears in the chairman's office. His two-year contract was a terminable one and would not, of course, be renewed: which he had known from the first, but now he was agitating to be rehired, writing letters, making speeches to his classes. Constance was, they assured her, only one of his campaigns. He was bitter, fantastical, perhaps even dangerous. He experimented with drugs, his landlord was very unhappy with the condition of his apartment. . . . "But why didn't any of you tell me before all this happened," Constance cried in exasperation. "Well, you seemed so fond of each other," they said. "You got along so well, and Thornton was so obviously infatuated with you. . . ."

Because of that unhappy young man Constance came dismayingly close to being expelled from her little paradise. But in the end Thornton was the one, of course, to leave; she need not have worried.

"What has happened to your former courtier?" people asked, the following year, as if it were all a joke, and there had never been any danger. As if Constance had not been deeply wounded. Thornton left no forwarding address; he simply vanished. Buffoonish and ungainly and childlike in his egotism, he was remembered as an unpopular teacher, an untalented poet. He was no longer frightening; he was merely silly. Anecdotes could be invented at his expense. "You see, Constance, there's a considerable risk in being too kindly, too attractive, for an unmarried woman," people said. Constance half-thought they were blaming her, for being unmarried: she *should* have had a man to protect her from misfits like Thornton.

Then again they flattered her, indirectly. She was made to feel as if she were a temptress of some sort, a seductive woman. "Your poor hapless admirer," they said, smiling, "whatever became of him—do you know?"

"Of course I don't know," Constance said irritably.

Now, this autumn, there was Mira Lindenthal.

Of course she was no Thornton. She was successful and talented and popular with her students; she was even on excellent terms with her former husband, a black musician who still helped her with her career. She was wonderfully ebullient: monkeyish, flamboyant, a tireless talker. Her first week in Fairfax, she approached Constance boldly on Main Street in her soiled blue jeans and near-transparent shirt, and seized both Constance's hands in hers, and leaned close, and told her that she had begun reading her novels when she was thirteen years old and that they meant more to her than anything—that Constance's work had saved her life, perhaps—though, as she said with an anxious smile, she didn't want to exaggerate—but she hoped Constance would understand.

Constance did not, and the girl's brash bullying admiration was disconcerting, but she managed to thank her, and to make a few courteous inquiries about Mira's impressions of the college and Fairfax. But it was hopeless: Mira with her dark shining eyes, her olive complexion that fairly glowed with life, her bitten nails, compulsive winks and grins, her long untidy frizzy hair, her bare toes wriggling inside filthy sandals, her unstoppable *essence*, was not to be diverted from her subject, which was Constance Shea, Constance Shea's novels, and what they had meant to the adolescent Mira Lindenthal. So Constance stood quiet; Constance endured ten or fifteen minutes of praise. Her face burned, her eyes misted over. The girl was, despite her slovenliness, despite her disturbing intensity, really quite attractive: almost beautiful.

As if reading Constance's thoughts she took hold of Constance's hands once again, in parting, and stammered: "You're even more lovely, Constance, than your photographs. . . ."

That was in September. By mid-October Mira had talked Constance into attending a "house-warming party" in her small, cluttered apartment (a noisy frantic unpleasant evening filled with too many people, most of them from New York City), and a rehearsal of *Mother Courage* which Mira was directing for the Drama Department (during which Mira shocked—and rather impressed—Constance with her strident voice, her unashamed temper, her frankness and exuberance and profanity: and Constance could see that the student actors, though frequently crushed by the young woman's criticism, were in awe of her), and, most inexplicable of all, a photography session in the Millstone River Arboretum that lasted for several exhausting hours. (Mira had been quite serious about her disapproval of Constance's dust-jacket pictures. So she arranged for a young black woman to come down from New York City, "a very gifted photographer, an artist really," and take Constance's picture one sultry afternoon. The girl was big-bodied, taciturn, not particularly friendly; she frowned a great deal; *she* did not flatter Constance. And after the long session, after Mira's excited promises, nothing at all came of it—no prints, no photographs. Evidently they did not turn out. The black girl did not care for them. Or perhaps she had not troubled to develop them. Or something had come up, some complication in her life. Mira never satisfactorily explained, and since she seemed embarrassed about the episode, Constance did not question her further. Word had gotten out of the photographing in the Arboretum, and Constance dreaded people at Elyria gossiping about her: her new-found vanity: her wish for a publicity photo that would do her beauty justice.)

And then, at the Dean's Christmas party in mid-December, Mira made a fool of herself so openly, so noisily, that Constance rebuffed her, and left the gathering. Mira had been drinking a great deal of the Dean's inexpensive sweet California wine, and jabbering about how much she loved Elyria, what a change it was from the heavy neurotic atmosphere of New York: what an honor it was to be on the same faculty with a genius like Constance Shea. She had even sat on the floor, at Constance's feet, and forced everyone in the room to drink a toast to Constance and the success of her new novel (which would not be published for several months), and somewhere in the midst of the girl's gay drunken speech Constance arose and said, "Stop. Please. This is intolerable. This is asinine," and got her coat and walked out. Her heart pounded so violently she was afraid she would lose consciousness on the street.

Mira hurried after her to apologize; and telephoned the next morning, insisting that she meant no harm, she hadn't realized that her remarks were upsetting Constance, she had no *idea* Constance was distressed. "I wouldn't embarrass you for anything in the world," she said timidly.

But there was speculation. There was gossip. A friend told Constance that odd anecdotes were making the rounds: there had been a quarrel in public, a sort of lover's quarrel, and Constance had stalked out, and Mira had run after her. . . . Constance was sickened as much by the mere fact of the rumors as by the substance of the rumors themselves. And then, it was intolerable that she could not control them. They constituted a kind of story, an elaborate ungainly buffoonish fiction, not of her own invention.

Mira disappeared over the mid-winter break, and Constance's life resettled. She began to think of the young woman as merely imprudent; certainly she was good-natured, and generous, and appeared to be highly talented—so students said, and they were not easily impressed. So when Mira telephoned Constance in late January, asking if she might drop by, Constance hesitated only a moment before agreeing.

Mira brought with her a belated Christmas present—a three-foot-high clay pot in a peculiar triangular shape, done by a friend of hers in the Village, a "very gifted" young Iranian artist. At the sight of the thing Constance's heart sank but she accepted it with a smile of polite gratitude. In a khaki windbreaker with sheepskin lining, and a jaunty crimson beret, and rather handsome leather boots, and her usual blue jeans, Mira was both penitent and exuberant; she was flushed as if from extreme cold, though the January evening was surprisingly mild.

Constance offered her a drink but Mira refused—"I want to cut down on that sort of thing," she said nervously.

She looked about Constance's attractive living room, and made appropriate comments, and seemed distinctly uneasy. Constance, sipping sherry, could not decide if she wanted the young woman to leave, or if she halfway hoped she would stay. There was plenty of food in the refrigerator, it would be no trouble to make dinner for the two of them. . . . But Mira kept jumping to her feet, pretending to be interested in one thing or another: Constance's cherrywood bookcase, Constance's books, Constance's emerald and gold Turkish rug, a gift from an old admirer. After thirty minutes of this Constance said curtly: "Did you have any particular reason for stopping by, Mira?"

It was the first time she had used the young woman's name, and Mira turned to her, startled and pleased. She had not really heard Constance's question; she had only heard her own name. She sat at the very edge of a chintz-covered chair and said shyly that she'd thought of very little since the Christmas party except the misunderstanding between them: it had been a terrible surprise to her, but maybe, "in the long run," it would come to seem a good thing. "I need awakening," Mira said, brushing her hair out of her eyes. "I mean, constant awakening. My husband, my former husband, he says I'm catatonic inside all my energy. . . . I don't really *see*, I don't really *listen*. . . . The sort of thing friends do for each other, you know. . . . Not just politeness, and hypocrisy, but genuine truth: standing up the way you did, that night, and picking my fingers off your skirt, and saying, what did you say, Constance?—you wouldn't tolerate anything more from me—you thought my behavior was asinine—And so you told me, and walked out; and I can't stop thinking about it. I mean, it was so *honest*. It was so *direct*. Friends who are genuinely fond of each other must tell the truth at all times, otherwise there's a kind of anarchy . . . and it's terrifying, you know, to be unable to determine truth from lies."

Constance, blushing, murmured something appropriate. She was relieved, she said, that Mira hadn't been hurt. . . .

"Oh I was hurt! I was hurt," Mira laughed. "I was crushed. But then I went away, to this friend of mine in Miami Beach, and brooded over it, and bored everyone out of their skulls, and came to the realization that it was exactly what I required . . . that sort of abrupt awakening, you know. Like a slap in the face. And since then I've been able to work again. Revising my new play, the one the Drama Department is supposed to put on this spring, you know, I was rather depressed about it for a while . . . but now it's coming along, I'm not totally ashamed of it. . . ."

Constance asked her about the play, hoping to divert her from the original topic; but she spoke of it perfunctorily, saying that "that side" of her could take care of itself. "What I really came here to talk about, Constance," she said, grinning uneasily, "is . . . is something very different. I suppose you would call it abstract, theoretical. The sort of thing people never talk about. In a marriage you don't talk about it, and in most friendships. . . . It's too primitive, I think. Or too exalted."

"Yes?" Constance said.

"Maybe I will have some sherry," Mira said.

And then, swallowing a large mouthful, she crossed one long leg over her knee and waggled her booted foot and told Constance, who was staring at her in dismay, that she wasn't certain about her existence.

"I don't understand," Constance said. "Your existence at the college . . . ? Or as a playwright . . . ?"

"My existence as a human being," Mira laughed forlornly. "Not even as a woman, a female. By that point you're pretty well specialized, and I'm not at that point, I'm somewhere far below. My mind drifts about on the level of protoplasm. Maybe algae. Do you know what I mean?" she said, fumbling in the khaki jacket for her cigarettes. "Sometimes I wake up in the morning and I just lie there, wondering who the hell I am, what the hell I'm required to do. The night's dreams, far from helping me, are a hopeless jumble: a ragbag: half appear to be the dreams of other people, strangers. Does any of this sound familiar to you?"

Constance remembered, but not clearly, a fictional character of hers, a young woman, long ago, in retreat from a bad marriage, enduring a winter in Colorado, alone; and this fictional character, of whom Constance had been quite fond at the time, had also doubted her existence; and had been quite eloquent about it. But she frowned now, and set down her sherry glass, and said nothing.

"Oh I realize I'm taking up your time, you certainly want to be working," Mira said. "I imagine half the misfits in Fairfax take you aside, and beg you for wisdom. . . . It's because, Constance, you seem to radiate such certainty. And knowledge. I mean," she said quickly, blushing, taking note of Constance's expression of displeasure, "I mean you're just such a fine calm fulfilled individual. You're centered—do you know the term?—no?—it's a sort of Eastern concept—or maybe it's just a fashionable Western concept now—Being centered means that your center of gravity is in *you;* in your own soul. Most people, you know, people like me, everyone I know, our centers of gravity are outside us—we're always running around getting reflections of ourselves from other people, or hoping to read about ourselves in the paper, we may be intelligent enough to know that it's ridiculous—it's hell—our 'delirious profession'—but we can't change our behavior; it's just the way we are. But you're very different, Constance."

Constance poured the young woman more sherry. She said lightly, "But my dear, aren't you simply telling me that I'm much older than you and your friends? After all I will be fifty-three in April—"

"*No.* Shit, no," Mira said. "People your age are the worst. I mean, the ones I know. The women, the men. . . . No, it has nothing to do with age, it's something in your character."

"But really. . . ." Constance said uneasily.

"Character. Like bone structure. Like the body's frame," Mira said emphatically. "It must be in the chromosomes. Determined. Biology is destiny, Freud said, but I mean something even more primordial than that. . . . Christ, am I embarrassing you again?"

Constance tried to smile. "I really don't get much pleasure, Mira, out of talking about myself. I don't imagine most people do."

"Most people—! Oh the hell with most people," Mira laughed. "They talk about nothing else. They see and hear and know only themselves. They're like Beckett's talking heads, stuck in jars. Oh they go on and on and it's amazing. . . . But you really are different, Constance," she said, lowering her voice. She fixed her dark shiny doggish eyes on Constance and was silent for a moment. "Somehow I knew you would be, before we met. I knew, from your writing. From your picture, even though it doesn't do your eyes—your marvelous eyes—justice. I *knew*. I've been telling everyone how we were fated to meet, it had to happen, there've been these queer dreams of mine for the past year, they have to do with turning thirty, will I survive or not—am I going to make it or not—Certain people I know haven't made it, and the ones who have might be better off dead: but I won't go into that. I'm certainly not going to bore you with my depressing life, and my crazy depressing friends. The thing is. . . . The thing is," she said vaguely, her gaze still fixed on Constance as if, for a moment, she had lost the train of her own thought, "some people are born beautiful and perfect. Their faces mirror their souls. Or their souls mirror their faces. Whatever Plato said. . . ."

"You exaggerate, Mira," Constance said softly.

But Mira did not hear. She went on to speak of the fact that some people *existed* more substantially than others. It might sound bizarre but it was nevertheless true. She spoke quickly, as if intoxicated, her cigarette burning forgotten in an ashtray, her long narrow foot wriggling with the intensity of her voice. An odd young woman! An endearing but most exasperating young woman, Constance thought. She was waiting now for her to leave; she would not suggest dinner after all. Mira Lindenthal's mere presence was exhausting, as if Constance's spirit were being drained from her though she did little more than listen.

Chatter about acquaintances in Soho, and the loneliness of Fairfax, Maryland, and Shakespeare's *Winter's Tale* (what relevance this had Constance did not catch), and one of Constance's early novels, and the fact that she, Mira, had hours of work awaiting her back in her ugly apartment, and could barely force herself to leave. . . . Constance prudently offered her no more sherry. Yet she remained seated, running a hand through her stiff hair, smiling and winking and squinting. "You won't tell anyone about our conversation, will you," she said.

"Of course not," Constance said.

"Because I wouldn't want certain things to get around. . . . This uncanny feeling that I don't exactly exist, or that the existence I find myself in isn't quite the correct one: I wonder if anyone shares it? But of course if anyone did, he might not confess, he might not want to confess," Mira said slyly. She waited, but

Constance did not reply. "I don't *think* I'm going crazy. I mean, I've gone a little off my head in the past, two or three times, but it didn't feel like this: it was primarily emotion and this is all intellect. The question of one's existence is theoretical, isn't it . . . ? By thinking of our own position aren't we also thinking of everyone's . . . ?"

"I don't know," Constance said gently, glancing at her watch.

Mira rose to leave. But then lingered. Her khaki jacket half-buttoned, her crimson beret dangling from a pocket. She apologized for having taken up so much of Constance's time—"I know, I know, your time is precious: I feel like a vandal, wasting it"—but still she dawdled, talking of the college, her most promising students, the over-priced food store in town, her need to get away to New York soon. And then, inexplicably, she was talking once again of Constance Shea: and staring at Constance in that peculiar hungry way. "I think what I really want to know," she said, nearly whispering, "is . . . how does it feel to be *you?* To stand where you are standing, to look out upon the world from your point of view, to know what you know, to have accomplished what you've accomplished. . . . You are such an extraordinary person, Constance," she said, her eyes shining, "you might almost forget the fact, now and then. And so someone must remind you."

A wave of sheer anger passed over Constance. She rose, her cheeks burning unpleasantly. "Exactly what do you mean by that, Mira?" she asked.

"Mean? Mean by what?"

"The hyperbolic things you've been saying."

"What things? That you're beautiful, that you're extraordinary?"

"And perfect too? I believe you said—perfect too?"

"Everyone knows it—"

"But how am I beautiful? How am I perfect?"

"By just—just *being* the person you are!" Mira laughed.

"Do you think so? Really? It's that simple?"

"I—I don't suppose it's necessarily *simple*," Mira said, taking an involuntary half-step backward.

Constance's pulses rang strongly. The sherry had done her good, she thought. It gave her courage, it gave her an uncharacteristic sense of righteousness. She stared without smiling at the young woman who had ruined her evening, and began slowly, quite deliberately, to unbutton her blouse. She noted with pleasure that Mira was now alarmed. Really alarmed. Was she so slapdash and daring after all, was she so flamboyant as she pretended . . . ? Merely a pale, frightened girl, staring as Constance Shea unbuttoned her blouse, and slid her slip and brassiere straps off her left shoulder. She thinks I have gone mad, Constance thought.

Constance faced her, defiantly. "Well. Do you see? Do you see, and do you understand? All those lies about perfection—Beauty and perfection—"

A pale, frightened girl. Now stammering an incoherent apology. Now backing away. Constance wanted to taunt her—Why are you suddenly so tongue-tied, when you've been jabbering away for hours?—for weeks? But she said only: "Good night, Mira."

The girl fled.

It had been a dramatic moment, a wonderfully theatrical moment. But Constance, standing alone in her living room, her scarred breast exposed, her flesh gathering itself into tiny goose bumps, felt only a sense of exhaustion. And bitterness. And hatred: for certainly she hated Mira Lindenthal, for having seduced her into behaving so crazily: for having behaved as Constance Shea never behaved.

"The impertinent little bitch," Constance whispered.

It was over. The relationship—it was not of course a friendship—was over.

And so Constance was appalled to receive a letter from the young woman two days later as if nothing were ended; as if Constance's contemptuous act had not been one of dismissal. She was so upset, she could barely force herself to read the poorly typewritten words: *My love for you has deepened. . . . The evidence of your suffering. . . . Your profound message. . . . Beyond words, the gesture of sheer mute anguish. . . . An intimate bond forged between us. . . . Between two women. . . . The sort of knowledge in the flesh that no man could comprehend. . . .*

As she tore up the letter Constance began to cry.

She began to hear wild tales about Mira Lindenthal. A drinking bout in Baltimore with a student, one of the actors in Mira's play; trouble with the police; classes missed. Evidently the young woman spent an inordinate amount of time in a tavern out on the highway, where she made a fool of herself with her long impassioned monologues, and was gaining a reputation as a whore (crudely put, but then it was a crude, clumsy situation) since she brought back to her apartment not only male students from Elyria but men from the area—truck drivers, handymen, construction workers, even a highway patrolman. When she taught her classes and when she showed up for rehearsals of her play she was evidently in control of herself: she was brusque and confident and bullying as always: and she had a small, highly vocal circle of supporters in the Drama School. But she was out of place at Elyria. She should never have accepted the offer from Elyria. Had she told Constance what was troubling her?—had she confided in Constance at all?

No, Constance said, she had not.

She was relieved to learn that Mira was no longer talking about her; at any rate, tales no longer wound their way back to her. Perhaps, Constance thought, she has found someone else to idolize. A man, a lover. A legitimate lover.

When Mira disappeared from Fairfax on the day before her play was scheduled to open Constance was one of the first people contacted: but of course she knew nothing. "You might try her husband, in New York. Her former husband," Constance said. During the three days Mira was missing—the play did open on schedule, and was well-received; and Mira did turn up, refusing sullenly to explain herself—Constance slept poorly, and had no appetite, and was forced to dismiss her classes after half an hour or so, since she felt not only her own apprehension over the young woman but her students'; and she felt, too, how they blamed her.

She wanted to address them. And her colleagues. She wanted to reason calmly with them. She would *not* be emotional, she was *not* like Mira. She would explain to them that she had nothing to do with Mira Lindenthal and that Mira Lindenthal had nothing to do with her. It was all exaggerated, histrionic. Constance was not to blame. How was she to blame? One must reject the sentimental drivel that insists we are all to blame for everything—we share in Hitler's guilt—that sort of thing—nonsense—dangerous nonsense. Absurd. "I did not deliberately attract Mira Lindenthal," Constance would tell them. Just as she had not deliberately attracted Thornton, or the others. The nameless others. And so she would *not* accept responsibility, no matter how they judged her. "You have no right to judge me," she would say, her voice rising.

But Mira did return. She simply showed up for her first class on Monday morning, and refused to explain herself, and of course she refused to apologize. It was said that she looked sickly and dishevelled: her clothes looked as if she had slept in them. Your play was quite successful, people told her. We missed you. . . . But she would not talk about it, she seemed really indifferent, she murmured something about the play being a failure.

The actors came to see her, the assistant director came to see her, even the chairman of her department—but she would not talk about it.

But aren't you even going to see it performed, they asked.

She shrugged her shoulders and smirked.

I don't like that kind of theatre, she was reported to say. I really prefer Chekhov. So why the hell should I sit through two hours of *that* . . . ?

Constance dreaded her call. Or perhaps Mira would come over, uninvited. I am not to blame for whatever you do to yourself, Constance would say. You should never have come here: you are out of place here. You must leave, go back to New York, go anywhere, and leave me alone. . . . She walked about her rented house, bringing her fists lightly together, whispering to herself. How dare people blame her for Mira Lindenthal! How dare people gossip about her, and tell grotesque lies!

Mira did not telephone, nor did she come to Constance's door. She sent another letter, as poorly typed as the first but much briefer. Constance did no more than scan it, holding it at arm's length; her hand trembled badly.

Why didn't you reply to my letter, Mira wanted to know.

Constance crumpled the sheet of paper and let it fall.

Some days later while she was having lunch with two of her colleagues in the faculty dining room, Mira Lindenthal appeared out of nowhere, pale and hulking and mockingly deferential. "May I have an audience with you, Miss Shea?" she asked. "It would only take up a few minutes of your time."

Constance stared at her. She felt that she had known Mira Lindenthal all her life, and that she had been fleeing her all her life.

"I realize your time is highly valuable," Mira said, licking her lips, smiling a queer wide smile. She seemed unaware of Constance's companions. "Perhaps I could pay you for your time. As one professional to another."

"I . . . I don't understand," Constance said.

"I'm asking for an audience with you. For a few minutes of your invaluable time," Mira said.

She stared at Constance. Her smile shaded into a grin.

She's mad, Constance thought.

"I am engaged at the moment," Constance said. "As you can see, I. . . ."

"I can *see,* I can certainly *see,* that hasn't been taken from me yet," the young woman laughed.

Constance felt as if she were slipping from her body. Losing her body—the weight of it—its gravity. A terrifying dizziness, airiness. . . . She heard herself stammer a sentence or two, heard the young woman's coarse mocking reply, and a pulse rang in her head, and she knew that she was close to fainting.

Someone intervened. Her luncheon companions, rising to their feet. A departmental colleague, sitting at another table.

"I simply want an audience with you, Miss Shea," Mira Lindenthal shouted. "Is that too much to ask? You don't answer your door—you don't answer your telephone! Did you get my letter? *You*—!"

People intervened, leading the angry young woman away. She resisted at first; then gave in; allowed herself to be led away like any disobedient child. Constance could hear her talking and laughing out in the hall.

"I—I don't understand—It isn't my fault—" Constance whispered.

The letter? Which letter?

She had crumpled it without reading it. And of course that mad young woman knew.

You did right to refuse her, to speak so calmly to her, everyone said. But isn't she *pitiful.*

Mira Lindenthal left Elyria three weeks before the end of the spring semester. She did not telephone, so far as Constance knew. (Of course Constance answered her phone only rarely these days.)

She did not write another letter, or leave notes in Constance's mailbox.

Still, there were rumors. About which Constance preferred not to think.

One night, very late, it was said that Mira turned up on Constance's doorstep—laughing drunkenly, trying the doorknob and pounding on the door. Imagine! The young woman was raving-drunk and her voice sounded coarse and guttural as a man's.

Constance naturally did not come to the door. She must have lain in bed, rigid beneath the covers, terrified.

Or was she terrified?—did she feel anything at all?

Elyria was divided on the subject of Constance Shea: whether she felt a great deal (which she suppressed), or whether she felt nothing at all (which was more likely).

At any rate, Constance did not answer the door that night, nor did she telephone the police. (For there *was* a disturbance—she would have been justified in calling the police.)

She lay in the dark, in her bed, trembling beneath the covers.

Trembling, or perfectly still. Calm.

And after ten or fifteen minutes the wretched girl went away.

You did right to refuse her, everyone told Constance, to her face.

Still, her life at Elyria was over.

She had to leave, she was expelled, there were too many rumors, too many fanciful lies. In public she could not mistake certain glances, certain intonations. It would do no good to protest: to point out that the young woman was clearly fated to destroy herself within a few years: and that it had nothing to do with Constance. They would listen, would pretend to sympathize; but secretly they blamed her.

And so Constance Shea resigned. And the president of Elyria College, who so much admired her, accepted her resignation with little more than a token protest.

Her life was over. She was expelled. It took her days to pack, to sort through her papers and letters—ah, she had accumulated so many letters!—and most of them had no value—had to be thrown out. The labor of sorting and packing exhausted her. A pulse beat oddly in her temple, her heart lurched, she was dizzy almost constantly, and found it difficult to keep her balance. Bodiless, weightless: like a ghost: drifting about the box-filled unfamiliar rooms like a ghost.

She did manage, however, to throw away useless things. And there were many of them. Letters, papers, parts of manuscripts, books given as gifts, books inscribed by fellow writers, outworn clothing, furniture with tiny scratches, soiled cushions and pillows, soiled curtains. It was too much trouble to have her carpets cleaned, she might as well throw them away. And snapshots kept untidily in manila envelopes, years of accumulation, years of clutter. She had meant to arrange the snapshots neatly in an album but there had never been any time, and now it was too late.

Despite the dizziness and weakness that buzzed close about her like a cloud of gnats Constance took distinct pleasure in certain chores. Like throwing away that Malaysian statue. It had been a gift from someone, from an admirer. A fairly recent gift. But she could not remember, for a space of several minutes, which one of them had given her the ugly thing.

BABY

IVY GOODMAN

Ivy Goodman was born in Harrisburg, Pennsylvania, in 1953. Her stories have appeared in *Fiction*, *The Ark River Review*, and other magazines. She studied at the University of Pennsylvania and at Stanford, where she was a Mirrielees Fellow. She is now working on a novel.

He shuttles from me, in Boston, to ex-wife and baby, in Baltimore, to me, to baby. He vacations three weeks alone with baby. He wants to get to know baby. He wants custody of baby. And when he gets custody (last month he shattered a tea cup to prove how certain he is of getting custody), he wants me to help love baby. I kissed his hands, one finger bloodied, sliced by a jagged piece of china, and agreed to love baby. Already, more carefully than if they were my own, I love both the man and his baby.

Five months ago, I met the man at a party. Clearly, he wanted someone at that party. He is particular to a certain point, and then beyond that point he is not at all particular. For hours I watched him dance with a married woman who I knew would eventually refuse him. Eye to eye, hip to hip. Overheated, she took her vest off and stared at him as if that vest and the tight blue blouse beneath it mattered. Perhaps they did matter. But when she and her husband left, he came to me and talked about his baby.

"And how old is this baby?" I asked.

"Ten months."

"Do you have a photograph?"

"Not with me."

"Not in your wallet?"

"I don't have a wallet. But I have hundreds of pictures at home. Do you want to see them?"

"Yes."

"Should we go now?"

"Yes."

At least he had the integrity to wait until afterward to bring out the baby. Naked, we sat in bed, turning over the baby in Maryland, the baby in Massachusetts, the drooling, farting five-toothed baby, holding his toes in zoos and botanical gardens, lounging in trees, hammocks, the arms of his father, his mother. No, I was not spared the eleven duo shots of the girlish ex-wife and mother kissing the baby.

The beautiful mother of the baby. Will he go back to her? He doesn't go back. He goes on. Unknowingly, I too, may be diminishing, a piece of the past that grows more evil with each new woman, each new recounting. The only unscathed one is that poor baby.

The baby. How does a woman who loves the father of the baby love the baby? By remembering that she is not the mother of the baby. When the father moves away, he will also take the baby. If I haven't already, I am doomed to lose both father and baby.

But why do I want them to begin with? When I could have an honest man and my own baby? Most days I am terrified by the thought of my own baby. About honest men: you must be honest in return, for who knows how long. But with the treacherous, you can be kind and honest while it lasts, knowing it won't last. In the end you suffer, of course. The surprise is how, and in which places.

Sometimes he held me all night. Sometimes when he heard me cry in sleep, he clawed my spine until I cried myself awake. When he planned a trip, I found the tickets on the bureau days before he told me he was leaving. ("By the way, I'll be flying to Maryland tomorrow." And after a pause, "Drive me to the airport at eight, would you?" Or, "Pack. You're coming with me.") For two weeks, he telephoned every midnight, though now I haven't heard his voice in sixteen days, and I tore open his last letter Saturday. It was all about the baby. The baby is walking perfectly. The baby is making friends with other babies. In so many gestures and baby words, the baby has stated his preference for road life with father, his dread of that split level crowded with mother, grandmother, grandfather, and every baby toy available in greater Baltimore.

Yesterday, in stores, on the street, I laughed, waved, and clicked my tongue at twelve babies, wheeled, cradled, backpacked, or carefully led by twelve women; yes, all twelve, women. He is probably the only man on the Eastern Seaboard walking into a grocery at ten A.M. without a wedding ring and with a baby. The woman he leers at over piled grapefruit will want to laugh but won't, because she's flattered, then will, because she's flattered. No wonder the baby is making friends with other babies.

But I can't compete with strangers, pretending to be lured, as I pretended to be, by his obvious glances, by his baby. He will stay with one of them or another of them, or he won't stay. He will come back, or he won't come back. Whatever his decisions, I knew from the start they would have nothing to do with me.

All last night I drifted, nearing sleep but never finding it. I miss him. According to plan, my ache spreads. I pit myself against myself. I'm losing.

I want another of our silent breakfasts, his head lowered to his bowl, his coffee spoon overturned near his mug. I want to break his mug. I want to do something to him.

He brooded. He thought he was entitled to brood. But his horrors, described on cold nights, were no more horrible than mine; he just thought they were. The stories he told and I listened to, I would never presume to tell. And if I did, who would listen to me?

Because he only liked my hair down, when I pinned it up to wash my face, I closed the bathroom door, but I closed the door for both of us. What he didn't want to see, and more, I wanted never to show him. And what he has seen I want now, impossibly, to take from him, before he mocks it to amuse his next woman.

His woman. His women. He's stuffed a battered envelope with snapshots of us, already including one of me, full lengths, with legs crossed or in a blur, crossing, heads turning, mouths speaking. He interrupted us and then, camera swinging from his shoulder, moved on. His ex-wife, mother of the baby, is actually his third ex-wife. From the glossy pile I try to guess the first two, but can't. Bodies, faces, wives, lovers, blend. We look tired; we are tired. Thinking practically, we want a good night's sleep and wonder if he'll leave soon. But we also think our shadowed faces have been brushed by moth wings. We feel more haunted than he. When he whispered what he thought was sad, we spared him what we knew was sadder. We let him pout, in a corner, alone. But even children keep their secrets. Right now, what is he thinking? All those silent times, what was he thinking?

In a friend's house, in a crowded room, I remember looking at him. He looked back. He shook his head. He could have been bedazzled. He could have meant we'll leave soon, but not yet. Or he could have wanted me to vanish.

Is he enigmatic, or is he just myopic? He's said himself that his eyes stare when he strains them. He should wear his glasses. I wonder, alone with the baby, does he wear his glasses? As a novelty, he was married the last time in thin gold framed glasses.

Wed in March, parents in August, estranged in November, and now, divorced, he and his ex-wife hate each other. If I said, "I'll give you another baby," would he marry me?

I don't want a baby. No, I do want a baby. I covet babies. But which are instincts, and which are yearnings? Do I feel heartbreak or the rattle of dwindling ova? What do I want so, when I lie awake, wanting? And what if I did have his baby? He would leave me and try to take his baby.

In green motel rooms, does he rest his elbows on the rails of portable cribs and watch the sleeping baby? When he slept with me, I watched him. His ribs, wings, spread, closed in, spread, closed in. He strained. I wanted to make breath easier for him.

He was losing hair. He was losing weight. His skeleton was rising out of him. Each night, new bones surprised me. My fingers stumbled. I want him again. I still want him. But my desire is diverted toward bed rolls, pillows, small animals seen from a distance, and other women's babies. Or is my desire itself diversion?

I worry about what I'll do because I know what I've done. Also, I worry about that baby.

And at dusk, when the telephone rings and I answer it, I recognize his whimper, wavering behind his father's voice, his father, who, after weeks of silence, has called to ask if I know it's raining. "Yes, here it's been raining. Where are you, where it's raining?"

"We're both in a phonebooth, about ten miles south at a Texaco."

"And you're coming back?"

"Yes. Soon."

Almost before I hear them or see them, I smell them, tobacco, baby powder, wet wool, cold; and after he puts the sleeping baby on the couch and touches me, just tobacco, wool, cold. "How's the baby?"

"A pain in the neck the last hundred miles, but fine now."

The baby, his face creased by the bent cap brim, stretches one fist, then brings it close, licks it.

"His cap."

"Would you take it off? I have to get another suitcase from the car."

When I bend down, the baby turns his head; his back curls. The cap slips, and I pull it free and put it on a chair. It is that simple. In the middle of the floor, where he'll be safer, I smooth a blanket for him. When I lift him, soft, willing, but weighted down by heavy shoes, he nestles. I untie the shoes. By the time the door slams, he is covered with his own yellow quilt and still sleeping. All the while, sleeping. His father says, "You've tucked him in, thanks. Too tired to talk. Tomorrow. And nothing's settled."

No, nothing's settled. In our bedroom now, flung across the bed, the other traveler also sleeps, his trousers damp, dragged black at the cuffs from the rain. I grab his sneakers by their heels and tug. When they hit the floor, he groans, rolls. His shirt wrinkles up above his rib cage.

"Too tired to talk. Tomorrow." If he hadn't been so tired, he might have laughed at his own joke. Why now, at the end, should we talk?

In the kitchen, I sit, the only one awake in this sleeping household. I don't want the man. I don't want the baby. But when the baby cries, I go to the baby.

THE WALTZ DREAM

BARBARA REID

Barbara Reid lives in New York City, and has an afternoon office job and writes in the morning. Her novella, *The Tears of San Lorenzo* was published by Apple-wood Press, and she has had three children's books published. Her stories have appeared in *Sewanee Review*, *Mississippi Review*, *Quartet*, *Descant*, and *Quixote*. She has just completed a new novella, and is revising a novel written under a Mary Roberts Rinehart Foundation grant.

They got in the car, all five of them for a change, Anna on the front seat with Bill, her cameo face turned away from him, screened by her long dark hair. Anna with him for once. In the back Mary Beth sat between the boys. She had wanted to sit with them because she did not feel so frightened, except they asked so many questions it tired her. It felt as if a hand had pulled down her features then, her eyelids drooping and her cheeks and mouth all gone slack and strange.

"Nana," said Lance now. "Will the doctor put another hole in your throat?"

"I hope not, dear," Mary Beth said in her voice which had suddenly gone whispery and strange.

They were bringing her to the hospital again, and the two boys, Lance and Sandy, stared at Mary Beth's throat though she was wrapped up in her old mink coat and a blanket as well.

"That's a dumb question," Sandy told Lance. "The doctor would use the same hole."

"Then it will be a bigger hole?" Lance went on, and Mary Beth clasped his warm small hand. "You will breathe through it, won't you, Nana? I know about that."

What they couldn't know was the dread—the baffling weakness, the double vision, she would see four little boys instead of two, and she would choke on a piece of toast. A few minutes ago she had choked on calf's liver, nothing went down, a pill was the size of a melon; she couldn't find her breath. She wondered if they would do another tracheotomy. She had had to explain that to her grandsons who peered through the doorway in fascinated silence as Lily, her nurse, cleansed and dressed her wound when she came home from the hospital, where she had been on the respirator. In the hospital, when she had at last come to, she had watched herself breathing, her puzzled blue eyes on the respirator as it went up and down, so even and steady it was a wonder it didn't lull her to sleep. What if it were unplugged? She felt useless beside the huge silver machine that kept her lungs filled with oxygen—useless and fragile—and she could not take her eyes from the long tube that was fastened from her throat to the respirator, going up and down, up and down. Sleep it said, but she could not.

It was such a struggle to breathe now she could not help thinking about it. She watched her breath going out in plumes in the icy air. She watched the boys' breaths too, only they moved about so much they reminded her of young colts snorting in a dawn workout. The back seat was filled with clouds of Spearmint. The blanket slipped and she had to ask the boys to pull it up. It was so cold! I wonder if it will be spring when I come home this time, Mary Beth thought.

"Why am I here?" she had asked the doctor when she came to.

He hesitated. Then because she insisted on knowing, Dr. Sloane said, his long face gentle as he held her hand, "You have myasthenia gravis."

The name frightened her almost more than the symptoms did. Spoken, the words had a knell, deriving from dead languages, myasthenia from the Greek for muscle weakness, gravis the Latin for severe. Anyway everyone called it MG, just as her husband Jules and her friends had shortened Mary Beth to MB and then they called her Emmy Bee. But she was Nana now to Bill and Anna, to the boys whom she saw more than she did anyone else after Lily left. Jules had been gone three years. Her friends had stopped in to see her occasionally, then they phoned Anna and asked solicitous questions, and then they sent cards and notes as though they were afraid they would catch it, this MG that caused her to shrink from size 12 to 8 and had altered her so, her expression droopy and peculiar, her limbs gone limp, that hump between her shoulders because she couldn't stand straight. Have I really lived with Bill and Anna two years? she marveled. She had and most of the time it seemed like one endless day. At the age of seventy-seven every day that passed was a day tricked from time, and when one was as ill as she was it was a miracle she had lasted at all. She had been on the respirator for weeks, or was it months? She was confused about that. Time got all muddled when you were this old, this ill. Sometimes she would make her way to the bureau and look at herself in the mirror and with surprise see barely a trace of the woman she had been. Her eyes were as large and as blue but filled with apprehension. Her dressing gown hung loose. Her hair looked like goose feathers. Everything about her was wispy. I was another woman, Mary Beth would think. Who was I? What happened to me?

Somehow, Dr. Sloane told her in his careful way, the electrical conductor between nerve and muscle was lacking, the communication was lacking. At least he didn't lie, Mary Beth thought. He treats me like I'm somebody. And when she asked why some days were worse than others her words were muddled, as if a thermometer were in her mouth. Only the boys could understand her when her voice slurred like that. But she could be mute and they would know what she wanted to say, just as they knew when their dog needed a run. Nothing frightened them, not even the change in her that scared her out of her wits whenever she thought about it, which was almost all the time. Her only comfort then was to let her mind roam over the past which had been full of excitement, such fun—such fun. . . . Sitting down, she would close her eyes and pretend nothing had changed but finally her reveries of all that happy gone time would leave her, and she would realize: I am here, in Bill and Anna's house, and how strange it is that it should be so, that I am like a little child now that has to be watched, a dependent. I never wanted that, never.

Port Washington, that was the town she was living in now. Weekdays Bill would catch the 8:10 train to New York, Anna would usually be at a committee meeting, the boys would be at school. Now that she was alone in the empty house so much Mary Beth couldn't wait till the boys came home, dashing in with the fresh air still about them, their cheeks red, eyes bright—Lance, the younger one, with his father's grave dark blue eyes and dark hair and square little jaw, Sandy dark-haired too but with his mother's beauty and more complicated nature. With them Mary Beth could pretend that her illness was only a game, that she could cut her meat herself if she wanted, zip her dress in the back, run to answer the phone. They weren't afraid. And so somehow she had conveyed to Bill just now that she wanted to sit with them in the car. "No, no, the back," she had managed to whisper, and then Bill had lifted her in.

He was driving slowly though it was no longer snowing. The yellow headlights lit up the furrows left by the snow plow. So deep was the snow on the sides of the road Mary Beth could hardly make out the familiar landmarks: the garbage dump, the golf course covered with skiers and sleds in the starry night, and now and then the houses almost lost behind great drifts, their lights tunneling through the shrubbery and fences.

Lance turned away from the window where he had been watching the sleighriding. "Dad has three scars," he said.

"No. He has four," Sandy said. "One from his appendix and three from the war."

"Three from the war," Lance said with awe. "Dad, do you have four scars?"

"Can't you boys talk about something else?" Bill said impatiently.

"Three from the war," Lance said to himself, in wonder.

Mary Beth took his hand under the blanket and the little boy leaned against her. His body was warm as toast. The bodies of little boys were fueled with energy, self-starting engines that needed just a touch to get going. She had had only one boy. One child. She looked at Bill. He had the window open and was hatless and the icy air rushed in.

Anna spoke for the first time. "It's freezing with that window open," she said.

"It's fresh air," Bill said in that tight voice he had these days.

"I don't care, I'm freezing. That's so goddamned typical of you, Bill. So thoughtless."

"You know damned well I'm allergic to cigarette smoke," Bill said.

"That's another of your crazy hangups," Anna said. "Like sleeping with all the windows open. God, I'm sick of sleeping with my robe and slippers on. That's just another instance of how selfish you are."

"Then stop smoking," he said.

"Never," Anna said. "Never." And she curled up against the door, pulling her scarf over her head, dragging on her cigarette and glaring at Bill. She had the profile of a saint, a beauty so pure, flawless that even angry she looked like an avenging angel. Tranquil she was a Della Robbia angel, so that it came as a shock to see her filled with fury as so much of the time she was. She flew at everyone with her shrill voice, possessed it would seem by a perverse demon, even the collie kept his distance. She was Italian, hot-hearted but not tender any more, not tender. Every day the marriage got worse, every day there was some new grievance that pulled Anna and Bill apart. Perhaps because Mary Beth sided with Bill, though only in silence with quivering lips and pained eyes, Anna was withdrawing with greater resentment than she would if Mary Beth were not living with them. Mary Beth looked at Bill's hair blowing in the wind and remembered when he was small and wore a Dutch cut, a gentle little boy who had not wanted to be fondled at all. He had come when she was almost forty, but she had been careful not to fondle and stroke him, thinking also he might grow up with a complex and develop emotional attachment to men if he were to become too close to his mother. Oh, no, she had kept hands off, and Jules had done the same, and Bill had grown up independent of them. Now how he needed to be touched! She longed to put out her hand and stroke his cheek where that small pulse of tension beat, put her arm around his shoulders and tell him everything was just fine. But he would never let her—he had his own need of pretending, and her touch would only tell him what he knew too well, that he was a stranger in his own house as was she, that Anna didn't love him. What a terrible thing! Mary Beth couldn't bear thinking about it. When Bill came home from work, late, from his brokerage firm in Wall Street where he escaped in the highs and lows of the stock market, he'd stand in the door of her room a minute or two. By then she would be propped up with pillows on the high bed, watching the news on television. Bill's face would be tense, uneasy, as if he didn't know what to expect and was bracing for the worst. The crystal ball was clouded. Soon it would be shattered. He was prematurely grey. He had an ulcer. He'd say in his edgy voice, "Hi—how's it going?" then leave her alone with Walter Cronkite or John Chancellor. Sometimes he'd stop in with a magazine or the newspaper. "Good piece on Washington," he'd say. She would be alone with James Reston. He hardly spent any time with her. It was as if he couldn't bring himself to look into her eyes, for she couldn't bear thinking about it and couldn't dissemble; no matter how she tried there were signals of distress. So left alone as she was Mary Beth fondled the boys, stroked their tousled hair, tickled them, let them climb over the bed, let their gerbils climb over her when the dog was out of the room. If she felt strong enough and her voice was good she would tell them about the past she would make believe was close, so close she was right back in those magical days, as full of spirit as they, as free. "Do you know I grew up in Harlem?" she would say. "Oh, yes, I did and it was wonderful. We lived in a townhouse that was opposite the Mott estate. I wonder what's happened to it now. Then we moved to Twenty West Seventieth Street. After school I went roller-skating in Central Park, and in the winter I went ice-skating with a boy named Mons Osterberg. He sent me Valentines addressed to Cupid's Terrace, Lovingdale and they were postmarked Lika You Much. I remember that so clearly! Yes, and I had elocution lessons and learned delsarte and carried my dancing slippers in a little velvet bag to the Hotel Majestic on Seventy-second Street and Central Park West—that's where the dancing school was—and I danced the waltz and two step and all the boys signed my card for each dance. They wore white gloves and bowed. Manners were as important as morals," Mary Beth would say, "and then we stepped out on the ballroom and we danced the two step and the waltz and we whirled round and round and wanted to dance forever."

"*Dancing* school!" Sandy would say with scorn, looking up from the Indian he was drawing. "Oh, *Nana!* Dancing school—that's sissy stuff!"

"I wouldn't like dancing school," Lance echoed. "That's sissy stuff!"

Mary Beth was transported, her blue eyes wide as she gazed out the window at the old oak that in her memory had become a stage. "Yes, and when I was in my teens I played in theatricals with the Columbia boys from Gamma Delta Psi fraternity. We played at the Hamilton Grange Reform Church at One Hundred Forty-ninth Street and Convent Avenue, and I was a moon-maid in *The Moon in the Picture.* I wonder what's happened to that church. Everything's changed so much."

She had talked too long. Suddenly her neck felt weak and she slumped down. Her eyelids fluttered, then closed.

"Are you asleep, Nana?" Lance asked.

"No. She's trying to breathe," Sandy said, coming closer.

"Through the hole?" Lance asked, fascinated.

"Does it hurt?" Sandy asked.

Their questions tired her though. They surely did. Sometimes she was so exhausted it was all she could do to take her pill, the Mestinon that was keeping her alive. "You're my water boy," she whispered to Lance as the child brought her the glass of water filled to overflowing and the pill dissolved at last. "You're my TV boy," she whispered to Sandy as he turned on the set. "That's the way it is," Walter Cronkite would say.

That was the way it was. When Anna and Bill were together there was either an uproar or they weren't speaking to each other, and then it was a different pain that consumed and grieved her and that was as hard to live with as MG. Lily stayed until Mary Beth's throat healed. The boys dashed in and out of her room until it seemed as full of commotion as Penn Station. They would tease each other and carry on and glad for the diversion she would let them. They would tease her. "What is a Baltimore Oriole, Nana?" "Why, that is a black and orange bird that sings a pretty song." "No, it isn't—it's a bird that plays *baseball!*" "Where's the great planes, Nana?" and she would say, "Oh, they're in Nebraska and Oklahoma." "No, they're not—they're in the great *hangars!*" She would laugh then. She would caress them and they would let her. Stroke their silky heads at bedtime as if to comfort them that their long day was over, they resisted it so. Time flows, Mary Beth thought. But where has it gone? Where is it? And what is it? It is us, and I cannot catch up. . . . The boys would settle down beside her, quiet at last. Then Anna would be on the scene. "Boys!" Anna would command, pulling them up. "Nana needs her rest. I want you to clean up your room right this minute. You've left it a mess. You know how that aggravates me. You're not two years old." Anna told Mary Beth she must not fuss over the boys so much, that she was spoiling them and making them difficult, and it touched the quick. We all touch each other's quick, Mary Beth thought, that is what hurts the most. In my house we were careful of each other's feelings. Oh, she hadn't wanted to live with Bill and Anna after Jules died, to be an in-law and a dependent at that, no longer her own woman, having to ask for everything, indulged then and humored and chastized even as the children were; but she came down with MG and it was either live with them or in a nursing home, and there wasn't enough money for a nursing home.

Bill was driving carefully on the snowy road. She had had an attack at dinner. The calf's liver wouldn't go down, it stuck in her windpipe and she lost her breath, her balance. She tried to get up and fell, lying there on the floor clutching her throat and gasping for air in wild terror. Bill phoned the doctor. It was another crisis. Then he bundled her up in her coat and hat and took her small suitcase with the few things she kept in it in case of emergency, her nightgown and bed jacket and toothbrush and all, and he carried her to the car, stepping over the roots of the old oak that thrust up through the snow. The tree was just outside her window and she would see its trunk all gnarled and full of boles and knots and think how it was like her life . . . its roots coming up all doubled-over with those knots, weathered from living so long, or loving, it came to the same thing in the end. . . . She looked at Bill and Anna, wanting to tell them: Speak to each other, say something nice even if you don't mean it, that's all it comes to in the end. . . . But they were silent. They had retreated within themselves. People in an unhappy marriage get enclosed in glass, Mary Beth thought. They have passed through fire and hardened, and I want to touch my boy and make everything right, and I can't, he just draws away. . . .

Last night Anna's voice had been so loud down the hall. "God, Bill, don't you ever think of someone besides yourself?"

"You're a great one to talk," Bill had said.

"Somebody's got to see to the house," Anna said.

"Hell, you're never around. Who gets the kids to bed, gives them their baths?" Bill said.

"Somebody's got to serve on the PTA who understands children," Anna said. She was so restless, spending hours on the phone and at her meetings, busy with clubs, activities, causes.

"Oh, for Christ's sake!" Bill said, his voice rising.

"You say nothing that's constructive," Anna stormed. "You *do* nothing that's constructive. That's right. Walk away. You've walked away from every issue the ten years I've been married to you. Because you're passive. *Passive.*"

Bill had turned on his heels and walked away. Sometimes after one of their scenes he would stop at Mary Beth's door to see if she'd heard and his cheek would twitch. He would look slighter, smaller, diminished by Anna's words as he gazed at her in silence. And Mary Beth would feel the weakness come over her from her head to her toes. His misery and her MG seemed one and the same. If she'd been able to, she couldn't touch him. He would just look at her and turn away and her heart would ache. Sometimes when she heard Bill and Anna at it, she would ring the little bell on her nighttable; but usually it would be one of the children who would come and hand her the glass of water for her pill. At least they were there. She didn't know what she would do without them. It was so hard living with Bill and Anna. It was so lonely she thought she could die of it. . . .

She looked at the boys again, Lance still curled up next to her, and she reached over to Sandy and held their hands together with hers under the blanket, but they began to push each other and Sandy kicked the front seat and his father said, "Stop doing that!" and they drove on without talking.

They were on the road to Glen Cove and the lights of the town turned the sky pink and the trees stood out against it with branches dark under the snow. Mary Beth would have loved the ride had she felt well, outings were a rarity, but they had been gone an eternity. The boys were giving each other pokes behind her back. It would end in a fight. She would try to distract them. First Lance, then Sandy who was the more intractable. Suddenly the moon began to rise, even as she watched, round and yellow and incredible as an eclipse. "Look, Lance," Mary Beth said slowly. "Over the hill there. See the moon?"

"It goes where we go," Lance said.

"No, it doesn't really," Sandy said. "It just seems to."

"The moon," Lance said, as if he could touch the word.

"Later tonight it will be white, not yellow, and it will shine on the snow," Mary Beth said in her slow weak way. "Won't that be lovely, Sandy?"

"The moon," Lance said, enchanted.

"It's getting white now," Sandy said with delight.

It rose even as they looked at it. They were in fairly open country and already it had left the hill, rising incredibly. Mary Beth remembered when she and Jules had looked in this section for a house. She felt the pang of loss again, a longing so keen for Jules that she let go the boys and put her hand to her breast, under the waning moon of her life she missed the past, or was it the loss of the future that held out so many options? "Shall we rent this house, or did you like the one with the fireplace? . . . Do you want to have dinner in the city, or shall we just go to the Club?" She remembered the large white bedroom she used to have with the dormer windows—which house was that in, the house on Brookside Drive, or Arleigh Road, or was it on Westgate Boulevard?—the wide bed under the windows, the highboy where every night Jules hung his pants from the top drawer when there was a whole closet for him to hang them in, and they would have words about it, laughing though, oh, yes, and the vanity table, yes, with her perfumes and silver brush and comb and flowers and pictures of the family all as much a part of her as her two hands. They moved so often and each time they did it was a wrench, but Jules had never wanted to own property, and either the landlord came back or something went wrong with the house the landlord wouldn't take care of, and with each move they lost a little of themselves. The dreams they had each time they moved! They had come to Great Neck because theater people and writers lived there, Jane Cowl and H. B. Warner, Ring Lardner and P. G. Wodehouse and Scott and Zelda Fitzgerald, and then when the amusing people drifted to Hollywood or abroad, they stayed on, moving from town to town as if they were in repertory. But Jules was a dear. She'd have gone anywhere with him. She thought how handsome he was with his mane of dark hair and strong features that made him look so commanding. He looked like an actor, she said. Even a great one, he said, and then he would act the part when they had company, turning his profile like John Barrymore and waving a white handkerchief at her as if she were Ophelia. Oh, he was a dear. Before Bill came along they spent almost every weekend in the city—New York was always "the city"—they would get on the Long Island Railroad with its yellow straw seats and in an hour they would check in at the Algonquin where they would say hello to George Kaufman and Dorothy Parker and all those wonderful people, and then they would go to the Café Martin, or Jack's, or the St. Regis roof garden, or the Brevoort where they threw confetti at Lindbergh in his thrilling parade. And they went many times to speakeasies where good Scotch was plentiful and Mary Beth felt daring and took off her wedding ring just to pretend she was having an affair with this handsome devil.

Time flows. The memories rushed back, so many they made her head spin, and who was there to listen, who could make them seem something she had not dreamed? To Lily who was so kind, Mary Beth said, "I have seen apple blossom time in Normandy, lilac time in Kew, cherry blossom time in Washington. I have seen the three crossroads of the world—the Rue de la Paix, Hollywood and Vine, and Times Square. One New Year's Eve Jules and I went to Times Square and a woman asked him if he was Douglas Fairbanks and Jules said yes, he was and he signed his autograph! That's how dashing he was!" "That's nice to think about, isn't it?" Lily said, gently brushing back Mary Beth's hair. She had wept when Lily left. Now she was truly alone. And the days were truly endless and seemed like a single black night as, desolate, she wondered how someone as vivid as Jules could be gone.

So she told the children about him when they sat quietly drawing pictures or looking at comic books. "I met your grandfather," she said, "at the *Dramatic Mirror* when we both were working there. I wrote the movie reviews and signed my name Mademoiselle Rialto, and he was the Editor, and we went to all the first nights, we saw every show that opened on Broadway! I had an original Patou dress that was black with yellow sleeves and I wore it to the musicals. We loved the musicals! Your grandfather knew Fred and Adele Astaire and Florenz Ziegfeld and Marilyn Miller. He knew Cole Porter and Irving Berlin and George Gershwin and everyone! He wrote songs himself. He wrote one for my cat. That's why I married him."

"He wrote a song for your *cat?*" Sandy asked with surprise. "Can you sing it?"

"'Oh, Marse Wheeney comes a-walking down the lane,'" Mary Beth sang. "'Sees a girl a-looking through the windowpane.' He was so much fun. I'd never met anybody like your grandfather. He wrote this *lovely* song for my cat and he sang it to Marse Wheeney."

"I like cats," Lance said softly.

"So do I!" Mary Beth said as she pulled the boys closer. "Oh, I remember when your grandfather was doing publicity for the Shuberts and he got the orchestra from *Blossom Time* to come to Central Park Zoo. They played the lovely music from that show to the lions and tigers in their cages, and those big cats stopped pacing around and stood still and listened!"

Jules, the charmer. The magician. The exact sense of that day came back to her as she closed her eyes then and saw the azaleas and cherry trees in bloom, their petals floating with the balloons in the flawless blue sky. Standing with Jules behind the orchestra, her foot keeping time to the music that always seemed to surround him. Jules, the composer. He could be as famous as Cole Porter, she used to tell him, if he'd just work at his songs, the entire world would sing them. . . . "Yes, the lions and tigers stopped roaring and listened!" she said.

"They did?" Sandy and Lance exclaimed, together.

"Oh, yes, they did!" Mary Beth replied. "But that was because your grandfather was standing behind the orchestra and holding up a big piece of meat! And so the photographer took this wonderful picture of those lions and tigers looking so intent with their shining eyes, as if they *loved* the music. The picture got in all the newspapers." She paused, thinking a lot more than that day had been lost. "I wonder what happened to that picture. I wish I had it to show you."

Anna and Bill had cleared out Mary Beth's house of all those photographs and clippings and treasures. God knows what they'd done with them, carted them to the garbage dump probably. Only the photograph of Jules was left, the one of him sitting in the hollow of a tree, with his Cheshire Cat grin and his hat at a jaunty angle. That was taken when Jules had settled down to being a reporter at the *World-Telegram* if it could be said he'd ever settled down. Often when he wasn't on a story he'd phone her to come to the city from Great Neck or Manhasset or Plandome or wherever it was they were living. She wasn't working then and she'd leave Bill with her sister and brother-in-law who lived near those towns and get on the train and meet Jules at the Algonquin, and then they'd have dinner and go to some wonderful show or party.

"Your grandfather did the most *fantastic* things!" Mary Beth told the boys as another memory flashed into her head. "He was a member of the Cheese Club that was made up of newspaper people and theatrical agents, and one day they all marched in a parade down Eighth Avenue from Fifty-ninth Street to Thirty-fourth Street and then over to Broadway and back up again. The Fifth Avenue Association wouldn't let them march down Fifth, because they were wearing overalls and there were elephants too."

"Were there many elephants, Nana?" Lance asked, enthralled.

"Oh, yes," she said, enthralled herself at the idea of it. "Many elephants with show girls sitting on them! Everyone was wearing overalls because they were so practical, you see—the parade was to call attention to the high cost of living. Then when the parade ended everyone went to the Waldorf and had a wonderful party. He was such a gadabout, your grandfather, and so was I!"

She started to tell the boys about a party at Texas Guinan's nightclub where a man had taken *her* for a movie actress, Ruby Keeler, because she'd had her dark hair bobbed in bangs and had tap-danced around the table to Jules. But Sandy and Lance had lost interest and were down on the floor racing their small Ferraris and Porsches about. Mary Beth looked at Jules's picture on the bureau, then out the window, and then closing her eyes she tricked back the memory till she could see Jules standing at the window grinning at her, blowing his breath on the misty pane and writing on it: IT'S WONDERFUL! MLLE RIALTO. DON'T MISS IT! MLLE RIALTO. God, do I! she thought, her eyes blurring. For she longed for him with a knowledge of her own extinction, soon maybe this awful lingering would be over and she'd be with him, her endearing and restless ghost.

Lost in memory, she asked the boys one day: "Do you ever pretend?"

"Sure!" Sandy smiled.

"Sure I do," Lance said eagerly. "Do you, Nana?"

"All the time," Mary Beth said. She liked to pretend Jules was going to walk in any minute, saying he had news for her, his arms wrapped around her. Or maybe he would be playing Cole Porter's songs on the piano. Gershwin's songs. College songs.

> Oh, the red hot spot
> To cast your lot
> Is with old DKE. . .

Where was the Deke pin? Mary Beth missed the tokens of his presence. She hadn't seen it in months—in two years in fact. "I will give you each a dollar if you find my little Deke pin," she said to the boys. "It's shaped like a diamond and is black and has gold letters DKE on it. Your grandfather gave it to me and it's precious." They couldn't find it and Anna was irritated when she saw them rummaging through the living room desk. "What on earth are you doing?" Anna asked. "Looking for Nana's Deke pin," they said. "Fraternities are an evil. In fact they're stupid and passé," Anna told Mary Beth. So that answered that. But what had happened to all Jules's things? His lucky silver dollar he always stroked before he bet on a horse or bought a new suit? Where was the Working Press card that he wore on his hat? The watch Jack Dempsey had given him? After Jules died Mary Beth had sat down on the floor with his writings heaped about her, bewildered by their sheer profusion and devastated by their vitality. "Nothing as dead as yesterday's newspaper," Jules used to say, but here were his best newspaper pieces, his unproduced plays, his songs carefully scored, his journals, those wonderful journals in which he listed wines he'd drunk, restaurants he'd been to, shows he'd seen, celebrities he'd known, the names of winning pitchers, racehorses, boxers, the Great Books he'd read. How she'd loved his journals. And she had marveled how things lived on when the person to whom they had meant so much was gone, that the chair he always sat in had survived him, that the silver cup he drank milk out of as a little boy had outlasted even his old age. Only what had happened to the things he loved, that were invested with such passionate caring they had a life of their own, a luster and patina that comforted her, touched as they had been by him? After his death, numbed with grief she had walked around touching his things. She hated to think they had been thrown out with the garbage. So in time she came to play a game of pretense, with eyes shut she would imagine that Jules would be there, that he would be telling her again about when he was a Deke at Yale—he was so proud of making Deke—and about the great time he had when he wrote, directed and acted in the college musical, *New Havenights,* and about the tables down at Mory's, and his old girls who never had her appeal. . . .

Then she would hear Jules playing his own songs on the piano.

"I just want to be your lit-tle love, tur-tle dove, and all the other names too."

"You must write it down!" Mary Beth had told him.

"I just did," Jules said as he bent over the keys. "Listen to *this*, Emmy Bee! 'I know the day when you're going to pop the question. Saw it in your eyes. You al-ways seem to dis-cover my in-tentions. You are ex-tremely wise. . . .' "

Oh, yes, and Jules phoning her from the Shuberts' one morning. "We're sailing at midnight on the 'France'! Pack the bags!"

"But we can't. I haven't the right clothes!" Mary Beth had cried.

"Buy them," he said. "We've got our passports . . ."

She'd packed their suitcases and then in the city she'd bought a pale yellow chiffon dress and a chartreuse velvet evening wrap and a navy knit suit and cloche and sensible shoes, and the entire crossing to Cherbourg she hadn't worn her wedding ring. At the Captain's table, where they sat, Senator Wadsworth played footsie with her and Jules flirted with all the women, and in the lounge in the evening they listened to Helen Morgan sitting on the piano and singing "My Bill." It was like *Show Boat* being married to Jules. The curtain went up on a new act all the time. Paris. How marvelous it was. In bed with each other and the reflections of the street lights thrown up and moving over the ceiling, moving over them, and it was as if it had never happened so excitingly before, they were new to each other. That was Paris. Everything new . . . And then the "Golden Arrow" to Calais and the Channel steamer and Dover and again the train flying past the lovely villages. Then London. Mayfair and pageantry. More shows. More shops. More dancing and love and fun. For a few years it almost seemed they commuted abroad. Yes, it made the painful drift of her days bearable when she could remember how it was living with Jules. . . .

But then Mary Beth would recall when he went into the hospital with cancer. "Should I wear the grey suit for the Confederacy or the blue suit for the Union?" he'd asked with a gleam in his eyes, fighting the ordeal in his whimsical way. When they wheeled him in he had on his blue suit and Charvet tie with little fishes swimming on blue silk, and for a few days after the operation his spirits were high and she had laughed as he told her how he'd had a hallucination the man in the next bed was she. "Yeah,

I tried to get up," said Jules, "and get in with him. I thought he'd be all warm and snuggly." His eyes had rested with relief and gratitude on the bottle of intravenous attached to his hand; but his stomach was still swollen like a football from the cancer—the operation had been unavailing, it was all through him. On his last good day Bill and Anna had stopped in, then they left and stood on the ground below with the children who were waiting with Mary Beth's sister Connie, Lance just two years old, Sandy only four. Mary Beth had cranked up the bed so that Jules could see them from the window, and the children waved to him and he waved feebly back. Then Jules had turned and looked at her and that was the last time he talked to her.

"Emmy Bee!" he said urgently, and the little grimace she had come to fear passed over his face.

"What do you want, dear?" she asked.

"You," he said.

She held his hand tightly. "Oh, your pink Scotch cheeks and your blue eyes," Mary Beth said. "Bluebell," she said, stroking his hand.

Jules's eyes lingered on her face and then closed and he smiled.

Oh, I'd like to cry but I cannot let him see me, she thought. Stroking his hand which was curled up now like a little child's, she thought: How will I live without him? Words from the old hymn "the strife is o'er, the battle done" entered her mind. What battle? she asked herself, fiercely wanting to fight the dread invader in his body. It's not over and never will be.

Then she thought: Love is long too and never ends. It's all you have out of life really and it brings you such pain. Grieving she thought: I am barely holding on. This silence falls already. Knuckles in her mouth—silent screaming—watching now the tiny silver ball bounce up and down with his heartbeat on the monitoring machine. His vital sign . . .

Mary Beth remembered what transpired a few days later. She saw Jules in the coma without his dentures. Had he known that he would have had a fit, he was such a dresser, so vain—did he know what he looked like then? she wondered. His face like a mask, and without his dentures? Did he feel his hand in hers? Could he hear her? "Jules, this is Emmy Bee. I'm here, darling." Did his forehead seem to clear as she spoke? What time do you leave the body? There were times now Mary Beth felt she had already left hers.

It was a back road Bill had taken where the traffic was light and he could make better time, though they still crept along over the furrows and patches of ice the snow plow had cleared. There was an occasional house and now and then a car went by coming the other way. That was a sound Mary Beth liked, the sound of cars rushing past in the night, making a whoosh . . . life rushing out in a whoosh . . . yes, that's what it was like whether or not you were on the respirator. One second you were there and the next you were gone. Where had Jules gone inside himself in the coma? Where was he now? She could hear herself breathing. It sounded labored, loud in her ears. It sounded like a whoosh.

This knocking in the blood was a sexual thing. Is it you after all this time, Jules? Mary Beth wondered. I seem to hear your voice just the way it was, but like a whisper, dear. Are you really there? I wish it so. Suddenly she felt her strength leaving her. She fell into a semi-conscious state, not feeling anything but a dark hollow place which opened to her, so easeful it was. Close your eyes in the warm dark, stop fighting for breath—that hurts dreadfully—let it have its way, this thing pressing down on your chest like all the weakness has coalesced there and weighs so heavily that you gasp with each breath. You are exhausted, so give over, that's it, just lapse and let go. Deeper she fell into the pulsating dark. And she wanted to go, though life had been like a cloud rainbowed by the sun, so bright it had been, so variously bright it had been. Perhaps that was why she couldn't go, because the cloud touched her still, things she had to do. . . . A stirring of will, deep within and stabbing needles of pain into her spine, jolted her awake with her eyes on Bill. I diapered you, she said to the back of Bill's head. I kissed your fuzzy head when you were sleeping. She saw his stricken face bent over the respirator, saying something she couldn't understand. He had sat down and then it seemed like he was breathing with the respirator, up and down, breathing with her and it was like when she'd carried him. She would try for Bill. She struggled to stay awake and let the needles do their work. Your father wrote his poem "The Good Ship Bassinet" when you were just two weeks old. You were "the captain, mate and crew," Bill. Do you remember? And Jules wrote

I dread the coming of the morn
When he will sail no more
To leave the good ship Bassinet
To take on years and youth (my pet)
And reach a worldly shore.

The poem had been lost along with everything else, but Mary Beth took it as a positive sign that she remembered how it ended. Bill had reached that worldly shore and it was filled with anguish and peril. For him, for the boys, for Anna even she would try.

He and Anna were sitting as far apart as they could get from each other, and Anna was looking at Bill with narrowed eyes, her face a study. Mary Beth felt it coming on again—the band of pain pressing in her lungs, choking and strangling her, it was so heavy now that her breath came in short gasps. She was in that state again where each breath was like a hill to climb, and when you got to the top, if you ever did, you couldn't breathe for the weakness that pulled you down, paralyzing you into stone. She was seized with terror that she couldn't breathe—couldn't move. When would they get there? Would they do another trach—put her on the respirator? She'd rather die than go through that. "I can't breathe, Bill!" she called out in fear. "Hurry!" But her voice was so whispery, and the children were fighting. Sandy was shoving Lance behind her back. "Give me the space helmet. It's mine," Sandy said.

"Daddy gave it to me. It's not yours," Lance said.

"We traded it, stupid," Sandy said. "Because I traded you my Ferrari."

"Oh, boys," Mary Beth whispered, but they didn't hear her.

"I can beat you up," Sandy said.

"You cannot," Lance said.

"I'll punch you in the nose if you don't give it to me," Sandy said.

"Dad," Lance said. "Sandy's messing around."

"Will you kids behave?" Bill said.

"It's not me. It's Sandy," Lance said.

"I want you to behave, both of you," Bill said. "Just shut up."

"Don't talk to them like that," Anna said. "That's no example."

"Listen, you're no rose," Bill said.

Anna leaned over and blew cigarette smoke in his face.

"You're such a sweet thing," Bill said.

"Damn you, Bill," Anna said. "Why did I come along anyway? What am I doing here? I don't know what I'm doing here."

"Mighty like a rose," Bill said.

"Oh, damn you for dragging me along," Anna said. "I mean that but you don't understand a word I'm saying and never have. I wish I'd stayed home."

Their loud voices startled Mary Beth, summoning new anguish. Hate-love. If only she could believe that there was love underneath. If only she could tell them how fine it was with someone. That was something she had to do. . . .

Smoke blew back with the wind. "Mommy," Lance said. Anna didn't answer him. Anna blew a smoke ring and then she said, "I'm the one that should be going to the hospital. I'm having a nervous breakdown. I'm blowing up a storm and it's such fun. When people don't expect you to cope, then you don't. Tell me what you expect of me, Bill. What you really think of me, I mean."

"Quit bitching, will you?" Bill said. "I'm sick and tired of it."

"I'm having a nervous breakdown. It's fun exploding into little splinters. It's like a strait jacket being around you," Anna said.

"I wish you had stayed home," Bill said.

"Well, I wish I had," Anna said. "It's how you're *treated* that matters. Only you wouldn't know that."

"How *you're* treated," Bill said. He put his foot on the brake so hard the car skidded. "For Christ's sake, Anna, I'm trying to drive!"

"What's that story about the splinter of glass that gets into the boy's eye and he can't see what's good anymore?" Anna said.

"It's 'The Snow Queen,'" Sandy said.

"Yes, and I'm the Snow Queen, only it's me that's exploding into little splinters," Anna said. "Oh, hell, what's the good of talking? It's such a bloody bore."

The moon went slipping and gliding through the trees, whiter now, so full, the man in it smiling, do you see him, boys? Only Mary Beth didn't know where their thoughts were or even where her own were, everything was so muddled now, time was all muddled. She was in the car with Bill and Anna and they were quarreling and it grieved her so much she had to shut it out. She had to reach back to her memories. Now she was a young woman lying on that big white bed under the dormer windows. Now she was a child swinging her dancing slippers in a velvet bag. She and Jules were fanning themselves with newspapers on the Long Island Railroad, sighing at the heat. Only it was as if she'd dreamed it all. Was that what you lived for, to fill your head with dreams that had no more reality than the man in the moon? Once someone's gone, he's gone forever, she thought. Once something's gone, it's a fantasy. Through the trees, over the hills, like a great round lamp the moon went. It's the man in the moon, Mary Beth thought. It's as if I made them all up, the memories. It's "The Waltz Dream" as Jules would say. Life wasn't a single dream, it was many dreams, so many they dazzled and left her with unsatisfied longing. And now it was as if she were only looking on for what she saw in her memory had no reality. If there was just someone I could talk to, she thought. There's no one. There's just myself, and I've a clenched fist in my chest where it strangles me to breathe and my heart's a lump of ice like in "The Snow Queen," chilled through with dread, I cannot shake it from me. Oh, what? The boys are whispering something. They seem so far away. . . .

They were whispering behind her back. "I know a secret," Sandy said.

"Tell me," Lance said.

"If you let me have the helmet," Sandy said.

"All right. *Tell* me!" Lance said.

"The moon's made of cheese," Sandy said.

"That's no secret," Lance said.

"It's craters and rocks and dust and things and the astronauts walked on it," Sandy said.

Lance looked out the window. The white hills shone in the moonlight. "Oh," he said in a hushed voice. "The moon."

"Give me the helmet now," Sandy said.

"All right," Lance said. He took the helmet off his head and gave it to Sandy who put it on.

"I love night," Sandy said in a moment. "There are so many things to see. That star. It's so bright."

"What star?" Lance said.

"That one. It's part of a constellation. It's part of the Big Dipper," Sandy said, pointing to it.

"I see it," Lance said. Then he was looking at the moon again. "The *moon.* The *moon,*" he said in hushed wonderment.

"The *moon,*" breathed Sandy.

The boys collided behind Mary Beth's back, their voices marveling as overhead rose the full white moon. They were laughing and telling each other secrets. They were caught up in their own secret world that had nothing to do with anyone else. Mary Beth felt she had accidentally collided with them. She felt the moon and the stars were riding along with them on a mysterious course whose trajectory went in circles and whose silence you could never enter. You were just thrown against this person and that person and then everyone was separate again. Yes, she felt, when all was said and done it was an accident—she had accidentally collided with Jules and Bill and Anna and the children, and her friends she used to see all the time, and Lily who was so kind—and then you all were separate again. You touched each other for a little while and it was as accidental as your fingernail scraping the icy whorls on the windowpane—you couldn't really see what it was like outside, you couldn't make anything out, it was as if no one was there, only a glimmer, something shining. "I'd like to call on you, dear, and talk to you of love." That was another of Jules's songs. Maybe if she sang it to herself long enough she would believe it.

"If you'll be con-de-scending I'll promise to be true. I won't be late if I make a date to call on you." That one came back now in his voice that was a tender whisper. "I'd like to walk with you, dear, with just the stars a-bove." But she couldn't remember how the rest of it went.

They were finally in the town. Bill drew the car up beside the hospital entrance. It was ablaze with lights. Mary Beth could not lift herself up and an attendant wheeled out a chair and put her in it. She slumped down, and taking the chair a nurse put her hat securely on her head. Mary Beth felt like closing her eyes, for so distant were they all now, Bill and Anna and the children, as if memory had made them all smaller, already leaving her, she could hardly make them out.

Then Lance, slim and serious, was standing next to her. "Nana," he said, looking at her. "Are you younger than Mommy?"

"Of course she's not, dopey," Sandy said.

"But you're so little," Lance said to her.

"Yes, I'm little now, honey," Mary Beth said in a whisper he didn't hear as she tried to bring his hand to her lips. He looked so like Bill, and like Bill he darted away to look in a shop window that was filled with gifts. Then Sandy ran over to him and put his arm around Lance's shoulders and said something that made them laugh. Come back, Mary Beth wanted to say to them. Don't go away just yet. You'll be big before I know it, and what I'll never know hurts. Everything hurt: the needles in her spine, the ache in her lungs as her breath came in shallow gasps. And she wanted to say don't go away to the rainbowed cloud of her life, but what she said to the nurse was, "This is my home away from home!" with a toss of her head that made the nurse smile.

THE PHOTOTROPIC WOMAN

ANNABEL THOMAS

Annabel Thomas is from Columbus, Ohio. She has published twenty-five short stories in such magazines as *Epoch*, *Prairie Schooner*, and *Kansas Quarterly*. One of her stories appeared once before in the O. Henry Awards (1979), and she is now working on her fifth novel. She lives in Ashley, Ohio, with her husband.

The woman was rolled up in a woollen blanket. It covered her body and even her head so that her world was warm and soft as an unborn's. When the alarm went off, she got out of bed and poked up the stove.

She put water to heat and when it was steaming she stripped to the waist and washed in the basin. She pulled a sweater over her head and plaited up her hair. While she drank a mug of strong black tea, she read the survival book.

After she put the shack in order, the woman took a coil of rope and a box of candles and walked up the sun-speckled path through the locust thicket between the green mossed rocks big as sheep sheds. She had worn the path carrying and dragging the provisions the book recommended to the cave.

The cave smelt of damp sandstone and of dust and still air. She dropped the rope beside the boxes of canned goods and was counting the candles when she heard a noise like hundreds of nine pins falling onto a wooden floor. When she turned round she saw dirt and rock pouring into the mouth of the cave. Before she could move toward it, the opening was completely closed and she stood coughing in blackness.

The woman felt her way to the boxes and found the coal oil lantern and the matches. When the wick caught, the light

First appeared in WIND/*Literary Journal*, Vol. 10, No. 36. Reprinted by permission.

reflected from a hundred rock surfaces overhead and around the edges while the middle was murky with floating dust. It was like standing inside a gem.

She took a pickax and dug where the entrance had been. She kept digging until she was too tired to dig anymore.

"There's no use to that," the woman said.

In fact she wondered if she should try to get out at all, at least right away. Had she seen a flash of light just before the dirt came down? The woman stood still a long time thinking what she should do.

She began by pacing off the room. It was twenty by fifteen feet. Then she felt the roof, tracing it back to where it closed down like a clamshell.

She took the pickax and pried gently where the roof joined the floor. As she widened a crack in the stone she felt air rush through. She worked slowly and hesitantly, half afraid of digging out into poisoned air.

When the hole was large enough, she took the lantern and crawled into the opening. Working forward on her belly, she wriggled down through the mud thick as grease. Her hair became caked and her clothes clogged with it. It went up her sleeves and down into her shoes.

The tunnel began to spiral like a corkscrew and to taper so that she got stuck sometimes, then squirmed loose and so at last came out of the tunnel onto the floor of a large room.

Wherever she shined the light she saw pillars with rock hanging from them in folds like cloth. She couldn't see the top of the room. She circled the walls. There was no way out except the way she'd come in.

Back in the upper room, she scooped out a trench with the pickax, laid large flat stones over the trench and closed the cracks with pebbles and mud. At the higher end she built a chimney from a small hollow tree limb. At the lower end she placed a handful of shredded bark and struck a match to it. She added twigs, then larger sticks from the supply of squaw wood she had gathered and stored in the cave. She kept the fire small. Every move she made came straight out of the survival book. She called up the pages in her mind's eye, then did what they said. When the fire burned steadily, she cooked soup.

Working and resting, then working again, the woman slowly

enlarged the tunnel, hacking out handholds and footholds until she could pass up and down easily. At the far end of the lower room she found a trickle of water spreading thin and soundless over the face of the rock. She set a bucket to catch it where it dripped off a projection. By feeling her pulse, she calculated the minutes it took for the dripping water to fill the bucket. Each time she judged twenty-four hours had gone by she made a mark on the cave wall with a piece of sandstone. One day she totaled up the marks. She had been in the cave somewhat over twelve days.

As time passed, the woman gradually made herself a proper home in the upper room. She arranged the boxes for chairs and a table, cooked good meals on the fireplace she had built and after she had eaten, spread a blanket over the warm stones and slept.

She wondered what was going on outside. Was the world burnt to ashes? Were scarred people picking about through swelling corpses, twisted metal, broken glass? Or was everything as it had been and the sun shining calm and warm down through the leaves spotting the path. The thought of the sun gave her heart a twist as if a coal of fire had touched her in her breast.

Below the water trickle in the lower room, the woman discovered a small underground pool in a rock basin.

"The old fishing hole," she said for in the pool were strange white fish.

Instead of swimming away from her, they froze in the water when she reached for them. She seined them out easily with her skirt. They were three or four inches long. On either side of their heads, she found bulges covered with skin where the eyes had been.

She slit the fish open, gutted them and pinned them with thorns to a smooth log which she propped close to the fire. The book had told how.

"Survival," the woman said to the fish. "Mine, not yours."

On one of her fishing trips, she noticed, in a small recess filled with boulders on the far side of the pool, what appeared to be a piece of cloth caught beneath the bottom stone. It was of a coarse weave like burlap. She couldn't pull it free. Every day she passed by it she felt of the cloth.

"What is it?" she said.

Finally she took along the pickax and pried the boulders loose, rolling them off, one by one, across the floor. She worked gingerly, afraid of starting a cave-in and burying herself. As each boulder fell away, more of the cloth showed until she could see a large bundle wedged into a depression. She bent forward and lifted away the final stone, then started back, giving a little shriek.

"God in heaven," she said. "It's an Indian!"

"He won't scalp you," she added a moment later, peering down. "He's been dead so long the meat's gone dry on his bones."

Although the long hair was much as it had been in life, the skin was blackish and hard and part of the skull was bare. The fiber blanket lay in patches over the rib cage. Beside the corpse was a small piece of gourd and a bundle of reeds tied together with grass.

"Came in out of a storm," the woman said, "and here he is still, poor bastard."

Leaning down to touch the Indian's blanket, the woman saw that the recess was a crawl way into yet another room.

She called the upper cave, "Home," and the second chamber, "the Indian Room." The third, the new one, became, "the Bat Room." The third room was fair sized though not so big nor so beautiful as the Indian Room. When the woman first heard the bats squeaking from a great distance overhead, she set the lantern on a rock and dug out handholds and footholds in the wall with a can lid. Following the method described in the survival book, she slapped the hand grips first and listened to hear if they sounded loose or cracked before going up carefully. She eased her foot into the vertical slits, twisting her ankle sideways, slipping in her toe, then straightening the ankle.

Now and then she paused in her climb to light a candle and have a look around. Once she saw a cave cricket, palest white and long-legged, creeping up the rock. Later she came upon the disintegrating body of a millepede with a white fungus encasing it like a shroud.

Pulling herself onto a ledge, she suddenly clapped her hands over her ears to shut out what sounded like the roaring of the biggest airplane motor in the world. Stretching her candle up at arm's length, she saw the bats, very high up, in a vast smoky cloud.

The ledge where she stood held a pool of bat droppings, a wide brown lake smelling of ammonia. As the candlelight slid across it she saw it move. She bent over, shining the light full on it. It was seething with living creatures. Tens of thousands of beetles, flat worms, snails, millepedes and mites were swimming on the surface or crawling on the bottom of the guano. All of them were colorless and all of them were blind.

Where the bats came in, she couldn't tell. She felt no air and saw no light. When the rock of the walls grew too hard to dig, she had to climb back down. She never came in sight of the ceiling.

Next she explored a number of small passageways opening off the Bat Room. Most dead-ended, choked with fallen rock. The rest opened onto horrifying drops. One descended and became an underground stream which she waded until the roof closed down to the water. Then she turned back.

The woman now believed that she had examined every room and passageway accessible to her and that there was no way out of the cave.

She settled into a routine of fishing, cooking, eating and sleeping. Time flowed on, sluggish and slow. She hung in it, drowsily.

But she dreamed strange dreams. And all her dreams were about light. At first she couldn't remember them but woke with only the imprint of brightness on her eyes like an aftertaste on the tongue.

Later, she recalled scenes in which she lay doubled inside a giant egg, walled away from the light. As she beat on the shell, stretching toward the light, she could feel the light outside straining toward her. At last, with a cracking like a mighty explosion, she straightened her arms and legs sending the shell into bits. As she thrust forth into hot brightness, she looked to see if it were the sun or the flash of an explosion that beat upon her but she never found out.

When the coal oil was gone and the woman began to use the candles more and more sparingly, the shape of day and night blurred and faded from her life. Her meals became irregular. She ate as often as she felt hungry. Sometimes she forgot to eat at all for long stretches. She let the bucket overflow or forgot to mark the wall so often that at last she lost all track of how long she had been in the cave.

Once, as she opened a can by candlelight, she lifted the lid and looked at her reflection in the shiny tin circle.

She saw that her face and arms had grown pasty. Her clothes

were colorless from dirt and wear. She had broken her glasses when she climbed the wall of the Bat Room so that she peered at herself through eyes slightly out of focus. The skin hung loose on her cheeks and drew taut across the sharp bridge of her nose. Her hair, trailing loose on her shoulders, was pale with dust.

The candle sputtered, brightened, then, burned to its end, died. She reached for another. The candles rattled against one another in the box. So few left? Her hands shook, counting them. How many more hours of light? Not many. Then the dark.

As the woman let the candles fall from her fingers, a strange restlessness came upon her. She moved to the cave mouth and felt of the mass of dirt and rock which covered it. She caught up the pickax and dug until she couldn't lift it for another stroke.

After that she often counted the candles and as often dug at the entrance. Blisters broke on her hands and bled. Sweat dripped off her chin. Her body burned. It was as if she felt the light through the tons of dirt over her head, pulling her toward it whether she wanted to go or not. She dug until her arm went numb. Then she threw herself on the floor and slept. When she woke, she dug again.

Sometimes she dropped the pickax and fell to tearing at the dirt and rocks with her fingers. Afterward she cleaned her hands and wrapped them in strips she tore from her skirt.

At last she left off digging and circled the Indian Room and the Bat Room each in turn again and again, feeling of the walls, climbing where she could gouge out a hand and foothold, going as far up as she was able, then dropping back.

Next she re-examined each of the passageways at the end of the Bat Room. One passage ended in a shallow pit carved into the stone with walls round like a chimney and stretching up out of sight. Down this chimney, it seemed to the woman, there poured like steady rain a strange dark light.

She placed her back against one wall of the chimney and lifted both her feet onto the wall opposite. She pressed a hand against the rock on either side of her buttocks and so levered her body off the wall. She inched her way up, alternately pressing her feet against one wall and her back against the other. Soon the chimney narrowed so that she was forced to use her knees instead of her feet and after a time she began to slip.

She slid down, caught herself, and started up once more. Her back and knees were raw and bleeding. The portions of her sweater and skirt covering them had worn away. She slipped again, reached out her hands to catch herself, tried to hold onto the sides of the pit, could not, and fell heavily, shot down like a stone, and hit the cave floor with a yell loud enough to wake the dead Indian.

When she tried to stand, the woman's ankle wouldn't bear her weight. It took her a long time to drag herself back to the Home Chamber. Once there, she mixed a poultice of mud and spread it on the ankle from the middle of the calf to the instep. Gradually it hardened into a cast.

The woman lay wrapped in her blanket on the warm stones while, slowly, her bruises and scrapes began to heal. She had used to talk to herself aloud a good part of the time. Now, she fell deeper and deeper into silence until her thoughts lost the shape of words and shot through her brain in strange flashes of feeling and impulse.

In her dreams she repeated the accident and repeated it, always waking with the sensation of having been, in falling, drenched with light. She slept, woke, ate, slept again. Her ankle ached less, then not at all. When she judged enough time had passed, the woman took a small stone and pounded the mud cast gently so that it cracked and fell away. She walked up and down the Home Cave until her ankle grew strong.

When she was able to return to the Indian Room and the Bat Room, she again explored the walls and passages, ending at last with the underground river. She waded the stream to the point where the overhead rocks narrowed down to touch the water. The river deepened as the roof came down so that she stood in water to her armpits.

She filled her lungs and swam downstream under the rocks. Feeling with her fingers that the roof still touched the water and still touched and still touched, she swam back.

She tried again. Then again. Before each try she breathed in and out rapidly and so was able to stay under water longer. With each attempt she went further until, when she felt the roof begin to rise, she pushed on and broke from the water into a narrow tunnel with air at the top and headroom enough to stand upright.

Back in the Home Chamber, the woman took the rope into her lap. She ran a few feet of its cold damp length through her fingers. The day she had carried it to the cave, it had been warm from the sun. She tore a strip from the bottom of her blanket and tied it to the rope. She added another strip and another until she had tied on the whole of the blanket.

At the river, she knotted one end of the rope around her waist and looped the other over a rock projection. Wading slowly downstream, she felt a slight push of current at the backs of her legs. Her thigh touched a fish hanging still in the water.

Swimming to the spot where she had stood before, she walked on in waist-high water. She could reach out her hands and touch both walls of the tunnel that held the river. The roof hung a few feet above her.

The woman moved on in blackness, trailing the rope. When she rubbed her eyes she saw pale flashes far back inside her head.

Several yards beyond the point where she'd turned back before, she began to feel the roof closing rapidly down again, grazing her head so that she must stoop to go forward. When her feet lost touch with the bottom she began to swim.

The water was numbing cold. Her clothes hung on her like the metal plates of a suit of armor. Only her head was above water and still the roof brushed her hair and she felt it closing, closing.

The woman took several quick, deep breaths, filled her lungs, and dove down through the water. Leveling off, she shot ahead rapidly, keeping a steady forward push with arms and legs, hands and feet. She continued on for the length of her body, then her body's length again. And again. As she swam she waited for the tug at her waist that would tell her she had reached the rope's end, the point of no return. When it came, she slipped the knot and swam out of the rope, leaving it to curl in the water behind her.

Her lungs began to ache in earnest. The blood, pounding behind her eyes, filled her head with flashes of bright color. Stubbornly she kept up her steady breast stroke, her frog kick, until the expanding and contracting of her muscles became the structure of her consciousness.

She tried to remember her life outside the cave but she could not. She tried to recall the details of her days in the Home Chamber, the Indian and the Bat Rooms but they were washed from her brain leaving only the sensation of inward scalding light creating, destroying her in its struggle to be born.

BRIEF LIVES IN CALIFORNIA

JOHN L'HEUREUX

John L'Heureux, from South Hadley, Massachusetts, is Associate Professor of English and Director of the Writing Program at Stanford University. He is the author of ten books of poetry and fiction. "Brief Lives in California" will appear in his next collection of stories, *DESIRES*, to be published this year by Holt, Rinehart and Winston.

Leonora started out pretty and bright.

"She could be a movie star," her mother said, "but I would never do that to my child. I would never allow a child of mine to be in the limelight. I want Leonora to be just normal."

So Leonora took ballet and tap and piano.

"Perhaps she has other gifts," the dance teacher said. "Perhaps she has a gift for music."

The piano teacher was more to the point. "She has nothing," he said. "And she's driving me crazy."

"You could be a movie star," her mother said.

In junior high Leonora was one of the first to grow breasts; the other girls resented her for that. But in high school her breasts made her popular with the boys, so she didn't care about the girls. She became a cheerleader and after every game she and the other cheerleaders crowded into the booths at Dante's and waited for the team to arrive. Then they all drank Cokes and ate cheeseburgers and grabbed at one another in the booths—nothing serious, just good fun—and made out on the way home.

In November of her senior year Leonora was parked in front of her house in Chuckie's car.

"Why won't you do it?" Chuckie asked. "Everybody does."

"I don't know," she said, miserable. "I want to, but I can't. I just can't."

"Nobody saves themselves for marriage any more. Is that what you think you're doing?"

"I think I was meant for better things," she said, not really knowing what she meant. "I mean, I get straight A's and B's."

"Ah shit," Chuckie said. "Just put your hand here. Feel this."

"No, I was meant for better things."

"But you've got to start somewhere," Chuckie said. "Hell, I'm captain of the team."

But Leonora was already getting out of the car, feeling chosen, feeling—she searched for the word—exalted. Yes, that was it. She was meant for better things.

In the Admissions Office at Stanford, Leonora was a floater, somebody who hadn't yet sunk to the bottom but somebody who wouldn't get picked out of the pool unless a real Stanford freshman decided to go to Yale or somewhere. That year a lot of freshmen went to Yale and so Leonora, floating almost to the end, was admitted to Stanford.

"You could be a college professor," her mother said. "Or a famous writer. You could win the Nobel Prize, maybe."

"Dry up," Leonora said. "What do you know about it? You never even went to college."

"Oh baby," she said. "Oh sweetheart, don't be mean to your mother, Leonora. I only want what's best for you. I only want you to be happy."

"Then dry up," Leonora said.

The worst part about Stanford was that they made her take Freshman English. She had been among the top thirty in high school and now she was back to writing compositions. At first she had just been a little nasty to the teacher in class, to let him know how she felt about being there. But after she had written the first assigned paper, she decided to go see him and demand an explanation. He gave it to her. He explained that it was a requirement of the college that every student demonstrate a basic competence in expository writing and that she had not, in the qualifying tests, demonstrated that. And then he handed her the corrected paper.

It was covered with little red marks—diction? antecedent? obscure, no no no—and there was a large black C at the bottom of the page.

"You gave me a C," Leonora said. "I've never had a C in my life."

"There's nothing wrong with a C," he said. "It's a perfectly acceptable grade. It's average, maybe even above average."

"You gave me a C," she said and, choking on her tears, ran from his office.

Her next two papers came back with C's on them also, so she knew he was out to get her. His name was Lockhardt and he had written a couple of novels and thought he was hot shit.

Leonora went to the ombudsman and complained that she was being discriminated against. She should not have to take Freshman English in the first place, and in the second place Lockhardt was guilty of unprofessional conduct in browbeating her and making her feel inferior.

The ombudsman went to the Chairman of the English Department who called in Lockhardt and then called in Leonora and finally checked her papers himself. The next day he told Leonora that yes, she would have to take Freshman English like all the others, that the grades Professor Lockhardt had given her seemed fair enough, that he was sorry Professor Lockhardt had made her feel inferior. He told Lockhardt for God's sake go easy on the girl, she's half crazy, and whatever you do don't be alone with her in your office. He told the ombudsman that the problem had been settled to everyone's satisfaction and there was no need to take all this to the Provost. So everyone was miserable and satisfied.

Leonora's final grade was a C, all because of that bastard Lockhardt.

Patty Hearst was wrestled, struggling, into the trunk of a car in Berkeley and the next day she was headlines in all the papers. Leonora narrowed her thin eyes and thought, why couldn't they have taken me?

In her junior year she moved in with Horst Kammer. He was clearly one of the better things that she was meant for. He was very smart and spent a lot of time with the housemaster, so that in Horst she had not only a roommate, she had instant acceptance as well. Horst was too intellectual to be much interested in sex, but he didn't mind occasional sex with Leonora and that was enough for her.

Horst dressed in army fatigues and spent a lot of his time protesting Stanford's investments in South Africa. Leonora protested along with him and they were arrested together during the spring sit-in at Old Union. Leonora felt proud to be involved in something historical, something that mattered. There were over a hundred students arrested and they were each fined nearly two hundred dollars. Leonora's mother sent the money, and with it a note saying "You're like Vanessa Redgrave or Jane Fonda. You're doing your part."

"God, that woman is hopeless," Leonora said.

Two photographs.

One. Leonora is home from college and all the relatives have come over for dinner. Afterward somebody snaps an Instamatic of Leonora and her mother and father, sitting on the floor in front of the Christmas tree, surrounded by gifts. The mother and father each have an arm around Leonora and they are smiling directly into the camera. Leonora is smiling too, but she is looking off to the right of the camera, as if at the very last minute she decided the picture is not what she wants; she wants something else.

"She could be a photographer's model," her mother says, examining the picture. "She could be on all the covers."

Two. Leonora has just crested the hill on Campus Drive and is about to make the long clear descent on her new ten-speed bike. She passes two professors who are taking a noon walk, looking like anybody else, just enjoying the California spring. Leonora does not notice them, does not see that one of them is Lockhardt. She sees only the long hill before her, and she feels the warm wind blowing through her hair. She sits high on the seat, no hands, and lifts her arms straight out from the shoulders, surrendering completely to the sun and the wind and being young and pretty with everything, every wonderful thing ahead of her.

"Look at that girl," Lockhardt says. "God, somebody should photograph that."

In her senior year, her second year with Horst, Leonora was all showered and getting ready to go to a frat party when Horst said "Come on, let's do it." He wasn't interested in doing it that often, so she said "I'm all ready for the party, but if you're sure you want to . . ." "I want to," he said. "I'm up for it. Look." And so he chased her from the bedroom into the living room and then back into the bedroom where she collapsed on the bed, laughing and tickling him, and they made love. "Was it wonderful?" she said. "Was it better?" "You're terrific," he said, "you're great. Where the hell is my deodorant?"

At the party everybody drank a lot of beer and sunrise tequilas and after a while they got to the subject of how often you ball your roommate. When Horst's turn came, he gave a long and funny speech about the primacy of the intellect and the transitory nature of sexuality. He described the postures you get into and he made them sound new and funny, and he said the real problem is that an hour later you're still hungry for more. He had everybody with him and he was feeling really good about his performance, you could tell, and then he paused and said, anticlimactically, "Let's face it, folks, what we're dealing with here is just two mucous membranes rubbing together."

Everybody laughed and applauded and spilled beer. Horst shook his head and smiled sneakily at Leonora.

But then somebody added, "They're sebaceous membranes, actually. Get your membranes straight, Horst."

Everybody laughed even louder and Leonora laughed too and Horst saw her do it.

So he was furious and, on the way home, when Leonora leaned against his side, her head on his shoulder, Horst put his hand on her breast. He felt for the nipple and when he had it firmly between his thumb and forefinger, he twisted it suddenly and violently, pressing down with his thumbnail. Leonora screamed in pain.

"You bitch," he said. "You fucking whore. Why don't you get out of my life. You're just a nothing. You're a noose around my neck."

"No," Leonora said. "No."

Patty Hearst was arrested in an apartment in San Francisco. Her picture appeared in all the papers, laughing like crazy, her fist clenched in the revolutionary salute. She listed her occupation as "urban guerrilla." Leonora was done with all that now that she was done with Horst. And who cared about Patty Hearst anyhow.

Leonora got her diploma in June, but she had to take one more course that summer before she had enough credits to officially graduate. She signed up for creative writing, taught by "staff." But staff turned out to be that bastard Lockhardt. He didn't seem to remember her, and everybody said he was a really good teacher, and she wanted to write a novel some day, so she decided to give him another chance.

Lockhardt wasn't interested in the things that interested her. She wanted to write something different, but Lockhardt kept talking about the initiating incident and the conflict and the characters. Old stuff. She wrote a story about a shoplifter named Horst, following him from the moment he picked up a tie until the moment he got out of the store, and she wrote it completely from within his mind, what he was thinking. Lockhardt said that the reader had no way of knowing that Horst was stealing, and that she should simply say so. But she explained that she was trying to be more subtle than that. She explained that the reader was supposer to find out Horst was stealing only after the fact, after he was outside the shop, otherwise the story would be just like any other story. They argued back and forth for a long time and then Lockhardt just shrugged his shoulders and said, "Well, I guess you've accomplished what you set out to do. Congratulations." The same thing happened with her next two stories. He didn't like them, so he said the reader couldn't follow them. He couldn't seem to understand that she was trying to do something different.

And then in August she got her grade. A flat C. She went straight from the Registrar's office to Lockhardt.

"I have to speak to you," she said.

"Sit down," he said. "Have a seat. But I've got to see the Dean in five minutes, so if you're going to need more than that . . ."

"You gave me a C."

"Right. I hope you weren't too disappointed."

"You," she said. "You," but the words wouldn't come out.

"Well, your work was not really extraordinary. I mean, I think you'll agree that it wasn't A work."

"It was C work, I suppose. It was only average."

"There's nothing wrong with being average. Most of us are. Most of our work is average."

She stood up and walked to the door. "What do I care," she said. "I can live with a C." And she slammed the door behind her.

She came back late the next afternoon, she was not sure why, but she knew she had to tell him something. Lockhardt was at his desk, typing, his back to the open door, and Leonora stood there in the corridor watching him. Nobody else was around. She could kill him and no one would know she had done it. If she had a knife or a gun, she could do it. That bastard.

He kept on typing and she just stood there watching him, thinking. And then suddenly he turned around and gave a little shout. "My God, you scared me half to death."

Leonora just stared at him, and he stared back, looking confused or maybe frightened. Then she turned and walked away.

She had not told him what he had done to her, but she would some day. She'd let him know. She'd let him know.

Leonora moved to San Francisco to be on her own. She got a studio apartment with a fire escape that looked down onto the roof of the Jack Tarr hotel and she applied for jobs at Gumps and at the St. Francis—they had asked her "doing what?"—and she shrugged and said to hell with them, she had a Stanford education. But her money ran out eventually and she took a job at Dalton's selling books.

Nothing interesting ever happened at Dalton's, and besides you had to press sixty buttons on the computerized register every time you rang up a sale. The worst part was that everybody kept buying a novel called *The Love Hostage*, written by that bastard Lockhardt. After the first four sales, she refused to sell any more. "I'm on my break," she'd say and make the customer go to another register.

Leonora hated her job, hated the people she worked with, hated books. Somewhere there must be something different happening. Even Patty Hearst, who was a zilch, a nothing, even she had things happen to her. With a name like Patty.

One night when she had worked late, Leonora decided to take a walk. She would make something happen. She moped along Polk Street to Geary and then back, but nothing happened. There were a million or so faggots eyeing each other, but nobody eyed Leonora. She went up to her studio and had a beer and then came down again and set off deliberately in the direction of Golden Gate Park. She knew what she was doing. She could be raped. She could be murdered. Lockhardt used to talk all the time about

Joyce Carol Oates characters, how they set up situations for themselves, getting trapped, getting murdered, having their pink and gray brains spilled out on the sidewalk. She liked Joyce Carol Oates. She got as far as the Panhandle and was about to turn around and go home when she realized somebody was following her. For a block, then for a second block. She could hear the heels go faster when she went faster, slow down when she did. Her heart began to beat very fast and she could feel the vein in her forehead pulsing. She wanted it to happen, whatever it was. She turned around suddenly, hands on hips, her head thrown back, ready. At once the man following her crossed the street and headed in the opposite direction. Leonora walked for another hour and then went home. Would nothing happen to her, ever?

The Women's Support Group was having a terrible time with Leonora.

"You've got to open up to your feelings as a woman," they said.

"Men have done this to you. They've refused to let you get in touch with your feelings," they said.

"What is it you feel? What is it you want?" they said.

"I want," Leonora said, "I don't know, but I think I want to die."

"No, what do you really want?" they said.

Leonora bought a gun and a copy of *The Love Hostage* on the same day. There was no connection she could see. She wanted them, that was all. It was time.

She loaded the gun with six bullets and hid it in a Kleenex box under a lot of tissues. It was for protection in this crazy city. It was a safeguard. It was just something nice to have around.

And then she sat down to read *The Love Hostage*. From the first page she was fascinated and appalled. The dust jacket said it was a novel about a young heiress who is kidnapped and brainwashed and all the other stuff that would make you think it was about Patty Hearst. But it wasn't about Patty at all; it was about her, it was about Leonora. Lockhardt had changed things to make it look as if it were about Patty, but she knew he meant her. He described her as an ordinary girl, a normal girl, average in every way. So now he had finally done it. He had killed her.

Leonora put the gun to the side of her head and pulled the trigger. There was an awful noise and the gun leaped from her hand and she felt something wet on the side of her face. She had only grazed her scalp, but inside she was dead just the same.

On the night she was committed to Agnew Mental, Leonora had forced down the beef stew her mother served for dinner and then she had gone back to her room to lie down. Almost at once she threw up into the wastebasket by her bed and then she went to the bathroom and threw up again. Back in her room she put on Phoebe Snow's "Poetry Man." She played the album through twice, though she was not listening. She was thinking—as she had been for these last three weeks—of Lockhardt and how he had ruined everything and how some day she would let him know. But not now. Some day.

And then, as if it were somebody else doing it, she got up and got dressed and drove to the Stanford campus. She found Lockhardt's house with no trouble at all, and it was only when she had rung the doorbell that she realized she didn't know what she was going to say. But it didn't matter; somehow she would just tell him, calmly, with no tears, that he had degraded her, humiliated her, he had ruined her life.

"Yes?"

"I want to talk to you. I want to tell you something."

"Are you a student of mine? A former student?"

And then she realized that this was not Lockhardt at all, this was a much older man with a beard and glasses. The Lockhardts, it turned out, had moved to San Francisco.

Leonora got back into her car. She was frantic now, she would have to find a phone booth and get his address. She drove to Town and Country Shopping Center and found a booth, but there was no San Francisco directory. She drove to Stanford Shopping Center, and again there was no directory. Never mind. She would drive straight to the city, she would find him, he wouldn't get away from her now. She would let him know.

Traffic on 101 was heavy and it had begun to rain. Leonora passed cars that were already doing sixty. She had to get there. She had to tell him. The words were piling up in her brain, like stones, like bullets. Bullets, yes, she should have brought the gun. She should kill the bastard. A car pulled into her lane and then began slowly to brake. Leonora braked too, but not fast enough.

Her car fishtailed and, with a short crunching sound, it smashed the side of a Volkswagen. She tore on ahead, though she could see in her mirror that the Volkswagen had ground to a halt, that its lights were blinking on and off. Tough. Yes, she should kill him, she thought, and she pressed her foot harder on the accelerator.

She couldn't find a parking place and so she left the car in a tow zone a block from the Jack Tarr hotel and ran back in the rain. She found the phone booth, the directory, she opened it to the L's. Lockhardt lived in North Beach. Of course he would, with all that money from *The Love Hostage*. She ran back to her car. A tow truck was backed up to it and a little bald man was kneeling down trying to attach a bar under the front bumper. "No," she shouted. "Stop it. Stop it. Stop." He stood up and looked at her, a screaming woman with her wet hair flying all around, a real crazy. "Okay, lady, okay," he said. "Okay." And then she was in her car again, tearing up Van Ness, running yellow lights, turning right on Pacific. In a few minutes she was there, at Lockhardt's blue and gray Victorian.

Leonora's head was pounding and her back ached. She wanted to throw up, but there was nothing left to throw up. She wanted a drink. She wanted a pill. She wanted to take Lockhardt by the hair and tear the scalp off him, to expose the pink and gray brain that had written those things, that had done this to her.

She put her finger up to ring the bell, but she was shaking so much she couldn't do it. She began to beat the doorbell with her palm and then with her fist. Still the bell made no sound. She struck the door itself, with her hand, and then with her foot, and then she leaned her entire body against it, beating the door rhythmically with her fist and then with both fists, the rhythm growing faster and faster, the blows harder and harder, until there was blood on her hands and blood on the door and she heard a voice screaming that sounded like her own.

The door opened and Lockhardt, with a book in his hand, stood there looking at the young woman whose wet hair was streaked across her face, a face distorted beyond recognition by her hysteria, and he listened to the screaming, which made no sense to him until her voice broke and he could make out the words. "I am not average," she sobbed. "I am not average. I am not average."

It was nearly a half hour before the orderlies came and took her away.

The world had gone crazy, that's just the way it was. Leonora's mother stared at the television where for days she had been watching pictures of the 911 corpses in Guyana. They had taken poison mixed with grape Kool-Aid and in five minutes they were dead. Every one of them. And Patty Hearst had been refused parole. And so had Charles Manson. And her own Leonora in that looney bin. Leonora could have been something once. She could have been . . . but nothing came to mind. It was Lockhardt's fault, Leonora was right. It was all Lockhardt's fault. Leonora's mother turned up the volume on the TV. And now somebody had shot Mayor Moscone and that Harvey Milk. It was the way you expressed yourself today, you shot somebody.

She thought of the gun hidden in the Kleenex box and suddenly it was all clear to her. She got in the car and drove to North Beach. She had no trouble finding Lockhardt's house; she had been there three times since Leonora was taken away. She had just parked opposite the house and sat there and watched. But this time she went up the steep wooden stairs and rang the bell. She rang again and as she was about to ring a third time Lockhardt opened the door, laughing. She could hear other people laughing too; he must be having a party. Over his left shoulder, in the entrance hall, she could see a chandelier, a deep green wall, the corner of a picture. She couldn't make out what it was a picture of, but she could see that he was rich. He had everything. "Yes?" he said, and there was more laughter from that other room. "Yes?" he said again.

"Leonora," she said. "She could have been something."

And then she took the gun from her purse and leveled it at his chest. There were three loud shots and when his body slumped to the floor, Leonora's mother could see that the painting on the green wall was one of those newfangled things with little blocks of color, all different sizes, that really aren't the picture of anything.

ISAAC AND THE UNDERTAKER'S DAUGHTER

STEVE STERN

Steve Stern was born in Memphis, Tennessee, where, after several years of transplantations, he currently resides. His stories have appeared in *Epoch, Nimrod, Barataria, Eureka Review,* and in several collections of ghost stories published in London, where he lived for a while. He teaches English part-time at a local college and is working on a novel about pretending it isn't so.

Above the little lake where they were burning Mama in her dinghy, there was an old windmill with a tower of green stone and a cap of copper. The tower was tangled in woodbine and wildflowers, and canvas hung in beggar's beards from its great sails. But the sails still turned in the least hint of a breeze, and the mossy legend on the foundation stone could still be made out to read: The Widow.

It was dusk and Mr. Goldfinch, the widower, stood in the tall grass at the side of the lake. In his swallow-tailed mourning and rostrum-beaked profile, he resembled a pot-bellied rook. The russet tufts of his otherwise bald head imitated in miniature the burning boat. Beholding the windmill over the rims of his nickeled spectacles, he confided in his son.

"You know," he said, "for a schmuck I see a lot of beauty."

Up to his ankles in mud, Isaac was skipping stones and shedding tears. The cremation of Mama was the cremation of the wideawake world; all that was left was a dream. Salamanders of flame leaped from the dinghy; above them stood the Widow. The sky itself had been kindled vermilion.

"Dumbwaiter," continued Mr. Goldfinch, addressing his son by a nickname, "stop scaring the fish. Get out of the mud and I'll tell you a secret." Obediently Isaac flung away his stones and hobbled on his crooked leg into the grass. His father pointed. "For your information, that windmill is the earth's propeller. So long as it turns, the earth spins and time passes."

Isaac knew that his father was crazy. He also knew that things which were not so were often made so by his father's saying them.

While she lay, still breathing, on her canopied deathbed, Goldfinch & Son, the costumers, had outfitted Mama in the full battle dress of a Viking. Pulling the folds of her midnight skirts off over her head had been like turning a parasol inside-out. So wasted away was her body that she weighed no more than her bones. They padded her with pillows and girded the pillows with barrel hoops. They burdened her with breastplates and ermine, clasped with a bronze fibula. They stuffed plum pits in her gaunt cheeks and newspapers in her antlered helmet. Then, when only her face and hands the texture of raisins remained exposed, they lit the Sabbath candles and sat down to gin rummy. Isaac wondered if, had she been able, Mama would have chosen to seek her reward in such attire. She'd always been a modest woman, even before she'd begun to shrink. But Mr. Goldfinch assured him that in her soul Mama was a warrior. The room was full of a musk as from mildewed fruit, and when she gasped her last breath, Mama's amulets rattled like the wind chimes.

"We'll give her a hero's send-off," resolved Mr. Goldfinch, but Isaac hung his head, because it would be a funeral for a broken doll and not for a woman who had waltzed with her husband, stout in the heyday of her knishes and strudel.

For want of a longboat, Mr. Goldfinch acquired an old barnacle-hulled fisherman's dinghy. They laid Mama in the bottom alongside her needlework and a picnic basket of pastries Isaac had commissioned some friends to steal from the market. At her head they placed the gramophone with its spiderweb frock and its scratched Strauss on the turntable. They closed the costume shop for the afternoon and loaded the boat onto a lorry with the help of its top-hatted driver. Then they drove round to the storefront mortuary, where the dinghy was carried into a small chapel and mounted on a catafalque of pastel chrysanthemums. The lorry driver, doffing his top hat and tendering his terret face, became the undertaker, conducting father and son to a private alcove reserved for the next of kin. An organ played a dirge like a trodden concertina. The undertaker undressed as he ducked behind a curtain.

After a minute a rabbinical gentleman in porkpie hat and corkscrew earlocks came into the alcove. He approached with mincing steps, as though his trousers had fallen down around his ankles. Taking Mr. Goldfinch's hand in both of his own, the rabbi fiercely condoled.

"She was a woman like a good droshky," he said, moving to Isaac whose hand he felt quivering as from a transferred palsy. As he passed by Mama in her open boat, the rabbi held up three fingers to fend off the evil eye and told the Lord she was a woman like a troika.

Another minute and a man entered with the graying temples and pointed beard of one who demands his business contracts signed in blood. He wore a silk cravat and a blue-petaled boutonniere.

"I had to come," he challenged, officially tapping the floor with his jeweled walking stick as he bowed once to the husband, once to the son, and once to the bier. Before turning on his heel, he plucked the boutonniere and tossed it wistfully into the boat, as into a pool where a lover has drowned.

A veiled woman in scarlet lamé and extravagant bosom collapsed onto Mr. Goldfinch, blubbering tears that were distinctly crocodile. Isaac had not been fooled for a moment. He protected himself from her kisses as from sucking eels. Even through her veil he could see that she had in common with the rabbi and the formal gentleman the undertaker's ferret eyes.

Afterward, restored to his top hat and mufti, the undertaker drove a one-vehicle procession through the town and up the old heath road. In the lorry's rocking cab Isaac, despite himself, admired the man's competence in his chosen trade. Unlike his father, Isaac was no orthodox believer in ceremony. But having risen in the space of a year from apprentice to partner in his father's shop, he fancied he could recognize a fellow professional. When the dinghy had been hauled down a ramp into a nest of bullfrogs and water lilies, the undertaker touched the brim of his hat and discreetly withdrew.

Then Mr. Goldfinch presented Isaac with a green-tinted wine

bottle full of gasoline and produced from a coat pocket a grainy leather prayer book.

"*V'yish kadol, v'yish kodosh, sh'may rabo,*" he intoned, as if reading the words to a sentimental song, while Isaac waded into scum and smashed the bottle over the bow of the boat, christening it in his mind the Fast Asleep. He launched the boat with a shove, averting his eyes from the antlers and ermine and the shucked shell of his mother. Then Isaac did to her what she had done to his father's books, which were themselves like shells whose contents Mr. Goldfinch had devoured in order to become himself. He struck a match and flung it like a curse at the dinghy, which burst into flames. He looked above the flames to see his Mama in her nightcap and beefsteak cheeks, sleepwalking leisurely to heaven; instead he saw only a windmill. So he stood in the mud like a broken wishbone, until his father recalled him into the sword grass, told him a secret, and hugged him the way an enormous rook hugs a scarecrow.

Later that evening in the kitchen above the costume shop, Mr. Goldfinch treated Isaac to his first glass of wine. He poured it from a cracked crystal decanter which was coated in dust.

"Your mother died so that we could stay here and be fools. Drink to our eternal partnership," he proposed, clinking glasses with Isaac. When he removed his spectacles, his closed eyes appeared pinched by dirty fingers. Light from a gas jet got trapped in the tears which streamed out of the bags beneath his eyes and fell like talismans, spiking his wine.

"It smells musty," said Isaac, sniffing before sipping; and by the time he'd helped himself to a second glass, the bouquet had begun to duplicate itself inside his head. Across the kitchen table his father sat massaging the bridge of his nose, condemned to relive forever the time when he transformed the cafe into a costume shop, and his wife began to wither and lose faith. But Isaac was set free; slouched in his chair, he had escaped through a skylight and was careering across the rooftops as in the days before his fall. He was climbing trellises and vaulting balconies on his way to becoming the complete catburglar, the one who eventually steals the Holy Grail. His headlong flight was interrupted by the ringing of the bell over the door downstairs. Rising, he found that the floor was tilted beneath him. This was because he was drunk, he reasoned before remembering that it was because he was lame.

The recollection gave him a certain tranquil sense of responsibility which lately had made him—though he'd just turned sixteen—want to begin to look for a wife.

Isaac roused his father and led him by the hand out of his mood, down the stairs, and between the dark racks of mantles and plumes. He turned on fixtures and unbolted the front door, standing aside for a man in top hat and plaid trousers pushing a wicker-backed wheelchair into the emporium. The undertaker had come for his pay.

"Jimmy Pin's the name, squire," and he tipped his hat, "formerly from the world of footlights and curtain calls, and currently the sole owner and proprietor of the Farewell Funeral Establishment. This here's Lily, my little girl."

Mr. Goldfinch welcomed them with a nod.

"Now you are of course familiar with my services. I deal with them that's gone." In deference he inclined his head. "But, as I understand it, you deal with them that's going. Am I right?"

He was. Goldfinch & Son catered costumes for every occasion, but appareling the moribund was their speciality.

"Righto," said Mr. Pin. "Now I've tucked away my artistic past in steamer trunks. I've got costumes galore and I use them, as you know, in my own line of work. I've got Shylock and I've got Charley's Aunt, but I've got nothing seemly for a young lady of Lily's complexion."

For a moment Mr. Goldfinch was puzzled, not to mention distracted, by his son and colleague who was most unprofessionally stalking about the perimeter of the shop with as much stealth as his game leg would allow.

"What exactly can I do for you, Mr. Pin?" he inquired.

The undertaker seemed surprised. He stepped away from the wheelchair and outstretched an arm as though it were all perfectly obvious.

"She's dying," he explained.

Meanwhile Isaac tried not to be too hasty in considering the matter of the undertaker's daughter. He'd circled her wheelchair like a discriminating vulture, admitting to himself that for practical purposes she appeared half a carcass already. Viewed from the rear her dingy brown hair was tied in a knot like a cowpat. From the flank she was a ghost or a dishrag in her white invalid's smock, uncontoured by a hip or a suggestion of breast. Her face was a mousy soup-stained oval with paraffin flesh, cheekbones like bunions, an expression entirely bored. She was a thing for fastening to a broomstick. So why, he wondered, did his bowels turn over like a lottery barrel? The streets were full of well-scrubbed girls in bright frocks that smelled of orchards, but this one was an empty hand-puppet. Why, then, did he want suddenly to strip off his mourning and dance in his underwear? He groped for reasons, his brain in disarray. The gas jets burned hieratically, but Isaac held his peace. It might be the drink, he told himself. It might be the devil. She was, after all, a shiksa. So he continued to gape, and for her part, she suffered his stare with perfect indifference. She fanned herself with a fly swatter during her father's speech and merely yawned when Mr. Goldfinch brought forth from the racks a gown made of gold thread and moth's wings. It was only when Isaac, whose mind was made up, hobbled forward and announced:

"She's not going to die, because she's going to be my wife!" that Lily's lips curled at their corners in the faintest amusement.

Mr. Goldfinch felt called upon to interpret.

"It's his obsession. I gave him wine; he got ideas. Isaac, go to bed."

He was already on his way, putting swagger into his limp, turning flamboyantly on the stairs to smile with his impish face. Then he saluted as with a riding crop and bounded up the stairs.

"Oi," sighed Mr. Goldfinch.

Lily looked up at her father and twirled the wire handle of her fan in the vicinity of her ear. Jimmy Pin concurred with a wink.

During the seven-day mourning which he observed with his father, Isaac concocted his scheme. After dinners, while his father sat shiva by the flickering yahrzeit light, Isaac had slipped from the kitchen and lurked about the lamplit streets. He'd contacted old friends. He'd loitered on the pavement adjacent the mortuary, marking the time when Jimmy Pin left his flat to nip round for his hour of billiards and beer. Then on the evening of the eighth day, Isaac borrowed a black hooded cape from the shop and went to abduct Lily Pin.

Having seen the undertaker well off to his tavern, Isaac ducked into an alley and, hoisting his bad leg over a topless hogshead, immersed it to the thigh in collected rainwater. Unabashed, he took hold of the drainpipe and limped up the brick wall to where a pink curtain was blowing through an open window like a waved kerchief. He rested his chest on the window-ledge, convulsed, and rolled headfirst into the room. Sitting up, he smelled frankincense and saw strangely in mid-air a sailing enamel bowl. When the bowl struck his forehead, Isaac's hood fell backward, followed by himself. He lay for a bit on the carpet and watched the catherine wheels until they dissolved, and felt his forehead sprout a horn. His hand before his eyes was covered with the scarlet liquid which trickled over his face and tasted, when he licked his lips, of garlicky tomato soup. Venturing with caution to sit up again, he wiped his face in the satin of his cape.

The room was kaleidoscopic with color posters of melodramas, religious paintings, plaster icons, and a smoldering thurible which hung from an electric chandelier. The centerpiece was an unfolded Murphy bed, decked out like a funeral barge in flowers and black bunting, upon which lay a body in violent motion. Lily Pin lay on her deathbed, laughing fit to be tied.

"I thought you were the Grim Reaper," she cackled, raising herself and collapsing.

It was the first time that Isaac had heard her voice. When she'd exhausted her laughter, she closed her oyster-gray eyes as if content to have dreamed her intruder. She was wearing the gown of wings and gold veins, through which her nipples showed like copper coins. Her lips had been carmined and her sallow cheeks rouged till she resembled a china clown; but the clot of her hair, as if it had been distilled, poured like whiskey over the sheets. Isaac was on his feet; he was damp with rainwater and sticky with soup, aching with injured forehead and pride, embarrassed by the nuisance of his cape. He was resolute. Lily was all done up for a bride, and Isaac meant to replace the groom she'd been prepared for. He cleared his throat with a cranking sound.

"I love you," he explained.

Lily reopened her eyes, propped herself on her elbows, and yawned. Isaac squeaked as he swallowed, and added,

"We're going to elope."

She examined him with mild curiosity. "You've a screw loose," she observed, and reclined again.

Having seen the truth of her remark, Isaac nodded gravely and broke wind. Love had undone him like one of Mama's clysters. In his brain spun the hands of a clock gone berserk. Approaching Lily's bed, he dipped his fingers in the puddle of her hair.

"So what?" he said. "You're like something out of a Jack-in-the-box. You got the face of an Easter egg. I got a screw loose. So what!"

As if to prove his point, he scratched his scurfy scalp till the hair stood up like bracken in a blizzard. This, along with the unicorn knot on his forehead, gave him an appearance of authentic derangement to which he added a wild grin. He was having the time of his life.

"Look at me," he said to whoever might be listening. Lily had pulled a pillow over her head. He lifted her easily from the bed and deposited her in the wheelchair that kept vigil in a corner. She weighed no more than an infant. The fabric of the dress was flimsy as membrane so that she was slippery in Isaac's arms, like a water snake.

"Put me back!" she screeched, making Isaac think of poison pilfered from a medicine chest. "I'm a dying woman, you grisly geek."

"But you're not a woman," he contradicted.

"Then what am I?"

He considered.

"You're a cripple like me."

For want of a lift, he pushed her out onto a back landing and down a flight of wooden steps whose groaning echoed Lily's complaints. He rolled her through narrow streets where the darkness oozed between islands of gaslight, and the gables of tall houses tilted like witches' hats. Lily taunted him with a variety of titles: fish features, frog prince, phantom of the outhouse, kosher gargoyle, bowel breath; the last of which she dropped the way a child in the woods might drop a last breadcrumb, and fell silent. Isaac tried not to imagine her face in the dark; instead he pretended they were a couple on their way to a court of miracles. Where the houses grew sparse he pushed the chair over railroad tracks and uphill onto the heath. He was stumbling against the woven wicker, puffing with fatigue, when they finally reached the pond upon whose black water Mama's ashes passed over the moon.

Isaac caught his breath. Beyond the bank of honeysuckle stood the Widow, her four great sails turning in the wind with a sound like a giant's heartbeat. Stars above the mill were pitched and stirred into whirlpools; the crescent moon rocked like a pendulum. A lamp burned in the window of the millwright's quarters.

"You'll go to hell for this," Lily mumbled sleepily, as Isaac carried her across the threshold and unloaded her into a crazy-quilted bunk which was recessed in the wainscotted wall. "Bum-faced twit," she yawned, and her gown whistled with friction as she stretched and turned over. Isaac wanted to tease her that the sandman had beat out the angel of death. He drew a checkered curtain across the bunk and looked around.

His friends had done their work like cobbler's elves; the room was swept tidy and arranged as snug as a cedar hope chest. At Isaac's request, his old street companions, with whom he had run in the days before his apprenticeship, had prepared his honey-moon dwelling. Isaac still commanded respect in the neighborhood, because once he had jumped from a house top over the market square, plummeting through the canvas marquee and shattering his leg in a crib of fruit. For his sake his light-fingered associates had been happy to break into the derelict mill and knock down cobwebs from mouse hole, settle, and hearth. They'd replaced a petrified bread loaf with several freshly baked, left on an oak table beside the miller's Bible, itself like a hunk of burned toast. They'd laid in a larder of pinched provisions: ripe pears and sharp cheeses, smoked cold cuts and kippered herrings, a basket of truffles, a saucer of sour cream, a bottle of champagne. Then they'd ridden the mill stocks like a carnival wheel and removed themselves to trees to sit sentinel. Isaac inhaled the grocery fragrance. There was only one thing left for him to do.

He mounted the ladder whose wide spoon-shaped rungs led through a trap door into the Widow's works. In the intestines of the mill the ghosts of dead millers seemed to be rattling their chains; there was a creaking of rafters and a grating of runners. Through a narrow window in the sack loft, star light fell into a hopper and was fed to three separate sets of millstones in the flour loft and ground into phosphorescent dust. Isaac climbed past the great spur wheel to the top of the tower, where bats darted through the spokes of the cast-iron spider in the hub of the massive brake wheel, and the timber-toothed wallower rumbled like an infernal carousel. The air was heady with the smell of dampness and rust. Isaac followed his friends' directions. He placed his shoulder under the brake staff, which was cradled in an iron hook, and heaved up until it was disengaged; then he leaped out of the way. The brake wheel ratchetted and the wallower thundered to a halt. The bats scattered into the cupola. The wind shaft twisted like a ship's helm, as the stocks reversed themselves, then ceased. The mill shut down as did, with a universal shudder, all the gears in the correspondent machinery of the night.

When Isaac had come down from the tower into his bridal chamber, he pulled back the curtain over the bunk and saw Lily sleeping beneath the crazy quilt, sound as a lump of landscape. Then he recalled further instructions his friends had given him. The kid with the wall-eye, who'd been assaulted as a child by a woman with dugs like sacks of meal, had revealed much. So had the gap-toothed kid, who'd been nineteenth in line in a jakes where a chartreuse-haired woman was chained to the plumbing. But nothing that they'd told him seemed now to apply. Hands trembling over his buttons, he stripped down to his spindle shanks. He blew out the spirit lamp and, as if testing bathwater, lifted the leg, which had earlier tested rainwater, over the side of the bunk. Then, holding his breath, he rolled onto the mattress and lay beside Lily as in a cradle on the open sea. A disturbing thought occurred: What if his releasing the brake staff had done mischief to Lily's frail pulse? That would account for her stillness. He bent an ear to her beast and listened. What he heard astonished him at first, because Lily had begun to snore as if in her dream she were sawing the peg leg off an old sailor. And in a bit, as is inevitable with those who eavesdrop on another's dreams, Isaac too fell asleep.

It was still dark when he awoke, but he felt as though he had slept for hours. He was pleased with his successful theft of a wife and sought to kiss the mascara'd lids of her eyes. This he accomplished before her lids opened and she shouted, "What are you doing!" as she shoved Isaac out of the bunk.

"I was putting the pennies over your eyes," snapped Isaac, picking himself up off the straw mat.

"You poxy maniac!" Lily was started. "Your mother strained a turd through cheesecloth and you were born."

Isaac had lit the lamp and lurched toward the pantry which he ravaged for the bottle of champagne.

"Crikey, you're naked!" She was awed. "Your little sack's like a wee walnut shell."

He would have liked to have broken the jade-green bottle over her crown as over the bow of Mama's dinghy, but instead Isaac fell back upon what he knew of tradition.

"It's time for your mikvah, my funny bride," he said and stood before her with the champagne between his knees, prying with his thumbs until the cork popped and liquid fireworks spewed over Lily's indignation. Though she wrestled with him savagely and called him a remarkable assortment of names, including puke-brained cretin gowk, Isaac still managed to erase her clown face in the folds of the patchwork quilt. Amazed at her strength, he struggled to hold firm her thrashing wrists. She made a noise in her throat like a bubbling cauldron and spat full in his face; then she looked a little sorry. Isaac let go and wiped his stinging eye.

"See," he said, as if the truth were finally out, "you're not going to die." But Lily was obstinate.

"Yes I am!" she insisted, and having reminded herself, she lay back, spent, fanning her cheek and batting her eyelids in boredom.

But Isaac would not hear it. Though she bolted from her torpor, crying, "Here, stop that!", Lily cackled despite herself, because Isaac had knelt between her legs and ducked beneath the fantasy fabric of her gown. She twisted and kicked and screamed for him to get his wooly head the hell out, it tickled. But Isaac was single-minded; in the choppy waters of her skirts he was diver and spelunker, nosing after the rumor of a grotto. And with a tongue, which he'd been told could catch flies, he explored. Then Lily let loose a whimper as if her soul had been pricked by a spindle. Isaac surfaced with a mouth bright with blood.

"What did you do?" Lily was livid with wonder.

"I think I made us relatives," said Isaac.

When she'd frantically shed her gown and pressed herself to him, Isaac felt that warm milk was spilling down his front. They coupled in a fever, their bodies flickering like a deck of cards shuffled with breathless dexterity. And when they were done and lay with their bellies glued in perspiration, Isaac wiped the tears of relief from his eyes so that he could see the tears of outrage in Lily's.

But as the stars continued to hang motionless in the windows and it became apparent that their wedding night was not going to end, Lily began to forgive Isaac for pulling her so rudely back into the world of the living. She even began to temper her exotic vocabulary, limiting herself to calling him frog prince and then dumbwaiter, a pet name which Isaac himself volunteered. She walked; she blushed. She left the bunk and broke her fast heartily on wedges of cantaloupe and slices of bread smeared with viscous cheese and tinned sardines. She made a porridge of oats and honey over a fire that Isaac had built in the hearth. They washed down everything with the sparkling champagne, sitting in the settle despite the warm weather—Lily in her spectral dress and Isaac girdled in patchwork. They stared at the coals which Isaac said were a nest of phoenix eggs, and Lily said were the sapphires she'd swallowed once as a child and later passed in her chamber jordan. Laughing, they became skittish and self-conscious, lit up by embers and alcohol until they were like a pair of glowworms. Then they took turns pretending to meditate so that each could study without inhibition the other's profile. Finally, when one of them refused to turn away, they held hands and made for the bunk, as if afraid it might sail without them. They clove to each other in order that neither might fall off the bucking animal that they were riding to paradise. And they each stifled with kisses the sobs of the other, so they would not give away that place where Isaac had kidnapped time and held it a secret hostage.

They slept and when they woke exchanged dreams. Isaac would say: "I dreamed I swung from the clapper of a tolling bell," and Lily would squeeze him for the loveliness of it. Lily would say: "I dreamed I was a marionette hanging from silk strings held by a bloody great spider," and Isaac would squeeze her because he was scared. They read aloud the dirty passages from the miller's Bible and Lily flogged Isaac with her hair. They pelted each other with food and scrubbed each other with water from the hand pump, until Lily was pink as a shrimp and Isaac was rosily mottled from the furuncles that Lily had ruptured. Once, recalling his responsibilities, Isaac told Lily how she would be the proud mistress of the costume shop and a daughter to her father-in-law, who was crazy and believed himself in league with dark angels. But Lily told him to shove it, and Isaac conceded that so long as they hid beneath the Widow's skirts, they at least remained impervious to age. Out in the world Lily might be dying again.

Occasionally during the long night, they looked out the window and down the hill to where the town swam in a shoal of lights. They saw, pinching each other to confirm it, a man with a bandanna over his head, wearing sabots and balloon sleeves, carrying a violin. He was coming over the honeysuckle path, when Isaac's friends, the market arabs, dropped from the Chinese elms and began to shove and snatch at his lapels. They broke the neck and smashed the box of his violin, then sent him on his way. Later on a uniformed man appeared in a cocked hat and a long coat with frog braids and epaulettes. His saber rattled as the boys pushed him backward over a kid on all-fours. An old woman on crutches received similar treatment, as did a blind priest. Isaac and Lily were so entertained that they forgot about going to bed. But after the first trespasser, they became a little less amused. They watched until a bald, bespectacled gentleman of middle years approached with the tails of his gaberdine in flight. Although they left their sentinel branches, the boys, who were familiar with his shop and with his son, let him pass without intervention.

"It's my old man!" said Isaac mistakenly, hopping to open the door before Lily could shout for him not to do it, you dumbwaiter.

"So Isaac," said the intruder, stepping inside, "the world should stop when you're in love?" His ferret eyes blinked and a pillow fell from his gut, as Jimmy Pin crossed the room and started up the ladder.

"Life goes on, mate," he said, disappearing through the trapdoor.

Lily clung to Isaac until the Widow's works had begun to grate and slog again and her sails to stir about the Milky Way. Then she put her lips to his ear and whispered brokenly,

"We're done for, you clod-pated freak."

After which she freed herself from Isaac and fled up the ladder after her father. It took Isaac a giddy few moments to shake off his confusion and follow.

He was lumbering up through the flour loft when the Widow was brought to a halt once again. Over the screaming of her machinery could be heard the screaming of a girl. The mill staggered, stocks cracked at the poll end, and a firefly shower of sparks sprayed from between the dry millstones. In the tower the undertaker endeavored to pull his daughter from where she'd thrown herself beneath the cogs of the turning brake wheel.

When Jimmy Pin drove his lorry down the hill with his dying daughter, Isaac was standing in sword grass on the bank of the little lake. In front of him the rising sun ran molten over the town. Behind him, the Widow crumbled into her burning skirts. On the surface of the water, framed by fire, Isaac's reflection shimmered like an oil slick with which, stooping, he anointed his ash-sprinkled head.

He went home. The streets were jocular and loud, and the shop, through which Isaac passed blindly on his way upstairs, was unusually full of customers. Ringing up a sale on the gilded cash register, Mr. Goldfinch excused himself. He found his son in the kitchen, drawing the shades to keep the sun out.

"Well Isaac," he said, "we had seven days of mourning, then seven days of evening. Today we're rich. Still it's a sad business."

"What should I do now?" asked Isaac, going to meet his father's embrace.

"Stick around and grow wise," said Mr. Goldfinch.

At sunset it was Isaac's turn to pour the wine and propose the toast to everlasting partnership. Father and son drank into the small hours and wept elegiacally over their memories, while outside the festival was yet in progress. When Mr. Goldfinch had inclined his several chins upon his chest, Isaac stumbled out into the night. The streets were a masked ball, celebrating the end of the hiatus and the reappearance of the sun. Flare-waving revelers strutted and fell down, outfitted as columbines and cavaliers, harlequins and zanies, their costumes bedizened with bells.

Isaac wandered into an alley and salvaged a broken-necked fiddle from a crate beside a rainbarrel. Plucking at the slack strings, he wrung forth a bellyache of chords to which his imagination supplied a tune and some lyrics.

"O Lily, I'm so silly," he sang, and an afterthought, "Lily's asleep and I'm in her dream."

Pleased with his composition, he repeated it at an unholy pitch. A lamp came on in an upstairs window and Jimmy Pin appeared, sober in his ferret face, saying something that could not be heard over the hell that by then had broken loose. Dogs howled and a party of drunks, attracted by the serenade, assembled in their noisy costumes. They made such a clamor that even the moon, throwing buckets of light on their heads, could not shut them up.

They blew on toy horns and jostled each other like tambourines; Isaac flailed the fiddle by its own fractured neck, singing,

"O Lily, I'm so sorry," while, catcalling and hiccuping like a glee club in bedlam, the choir had picked up the refrain:

"Lily's asleep and we're in her dream . . ."

THE SEPARATION

ANNETTE T. ROTTENBERG

Annette T. Rottenberg was born and raised in Washington, D.C. Now assistant director of the Rhetoric Program at the University of Massachusetts in Amherst, she is teaching English in several other colleges, including Duke University, State University College at Buffalo, and Chicago City College. Her stories and articles have appeared in *Story* magazine, *New Mexico Quarterly, College English, Studies in Short Fiction,* and other periodicals.

A few days after my twelfth birthday my father and mother separated. The separation came as a shock to all of us, except my father, of course. I didn't hear about it from them. I was standing on the terrace of our villa in Cologny looking across Lake Geneva to the park where there was a hotel—so I had just been told—in which Byron, Shelley, Queen Victoria and others had stayed. It was late afternoon, August, I was using a pair of field glasses which I had received as a birthday gift. It seemed strange enough that I had never seen the hotel, but even stranger that I had recently encountered Byron in so many places; first, reading "The Prisoner of Chillon" and exploring the castle (where I confused Byron with the prisoner); then, learning that our house was not far from the Villa Diodati where Byron had lived one summer, visiting his friends the Shelleys and writing part of *Childe Harold;* finally, to my delight, overhearing someone say that my father resembled Byron. I took this to mean physically, but later when I saw a picture of Byron, I knew that I had misunderstood the remark. (And here I confess that, although Byron has nothing to do with this story, it has always been impossible for me to tell it without associating him with the separation.) My father, who was an architect, had designed our house, in its airy site and its light-filled serenity like an exquisite small temple high above the lake, surrounded by roses and pear trees, facing the gentle slopes of the Jura; the fact that it was near the Villa Diodati seemed to me now both mysterious and satisfying. My parents were Peruvians who had met in Geneva. Sometimes they spoke of Lima in such a way as to suggest that the mists, the waters, the mountains of that other city were comparable to those of Geneva, but I didn't believe there could be another place like this one.

As I peered across the lake, seeing nothing but vague shapes, suddenly I heard above me from the open window of my parents' bedroom, the sound of their voices, my mother's raised in anger, my father's less strident but tense and urgent. I had never heard them quarrel before, never, and the sound of it was terrifying. I couldn't distinguish the words, but whatever it was that had hurt or divided them, I didn't want to know about it, and I ran into the house, pulling the french doors shut behind me so that the sound couldn't follow me.

At the bottom of the stairs I saw my sister Sylvia with a white closed face, holding onto the bannister. So she had heard it, too. She turned as I came in and before I had moved from the door, she said in a harsh whisper, "Papa's leaving. He's got—" Without finishing the sentence, she looked at me darkly as if her meaning must be clear.

"Leaving," I repeated. I had only a vague notion of what this meant, but surely something terrible had happened. My sister's strained voice, her secretive face frightened me as much as the voices I had heard a few moments before. Sylvia was almost fifteen and knew much more than I did about everything, but especially about the bewildering relationships between adults.

"Yes, leaving," she said and stopped. Then, after a short silence, she broke out angrily, "What are you staring at? You know what leaving means, don't you, stupid? He's got another woman."

For some reason it took me a minute to absorb the last part—I had trouble with the meaning of the verb—then I began to cry, although I knew that that would make Sylvia even angrier. When she saw my tears, she gave me a withering look and vanished into the dining room. I stood in the hall, letting the tears fall and licking the salt from my lips, not knowing where to go. Then I heard a door opening and closing upstairs, and my father came down, almost running. When he saw me, he stopped—reluctantly, I thought—and said, "Why are you crying, Ana?"

I examined him hungrily, but there was nothing in his face or manner to disturb me. He looked the same as always, pale and smooth—pale, smooth face, smooth brown hair, his body relaxed and graceful, like that of a dancer or a bullfighter (though, in fact, he hated all forms of exercise). Only his suit was different, a beige silk which I hadn't seen before. And yet, despite his beauty and his marvelous assurance, he seemed vulnerable, at least to me, like someone who might die early of an old-fashioned disease, one that lingered but would not disfigure. I loved to stroke the back of his neck, which was as fine as a girl's. Sometimes I imagined him as a boy of my own age, growing older as I did, but at the same time never changing.

"I'm not crying," I answered.

"Of course, you're crying." He took out his car keys and moved a few steps toward the door, then stopped again. "Has Sylvia said something to hurt your feelings?"

"She called me stupid," I said. I lowered my head and began to sob noisily.

He shook his head and frowned. "That's enough, Ana. You're too big for that." He came forward and kissed me on the top of my head. "Now stop crying and go upstairs and talk to your mother. She's not feeling well."

I tried to cling to him, but he pushed me gently away.

"What's the matter with her?" I asked.

For a moment he stared abstractedly at the carpet. He seemed at a loss for words. When he spoke, he glanced at me briefly, then looked away.

"Listen, Ana, I'm going away for a few days. Till Sunday. I'll be here for Sunday dinner. Now go upstairs and say something cheerful to your mother."

I watched him as he went out, waiting until I heard the sound of the Maserati going down the driveway. Then I turned and climbed the stairs, walking as slowly as possible. I didn't want to disobey my father, but I didn't want to see my mother either. What could I say to her? I stood and listened outside the bedroom before I knocked. I couldn't hear anything, even when I put my ear against the door—no crying, no movement. I knocked timidly and waited. After a moment I heard my mother walk toward me, but the door remained closed.

"Who is it?" she asked.

"It's me, Ana. May I come in?"

"Go away," she said in a muffled voice. "Go away."

I could feel the sobs rising again. "Please, Mama, I want to tell you something."

My mother struck the door softly.

"Ana, don't make me angry. Leave me alone. Get away from the door."

Her voice sounded tired and tremulous as if she too had been crying. I turned away and went downstairs and out onto the terrace where I saw Sylvia sitting on the low stone wall, picking at the mortar with a garden tool. I waited for her to speak to me, afraid that whatever I might say would irritate her. But when she looked up and saw me, her face seemed sober, not angry.

"Come here," she said, glancing up at the bedroom window, and when I came closer, she asked me in a whisper, "What did Papa say to you?"

"He said he was going away for a few days. Where is he going?"

"He's not coming back," she said, bitterly. "That's his way of saying he's moving out. He's rented a house in Petit Sacconex, and he's going to live there with that woman."

I sat down on the wall next to her and watched her face. She looked sullen and unhappy, already grown-up; I realized then that this inexplicable crisis, instead of bringing us together, might widen the differences between us, perhaps forever.

"But he said he was coming back for Sunday dinner," I said, forgetting to whisper. Sylvaia gave me a warning glance.

"Oh, yes, very good," she said. Her lips parted in an imitation of a smile. "Sunday dinner. That'll be nice."

A thin haze had begun to drift across the lake. A few lights, like insect fire, appeared on the other side, and suddenly I imagined that I could see the lights of the very house where my father would be living. Could he have arrived there already? I felt a thrill of jealousy.

"Sylvia, do you know who the woman is?" Even as I asked, I hoped that she would say no, that the woman would remain disembodied, a phantom who would never acquire any more reality than a bad dream.

Sylvia continued to pick savagely at the wall, tossing out small chunks of rock and cement.

"Oh, I saw her once. I don't know who she is. They were coming out of *Roberto's* after lunch, but Papa didn't see me."

I tried unsuccessfully to imagine my father with another woman on his arm.

"What did she look like? Was she pretty?"

Sylvia bent over the wall; her hair swung forward and covered her face.

"She's an Indian," she said. "She was wearing a sari." A sizable stone dropped to the floor of the terrace. My sister picked it up and put it back carelessly. "I didn't look at her," she added.

There was a long silence while I tried to think of something to say. I wanted to summon up a more appropriate feeling, but I felt only a vague anxiety, nothing like the fear I had felt a few moments ago. The information that Sylvia had given me floated like a cloud somewhere above me, like gossip about people I hardly knew. One of the girls at school was an Indian. I had seen her mother several times, a small, wizened, heavily made-up woman with a shrill scolding voice. I felt reassured when I thought of her. Never would my father have chosen such a woman. If he had, then there had been a terrible mistake which would soon be rectified.

The maid Angelica came to the door to call us to supper.

"I'm not hungry," said Sylvia.

Angelica made a noise of exasperation. "What's come over this family?" she said in Spanish. "First your mother, now you. Well, come, anyway. I'm putting it on the table. Tito is waiting."

"Let him wait," said Sylvia under her breath—Tito was our nine-year-old brother—but she got up, dusting off her hands, and followed Angelica into the house. I sat on the wall for a while longer, watching the lights across the lake grow more numerous; then I went in, too, not because I was hungry but because I didn't want to be alone.

But at the table we sat like strangers in a hotel dining room. Neither Sylvia nor I had anything to say, and Tito, who always ate rapidly with full attention to his food, jumped up as soon as he had finished and disappeared. Angelica took a tray up to my mother's room. An hour or so later I saw her come down with it.

Oddly enough, my mother, unlike Sylvia or me, had eaten everything.

My father had left the house on a Thursday afternoon. The next few days were a mixture of normalcy and nightmare. None of us talked about what had happened. On Friday and Saturday Sylvia and I attended school, took our tennis lessons, went to the dressmaker, and on Saturday afternoon I saw my mother for the first time in two days, talking to Angelica in the kitchen. She was still in her housecoat, without make-up, her hair uncombed. She looked like an ambulatory patient in a hospital. But apart from her tiredness, she didn't seem much changed, not as I had been imagining her behind the closed door. I was somewhat relieved, although that absent-minded weariness, which I had never seen in her before, put me off, and I didn't try to talk to her. Nor did she try to talk to me. What worried me a little was that she hadn't gone to work. She was one of the editors of a woman's magazine.

When Sunday came I was exhausted. For two nights running I had had dreams of phone calls from my father saying he was on the way but having trouble with his car which prevented him from getting to the house and of myself standing on the terrace in a fever of anxiety watching the cars on the road and waiting until it grew dark and I couldn't see them any more. Once I woke up crying.

My mother didn't come down to breakfast. I began to worry that when my father arrived she would drive him away with her anger or her silence. I wanted to talk to Sylvia about it, to get her help in mollifying my mother, but Sylvia had gone into her room and locked the door and wouldn't answer when I called her.

At half-past one—my father was expected at two, Angelica said, and I should have been reassured by the fact that she seemed to be preparing a feast of unusual size and complexity—I was lying on my bed trying to read when someone knocked. Anxiously I opened the door, and there was my mother, already dressed for dinner. I stared at her as if she were a stranger, the transformation from the haggard and disheveled woman of yesterday was so extraordinary. My mother was slender and delicately built with enormous eyes and dark hair cut short like a boy's; she had dressed in a way to emphasize that appealing blend of innocence and seductiveness which even as a child I knew the power of, though, of course, I couldn't have defined it. She had made up her eyes and mouth more heavily than usual and put on a wide-sleeved cerise silk blouse, buttoned low, and white linen pants. I thought she looked like a movie star, and I told her how beautiful she was.

She bent forward and touched my cheek with her lips, then said briskly, "Get dressed now, Ana. Put on your embroidered dress. And don't be long. Get Sylvia to help you with your hair." She was nervously fingering a silver bracelet while her eyes moved back and forth over my face as if she were trying to remember a great many things at once. "We're going to eat on the terrace. Papa is always on time, so don't be late." She turned and ran downstairs.

Even Sylvia had made some slight concession to the occasion; I noticed that she was wearing lipstick. And she was excited, too; not exactly happy, but nervously excited, like my mother and me.

A few minutes before two, we went out to the terrace where Angelica had set the table with our flowered Peruvian dishes and pots of pink and white cyclamen. It was a brilliant day, a day of Mediterranean splendor, of white sunlight and southern breezes, the lake spangled with reflected light and hundreds of sails. The striped red and white canopy over the table, billowing in the wind, made a loud smacking noise. If I looked at the water, I could imagine myself and my father on board a sailing ship, bound, like Byron, for the Grecian isles.

And at two o'clock the Mascrati came up the drive, and my father emerged, smiling and stretching out his hands to us. There was no sign of hesitation or embarrassment. When he reached my mother, he held her at arm's length to admire her, then kissed her on the cheek. How could he prefer any other woman to her, I wondered, and in a sudden rush of bitterness, I hated him for making her suffer. But my mother didn't seem to be suffering; on the contrary. How could that be? While they drank their apéritifs, I watched them as if they were spies, trying to find some way to reconcile Thursday and today. There had been an astonishing leap, a quantum jump, from unhappiness, even misery, to radiant joy; during those three days something had been mysteriously at work; a secret had passed from one hand to another which changed everything, but at the crucial moment I had missed it. If I had not been so happy myself, I would have felt angry, cheated. In my stupidity I had not known what to look for.

Later we sat under the striped canopy, eating chilled consommé with caviar, poached salmon, salmis of duckling, cold lemon soufflé, drinking the Chateauneuf-du-Pape that my father had brought. Even Tito drank as much as he wanted. As the afternoon lengthened, the sunlight slanted in under the canopy and shimmered below our faces; the wine-filled crystal threw off shafts of ruby light, and my father, who was facing the sun, put on his dark glasses and took out a cigar. Now it is easier for me to remember that day as a work of art than as an event in my life—a Bonnard, perhaps, the whole scene arrested forever, every color, every shadow intact whenever I summon it to mind. No wonder that my father seemed so happy. For him the perfection of life lay in those moments of its proximity to art, especially Impressionist art, in its smiling changeless serenity, all the elements arranged to capture and immortalize the sense of delight. He had no "Germanic" notions, as he called them, about the virtues of suffering and sacrifice. When I asked him to repeat our favorite anecdotes—a series of stories about his high-school chemistry teacher, who called himself the greatest chemist in the Andes—he launched into them with pleasure and even added a few touches which may or may not have been authentic. Then it was time for poetry. My father read it aloud with an old-fashioned dramatic eloquence which might have appeared ridiculous in anyone else, but, after all, he himself was not entirely a man of his time. Although he was modish and worked hard, loved fast cars and movies and modern art, there was also something belonging to an earlier age in the elegance of his manners, in the romantic idealism which sat easily beside fastidious notions of his own place among the elite. His attraction for women and his love of the classics and of poetry, in those days made me think of him as the reincarnation of Byron that I seemed to be looking for, but after I knew more about Byron, I realized that my father lacked Byron's cynicism. He had an unbreakable confidence in the goodness of people and, like a well-loved child, lived comfortably in the belief that no harm could come to him.

Carrera Andrade, the Ecuadorian poet, was one of his favorites, and after finishing his coffee, my father went into the house and came out with a volume of his poetry. Although neither Sylvia nor I, and certainly not Tito, knew literary Spanish well enough to understand those dense metaphors, except for occasional phrases, we always listened intently to the music of my father's somewhat high-pitched voice and the cadence of the lines.

> Yo amaba la hidrografia de la lluvia,
> Las amarillas pulgas del manzano
> Y los sapos que hacian sonar dos o tres veces
> Su gordo cascabel de palo.
>
> Sin cesar maniobra la gran vela del aire.
> Era la cordillera un litoral del cielo.
> La tempestad venia, y al batir del tambor
> Cargaban sus mojados regimientos;

I remember that by a curious transference I thought of the long afternoon on the terrace as the inspiration for Carrera Andrade's poem, especially as the sunlight faded and rain clouds appeared over the Jura. So we sat there until Angelica came to clear the table and my father went away.

After that our lives revolved around his visits. The Sunday dinners became less elaborate but more ceremonial, like holidays which commemorated some joyful and significant event. The rhythm of the weeks altered abruptly for all of us, but we accepted the changes as if they were part of a natural alteration in the night sky, say, or the seasons. Even Sylvia, now beginning to have a life outside the family, seemed reconciled although her attitude was far more complicated than mine. Of course, the changes were greatest for my mother. Before the separation my mother, who loved skiing, used to go with friends on weekends to Megeve or Villars while my father stayed home or visited other friends. But after he left, my mother gave up her skiing and refused to accept almost all other invitations. Her days were filled with work, lessons in painting and music, and shopping. She was preoccupied with her appearance. Every week she brought back something from her favorite boutiques: dresses, perfume, jewelry, which she wore on Sunday afternoons for my father's admiration. Now and then he called my mother during the week. They would talk for a long time; my mother smiled and laughed often during those conversations. She acted like a young girl being courted by a favorite suitor. Once or twice my father stayed very late, after Sylvia and I had gone to bed. I don't remember that my father ever missed a visit in more than two years; even when we took a house in Talloires for a month during the second summer, he drove down faithfully every week.

From time to time my mother invited people in. Then the visits became celebrations; full of loud, vigorous conversation, dramatic recitations, music, even dancing on the terrace. I was always jealous of guests and preferred the times when we were alone. On cold or rainy days we ate in the dining room, a white room furnished very simply and decorated with a few of my mother's paintings. There were french doors curtained in white silk which faced south, and years later when I read the lines,

> The light of early evening, Lisadell,
> Great windows opening to the south,

I thought at once of the diffused light and the gleam of rain or snow outside the dining room in Cologny. But the best afternoons were those when we sat on the terrace above the lake like excursionists in the gondola of a great balloon, feeling the air rush through the sails of the canopy, looking down on the lake and the city which receded endlessly toward the mountains.

One day a few months after my father had left the house, I overheard a telephone conversation between my mother and one of her friends. The bedroom door was open, and as I passed, I heard my mother saying, "What's the difference, Louise? Believe me, nothing has changed." Her voice was light and untroubled. I stopped in the hall out of sight and listened. There was a silence, then, "You don't understand. I don't think about that. What's the difference?" she asked again, and after a short pause, "What if he were a secret agent? Or a traveling salesman?" I could tell that the idea amused her. Then she changed the subject.

I went back to my room and sat down to think about what she had said. A traveling salesman, a secret agent. So she believed that my father still belonged exclusively to us. For a moment I wondered if Sylvia's detective work in uncovering the other woman's name, age, marital status, and other facts had been a joke. Once Sylvia and I had even driven past a small chalet near the United Nations building where the other woman worked, *their* house, Sylvia had told me. I had never doubted that all these things were true; why should Sylvia have invented them? And yet I partly understood what my mother meant. What did his absence matter, the little house, even the other woman, if everything was just as it had always been?

At first Sylvia and I used to entertain fantasies about our father's life with the other woman. The fantasies took different forms; sometimes they were sublimely happy together, like lovers in a dream by Chagall; sometimes living in a state of perpetual warfare. I suppose we preferred the unhappy scenarios, though they made little sense. But after a while even those lost their interest. On his Sunday visits my father never spoke of his other life, never even mentioned Krishna's name to us, and it became harder and harder to imagine anything either real or probable.

Now it seems incredible, but one thing I didn't question was a kind of agreement between Sylvia and me not to speak about the separation to our parents—with one exception, which turned out to be a mistake. It's true that in the beginning we cast about, desperately, for something to say to either of them—a question, a reproach, a plea, a magic formula which would open the door behind which they seemed to have barricaded themselves. I used to lie awake at night composing long speeches which would move my parents so deeply that they would fall into each other's arms, weeping. But in the light of day the words always died in my throat. Sometimes I even wondered, so vivid were those interior monologues, if I hadn't already uttered them and received the assurances I wanted. When Tito asked why our father wasn't home during the week, Sylvia and I offered him an implausible story about the necessities of a house he was designing which required him to stay on the site. The explanation didn't satisfy him (and surely he spoke to my mother without telling us), but in September he went away to school in Lausanne and came home only on weekends so that my father's absence no longer seemed unnatural. And after a few days had passed, a few weeks, speaking about it became not only more difficult but finally pointless. There were hours, I remember, when my mother was suddenly struck by a numbing listlessness, like the malaise of those first few days, and I longed to comfort her, but at those times, even less than at others, did it seem possible to break in with words. And in the end we lived blissfully in silence, secrecy, and evasion, in a cocoon of mystery. Perhaps it was the mystery that we loved.

But shortly after that telephone conversation I followed my

mother to her room one afternoon when she came back from the magazine and sat on the chaise longue while she changed her clothes. There was something I had wanted to ask her for a long time, and she seemed so happy, so much the tender, gay creature she had always been, that I thought there could be no harm in mentioning it to her.

"Mama, do you think Papa ever talks to Krishna about us?"

My mother, in the process of pulling on her slacks, stopped and let her hands fall; the unzipped slacks rested on her hips. Her face, which always colored whenever she was angry or hurt, turned bright pink. She looked at me with repugnance, as if I had just committed some shameful act in front of her.

"Where do you get those crazy ideas?" she asked harshly. The lines of her face deepened, her nose seemed to lengthen. "You're a fool, Ana. Don't talk about things you don't understand." She zipped up her slacks and looked at herself in the mirror, running her fingers through her hair and moving her head from side to side in the mirror. Her expression changed. A smile came and went on her brightly-colored face.

"Have you ever seen her?" she asked. Not knowing how she would take an account of Sylvia's discoveries, I didn't answer. Besides, the question astonished me; I didn't understand it. Was it a request for information, a challenge, a sneer? I couldn't read her tone. It didn't occur to me to wonder how it was that, in such a small city as Geneva was then, my mother and my father's mistress had apparently avoided meeting each other. Or how it was that other people hadn't told my mother all the things she wanted —or didn't want—to know. As soon as I could, I got up and went out. I knew then how right we had been, Sylvia and I, not to violate the harmony of the arrangement with words.

I think I imagined that those Sundays would go on forever. Once in a while if I suddenly had a vision of the future in which the villa didn't appear—because I would be away at school or married or traveling around the world—I banished it. While everything else might change, I believed passionately, or tried to, that those days when my father came to visit us at the house in Cologny would go on as they always had. Of course, it must sometimes have occurred to me or to Sylvia that my father might give up his other life and come back to stay. But that possibility, too, appeared more and more remote as the months went by. So that the end, or the beginning of the end, seemed to come unexpectedly.

One rainy Sunday in October, more than two years after my father had moved out, we were sitting at the table after dinner, listening to my mother, who, like my father, had a gift for anecdote. She was telling a story about her guitar teacher, an elderly Spaniard with an interest in yoga; all of us laughed at her description except my father, who seemed to be thinking of something else. He waited until the laughter subsided.

"Anita, let's be serious." He was looking at my mother soberly but with affectionate indulgence as if he were speaking to Tito or me. "Listen." His eyes went round the table and came back to my mother. He said, gently, "Anita, I must have a divorce." He paused for a second, then went on, "Shall we talk about it now?"

My mother's face darkened, and she glanced at the three of us. Sylvia lowered her eyes. I felt a sudden sharp painful throb in my stomach, a rush of blood to my head.

"Pablo, not here," my mother said. "Not in front of the children."

Although his manner didn't change, he seemed taken aback at her answer. He said in the same gentle coaxing voice, "They're not infants, Anita. They know what's happening whether we talk about it or not." He looked around the table at each of us in turn. "Krishna is going to have a baby," he went on gravely. "We ought to be married as soon as possible."

There was a moment of terrible silence, then my mother said in a low strained voice, "I don't want to hear any more." I saw that she was struggling to keep her feelings under control, to remain dignified, no matter what my father said. He rose and came toward her, but she stood up and moved away.

"Don't touch me," she said, loudly this time. At the sound of her voice, Tito stiffened in fear. His eyes remained fixed on her face, like those of a dog waiting for a signal from his master. She added, more violently, "Don't say any more!" But to me there was something unnatural, even theatrical, in the way she said it. Or perhaps it was only that I had never seen her play such a part before. She seemed suddenly like an older, coarser version of herself.

"Anita, you don't understand." My father stopped and looked at her helplessly. "What can I do?" He seemed bewildered at her obstinacy; at the same time he was searching her face as if for a sign that would clearly reveal to him what he had done to evoke such a response. He moistened his lips nervously while my mother stared back at him, her eyes wide and brilliant with excitement.

"Anita, listen, you don't understand," he said again. "Krishna and I—"

My mother didn't let him finish. She took a step backward and said hoarsely, "Be quiet! Don't speak to me! I don't want to hear any more!"

My father held up his hands in a characteristic gesture which he used whenever he was asking for forgiveness, even in fun.

"Anita, don't say such things." They were still looking at each other with desperate intensity, in a kind of staring match. They seemed to have forgotten that there was anyone else in the room. "God knows I don't want to hurt you, darling. I love you." His voice had risen. I recognized the passionate tone of his poetry readings. He came closer to my mother; this time she didn't move. There were tears in her eyes and she had begun to sniffle like a small child. My father took her in his arms. She didn't resist but put her head on his shoulder and began to cry in earnest.

"Don't cry, darling," he whispered. "We'll still have the same good times. You've been happy, haven't you?" He lowered his head to touch hers. "Nothing will change. Why should it?"

Neither Sylvia nor I said anything. Sylvia continued to stare at her hands, but my own eyes were riveted on my parents as they clung to each other. I remembered that first Sunday dinner on the terrace more than two years ago: a meeting (a reconciliation?) that I did not understand, joy and summer light which did not penetrate the mystery. And now, in sick suspense, I watched them again without knowing whether they were friends or enemies.

His head still resting against my mother's, my father went on in a low voice, "If it weren't for the baby, Anita, I would never ask for a divorce."

At this my mother raised her head to look at him. She was no longer crying, and her expression had changed. She seemed watchful but entirely composed, even relaxed. She reminded me of a bird watcher who has just heard some unusual call which he cannot identify. My father didn't see her face. He smiled and stroked her hair.

"What can I do?" he said. "Krishna has been the soul of patience. You can't imagine what she's been through for me. Her husband and her children have gone back to India." He took a deep breath, like a sigh. "I'm all she has now, Anita. I have to think of her happiness."

My father's eyes were half closed as my mother twisted herself out of his arms and confronted him. Her face was flushed with weeping but enigmatic. She studied him for a moment without emotion. I was afraid that she was preparing some striking and irrevocable insult. But she said nothing, simply turned and walked out of the room. Tito sprang up and followed her. I sat waiting, stunned; I couldn't believe that she wasn't coming back to finish the scene. If she had spoken, what would she have said? That was what I wanted to know.

My father looked after them unhappily, then took out his handkerchief and carefully wiped his face. The odor of his cologne hung over the table. Suddenly he seemed aware of my sister and me and turned to us.

"Sylvia, Ana," he said, "talk to your mother. Tell her I don't want our good times to end. God forbid." He paused while he replaced his handkerchief. Sylvia's eyes remained downcast. She was rigid, I guessed with rage.

"I want things to be as they've always been," he went on earnestly. "I don't want anything to change. Do you understand what I'm saying?"

"Papa, will it be the same? Really?" I asked, reaching out my hand to him.

"The same, the same, believe me." He seized my hand and held it for a second, then glanced at his watch and straightened up.

"It's late. I can't stay." He looked at Sylvia again, trying to catch her eyes, but she would not lift her head. "I'm sorry our Sunday was spoiled." As if he had thought of a more appropriate farewell, he added, "But next week I'll have a surprise for you. Something special. Tell your mother."

Then he went away. As soon as he had left the room, Sylvia looked up and sent after him a long glance of purest hatred. "The greatest lover in the Andes," she said, mimicking someone I didn't recognize, "also the Alps." I was listening intently to the sound of my father's footsteps, the closing of the door, the starting of the engine. But when the sound of the car had faded, I turned to her angrily. "You heard what Papa said. What difference does it make?"

But Sylvia wouldn't answer me, and we sat there in silence until Angelica came to clear the table. Then I followed Angelica into the kitchen, hoping to talk to her, to have her explain to me what had happened to change things when, after all, my father hadn't lived with us for more than two years. But Angelica wouldn't talk either, and next day we had a terrible fright; my mother took an overdose of sleeping pills, and the doctor came only just in time.

WORLD'S END

PAUL THEROUX

Paul Theroux was born in Medford, Massachusetts, in 1941 and presently divides his time between London and Cape Cod. "World's End" is the title story of a collection that appeared in 1980. He was written sixteen other books on various matters.

Robarge was a happy man who had taken a great risk. He had transplanted his family—his wife and small boy—from their home in America to a bizarrely named but buried-alive district called World's End in London, where they were strangers. It had worked, and it made his happiness greater. His wife, Kathy, had changed. Having overcome this wrench from home and mastered the new routine, she became confident. It showed in her physically—she had unstiffened; she adopted a new hairstyle; she slimmed; she had been set free by proving to her husband that he depended on her. Richard, only six, was already in what Robarge regarded as the second grade: the little boy could read and write! Even Robarge's company, a supplier of drilling equipment for offshore oil rigs, was pleased by the way he had managed; they associated their success with Robarge's hard work.

So Robarge was vindicated in the move he had made. He had considered marriage the quietest enactment of sharing, connubial exclusiveness the most private way to live—a sheltered life in the best sense. And he saw England as upholding the domestic reverences that had been tossed aside in America. He had not merely moved his family but rescued them. His sense of security made him feel younger, an added pleasure. He did not worry about growing old; he had put on weight in these four years at World's End and began to affect that curious sideways gait, almost a limp, of a heavy boy. It was a game—he was nearly forty—but games were still possible in this country where he could go unrecognized and so unmocked.

Most of all, he liked returning home in the rain. The house at World's End was a refuge; he could shut his door on the darkness and smell the straightness of his own rooms. The yellow lights from the street showed the rain droplets patterned on the window, and he could hear it falling outside, the drip from the sky, as irregular as a weeping tree, which meant in London that it would go on all night. Tonight he was returning from Holland—a Dutch subsidiary machined the drilling bits he dispatched to Aberdeen.

Without waking Kathy, he took the slender parcel he had carried from Amsterdam and crept upstairs to his son's room. On the plane he had kept it on his lap—there was nowhere to stow it. A man in the adjoining seat had stared and prompted Robarge to say, "It's a kite. For my son. The Dutch import them from the Far East. Supposed to be foolproof." The man had answered him by taking out a pair of binoculars he had bought for his own boy at the duty-free shop.

"Richard's only six," said Robarge.

The man said that the older children got the more expensive they were. He said it affectionately and with pride, and Robarge thought how glad he would be when Richard was old enough to appreciate a really expensive present—skis, a camera, a pocket calculator, a radio. Then he would know how his father loved him and how there was nothing in the world he would not give him. And he felt a casual envy for the man in the next seat, having a son old enough to want the things his father could afford. His own uncomprehending son asked for nothing: it made fiercer Robarge's desire to show his love.

The lights in the house were out; it was, at midnight, as gloomy as a tunnel and seemed narrow and empty in all that darkness. Richard's door was ajar. Robarge went in and found his son sleeping peacefully under wall posters of dinosaurs and fighter planes. Robarge knelt and kissed the boy, then sat on the bed and delighted in hearing the boy's measured breaths. The breaths stopped. In the harsh knife of light falling through the curtains from the street Robarge saw his son stir.

"Hello." The word came whole: Richard's voice was wide-awake.

"It's me." He kissed the boy. "Look what I brought you."

Robarge brandished the parcel. There was a film of rain on the plastic wrapper.

"What is it?" Richard asked.

Robarge told him, A kite. "Now go back to sleep like a good boy."

"Can we fly it?"

"You bet. If it's windy we'll fly it at the park."

"It's not windy enough at the park. You have to go in the car."

"Where shall we go?"

"Box Hill's a good place for kites."

"Is it windy there?"

"Not half!" whispered the child.

Robarge was delighted by this odd English expression in his son's speech, and he muttered it to himself in amazement. He was gladdened by Richard's response; he had pondered so long at the gift shop at Schiphol wondering which toy to buy—like an eager indecisive child himself—he had nearly missed his flight.

"Box Hill it is then." It meant a long drive, but the next day was Saturday—he could devote his weekend to the boy. He crossed the hall and undressed in the dark. When he got into the double bed, Kathy touched his arm and murmured, "You're back," and she swung over and sighed and pulled the blankets closer.

"I think I made a hit last night," said Robarge over breakfast. He told Kathy about the kite.

"You mean you woke him up to give him that thing?"

Kathy's tone discouraged him: He had hoped she would be glad. He said, "He was already awake—I heard him calling out. Must have had a bad dream. I went straight up." All these lies to conceal his impulsive wish to kiss his sleeping child at midnight. "We'll fly the thing today if there's any wind."

"That's nice," said Kathy. Her voice was flat and unfocused, almost belittling.

"Anything wrong?"

She said no and got up from the table, which was her abrupt way of showing boredom or changing the subject. And yet Robarge was struck by how attractive she was; how, without noticeable effort, she had discovered the kind of glamour a younger woman might envy. She was thin and had soft heavy breasts and wore light expensive blouses with her jeans.

Robarge said, "Are you angry because I travel so much?"

"You take your job seriously," she said. "Don't apologize. I haven't nagged you about that."

"I'm lucky I'm based in London—think of the rest of them in Aberdeen. How would you like to be there?"

"Don't say it in that threatening way. I wouldn't go to Aberdeen."

"I might have been posted there." He said it loudly, with the confidence of one who has been reprieved.

"You would have gone alone." He guessed she was poking fun; he was grateful for that, grateful that things had worked out so well in London.

"You didn't want to come here," he said. "But you're glad now, aren't you?"

Kathy did not reply. She was clearing the table and at the same time setting out Richard's breakfast.

"Aren't you?" he repeated in a taunting way.

"Yes!" she said, with unreasonable force, reddening as she spoke. Then she burst into tears. "There," she stuttered, "are you satisfied?"

Robarge, made guilty by her outburst (what had he said?), approached his wife to calm her. But she turned away. He heard Richard on the stairs, and the rattle of the kite dragging. He saw with relief that Kathy had fled into the kitchen, where Richard could not hear her sobbing.

He had dropped Kathy on the Kings Road and proceeded—Richard in the back seat—out of London toward Box Hill. It was only then that he remembered that he had failed to tell Kathy where they were going. She hadn't asked. Her tears had made her stubbornly silent. It was late May and once they were past Epsom he could see bluebells growing thickly in the shade of pine woods, and the pale green of the new leaves of beeches, and—already high and drooping from the weight of their blossoms—the cow parsley at the margins of plowed fields.

Richard said, "There are seagulls here."

Robarge smiled. There were no seagulls—only newly plowed fields set off by windbreaks of pines, and some crows fussing from tree to tree, to squawk.

"The black ones are crows."

"But seagulls are white," said Richard. "They follow the tractor and eat the worms when the farmer digs them up."

"You're a smart boy. But seagulls—"

"There they are," said Richard.

The child was right; at the edge of a field a tractor turned and just behind it, hovering and swooping—seagulls.

They parked near the Burford Bridge Hotel, and above them Robarge saw the long scar of exposed chalk, a whole eroded chute of it, and the steep green hill rising beside it to the brow of a grassy slope where the woods began.

"Mind the cars," said Richard, warning his father. They paused at the road near the parking lot. A motorcyclist sped past, then the child led his father across. He was being tugged by the child to the far left of a clump of boulders at the base of the hill, and then he saw the nearly hidden path. He realized he was being led by the boy to this entrance, then up the path beside the chalk slide to the gentler rise of the hill. Here Richard broke away and ran the rest of the way up the slope.

"Shall we fly it here?"

"No—over there," said Richard, out of breath at pointing at nothing Robarge could see. "Where it's windy."

They resumed, Robarge trudging, the child leading, until they were on the ridge of the hill. It was as the child had said, for no sooner had he walked to the highest point on that part of the hill than Robarge felt the wind. The path was sheltered, but here the wind was so strong it almost tore the kite from his hands. Robarge was proud of his son for leading him here.

"This is fun!" said Richard excitedly, as Robarge fixed the cross-piece and looped the twine, tightening and flattening the paper butterfly. He took the ball of string from his pocket and fastened it to the kite.

Richard said, "What about the tail?"

"This kite doesn't need a tail. It's foolproof."

"All kites need tails," Richard said. "Or they fall down."

The certainty in the child's voice irritated Robarge. He said, "Don't be silly," and raised the kite and let the wind pull it from his hand. The kite rose, spun, and then plummeted to the ground. Robarge tried this two more times and then, fearing that he would destroy the frail thing, he squatted and saw that a bit of it was torn.

"It's broken!" Richard shrieked.

"That won't make any difference."

"It needs a tail!" the child cried.

Robarge was annoyed by the child's insistence. It was the monotonous pedantry he had used in speaking about the seagulls. Robarge said, "We haven't got a tail."

Richard planted his feet apart and peered at the kite with his large serious face and said, "Your necktie can be a tail."

"I don't know whether you've noticed, Rich, but I'm not wearing a necktie."

"It won't work then," said the child. Robarge thought for a moment that the child was going to stamp on the kite in rage. He kicked the ground and said tearfully, "I told you it needs a tail!"

"Maybe we can use something else. How about a handkerchief?"

"No—just a tie. Or it won't work."

Robarge pulled out his handkerchief and tore it into three strips. These he knotted together to make a streamer for the tail. He tied it to the bottom corner of the kite, and while Richard sulked on the grass, Robarge, by running in circles, got the kite aloft. He tugged it and paid out string and made it bob; soon the kite was steadied on the curvature of white line. Richard was beside him, happy again, hopping on his small bow legs.

Robarge said, "You were right about the tail."

"Can I have a go?"

A go! Robarge had begun to smile again. "You want a go, huh? Think you can do it?"

"I know how," said Richard.

Robarge handed his son the string and watched him lean back and draw the kite higher. Robarge encouraged him. Instead of smiling, the child was made serious by the praise. He worked the string back and forth and said nothing.

"That's it," said Robarge. "You're an expert."

Richard held the string over his head. He made the kite climb and dance. The wind beat against the paper. The child said, "I told you it needed a tail."

"You're doing very well. Walk backward and you'll tighten the line."

But Richard, to Robarge's approval, wound the string on the ball. The kite began to rise. Robarge was impatient to fly the kite himself. He said he could get it much higher and then demanded his turn. He got the kite very high and while it swung he said, "You're a smart boy. I wouldn't have thought of coming here. And you're good at this. Next time I'll get you a bigger kite—not a paper one, but plastic. They can go hundreds of feet up."

"That's against the law."

"Don't be silly."

"Yes. You can get arrested. It makes the planes crash," said the child. "In England."

Robarge was still making sweeping motions with the string, lifting the kite, making it dive. "Who says?"

"A man told me."

Robarge snorted. "What man?"

"Mummy's friend."

The child screamed. The kite was falling on its broken string. It crashed against the hill and came apart, blowing until it was misshapen. Robarge thought: I am blind.

Later, when the child was calm and the broken kite stuffed beneath a bush (Robarge promised to buy a new one), he confirmed what Robarge had feared: He had been there before, seen the gulls, climbed the hill, and the man—he had no name, he was "Mummy's friend"—had taken off his necktie to make a tail for the kite.

The man had worn a tie. Robarge created a lover from this detail and saw someone middle-aged, middle class, perhaps prosperous, a serious rival, out to impress—British, of course. He saw the man's hand slipped beneath one of Kathy's brilliant silk blouses. He wondered whether he knew the man; but who did they know? They had been happy and solitary in this foreign country, at World's End. He wanted to cry. He felt his face breaking to expose all his sadness.

"Want to see my hide-out?"

The child showed Robarge the fallen tree, the pine grove, the stumps.

"Did Mummy's friend play with you?"

"The first time—"

Kathy had gone there twice with her lover and Richard! Robarge wanted to leave the place, but the child ran from tree to tree, remembering the games they had played.

Robarge said, "Were they nice picnics?"

"Not half!"

It was the man's expression, he was sure; and now he hated it.

"What are you looking at, Daddy?"

He was staring at the trampled pine needles, the seclusion of the trees, the narrow path.

"Nothing."

Richard did not want to go home, but Robarge insisted, and walking back to the car Robarge could not prevent himself from asking questions to which he did not want to hear answers.

The man's name?

"I don't know."

"Did he have a nice car?"

"Blue." The child looked away.

"What did Mummy's friend say to you?"

"I don't remember." Now Richard ran ahead, down the hill.

He saw that the child was disturbed. If he pressed too hard he would frighten him. And so they drove back to World's End in silence.

Robarge did not tell Kathy where they had gone, and instead of confronting her with what he knew he watched her. He did not want to lose her in an argument; it was easy to imagine the terrible scene—her protests, her lies. She might not deny it, he thought; she might make it worse.

He directed his anger against the man. He wanted to kill him, to save himself. That night he made love to Kathy in a fierce testing way, as if challenging her to refuse. But she submitted to his bullying, and at last, as he lay panting beside her, she said, "Are you finished?"

A few days later, desperate to know whether his wife's love had been stolen from him, Robarge told Kathy that he had to go to Aberdeen on business.

"When will you be back?"

"I'm not sure." He thought: Why should I make it easier on her? "I'll call you."

But she accepted this as she had accepted his wordless assault on her, and it seemed to him as though nothing had happened, she had no lover, she had been loyal. He had only the child's word. But the child was innocent and had never lied.

On the morning of his departure for Aberdeen he went to Richard's room. He shut the door and said, "Do you love me?"

The child moved his head and stared.

"If you really love me, you won't tell Mummy what I'm going to ask you to do."

"I won't tell."

"When I'm gone, I want you to be the daddy."

Richard's face grew solemn.

"That means you have to be very careful. You have to make sure that Mummy's all right."

"Why won't Mummy be all right?"

Robarge said, "I think her friend is a thief."

"No—he's not!"

"Don't be upset," said Robarge. "That's what we're going to find out. I want you to watch him if he comes over again."

"But why? Don't you like him?"

"I don't know him very well—not as well as Mummy does. Will you watch him for me, like a daddy?"

"Yes."

"If you do, I'll bring you a nice present."

"Mummy's friend gave me a present."

Robarge was so startled he could not speak; and he wanted to shout. The child peered at him, and Robarge saw curiosity and pity mingled in the child's squint.

"It was a little car."

"I'll give you a big car," Robarge managed.

"What's he stealing from you, Daddy?"

Robarge thought a moment, then said, "Something very precious—" and his voice broke. If he forced it he would sob. He left the child's room. He had never felt sadder.

Downstairs, Kathy kissed him on his ear. The smack of it caused a ringing in a horn in his head.

He had invented the trip to Aberdeen; he invented work to justify it, and for three days he knew what madness was—a sickening and a sorrow. He was deaf, his feet and hands were stupid, and his tongue at times seemed to swell and choke him when he tried to speak. He wanted to tell his area supervisor that he was suffering, that he knew how odd he must appear. But he did not know how to begin. And strangely, though his behavior was clumsily child-like, he felt elderly, as if he were dying inside, all his organs working feebly. He returned to London feeling that a burned hole was blackened on his heart.

The house at World's End was so still that in the doorway he considered that she was gone, that she had taken Richard and deserted him with her lover. This was Sunday evening, part of his plan—a surprise: He usually returned on Monday. He was not re-assured to see the kitchen light on—there was a telephone in the kitchen. But Kathy's face, when she answered the door, was blank.

She said, "I thought you might call from the station."

He tried to kiss her—she pulled away.

"My hands are wet."

"Glad to see me?"

"I'm doing the dishes." She lost her look of boredom and said, "You're so pale."

"I haven't slept." He could not gather the phrases of the ques-tion in his mind because he dreaded the simple answer he saw whole: yes. He felt afraid of her, and more dead and clumsy than ever, like a helpless orphan snatched into the dark. He wanted her to say that he had imagined the lover, but he knew he would not believe words he craved so much to hear. He no longer trusted her and would not trust her until he had the child's word. He longed to see his son. He started up the stairs.

Kathy said, "He's watching television."

On entering the television room, Robarge saw his son stand up and take a step backward. Richard's face in the darkened room was the yellow-green hue of the television screen; his hands sprang to his ears; the blue fibers of his pajamas glowed as if sprinkled with salt. When Robarge switched on the light the child ran to him and held him—so tightly that Robarge could not hug him.

"Here it is." Robarge disengaged himself from the child and crossed the room, turning off the television as he went. The toy was gift wrapped in bright paper and tied with a ribbon. He handed it to Richard. Richard put his face against his father's neck. "Aren't you going to open it?"

Robarge felt the child nodding against his shoulder.

"Time for bed," said Robarge.

The child said, "I put myself to bed now."

"All by yourself?" said Robarge. "Okay, off you go then."

Richard went to the door.

"Don't forget your present!"

Richard hesitated. Robarge brought it to him and tucked it under the child's arm. Then, pretending it was an afterthought, he said softly, "Tell me what happened while I was away—did you see anything?"

Richard shook his head and let his mouth gape.

"What about Mummy's friend?" Robarge was standing; the question dropped to the child like a spider lowering on its own filament of spittle.

"I didn't see him."

The child looked so small; Robarge towered over him. He knelt and asked, "Are you telling the truth?"

And it occurred to Robarge that he had never asked the child that question before—had never used that intimidating tone or looked so hard into the child's eyes. Richard backed away, the gift-wrapped parcel under his arm.

At this little distance, the child seemed calmer. He shook his head as he had before, but this time his confidence was pronounced, as if in the minute that had elapsed he had learned the trick of it. With the faintest trace of a stutter—when had he ever stuttered?—he said, "It's the truth, Daddy. I didn't."

Robarge said, "It's a tank. The batteries are already inside. It shoots sparks." Then he shuffled forward on his knees and took the child's arm. "You'll tell me if you see that man again, won't you?"

Richard stared.

"I mean, if he steals anything?"

Robarge saw corruption in the unblinking eyes.

"You'll tell me, won't you?"

When Robarge repeated the question, Richard said, "Mummy doesn't have a friend," and Robarge knew he had lost the child.

He said, "Show me how you put yourself to bed."

Robarge was unconsoled. He found Kathy had already gone to

bed, and though the light was on she lay on her side, facing the dark wall, as if sleeping.

Robarge said, "We never make love."

"We did—on Wednesday."

She was right; he had forgotten.

She said, "I've locked the doors. Will you make sure the lights are out?"

So he went from room to room turning out the lights, and in the television room Robarge sat down in the darkness. There, in the house which now seemed to be made of iron, he remembered again that he was in London, in World's End; that he had taken his family there. He was saddened by the thought that he was so far from home. The darkness hid him and hid the country; he knew that if he appeared calm, it was only because the darkness concealed his loss. He wished he had never come here, and worrying this way he craved his child and had a hideous reverie, of wishing to eat the child and eat his wife and keep them in that cannibal way. Burdened by this guilty thought, he went upstairs to make sure his son was safe.

Richard was in darkness, too. Robarge kissed the child's hot cheek. There was a bright cube on the floor, the present from Aberdeen. He picked it up and saw that it had not been opened.

He put it beside Richard on the bed and leaning for balance he pressed something in the bedclothes. It was long and flat and the hardness stung his hand. It was the breadknife with the serrated blade from the kitchen, tucked beneath these sheets, close to the child's body. Breathless from the shock of it Robarge took it away.

And then he went to bed. He was shaking so badly he did not think he would ever sleep. He wanted to smash his face against the wall and hit it until it was bloody and he had torn his nose away. He dropped violently to sleep. When he woke in the dark he recalled the sound that had wakened him—it was still vibrant in the air, the click of the front gate: A thief was entering his house. Robarge waited for more, and perspired. His fear left him and he was penetrated by the fake vitality of insomnia. After an hour he decided that what he had heard, if anything, was a thief leaving the house, not breaking in. Too late, too far, too dark, he thought; and he knew now they were all lost.

MAGAZINES CONSULTED

Antaeus
Ecco Press, 1 West 30th Street, New York, N.Y. 10001
Antioch Review
P.O. Box 148, Yellow Springs, Ohio 45387
Apalachee Quarterly
P.O. Box 20106, Tallahassee, Fla. 32304
Appalachian Journal
P.O. Box 536, Appalachian State University, Boone, N.C. 28608
Ararat
Armenian General Benevolent Union of America, 628 Second Avenue, New York, N.Y. 10016
Arizona Quarterly
University of Arizona, Tucson, Ariz. 85721
The Ark River Review
Box 14, W.S.U., Wichita, Kan. 67208
Ascent
English Department, University of Illinois, Urbana, Ill. 61801
Aspen Anthology
P.O. Box 3185, Aspen, Col. 81611
The Atlantic
8 Arlington Street, Boston, Mass. 02116
Bachy
11317 Santa Monica Boulevard, Los Angeles, Calif. 90025
Bennington Review
Bennington College, Bennington, Vt. 05201
The Black Warrior Review
P.O. Box 2936, University, Ala. 35486
Bloodroot
P.O. Box 891, Grand Forks, N.D. 58201
The Boston Monthly
20 Newbury St., Boston, Mass. 02116
Boston University Journal
704 Commonwealth Avenue, Boston, Mass. 02215

Brushfire
c/o English Dept., University of Nevada, Reno, Nev. 89507
California Quarterly
100 Sproul Hall, University of California, Davis, Calif. 95616
Canadian Fiction Magazine
P.O. Box 46422, Station G, Vancouver, B.C., Canada V6R 4G7
Canto
11 Bartlett Street, Andover, Mass. 01810
Carleton Miscellany
Carleton College, Northfield, Minn. 55057
Carolina Quarterly
Greenlaw Hall 066-A, University of North Carolina, Chapel Hill, N.C. 27514
The Chariton Review
Division of Language & Literature, Northeast Missouri State University, Kirksville, Mo. 63501
Chicago
500 North Michigan Ave., Chicago, Ill. 60611
Chicago Review
970 E. 58th Street, Box C, University of Chicago, Chicago, Ill. 60637
Christopher Street
Suite 417, 250 W. 57th St., New York, N.Y. 10019
Cinemonkey
P.O. Box 8502, Portland, Ore. 97207
Colorado Quarterly
Hellums 134, University of Colorado, Boulder, Col. 80309
Confrontation
English Department, Brooklyn Center of Long Island University, Brooklyn, N.Y. 11201
Cornell Review
108 North Plain Street, Ithaca, N.Y. 14850
Cosmopolitan
224 West 57th Street, New York, N.Y. 10019
Crucible
Atlantic Christian College, Wilson, N.C. 27893
Cumberlands
Pikeville College, Pikeville, Ky. 41501

Cutbank
c/o English Dept., University of Montana, Missoula, Mont. 59801
Dark Horse
Box 36, Newton Lower Falls, Mass. 02162
December
P.O. Box 274, Western Springs, Ill. 60558
The Denver Quarterly
Dept. of English, University of Denver, Denver, Col. 80210
Descant
Dept. of English, TCU Station, Fort Worth, Tex. 76129
Dog Soldier
E. 323 Boone, Spokane, Wash. 99202
Epoch
254 Goldwyn Smith Hall, Cornell University, Ithaca, N.Y. 14853
Esquire Magazine
488 Madison Avenue, New York, N.Y. 10022
Essence
1500 Broadway, New York, N.Y. 10036
Eureka Review
Dept. of English, University of Cincinnati, Cincinnati, Ohio 45221
The Falcon
Bilknap Hall, Mansfield State College, Mansfield, Pa. 16933
Fantasy and Science Fiction
Box 56, Cornwall, Conn. 06753
The Fault
33513 6th Street, Union City, Calif. 94538
Fiction International
Dept. of English, St. Lawrence University, Canton, N.Y. 13617
Fiction Magazine
c/o Dept. of English, The City College of New York, New York, N.Y. 10031
The Fiddlehead
The Observatory, University of New Brunswick, P.O. Box 4400, Fredericton, N.B., Canada E3B 5A3
Fisherman's Angle
St. John Fisher College, Rochester, N.Y. 14618

Forms
P.O. Box 3379, San Francisco, Calif. 94119
Forum
Ball State University, Muncie, Ind. 47306
Four Quarters
La Salle College, Philadelphia, Pa. 19141
The Gay Alternative
252 South St., Philadelphia, Pa. 19147
Georgia Review
University of Georgia, Athens, Ga. 30602
GPU News
c/o The Farwell Center, 1568 N. Farwell, Milwaukee, Wis. 53202
The Great Lakes Review
Northeastern Illinois University, Chicago, Ill. 60625
Great River Review
59 Seymour Ave., S.E., Minneapolis, Minn. 55414
Green River Review
Box 56, University Center, Mich. 48710
The Greensboro Review
University of North Carolina, Greensboro, N.C. 27412
Harper's Magazine
2 Park Avenue, New York, N.Y. 10016
Hawaii Review
Hemenway Hall, University of Hawaii 96822
The Hudson Review
65 East 55th Street, New York, N.Y. 10022
Iowa Review
EPB 453, University of Iowa, Iowa City, Iowa 52240
Jewish Dialog
1498 Yonge St., Suite 7, Toronto, Ontario M4T 1Z6
Kansas Quarterly
Dept. of English, Kansas State University, Manhattan, Kan. 66506
Kenyon Review
Kenyon College, Gambier, Ohio 43022
Ladies' Home Journal
641 Lexington Avenue, New York, N.Y. 10022
Lilith
250 West 57th St., New York, N.Y. 10019

The Literary Review
Fairleigh Dickinson University, Teaneck, N.J. 07666
The Little Magazine
P.O. Box 207, Cathedral Station, New York, N.Y. 10025
The Louisville Review
University of Louisville, Louisville, Ky. 40208
Mademoiselle
350 Madison Avenue, New York, N.Y. 10017
Malahat Review
University of Victoria, Victoria, B.C., Canada
The Massachusetts Review
Memorial Hall, University of Massachusetts, Amherst, Mass. 01002
McCall's
230 Park Avenue, New York, N.Y. 10017
MD
30 E. 60th St., New York, N.Y. 10022
Michigan Quarterly Review
3032 Rackham Bldg., The University of Michigan, Ann Arbor, Mich. 48109
Midstream
515 Park Avenue, New York, N.Y. 10022
Mother Jones
607 Market Street, San Francisco, Calif. 94105
The National Jewish Monthly
1640 Rhode Island Avenue, N.W., Washington, D.C. 20036
New Boston Review
Boston Critic, Inc., 77 Sacramento Street, Somerville, Mass. 02143
New Directions
333 Sixth Avenue, New York, N.Y. 10014
New Letters
University of Missouri–Kansas City, Kansas City, Mo. 64110
New Mexico Humanities Review
The Editors, Box A, New Mexico Tech, Socorro, N.M. 57801
The New Renaissance
9 Heath Road, Arlington, Mass. 02174
The New Republic
1220 19th St., N.W., Washington, D.C. 20036

The New Yorker
25 West 43rd Street, New York, N.Y. 10036
Nocturne
P.O. Box 1320, Johns Hopkins University, Baltimore, Md. 21218
The North American Review
University of Northern Iowa, 1222 West 27th Street, Cedar Falls, Iowa 50613
Northwest Review
129 French Hall, University of Oregon, Eugene, Ore. 97403
Northwoods Journal
Route 1, Meadows of Daw, Va. 24120
The Ohio Journal
164 West 17th Avenue, Columbus, Ohio 43210
Ohio Review
Ellis Hall, Ohio University, Athens, Ohio 45701
The Ontario Review
9 Honey Brook Dr., Princeton, N.J. 08540
Paragraph: A Quarterly of Gay Fiction
Box 14051, San Francisco, Calif. 94114
The Paris Review
45-39–171st Place, Flushing, N.Y. 11358
Paris Voices
37, rue de la Bucherie, Paris 5, France
Partisan Review
128 Bay State Rd., Boston, Mass. 02215 / 552 Fifth Avenue, New York, N.Y. 10036
Perspective
Washington University, St. Louis, Mo. 63130
Phylon
223 Chestnut Street, S.W., Atlanta, Ga. 30314
Playboy
919 North Michigan Avenue, Chicago, Ill. 60611
Ploughshares
Box 529, Cambridge, Mass. 02139
Prairie Schooner
Andrews Hall, University of Nebraska, Lincoln, Neb. 68588
Prism International
Dept. of Creative Writing, University of British Columbia, Vancouver, B.C., Canada V6T 1WR

Quarterly West
312 Olpin Union, University of Utah, Salt Lake City, Utah 84112
Quartet
1119 Neal Pickett Drive, College Station, Tex. 77840
Quest/79
1133 Avenue of the Americas, New York, N.Y. 10036
Redbook
230 Park Avenue, New York, N.Y. 10017
Remington Review
505 Westfield Ave., Elizabeth, N.J. 07208
Rolling Stone
625 Post St., Box 752, San Francisco, Calif. 94109
San Francisco Stories
625 Post St., Box 752, San Francisco, Calif. 94109
The Saturday Evening Post
110 Waterway Boulevard, Indianapolis, Ind. 46202
The Seneca Review
P.O. Box 115, Hobart and William Smith College, Geneva, N.Y. 14456
Sequoia
Storke Student Publications Bldg., Stanford, Calif. 94305
Sewanee Review
University of the South, Sewanee, Tenn. 37375
Shenandoah: The Washington and Lee University Review
Box 722, Lexington, Va. 24450
Silver Vain
P.O. Box 2366, Park City, Utah 84060
The South Carolina Review
Dept. of English, Clemson University, Clemson, S.C. 29631
The South Dakota Review
Box 111, University Exchange, Vermillion, S.D. 57069
Southern Humanities Review
Auburn University, Auburn, Ala. 36830
Southern Review
Drawer D, University Station, Baton Rouge, La. 70803
Southwest Review
Southern Methodist University Press, Dallas, Tex. 75275
Steel Head
Knife River Press, 2501 Branch St., Duluth, Minn. 55842

Story Quarterly
820 Ridge Road, Highland Park, Ill. 60035
The Tamarack Review
Box 159, Postal Station K, Toronto, Ont., Canada M4P 2G5
The Texas Review
English Department, Sam Houston University, Huntsville, Tex. 77341
The Threepenny Review
P.O. Box 335, Berkeley, Calif. 94701
Tri-Quarterly
University Hall 101, Northwestern University, Evanston, Ill. 60201
Twigs
Pikeville College, Pikeville, Ky. 41501
Twin Cities Express
127 N. 7th St., Minneapolis, Minn. 55402
University of Windsor Review
Dept. of English, University of Windsor, Windsor, Ont., Canada N9B 3P4
U.S. Catholic
221 West Madison Street, Chicago, Ill. 60606
Vagabond
P.O. Box 879, Ellensburg, Wash. 98926
The Virginia Quarterly Review
University of Virginia, 1 West Range, Charlottesville, Va. 22903
Vogue
350 Madison Avenue, New York, N.Y. 10017
Washington Review
Box 50132, Washington, D.C. 20004
The Washingtonian
1828 "L" St., N.W., Suite 200, Washington, D.C. 20036
Webster Review
Webster College, Webster Groves, Mo. 63119
West Coast Review
Simon Fraser University, Vancouver, B.C., Canada
Western Humanities Review
Bldg. 41, University of Utah, Salt Lake City, Utah 84112
Wind
RFD Route 1, Box 809, Pikeville, Ky. 41501

Wittenberg Review of Literature and Art
Box 1, Recitation Hall, Wittenberg University, Springfield, Ohio 45501

Woman's Day
1515 Broadway, New York, N.Y. 10036

Writers Forum
University of Colorado, Colorado Springs, Col. 90907

Yale Review
250 Church Street, 1902A Yale Station, New Haven, Conn. 06520

Yankee
Dublin, N.H. 03444